SHE WAS A WOMAN
WHO COULD DESTROY A MAN
WITHOUT EVER LAYING A FINGER
OR A FANG ON HIM.

"Come."

He jerked his head toward the door, then strode down the aisle and out the door.

Vanda's mouth fell open. What the hell was he doing, giving her orders? Though she had to admit his backside had looked really good.

She stalked out the door and spotted him across the hall, leaning against the wall with his arms folded. He'd always had rather big biceps for a mortal. "Look. This is a mistake. You're a mortal. You can't handle a Vamp."

"I made you leave the room, didn't I?"

Her anger flared. "Only because I didn't want to embarrass you in front of everyone while I kick your ass!"

His mouth tilted up. "Try it."

She stepped closer to him. "I've eaten mortals like you for breakfast."

His smile grew. "Lucky bastards."

She stepped back, huffing with exasperation. "Phil, this is crazy! You can't just . . . force yourself on me."

Something hot flared in his eyes. His gaze wandered down to her feet, then back to her face. "Sweetheart, no force will be necessary."

By Kerrelyn Sparks

FORBIDDEN NIGHTS WITH A VAMPIRE
SECRET LIFE OF A VAMPIRE
ALL I WANT FOR CHRISTMAS IS A VAMPIRE
THE UNDEAD NEXT DOOR
BE STILL MY VAMPIRE HEART
VAMPS AND THE CITY
HOW TO MARRY A MILLIONAIRE VAMPIRE

KERRELYN SPARKS

FORBIDDEN NIGHTS
with a
VAMPIRE

AVON
An Imprint of HarperCollinsPublishers

AVON BOOKS
An Imprint of HarperCollins*Publishers*
10 East 53rd Street
New York, New York 10022-5299

Copyright © 2009 by Kerrelyn Sparks
ISBN 978-0-06-166784-8
www.avonromance.com

First Avon Books paperback printing: May 2009

10   9   8   7

To my mother Charly.
Hurricane Ike demolished your house,
but it couldn't diminish your spirit.

Acknowledgments

*A*fter surviving another round of Deadline Hell, I wish to thank those people who helped keep me afloat. Many thanks to my husband and children; my critique partners MJ, Sandy, Vicky, and Vicky; my agent Michelle Grajkowski; and my friends at the West Houston and Northwest Houston chapters of Romance Writers of America. My thanks to Erika Tsang for being the most brilliant and understanding editor ever! Thanks also to all the professionals at HarperCollins for giving me the most awesome covers, marketing, and promotion. And finally, a big thank-you to all the readers of the Love at Stake series. Your letters and e-mails are like Chocolood for a hungry vampire.

Chapter One

"*Y*e're late." Connor greeted her with a disapproving frown.

"So?" Vanda Barkowski returned the Scotsman's frown as she stepped into the foyer of Romatech Industries. "I'm not a harem girl anymore. I don't have to come running whenever the great Master snaps his fingers."

Connor arched a brow. "Ye were sent an official summons that clearly stated the East Coast Regional Coven Meeting would start at ten o'clock tonight." He locked the door behind her and punched some buttons on a security pad.

Was she in trouble? That "official" summons had worried her all week, although she hadn't let anyone know. She would have arrived sooner if she'd been allowed to use her Vamp skill of teleportation, but the summons had warned her not to teleport inside Romatech. Such an act would trigger the alarm, interrupt the meeting, and result in a hefty fine. So she'd driven from her nightclub in Hell's Kitchen with a detour first to Queens to pick up some costumes she'd had custom made. The traffic had been awful all the way to White Plains, leaving her much too tense. Damn, she didn't want to be here.

She took a deep breath and fluffed up her spiky, purple-dyed hair. "Big deal. So I'm a few minutes late."

"Forty-five minutes. Late."

"So? What's forty-five minutes to an old goat like you?"

"I believe it is still forty-five minutes."

Was that a glint of humor in his eyes? She chafed at the thought of being considered amusing. She was tough, dammit. And he should have been insulted that she'd called him an old goat. Connor Buchanan didn't look a day over thirty. She would have considered him very handsome if he hadn't fussed at her so much over the years.

She adjusted the black, braided whip she wore around her waist. "Look. I'm a businesswoman now. I'm late because I had to open the club and run some errands. And I need to get back to work soon." She had a meeting scheduled at eleven-thirty with all the male dancers so she could give them their new costumes for the month of August.

Connor looked unimpressed. "Roman is still yer Coven Master, and when he requests yer presence, ye're expected to arrive on time."

"Yeah, yeah, I'm quaking in my little boots."

Connor pivoted toward a table, causing his red

and green plaid kilt to swing around his knees. "I'll need to search yer handbag."

She winced inwardly. "Do we really have time for this? I'm already late."

"I check every bag coming in."

He'd always been a stickler for the rules. How many times had he reprimanded her for flirting with the guards at Roman's townhouse? Well, just one guard. A mortal day guard who worked for MacKay Security & Investigation. A deliciously handsome day guard.

Connor worked for MacKay S&I, too, so he knew guards were never supposed to fraternize with their charges. As far as Vanda was concerned, that old rule needed to be tossed out. Ian had gotten involved with his mortal guard, Toni, and her love for him hadn't weakened her one bit. In fact, her love had empowered her, enabling her to kill Jedrek Janow in spite of the Malcontent's attempt to stop her with vampire mind control.

However, when it came to security at Romatech Industries, Connor had good reason to cling to his precious rules. Since the nasty Malcontent vampires hated the friendly, law-abiding, bottle-drinking Vamps, they also hated Romatech, where the bottled blood was manufactured. They'd managed to bomb Romatech three times in the past.

Vanda sighed. "I didn't bring a bomb. Do you think I would blow myself up? Do I look crazy to you?"

A glint of humor sparkled in his eyes. "I believe that will be determined at the coven meeting."

Damn. She *was* in trouble. "Fine." She tossed her

hobo handbag on the table. "Knock yourself out."

Heat crept up her neck as he rummaged through her bag. God, she hated embarrassment. It made her feel weak and small, and she'd sworn never to feel vulnerable again. She lifted her chin and glared at Connor.

"What's this?" He pulled out a scrap of fabric that looked like a stuffed yellow tube sock with a large brass nozzle on the end.

"It's a dance costume. For Freddie the Fireman. That's his personal fire hose."

Connor dropped the thong like it was on fire, then resumed his search of her handbag. He pulled out a sparkly flesh-colored thong with fake ivy twisted around the tube. "I hesitate to ask . . . "

"Our theme for August is 'Hot Jungle Fever.' Terrance the Turgid is doing an ode to Tarzan. He'll swing across the stage on a vine while he's stripping."

Connor tossed the male thong on the table and continued his search. "It does look like a bloody jungle in here." He pulled out a vine of large leaves.

"Hot Jungle Fever is highly contagious," Vanda said with a husky voice. "I'm sure we could find a fig leaf just your size."

He glowered at her.

"All right, a banana leaf, then."

With a snort, he fished her car keys from the pile of vines and dropped them into his sporran.

"Hey," she objected. "I need those to drive home."

"Ye'll get them back after the meeting." He crammed the costumes back into her bag. " 'Tis shameful for

Vamp men to dress—or rather, undress—like this in public."

"The guys enjoy it. Come on, Connor. You never wanted to take your clothes off in front of some pretty girls?"

"Nay. I'm too busy trying to keep Roman and his family alive. If ye havena noticed, we're at the brink of war with the Malcontents. And if ye havena heard, their leader Casimir is somewhere in America."

Vanda repressed a shudder. "I know. My club was attacked last December." Some of her best friends had come close to getting murdered that night. She tried not to think about it. If she did, the thoughts would mushroom into bigger, more horrid memories.

And she had no intention of reliving them. Life was simple and pleasant at the Horny Devils nightclub, where gorgeous men danced in skimpy costumes, and pints of Bleer could leave the coldest of Vamps feeling warm and fuzzy.

Each night could pass without pain as long as she concentrated on work and kept the past firmly locked in a mental coffin. Days were even easier, for death-sleep was painless and nightmare-free. She could go on like this for centuries if people would just leave her the hell alone.

Connor gave her a sympathetic look. "Ian told me about the attack that night. He said ye fought bravely."

She refrained from grinding her teeth. It was hard on the fangs. She grabbed her handbag and swung it onto her shoulder. "So what's the deal? How much trouble am I in?"

"Ye'll find out." Connor motioned to the double doors on the right. "I'll take ye to the meeting hall."

"No thanks. I know the way." Vanda strode through the doors and down the hall, her high-heeled boots clicking on the spotless and shiny marble floor.

The unpleasant smell of antiseptic cleanser couldn't completely mask the delicious aroma of blood. The mortal workers at Romatech manufactured synthetic blood all day. That blood was shipped openly to hospitals and blood banks, and secretly to Vamps.

Roman Draganesti invented synthetic blood in 1987, and in recent years, he'd come up with Vampire Fusion Cuisine. On weeknights, Vamp employees worked at Romatech, making lovely drinks such as Chocolood, Bleer, Blissky, or Blood Lite for those who overindulged. The combined scent of all these drinks lingered in the air. Vanda took a deep, satisfying sniff to soothe her frazzled nerves.

Her superior Vamp hearing caught the sound of crackling static. She glanced back and spotted Connor standing by the double doors. He was watching her progress with a walkie-talkie in his hand. Did he suspect she'd make a run for it? It was awfully tempting to teleport to the parking lot and speed away in her black Corvette. No wonder he'd confiscated her keys. She could always teleport straight home. But they knew where she lived and where she worked. There was no running away from coven law.

Of course, only Vamps who drank synthetic blood acknowledged Roman Draganesti as Coven Master of East Coast Vampires. As she neared the meeting hall, Vanda's steps slowed. If Roman had some kind of complaint against her, why hadn't he approached her in private? Why humiliate her in front of the other bigwigs in the coven?

Connor's softly accented voice carried down the long hallway. "Phil has arrived? Good. Let me talk to him."

Phil? Vanda wobbled on her heels. Phil Jones was back in New York? The last she'd heard he was in Texas. Not that she was interested. He was just a mortal. But an incredibly handsome and interesting mortal.

He'd spent five years as one of the day guards at Roman's townhouse when she'd lived there with the harem. Most of the mortal guards had considered the harem a silly bunch of nameless, undead women, connected to their real charge, Roman Draganesti. They had rated the harem's value somewhere below Roman's artwork and priceless antiques.

Phil Jones was different. He'd learned their names and treated them like real people. Vanda had tried flirting with him a few times, but Connor, that old grouch, always put a stop to it. Phil had followed the rule of noninvolvement and kept his distance—easy enough to do when he was usually at night school or asleep when she was awake; and she was dead during the day, when he was awake.

Even so, she'd suspected that he was attracted to her. Or maybe she'd just wanted him to be. Harem life had been so damned boring, and somehow, Phil had seemed intriguing.

But she must have just imagined it all. She'd been free from the harem for three years now, and in that time, Phil had never bothered to see her.

She paused to listen as Phil's voice replied on the walkie-talkie. She couldn't make out the words, but the sound reverberated through her with a surprising sizzle. She'd forgotten how sexy his voice was. Damn him, she'd thought he was a friend. But she'd just been part of the job, easily forgotten once he'd moved on to the next assignment.

She reached for the door to the meeting hall when it suddenly burst open. She jumped back to keep from being mowed down by a buxom woman and a cameraman. Vanda recognized the woman instantly. Corky Courrant was the hostess of the Digital Vampire Network's celebrity talk show, *Live with the Undead*.

"I reject this verdict!" Corky screamed, turning to catch the door before it swung shut. "I'll take this to the Supreme Coven Court!"

"My decision is final." Roman's voice sounded firm, but bored.

"You'll hear about this on my show!" Corky noticed Vanda for the first time. "*You!* What are you doing here?"

Vanda winced as the cameraman turned his camera on her. Damn. Now she was going to end up on Corky's show.

She smiled hesitantly at the camera. "Hi there,

fellow Vamps. I'm going to the coven meeting. I always go to the coven meetings. It's our civic duty, you know."

"Cut the bullshit," Corky snarled. "You came here to gloat. But I'm not dropping my suit against you, no matter what the Coven Master says."

Vanda kept her smile glued in place for the camera. "Can't we all just get along?"

"You should have thought about that before you attacked me!" Corky screeched.

Oh, right. That incident last December at the club. Vanda had leaped across a table to try to strangle Corky Courrant. After all the turmoil that had followed, that little incident had seemed unimportant in comparison. She'd had shrugged it off as one more minor tiff. Vanda had had a lot of minor tiffs over the years.

She faced the camera with a soulful look. "It was an unfortunate mishap, but we can all be eternally grateful that our dear Corky has not suffered from it. Her voice is just as loud and strident as ever."

Corky snorted, then made a cutting motion to signal her cameraman to stop recording. She leaned close, lowering her voice. "It's not over between us, bitch. I have a lot of power in the Vampire World, and I'll see you ruined." She stormed down the hall, her cameraman scurrying behind her.

"Have a nice day!" Vanda called after her. She turned to enter the meeting hall and noticed how quiet it was. Everyone was staring at her. Great. They'd witnessed that little scene with Corky.

The whispering began. Vanda lifted her chin. She estimated there were about thirty Vamps in attendance. Mostly male. The archaic Vamp world was still run almost entirely by men. Arrogant, stodgy old men who didn't approve of her nightclub where Vamp men stripped for Vamp women.

She noted the sour looks on their faces. Obviously, they also didn't care for her purple spandex catsuit or purple, spiky hair. Out of the entire crowd, she spotted one friendly, smiling face. Gregori. Unfortunately, he was seated on the front row. She tightened the whip around her waist and strode down the center aisle.

Roman Draganesti was seated in the big Master chair on the dais. In the old days, the Coven Master sat alone, but times had changed. Roman's chair was flanked by two smaller chairs. His wife Shanna sat on his left, and the priest, Father Andrew, sat on his right. They were obviously his chief advisors. And both were mortal.

What was the Vamp World coming to? Why had Roman given these two mortals so much power in a world where they didn't belong? With a disgusted huff, Vanda sat next to Gregori.

Roman acknowledged her presence with a regal nod. Vanda scowled back.

Seated at a table close to the dais, Laszlo Veszto scribbled notes with a fountain pen on antique-looking parchment. He was a chemist at Romatech, but also held the prestigious job of Coven Secretary. Vanda rolled her eyes. He might as well use a quill and inkwell. Or maybe a roll of papyrus and a stick reed.

"Sheesh, get the poor guy a laptop," she muttered to Gregori.

"He has one," Gregori whispered back. "But they like to stick with tradition for these meetings."

"These meetings are a joke," she grumbled. She supposed Laszlo was still writing down the decision that had upset Corky Courrant. "What happened with Corky?"

"Good news for you," Gregori whispered. "Roman dismissed her lawsuit against you."

"About time. I obviously didn't hurt her throat."

"Then Corky insisted that it would only be fair for Roman to drop the lawsuit that's been leveled against her, but he refused."

"What lawsuit?" Vanda asked.

"You haven't heard? The famous model, Simone, is suing Corky. Remember when I hired Simone to do *Fangercise*, an exercise DVD? Corky claimed on her show that Simone used fake teeth."

Vanda broke out in laughter, her voice echoing across the silent room. A dozen male Vamps shushed her. Laszlo dropped his pen and gave her a startled look. Then he glanced at Roman.

Vanda halted mid-laugh and cleared her throat. Damn. These old Vamps needed to pull the stakes out of their butts. She opened her mouth to say so, but Gregori touched her arm.

"Don't," he whispered. "Don't speak to him until he's spoken to you."

"Laszlo," Roman began quietly.

"Yes, sir?" The Coven Secretary fiddled with a button on his lab coat.

"Since Vanda Barkowski has finally arrived, let us proceed to the other suits against her."

Other suits? As in plural? Vanda glanced around nervously. Roman's wife gave her a sympathetic smile.

Anger sparked inside Vanda, and she clenched her fists. She didn't need anyone's sympathy. She was tough, dammit.

Laszlo fumbled through a stack of papers. He drew one page out. Then another. And another. Three pages? Her anger sizzled into a hot flame.

Laszlo gave her a nervous look, then proceeded. "Vanda Barkowski is being sued on three counts. Count one—unjustified termination of employment, resulting in loss of wages and mental trauma. Count two—reckless endangerment at the workplace, resulting in minor injury and mental trauma. Count three—assault with a deadly weapon, resulting in physical injury and mental trauma."

Vanda jumped to her feet. "That's a load of crap! Who's suing me?" Her face burned with heat as she scanned the room. "Where are you, you assholes? I'll show you some mental trauma!"

"Sit down, please," Roman said quietly.

"I have the right to face my accusers." She spotted three former employees hunched down in the back row. "There you are, you bastards!"

"Vanda, sit!" Roman ordered.

She whirled to face him. Dammit, he'd known

her since 1950, and he was believing this crap from those whiny troublemakers? She pointed a finger at him . "You—"

She gasped when Gregori grabbed her arm and yanked her down hard onto her seat. He gave her a warning glare.

She drew in a shaky breath. Okay. She needed to calm down.

"How do you plead, Ms. Barkowski?" Roman asked.

She gripped her hands together, knuckles white. "Not guilty."

"You didn't terminate the first plaintiff's employment?" Roman glanced at Laszlo. "His name?"

Laszlo scanned the first page, then plucked nervously at one of his buttons. "He wishes to be called by his stage name—Jem Stones."

Chuckles reverberated across the room, then halted abruptly when Roman cleared his throat. "Ms. Barkowski, did you fire Mister . . . Stones?"

"Yes, I did, but I had just cause."

"No, you didn't!" a petulant voice shouted from the back of the room. "I was the best dancer you ever had. You had no reason to fire me!"

Vanda glanced back at Jem. "You were trying to sell your services. I run a dance club, not a brothel."

"The ladies were begging for me," Jem argued.

"And you charged them money?" Roman asked.

Jem huffed. "Of course I did. And I'm worth it! I'm the best there is."

Roman looked unimpressed. "The first suit is dismissed."

"What?" Jem squealed. "But I need my job back. How will I make a living?"

Roman shrugged. "It appears you have already embarked upon your next career. You may leave."

Jem muttered some cusswords as he stalked out the door.

Vanda felt a small measure of relief. One accuser down and two to go.

"The second suit?" Roman asked Laszlo.

"Yes, sir." The secretary fumbled through his papers. "Reckless endangerment at the workplace. This plaintiff also wishes to go by his stage name." Laszlo fiddled with a button on his lab coat. "Peter the Great, Prince of P-P-Peckers." The button popped off and rolled across the table.

Roman's wife covered her mouth. The sound of snickering drifted about the room. Even the priest was smiling.

Gregori leaned close to Vanda and whispered loudly, "How many pickled peppers did the Prince of Peckers pick?"

Vanda snorted and elbowed him in the ribs.

Roman lifted his gaze with an exasperated look as if he were asking God, *Why me?* He schooled his features and regarded the crowd seriously. "Is Mister . . . Prince here?"

"Yeth!" A slender man in the back row stood. He flipped his long blond hair over one shoulder. "I'm the Printh of Peckerth."

"You were injured at work?" Roman asked.

"Yeth," Peter continued with his lisping voice.

"I wath danthing when I thlipped in a puddle of water."

"He wanted the water," Vanda interrupted. "Peter wanted to pull a chain and have ten gallons of water fall on top of him."

"You asked for the water?" Roman asked.

"Yeth. All the little water dropleth were glithening on my bare thkin. I wath incredibly beautiful."

"I'll take your word for it," Roman muttered. "And then you slipped?"

"Yeth! It wath awful. I fell on my nothe and broke it."

"You broke . . . what?" Roman asked.

"His nose," Vanda explained. "But we fixed it, and it's perfectly normal now."

"It ith not!" Peter planted his hands on his hip. "Now my voithe hath a terrible nathal quality to it, and everyone laughth at me."

The room filled with snorts of laughter.

"You thee?" Peter wiped at his teary eyes. "They're laughing at me. I'm thuffering from emotional trauma."

Roman sighed. "Mr. Prince, your accident was indeed regrettable, but I fail to see how you can hold Ms. Barkowski accountable when you requested the water yourself."

Peter crossed his arms and scowled. "She should have protected me."

"I reset your nose and gave you the rest of the night off," Vanda said. "You were the one who up and quit."

Peter pouted. "I want my job back."

"Is that all right with you?" Roman asked Vanda.

"Yes. I was always happy with Peter's work."

"Good." Roman nodded. "You'll hire him back, and we'll dismiss the second suit. Laszlo, the last suit, please?"

"Yes, sir." Laszlo shuffled through his papers. "Assault with a deadly weapon. The plaintiff goes by the stage name 'Max the Mega Member.'" Laszlo plucked at another button on his lab coat.

Roman gazed about the room. "Mister . . . Mega Member? Will you describe the alleged incident?"

"Alleged, my ass." Max jumped up from his seat. "She put a three-inch hole in my chest. If she'd hit my heart, I would have perished on the spot!"

"My mistake," Vanda muttered. "My aim was off."

"Then you admit to injuring this man?" Roman asked.

"He was calling me filthy names in front of my employees," Vanda explained. "I couldn't let him get away with that."

Roman frowned. "I believe firing him would have been a more reasonable course of action than stabbing him."

"She did fire me!" Max shouted. "The bitch claimed I was a lousy dancer, and that's total bullshit."

"You *are* a lousy dancer!" Vanda turned to Roman. "He did a dance with a fifteen-foot-long python, and it got loose and wrapped itself around one of my customers. She had to teleport away before it could crush her. I told Max to take his snake and hit the road."

Roman nodded. "A logical decision."

"But the bitch attacked me!" Max bellowed.

"Only after you verbally assaulted me!" Vanda shouted.

"What did you attack him with?" Roman asked.

"I wasn't going anywhere near him as long as he had that damned snake, so I grabbed one of my shoes and threw it at him." Vanda shrugged. "I guess I threw it kinda hard cause the stiletto heel sorta stuck in his chest."

"She nearly killed me!" Max hollered.

"And you nearly killed a customer with your snake," Roman reminded him. "Did your injury heal itself during your death-sleep?"

"Well, yeah, but that doesn't make it okay for her to attack me."

Roman drummed his fingers on the arm of his chair. "I am not going to find fault with a woman defending herself against a verbally abusive male."

"Yes!" Vanda punched the air.

"I'm not finished." Roman gave her a stern look. "Your method of defense was inappropriate. I'm sure you have some kind of security who could have removed Mr. Mega Member from the premises."

Vanda shrugged. She did have a huge bouncer.

"This is the third time since the opening of your club that you have been summoned here because of inappropriate and violent behavior," Roman continued. "In short, Ms. Barkowski, you have a problem with anger."

"Yeah!" Max yelled. "She's a crazy bitch!"

"Enough," Roman warned the ex-dancer. "I am dismissing the charges under the condition that Ms. Barkowski take a class in anger management."

Vanda grimaced. Not again.

"This is bullshit," Max declared. "That bitch owes me! I demand to be compensated for the trauma she caused me."

"I'll give you some compensation." Vanda shook a fist at him. "Let's meet in the parking lot—"

"Vanda, enough!" Roman glowered at her.

She glared back.

"You are exhibiting a serious lack of control," he stated quietly. "Obviously, one class of anger management wasn't enough for you."

"Yeah, she flunked anger management!" Max snickered. "You just wait, bitch. I'll give you something to be angry about."

"You are now officially under a restraining order," Roman told the ex-dancer. "You will stay away from Ms. Barkowski, or you will be fined five thousand dollars."

"What?" Max looked aghast. "What did I do?"

"Laszlo, call security to have Mr. Mega Member removed," Roman ordered.

"Yes, sir." Laszlo punched a button on his desk.

"All right, all right, I'm leaving." Max strode from the room.

"The third suit is dismissed," Roman announced, "and Ms. Barkowski has agreed to attend a second round of anger management classes."

Vanda gritted her teeth as amused whispering

sounded around the room. "I don't recall agreeing to anything."

"You will attend." Roman regarded her sternly. "Father Andrew has graciously offered to counsel you again."

She groaned inwardly. The mortal priest was a kindly old man, but he didn't have a clue about all she'd been through in her long life. And she really didn't want to tell him. Or anyone.

Father Andrew smiled at her. "I look forward to getting to know you better, my child."

Vanda crossed her arms. "Whatever."

"I will need a volunteer to be her sponsor," Father Andrew continued.

The murmuring in the room came to an abrupt halt. Absolute silence.

Great. With her superior senses, Vanda could hear the crickets chirping outside Romatech. She felt heat rising up her neck. No one wanted anything to do with her. "I don't need a sponsor."

"I'm convinced that you do," Father Andrew insisted.

More silence.

Vanda turned to Gregori. "Come on," she hissed.

"I sponsored you last time," Gregori whispered. "Obviously, I wasn't very good at it."

"Laszlo?" Vanda asked.

The short secretary jumped in his seat, and another button popped off his lab coat.

Anger sizzled in Vanda as she faced Roman. "You won't find anyone here to sponsor me. They're a bunch of cowards." She adjusted the whip around her waist. "And they're right! They should fear me. If any of them dares to reprimand me, I'll rip their heads off."

A collective gasp echoed across the room.

Roman regarded her sadly. "I don't believe you're entering into this exercise with the correct attitude."

She lifted her chin. "I've got plenty of attitude."

Roman sighed. "Is there no one here—"

"I'll do it," Shanna offered.

Vanda flinched. Roman's wife? She couldn't confess her horrid sins to sweet little do-gooder Shanna Draganesti.

Roman turned to talk quietly with his wife. Vanda's superior hearing picked up most of it. Shanna had a two-year-old son and a nine-week-old daughter to take care of. Watching Vanda would be too much of an added burden.

Vanda's anger spiked. She didn't need a damned babysitter. And she sure didn't want Shanna's pity. "Forget it! You won't find anyone here to sponsor me. None of the men here have the balls to take me on."

"I'll do it," a deep voice rumbled in the back of the room.

Vanda gasped. She recognized that voice instantly, but still, she had to turn to make sure it was really him. Oh, damn, he looked better than ever. He'd always been tall, but his shoulders looked broader than she remembered. His thick brown hair gleamed with red and gold highlights. And his eyes . . . his eyes had always taken her breath away. A pale icy blue that somehow managed to glitter with heat.

"I'll sponsor her." Phil marched down the center aisle.

God, no. She couldn't bare her soul to *Phil*. She'd confided a lot in Gregori when he'd sponsored her, but he was like a little brother. Phil could never be like a brother. "No! Ask Ian. Ian will do it."

Roman frowned. "Ian and his wife are still on their honeymoon."

Oh, right. Ian had told her they'd be gone for three whole months. So it would be the middle of August before he and Toni returned. "Then ask Pamela or Cora Lee."

Roman gave her a dubious look. "I can't imagine either of them being able to manage you."

Dammit, she'd had enough of this humiliation. "No one can manage me! I don't need a damned sponsor."

Roman ignored her and turned to Phil. "Thank you for volunteering."

"I'm not accepting him!" Vanda yelled.

Phil gave her a challenging look. "Do you prefer one of the other volunteers?"

She scowled at him. "I'll make you miserable."

He arched a brow. "What else is new?"

She blinked. She'd made him miserable? How? She'd always been nice to him. She noted the amused looks among the crowd. Dammit. They were enjoying this.

Roman cleared his throat. "Phil, do you understand the responsibilities that come with sponsorship?"

"Yes," he replied. "I can do it."

"Very well." Roman gave him a grateful smile. "The job is yours. Thank you. Laszlo, make a note of it."

"Yes, sir." Laszlo scratched away on his parchment.

"Wait a minute!" Vanda marched toward Phil. "You can't do this. I never agreed to it."

"Come." He jerked his head toward the door, then strode down the aisle and out of the room.

Vanda's mouth fell open. What the hell was he doing, giving her orders? Though she had to admit his backside looked really good. She glanced around and noticed the other Vamps watching her curiously. Well, maybe Phil was right, and they shouldn't discuss this fiasco in front of an audience.

She stalked out the door and spotted him across the hall, leaning against the wall with his arms folded. He'd always had rather big biceps for a mortal. "Look. This is a mistake. You're a mortal. You can't handle a Vamp."

"I made you leave the room, didn't I?"

Her anger flared. "Only because I didn't want to embarrass you in front of everyone while I kick your ass!"

His mouth tilted up. "Try it."

She stepped closer to him. "I've eaten mortals like you for breakfast."

His smile grew. "Lucky bastards."

She stepped back, huffing with exasperation. "Phil, this is crazy! You can't just . . . force yourself on me."

Something hot flared in his eyes. His gaze wandered down to her feet, then back to her face. "Sweetheart, no force will be necessary."

She swallowed hard. Did he think he could seduce her? Sure, she'd flirted with him in the past, but that had been nothing more than a little harmless fun. She couldn't actually get close to Phil. She couldn't open her coffin of horrors to him. Hell, she didn't open that door even for herself.

She took another step back. "*No.*"

A flicker of sympathy registered in his eyes before they hardened to an icy blue. "We all have an inner beast, Vanda. It's time for you to face yours."

"Never," she whispered, and teleported away.

Chapter Two

*N*ow that went well.

Phil frowned at the space Vanda had just vacated. Her scent lingered, something sweet and flowery like jasmine. He suspected it came from the gel she used to spike up her hair, but he might never get close enough to know. She was as fierce as a wildcat, hissing and showing her claws if anyone got too close. That alone made her intriguing. Combine it with stormy gray eyes, sweet lips, porcelain skin, and luscious curves, and the result was a woman who could destroy a man without ever laying a finger or a fang on him.

Entice, then push away. She'd done that for five long years while he'd worked as part of the security team at Roman's townhouse. Harmless flirtation, she'd called it, whenever his boss, Connor, had fussed at her. It had never been flirtation. Nor harmless. It was torture.

He'd always acted with honorable restraint. Honorable, he thought with a snort. That just meant he'd lusted for her in private.

When she'd left Roman's townhouse three years ago, he'd tried to forget about her and move on with his life. Unfortunately, seeing her tonight had unleashed years of pent-up, unrequited lust. All the memories flooded back. Memories of her teasing looks, flirtatious words, and light touches on his arms and chest. God help him, he still wanted her. He wanted her something fierce.

This time it would be different. He wasn't her guard anymore. Let her try that "harmless flirtation" with him now. A few scratches from her sharp claws wouldn't scare him away. He closed his eyes, imagining her soft, naked body beneath his, and her raw, explosive emotions erupting in a frenzy of passion. Yeah, that was the best way to cure her anger problem. He'd turn the raging tiger into a cuddly little kitty. She would be so wild and so sweet——

A door clicked shut, and Phil's eyes snapped open. Shit. He carefully refrained from looking down at the bulge in his trousers. "Father Andrew. Good to see you again."

"Mr. Jones." The priest extended a hand.

He shook it. "Call me Phil."

"Phil, then. Thank you for agreeing to sponsor Vanda."

"Glad to help." How could he have refused her?

She'd looked so fierce and defiant when no one would sponsor her. Was he the only one who could see how desperately she had covered up the pain of rejection?

"I tried to help her before," Father Andrew said, "but obviously I failed to get through that thick armor of hers. I hope you'll have better luck than I did."

"I'll do my best." He had an instant vision of Vanda's armor falling off to reveal soft naked skin underneath, but he quickly squelched that image. He couldn't afford the bulge in his pants to get any larger.

"I believe her anger is hiding a great deal of emotional pain," the priest continued. "The poor girl is in dire need of our kindness and compassion."

Now he felt like a dog. Which was fairly close to the truth.

"I'd like to know more about you, if you don't mind." Father Andrew regarded him curiously. "How long have you worked for MacKay Security and Investigation?"

"Eight years. I joined my sophomore year at NYU. I was stationed at Roman's townhouse."

"What was your degree in?"

"Psychology. Animal psychology."

"Ah. You were seeking insight into your own kind?"

Phil glanced at priest sharply. "You know about me?"

"That you're a wolfman? Yes."

Phil winced. "'Werewolf' is the correct term. Or 'Lycan.'"

"Excuse me. I find your kind fascinating, of course."

"Of course," Phil said wryly. Which was precisely why his kind wished to remain secret. The curious ones like Father Andrew would pester him with questions. The angry ones would want to kill him. The scientists would study and dissect him, and the government would seek to use him as a weapon. The cost of being fascinating was far too high.

Father Andrew removed a pair of reading glasses from his coat pocket and put them on. "I believe your special dual nature puts you in a unique position to help Vanda learn to control her violent emotions."

"Because I'm an animal?" Phil was beginning to find this conversation annoying.

"Exactly. I believe we all have . . . baser qualities that we struggle with. And since your struggle must be more tangible, you've probably developed a more practical approach of gaining control—"

"You mean I've learned to tame the beast."

The priest watched him over the rim of his glasses. "Have you?"

Phil returned the man's stare without moving a muscle. He did have control over the animal within, not that it was anyone's damned business. Then he realized what this wily priest was up to. "You're testing me, aren't you? To make sure I can control my own anger before I take on Vanda."

Father Andrew had the grace to look embarrassed.

"Forgive me, my son. But I did need to make sure. I fear Vanda will test your control to its limit. She will fight us every step of the way."

"I can handle her." Phil felt a growing curiosity about this priest. "Why do you care what happens to her? Or any of the Vamps? Why do you minister to the Undead?"

The priest's blush crept up to the fringe of silver hair above his brow. "I value all creatures who have been wrought by the Creator."

"But surely they've done things that make you cringe."

"Jesus broke bread with the tax collector and the prostitute. I'm fortunate to be able to follow His example."

Phil's mouth twitched. "In other words, with the Vamps, you've found the ultimate sinners. You must be thrilled."

"Everyone needs to know they're the children of God. That goes for shape shifters, too, I might add." He pulled a small day-timer from his coat pocket. "Now, I'd like to schedule a counseling session for you and Vanda. I may need your assistance to make sure she attends."

"No problem." It would definitely be a problem. Phil knew, from his psychology classes, that you couldn't force therapy on someone. A person couldn't change unless they really wanted to, and Vanda did not want it.

"All right." Father Andrew unhooked a small pen from the inside spine of the day-timer. "Let's see. I have a prayer meeting tomorrow night. Consultations on Thursday. Friday night is Jack and Lara's engagement party here."

"Let's do it then."

The priest glanced up. "During the party?"

"Why not? We could slip away to a conference room for fifteen minutes or so. It's the best way to get Vanda's cooperation. She'll know almost everyone in attendance, so I doubt she'll create a scene in front of them. Her sense of pride is bigger than her anger."

"She could simply refuse to attend the party."

Phil shrugged. "Then we won't tell her what we're planning to do."

"Young man, that is not how I normally do business."

"Vanda is not your normal customer."

Father Andrew winced. "That's true. But counseling should be based on trust. How will she ever trust us if we resort to trickery?"

"If we ask nicely, she'll refuse. Think of this as an intervention."

Father Andrew frowned as he considered. Then, with a sigh, he wrote in his day-timer. "All right, we'll try it your way. But I can't say I feel good about this maneuver. What if it triggers an extreme outburst of anger?"

"Then we'll help her learn how to manage it. That's the whole point, right?"

Father Andrew nodded slowly. "You're not afraid of her rage, then. That could be a good thing." He slid the day-timer back into his coat pocket. "That may be where Gregori and I went wrong the first time. I taught her relaxation exercises, and Gregori tried to keep everything very calm."

Phil shook his head. "You have to confront the beast in order to tame it. Believe me, I know."

"I see your point." Father Andrew extended a hand. "Thank you, Phil."

He shook the priest's hand. "You're welcome."

Father Andrew headed back to the meeting hall, then paused at the door. "There's one more thing. I . . . hesitate to even bring it up. You're probably already aware of the rules concerning sponsorship, and given the fact that you're two entirely different species . . . "

"What are you saying, Father?" Phil asked.

The priest removed his glasses and pocketed them. "I'm sure you don't need to hear it, but a sponsor should never get too . . . involved with his client."

Shit. Phil was careful to show no emotion, even though he was howling inside. Plan A had just gone down the tubes. So much for channeling Vanda's anger into a glorious eruption of lust. He'd have to resort to Plan B.

There was no Plan B. His thoughts had never progressed past the bedroom. The priest was right. He was an animal.

Father Andrew smiled apologetically. "I'm sure it won't be a problem for you. You've already shown that you can honor that rule when you were Vanda's guard. I'll see you Friday." He slipped back into the meeting room.

Phil stared at the closed double doors. *Double shit.* Once again he was overcome with lust for a beautiful

Vamp woman. And once again she was forbidden.

His hands balled into fists. He was an Alpha wolf now, one of the most powerful supernatural creatures on earth. If he wanted a woman, no priest was going to stop him. No ridiculous rules would stop him.

He had always felt a connection to Vanda. She'd never really fit into Roman's harem, just as he'd never fit into his father's pack. While the other harem girls had scurried about, trying in vain to gain Roman's attention and favor, Vanda had made it clear from the start that she answered to no one. She was a loner like him.

With a sigh, he trudged down the hall. Father Andrew was right. She needed his understanding and compassion. Unfortunately, his strongest feelings for her right now were lust and anger.

He'd been a starving, nineteen-year-old student, desperately trying to pay his way through college, when Connor had hired him. He would have put up with anything to keep a job that paid well, gave him free room and board, and allowed him to finish school. And he had put up with a lot. All from Vanda. For five long years she'd tortured him with her "harmless flirtation."

He'd tried his best to ignore it. The Vamps were his friends—more like his family, actually, since his father had disowned him at the age of eighteen. There was no going back. And over time, Phil had come to realize how valuable he was to the Vamps and their struggle against the Malcontents. He was protecting not just his Vamp friends, but the entire world.

He swiped his ID card outside the door to the security office, then pressed his palm against the hand sensor. These were a newly added security measures, reminding him how much the Malcontent problem had worsened over the past few years. The indicator light turned green as the door unlocked, and he entered the office.

Howard Barr, head of daytime security, was seated behind the desk, watching the wall of monitors connected to surveillance cameras. Because of the Coven Meeting, Howard was working late. Seated in front of the desk was Phineas McKinney, a young black Vamp from the Bronx. He'd been making a round earlier, when Phil had first arrived, so Phil had missed him.

"What it is, wolf-bro?" Phineas stood and raised a hand for a high five. "Lay a furry paw on me."

Phil smacked his hand. "How's it going, Dr. Phang?"

"Can't complain," Phineas said.

"Want a doughnut?" Howard pushed the box across the desk.

"No thanks." Phil shook his head, smiling. Howard Barr always had a box of doughnuts on hand, and he never seemed to gain weight. It must have something to do with having the metabolism of a bear.

Phineas settled back in his chair. "So are you stationed here now?"

"Yep." Phil was glad to be back in New York, where he could be more useful in the war against the Malcontents. He'd come earlier in the summer to help another MacKay S&I employee, Jack, rescue his fiancée, who had been kidnapped by Malcontents.

For the last year Phil's official assignment had been in Texas, where he'd served on the security team protecting Coven Master and famous fashion designer, Jean-Luc Echarpe. "I had to go back to Jean-Luc's place for a few days to take care of a problem."

"What kind of problem?" Phineas asked. "Did you have fleas, man? They make collars for that, you know."

Howard chuckled.

Phil gave them both a bland look. "It wasn't fleas. It was Billy."

"Billy?" Howard selected a bear claw from the doughnut box. "Isn't he Jean-Luc's new day guard?"

"Yes. He was the local sheriff," Phil explained, "but he retired, so he could work for MacKay S & I. I had a little trouble training him. He was sorta angry with me."

Phineas snorted. "Well, you did bite him, you know."

"He shot me first," Phil muttered.

Phineas grinned. "You looked at him funny."

"So what's the problem with Billy?" Howard munched on his bear claw. "He doesn't like being a werewolf?"

"He was shocked at first," Phil began.

"I'm sure he was." Howard stuffed the last of the bear claw in his mouth. "It can be a tough adjustment for those who become shifters as adults. It's a lot easier for us who were born into were families."

Phineas snickered. "So you had a Mama Bear and Papa Bear? Was your porridge too hot or too cold?"

"It was just right." Howard smiled as he licked the sugar off his fingertips. "So what happened with Billy?"

"After I took him out on his first hunt, he seemed okay," Phil said. "He was excited about having extra strength, superior senses, and a much longer life span. Everything was fine till about two weeks ago when Billy's girlfriend left him and he decided his life was ruined."

"Hey, I remember his girlfriend. She was hot!" Phineas sat up. "Do you have her number? She might need a little comforting from the Love Doctor, if you know what I mean."

Phil snorted. "If she rejected a werewolf, she'd probably reject a Vamp, too. Personally, I don't think she would have stayed with Billy even if he didn't go furry with the full moon. She was used to being a celebrity fashion model in New York and Paris. Life in a small town in Texas would have never suited her. I told Billy that, but he was convinced his life was over."

"What did you do?" Howard asked.

Phil had tried reasoning with Billy, but the new werewolf had sunk into a depression that logic couldn't reach. "I took him to New Mexico. I have an old friend on a Navajo reservation. Very old. And wise. He'd helped me before, so I figured he could help Billy. And he did."

"What did he help you with?" Phineas asked.

"He helped me undertake a . . . spiritual journey about six months ago. Hard to explain."

Phineas's brown eyes widened. "You got high, didn't you? What were you smokin', man?"

Phil crossed his arms. "I'd rather not discuss it."

Phineas snorted. "Ate some of those mushrooms, huh? Did you dream you were a giant iguana?"

Howard grinned, then cast a curious look at Phil. "I think that's when he became an Alpha."

"Cool," Phineas whispered. "Are you still keeping that Alpha stuff a secret?"

"Yes." Phil took a deep breath. "So, where did Connor go?"

"Oh, that was smooth, bro. We would have never noticed you changing the subject." Phineas motioned toward the monitors. "Connor's making the rounds."

Phil scanned the monitors and noted a blur of movement through the trees west of the parking lot. Connor was moving at vampire speed. "He's fast."

"Like the Flash, man." Phineas cocked his head. "I think he's slowing down. He must have seen something."

"There." Howard pointed at another monitor. "Someone's just teleported onto the grounds."

All three guards tensed, ready to spring into action. Phil relaxed. "It's Jack."

Phineas lounged back in his chair. "I guess he's just getting back from Venice."

Howard helped himself to another doughnut. "You two going to his engagement party on Friday?"

"I am." Phil watched the monitors. Connor had met up with Jack in the woods.

"Me, too," Phineas added. "Man, have you noticed how many of the guys are getting lucky? Roman, Angus, Jean-Luc, Ian, and now Jack—they're all hooking up with hot-looking babes."

Phil edged behind the desk to fill a cup of coffee from the pot Howard kept on a credenza. "I'm happy for them."

"So am I, but where the hell is *my* hot babe?" Phineas stood and planted his fists on his hips. "I'm the Love Doctor. The chicks should be climbing all over me."

Howard shoved a small canister toward Phil. "Sugar?"

Phil shook his head.

"Not for a long time, man." Phineas paced across the room. "It's been months since I had any sugar."

Howard offered Phil a canister of Coffee-mate.

Phil shook his head. "I like it black."

"I like 'em black, too." Phineas suddenly halted. "But I'm not prejudiced, you know. I have never failed to jump a woman's bones based on her color or religion. The Love Doctor never turns a lady away."

"That's real sporting of you, Phineas." Phil took a sip of coffee. He noticed on the monitor that Jack and Connor had reached the side entrance. Connor swiped his card, then activated the hand sensor.

Phineas's shoulders slumped. "I just don't get it."

"Get what?" Howard poured himself a cup of coffee, then dumped in a huge amount of sugar.

"All the married Vamps seem really happy."

Phineas resumed his pacing. "With just one woman. When there are so many hot chicks in the world, how can you settle for just one?"

"She has to be really special." And of all the women Phil had met in his twenty-seven years, it was Vanda who came to his mind. She didn't wear the facade of indifferent superiority like most Vamp women. She was raw, passionate, and painfully honest. She was in your face. She'd intrigued him from the start.

"I think it's called love," Howard said.

Phil flinched. "I wouldn't call it that. Infatuation, maybe."

Howard gave him an incredulous look. "You don't think Jack loves Lara? Or Roman loves Shanna? Or—"

"Oh, yeah." Phil realized he'd lost the trail of the conversation. "That's definitely love. I—I was thinking about . . . someone else."

Howard eyed him curiously. "Like who?"

Phil was saved when the buzzer sounded at the door. Connor had activated the security measures outside, causing the door to unlock. Connor and Jack walked in.

Jack smiled and shook hands as he greeted everyone. "You're all coming to the engagement party, yes? I want Lara to feel welcomed in the Vamp world."

"We're coming," Howard said.

"Where is Lara?" Phil asked.

"At her apartment," Jack answered. "I teleported her there first, so she could get some sleep. She's worn-out from sightseeing all day in Venezia."

"I'm glad ye're back." Connor stood next to the desk and folded his arms across his chest. "Phil just arrived tonight, too, so I'd like to catch everyone up to date."

"Good." Jack perched on the far corner of the desk.

Howard sat behind the desk, while Phineas and Phil took the chairs in front. When everyone was focused on Connor, he began.

"The latest information we have indicates that Casimir has moved to North America. We have no idea where he's setting up his base of operations, but we do know that he liked to visit his friend Apollo, in Maine. We're assuming he doesna know that Apollo and Athena have been killed."

Phil drank some coffee. Earlier in July he had helped Jack rescue his fiancée, Lara, who was being held captive at Apollo's Malcontent compound in Maine. Jack had killed Apollo, while Phil had teamed up with Lara to kill Athena. "We left the compound empty. Most of the mortals had their memories erased and were sent back home."

"What happened to the girl who wanted to keep her memory?" Jack asked.

"She's at Shanna's school," Connor replied. "She's going to be a teacher there. Carlos is doing security. Now my point is, there's no one at the compound to tell Casimir no' to come anymore. So Angus figured there's a good chance that Casimir might return."

"Are we setting a trap?" Jack asked.

"Aye." Connor smiled. "Angus arrived there two

weeks ago to do just that. He has a team of seven with him. That should be enough to capture Casimir."

Phil felt a twinge of envy. He would love a piece of that action. "What are our orders?"

"We're to stay here," Connor said. "Romatech is still a prime target. If Casimir decides to avenge the massacre at DVN, he knows he can always find a few enemies right here."

"We'll need to be extra careful the night of the engagement party," Jack said.

"Aye. We'll all be on duty that night. Any questions?" When no one spoke, Connor continued. "Good. With any luck, Casimir will be destroyed soon, and another vampire war will be avoided."

Jack glanced at the monitor that showed the coven meeting coming to an end. "I need to talk to Shanna about the party. See you all later." He rushed out the door.

"Phineas, will you make sure everyone attending the coven meeting leaves?" Connor asked. "We doona want anyone roaming about the facility."

"Gotcha." Phineas hurried out the door.

"Howard, see if Shanna and the children need a ride home," Connor said.

"Yes, sir." Howard lumbered out the door.

"Phil, ye're off for the rest of the night." Connor sat behind the desk and shuffled through some papers. "I'm glad ye're back, lad."

"Me, too." Phil finished his coffee, then returned the empty cup to the credenza. As a day guard, he was expected to sleep at night so he could be on duty during the daylight hours. He usually slept at Roman's townhouse in the Upper East Side. Phineas and Jack would show up there shortly before dawn to fall into their death-sleep.

"Good night, sir." Phil headed for the door.

"Good night. Oh, I was wondering . . . " Connor gave him a curious look. "I saw on a monitor earlier that you were talking to Vanda and then she teleported away."

Phil paused with his hand on the doorknob. "She was a little upset."

"Of course she was upset. Three of her former dancers were suing her for damages. Do ye know what Roman decided?"

"He insisted she take another session of anger management."

Connor snorted. "Like that will help. Vanda's been angry for as long as I've known her."

"How long is that?" Phil asked.

"Since Roman became Coven Master and inherited the harem in 1950."

"So she was already in the harem? She must have joined when the previous Coven Master was in power."

"Aye." Connor nodded. "Why are ye so interested?"

"I agreed to be her sponsor."

Connor's eyebrows rose. "Why would ye do that?"

Phil shrugged. "Someone had to do it."

Connor studied him a moment, then shifted his gaze to the monitors. "She left her car behind."

Phil glanced at the monitor that showed the front parking lot. "Which car is hers?"

"The black Corvette. I have the keys."

Phil's heart leaped in his chest. He could see her again tonight. "I'll be happy to return it to her."

"If she wants it, she can teleport back for it. Ye're officially off duty now."

"But I can drop it off on the way to Roman's townhouse," Phil insisted. "I really don't mind."

Connor removed the keys from his sporran. "She's probably at her club."

"I know where it is."

Connor handed him the keys. "Be careful, lad."

Phil snorted. "I know how to drive."

"I wasna referring to the car."

"I know what I'm doing."

Connor frowned at him. "That's what they all say."

Chapter Three

*A*lthough Phil knew about Vanda's nightclub, he'd never been inside before. The entrance to the Horny Devils was hidden at the dead end of a dark alley to keep unsuspecting mortals from stumbling across the place.

A huge bouncer stood guard at the dark red door. His nostrils flared as he took a sniff. Phil knew he didn't carry the usual mortal scent. Since most Vamps didn't know about shape shifters, they didn't realize the significance of his different scent. They simply thought he was a strange-smelling mortal.

"Place is closed," the bouncer grumbled. "Get lost."

"I'm here to see Vanda Barkowski."

"You know Vanda?" The bouncer took another sniff, and his beady eyes narrowed. "You're an odd duck."

"Not even close." Phil showed his MacKay Security & Investigation ID card, knowing the Vamp bouncer could see it in the dark. "I'm returning Vanda's car. She left it at Romatech."

The bouncer still eyed him suspiciously. "I'll have to frisk you."

"Fine." Phil raised his arms to shoulder height so the bouncer could pat his navy polo shirt and khaki pants—the MacKay uniform for guards who didn't wear kilts.

"What's this?" The man patted his pants' pocket.

"It's a chain. Silver."

The bouncer jerked his hand away. He hesitated, then asked, "You're not planning on using it on anyone?"

"No." Phil smiled, understanding the bouncer's predicament. The Vamp couldn't confiscate the silver chain without giving himself severe burns. Luckily for Phil, silver was only painful when introduced internally, as in silver bullets. "You can call Connor Buchanan at Romatech if you want to check on me."

The bouncer shrugged his massive shoulders. "I'll just keep an eye on you." He opened the door. "Go on in."

Phil was instantly bombarded with loud, pounding music and red and blue laser lights slashing across the large renovated warehouse. As his eyes adjusted, he noted the stage was empty. The male dancers must be on break.

A group of Vamp women were writhing on the dance floor. A few Vamp men sat at tables, drinking glasses of Bleer topped with pink-tinted foam while they watched the women dance. Their eyes narrowed when they spotted him. Competition.

He scanned the huge room but couldn't see Vanda. The bouncer was standing just inside the door, watching him. He recognized the woman behind the bar. Cora Lee Primrose, former member of Roman Draganesti's harem. She'd shed her Southern belle hoop skirts in favor of more modern garb—hip hugger pants and a sparkly halter top.

She did a double take when he eased onto a barstool. "Phil? Is that you?" she yelled over the loud music. "Land sakes, I haven't seen you in ages."

"Hi, Cora Lee. You're looking great."

"Why, thank you kindly." With a giggle, she flipped her long blond hair over her shoulder. "Would you like something to drink? We have a few mortal drinks like beer."

"I'll have one of those." He stood so he could pull the wallet from his back pocket.

"No, you don't. It's on the house." She cast a flirtatious look at him as she filled a glass. "Land sakes, you've filled out nicely over the years."

"Thank you." He settled back onto the barstool. "So, is Vanda here?"

With a sigh, Cora Lee set the beer in front of him. "I should have known you'd come to see her. The way she used to talk about you—goodness gracious, we were scandalized."

His first sip of beer went down with a gulp. "Why? What did she say?"

"What didn't she say? I do declare she would describe every part of your manly physique from the top of your head down to your toes." Cora Lee gave him a sly smile. "She was quite poetic about your buttocks."

He gulped down more beer.

Cora Lee wiped the counter, still smiling. "She always claimed you had a crush on her."

His hand tightened around the glass. "Did she, now?"

"According to Vanda, she can make you do anything she wants like a trained puppy."

He downed the last of his beer and slammed the glass onto the bar. "Where is she?"

Cora Lee pointed to a series of doors along the back wall. "The first one is her office."

"Thanks." Phil slid off the stool.

"Don't forget to knock," Cora Lee warned him. "Vanda's got the dancers in there. It could be kinda awkward if you just barge in."

He stiffened. "Why? What's she doing with them?"

Cora Lee shrugged. "The usual. She has to personally check out the costumes and dances before the guys go on stage. Quality control, you know."

Phil's jaw clenched. "You don't say."

"Oh, I do. One time I went in there, and Terrance was prancing around naked." Cora Lee giggled. "Vanda told him to put a sock on it."

"I understand," Phil growled. As he stalked toward her office, the music ended. With his superior hearing, he heard Vanda's voice through the door.

"Oh my God, Peter, it's *huge*!"

"They don't call me the Printh of Peckerth for nothing," a man boasted.

"You can't let him on stage with that," another man protested. "He'll make us look small."

"You *are* smaller than me," Peter insisted.

"We are not!" a third male shouted.

"Calm down!" Vanda's voice sounded agitated. "Peter, I'm glad you've come back to dance for us, but this—this is too much. You'll have to lose a few inches."

"No!" Peter screamed. "I won't let you touch it!"

"Don't tell me what I can't do!" Vanda yelled. "Where are my scissors?"

Peter squealed. Like a girl. Which he might be soon.

Phil threw the door open and charged inside. "Vanda, stop! You can't cut off a man's——" He halted, stunned to see Vanda standing behind her desk with her scissors poised on a sparkling red sheath.

It wasn't a dong. It was a thong. With a long sheath stuffed like a sausage.

Vanda's mouth fell open. "Phil, what are you doing here?"

He glanced around the office, noting that the three slender young men were fully clothed and regarding him curiously. "What are *you* doing, Vanda?"

Her cheeks grew pink as she lowered the thong to the desk. "I was conducting a business meeting."

"Vanda," one of the male dancers whispered. "Won't you introduce us to your handsome young friend?"

"Sure, Terrance." Vanda spoke through gritted teeth. "This is Phil Jones." She gestured to the other male dancers. "Terrance the Turgid, Freddie the Fireman, and Peter the Great."

"I remember you from the coven meeting," Peter said. "You thaid you would help Vanda with her anger problem."

"I don't have an anger problem!" Vanda pointed the scissors at Peter, then at Phil. "And I don't need your help."

Phil arched a brow at her. "As your sponsor, I suggest you put the scissors down."

She slammed them onto the desk. "You are *not* my sponsor."

Terrance smiled at him. "You can be *my* sponsor."

Vanda groaned. "Phil, we're trying to have a costume meeting here." She handed Freddie a thong that looked like a fire hose, and Terrance a thong covered with ivy.

Terrance dangled his costume in front of Phil's face. "Isn't it fabulous? I'm doing an ode to Tarzan."

"That's nice," Phil mumbled.

Peter made a grab for the red sparkly thong.

"No!" Vanda snatched it from his hand. "You're not dancing in this monstrosity. *I* design the costumes, and I'll tell you what to wear."

"That'th not fair," Peter whined. "I had that cuthtom made to fit me perfectly."

"No way," Freddie grumbled. "You would have to use padding."

Peter huffed. "I never uthe padding."

"You would have to." Vanda set the costume on the desk. "There isn't a man on earth who could fill that thing."

"I'm not so sure about that." Terrance glanced at Phil and winked.

Phil had had all he could take. "This meeting is over." He gave the men a warning look and motioned to the door. "You will leave."

"What?" Vanda's eyes flashed with anger. "You can't do that! This is my—" She paused when Peter and Freddie scurried from the room. "—office."

Terrance stopped halfway out the door and grinned at her. "Be nice, girlfriend. This one's a keeper."

"Out," Phil growled.

"Oooh." Terrance shivered. "Me Tarzan, you Phil." He ran out.

Phil shut the door. "Now we can talk."

Vanda glared at him. "I'm not talking to you. You're acting like a caveman."

"I suppose you prefer those pretty little boys who are easy to control. Easier to control than your own anger—"

"My anger's just fine!" She grabbed Peter's costume off the desk and threw it at him. "Get out!"

He caught the thong with one hand and turned it over as he examined it. "Thank you, Vanda. It's just my size."

She snorted. "A man would have to be aroused to fill that up."

He lifted his gaze to meet hers. "Not a problem."

Her gaze flitted down to his pants, then jerked away. "What—Why did you come here?"

He walked toward her. "You left Romatech in a hurry. We were in the middle of a conversation."

Her eyes darkened to a stormy gray. "The conversation was over."

"You left your car behind."

"Like I had any choice! That damned Connor confiscated my keys." She blinked when Phil jingled the keys in the air. "You—You brought my car?"

"Yes. It's parked across the street."

"Oh. Thank you." She skirted the desk and approached him. "That was very kind of you," she grumbled.

"You're welcome." He dropped the keys into her outstretched hand. "Now, about my sponsorship . . ."

Her hand fisted around the keys. "There is no sponsorship. You can't force me to take anger management."

"I believe we can. It was the court's decision. If you want the lawsuits against you dropped, then you have to comply."

She tossed the keys on the desk. "Do I look like the kind of person who *complies?* Only cowards and trained monkeys comply. I'm a free spirit. Nobody's going to tell me what to do."

Phil couldn't help but smile. Vanda's words were almost identical to the speech he'd given his father nine years ago before he'd stormed out of Montana. "Then what do you plan to do about your anger problem?"

"I don't have an anger problem!" she yelled. With a groan, she pressed a hand to her forehead. "Why won't people stop trying to force me to do things against my will?"

"Believe me, I understand." Phil's father had tried to force him into a preplanned life. At the age of eighteen, he hadn't possessed the maturity or strength to fight his father. He'd simply left. Then his father had banished him from the pack. "Things don't always go the way we want them to. And it's very frustrating when there's nothing you can do to change it."

Vanda frowned at him. "Are you sympathizing with me just to get me to agree to the program?"

"I'm saying if you want to talk, I'll listen."

Her face grew pale and she tightened the whip around her waist with a jerky motion. "Why should I believe you care? You haven't bothered to see me in three years."

She'd counted the years? Phil swallowed hard. What if he'd misinterpreted things? He'd felt sure that Vanda had considered him nothing more than a toy to relieve her boredom. Good God, what if she had genuinely cared about him? No, this had to be more of her fun and games. "I didn't realize you wanted to see me."

Her eyes narrowed. "What do you need, an engraved invitation?"

"You opened a male strip club, Vanda. You're surrounded every night with available men. Nearly naked, vampire men." He tossed the costume onto her desk. "I really didn't think you were lacking for companionship."

She lifted her chin. "I get all the companionship I need."

He gritted his teeth. "Good."

"Excuse me for thinking you might want to keep in touch. I had thought we were friends."

"We were never friends."

She gasped. "How can you say that? We . . . we talked."

"You taunted me."

She stiffened. "I was nice to you."

He stepped toward her. "You were bored, and you tormented me for the fun of it."

"Don't be silly. It was just a little harmless flirtation."

"It was sheer torture." He advanced another step. "I *hated* it. Every time you touched me, I wanted to rip your little catsuit off and make you purr."

Her mouth dropped open, then shut suddenly with a snap. Her cheeks flushed. "Then why didn't you? Why did you let a stupid rule stop you? Ian didn't let anything stop him from going after Toni."

He grabbed Vanda by the shoulders so quickly, she gasped. "I would have taken you in a second if I had thought you actually wanted it."

Her cheeks grew a deeper red. "How would you know what I really want?"

He leaned close. "I was on to you from the start. You're a tease. You like to get a man hard, then leave him panting. You enjoyed watching me suffer."

"That's not true. I—I really liked you." She winced as if she'd admitted more than she had wanted to.

He brushed his nose across her cheek and whispered in her ear, "Prove it."

She trembled in his arms. He could feel her breath coming in quick puffs against his skin.

He moved his mouth closer to hers. "Show me."

With a small cry, she turned her head away from him.

Shit. He had been right all along. He'd been nothing but a game to her. He dropped his hands from her shoulders. "Admit it. You flirted with me because you were bored and I was safe. I desperately needed the job, so I was going to follow the rules no matter how much you tortured me."

She pressed a hand to her forehead. "I—I didn't mean . . ."

"To make me ache for you? Tell me, Vanda, did you ever feel anything? Did you really care about me, or were you just being a cold-blooded bitch?"

With a gasp, she pulled her hand back and slapped him. "Get out!"

He rubbed his jaw and smiled. "I guess you're not too cold-blooded."

She pointed at the door. "Leave!"

He considered taunting her some more. God knew she deserved it after torturing him for five long years. But he noticed her hand was trembling and her eyes glimmered with unshed tears.

Now he felt like a dog. He'd only wanted to turn the tables on her and give her a taste of her own "harmless flirtation." He hadn't meant to hurt her.

He trudged toward the door, where he paused with his hand on the doorknob. "You've always intrigued me, Vanda. From the moment I met you. I could never figure out why a free-spirited woman would confine herself to a harem. What were you hiding from? And why would a rebellious, beautiful woman flirt with the one man she considered safe?"

She folded her arms and gave him a wary look. "So now you want to analyze me, *Doctor* Phil?"

He smiled slowly. "I want to do a lot of things to you, Vanda. You see, with me, you made one big mistake. I was never safe."

Vanda stood alone in her office, blinking back tears. Dammit, she wouldn't cry. She was tough. But she'd made Phil suffer. She'd never intended to do that. How could a little harmless fun go so wrong?

She circled the desk and collapsed in her chair. He'd seen right through her. He'd known she was bored out of her skull. When she'd first joined the harem in 1948, she'd welcomed the peace and serenity. But over time, boredom had set in, and she'd been desperate for a diversion.

Poor Phil had seemed safe. It was against the rules for him to fraternize with her. He'd made it clear from the start that he would honor the rules.

And she'd tortured him.

She bent her head and rested it on her hands. The coffin tucked away in the shadows of her mind slowly creaked open. Mental pictures floated out.

Mama, who had died in 1935 when Vanda was eighteen.

Frieda, her youngest sister, who died four years later when they fled from the Nazis. Frieda, with her chestnut curls and big blue eyes.

Jozef, her baby brother, who at the age of twelve insisted on joining his father and three older brothers to fight the incoming invasion. Vanda's eyes stung with tears. Jozef with his black curly hair and laughing, blue eyes. He'd marched off to war so proudly. And she never saw him again. A tear rolled down her cheek.

Ian had always reminded her of Jozef. She hadn't meant to become attached to Ian, but he'd slowly started to symbolize all the brothers she had lost. And she'd come so close to losing Ian last December. Ever since the battle at DVN, her nerves had been on edge.

More pictures drifted out of the coffin. Papa and her three other brothers—Bazyli, Krystian, and Stefan. Fuzzy and unclear.

A sob escaped. Oh God, she couldn't remember their faces. Her shoulders shook. How could she forget? After Mama died, she'd taken care of all her brothers and sisters. They'd been her entire life. How could she forget?

She squeezed her eyes shut. No! She wouldn't do this. She didn't need to punish herself just because she felt guilty for tormenting Phil. Mentally, she shoved all the pictures back into the coffin and slammed the lid shut.

She wouldn't let herself think about the past. How she'd lost everyone she loved. Her parents, her brothers, her sister. Even Karl, her first love and leader of the underground resistance.

All gone.

She took a deep, shuddering breath and wiped the tears from her face. She should have never flirted with Phil. He was a mortal with a short life. If she fell for him, she would only lose him, too.

It didn't matter that he intrigued her and excited her. It didn't matter that she wanted his arms around her, comforting her. It didn't matter that she admired his strength and intelligence. Or that she was so tired of being alone.

Screams erupted from the club, jerking her back to reality. What now?

"Vanda!" Terrance flung the door open. "Max the Mega Member just teleported in. He says you're going to die!"

Chapter Four

Vanda strode into the club, whip in hand, her eyes adjusting to the dim lighting. Only a handful of customers remained. The others must have teleported away at the first sign of danger. The remaining customers were crowded in a circle, gossiping with hushed voices.

"He's so incredibly strong," a female Vamp whispered to her friend.

"And so handsome," the friend replied.

Vanda snorted. There was no accounting for taste. Her bouncer Hugo was about as wide as he was tall. His massive head sat right on his huge shoulders. She often wondered how he'd ever gotten transformed when he had no visible neck to bite.

"Excuse me." She nudged the two gossiping girls aside.

"Vanda," a deep, gravelly voice spoke behind her.

With a start, she turned to find Hugo. "What? Then who—"

He rested a beefy hand on her shoulder. "I need to talk to you."

"Not now!" She pulled away from him and shoved her way through the crowd. She stopped with a gasp.

Max was flat on his back with Phil sitting on top of him. Phil's fists were planted on the floor on each side of the ex-dancer, and in them he gripped a silver chain that was stretched across Max's chest. The chain not only pinned Max to the floor, but it prevented the Vamp from teleporting away.

Vanda stared at them for several seconds. No wonder the crowd was whispering in amazement. It was practically unheard of for a mortal to be quick enough to catch a vampire and strong enough to hold one down.

On the floor, at her feet, a long dagger gleamed in the dim light. *Good Lord*. A shudder skittered down her spine. If Max had stabbed her in the heart, she'd be a pile of dust right now. Somehow, Phil had managed to disarm him. Phil had saved her life. And he didn't even look winded.

He glanced up at her and smiled.

Her knees nearly buckled.

The girls behind her sighed.

"What pretty eyes," one of them whispered.

Vanda's grip tightened on the whip, and she stifled an urge to snarl at the girls. But what could she possibly say? *Hands off, he's mine*? She had no claim to him.

She glanced away, irked with herself for succumbing to jealousy and being so easily flustered by a man's smile and pretty blue eyes. Her frustration flared into anger when she spotted her three dancers watching the scene from behind the bar. Those spineless cowards.

Hugo grabbed her arm and pulled her away from the crowd. "Vanda, I have to talk to you. It's about that mortal."

"I know," she spoke with gritted teeth. "He's incredibly strong and handsome. You want to join the fan club?"

Hugo looked confused. "No. There's something strange about him. He moves too fast."

"Tell me about it. He captured a psycho and protected me from certain death, which is *your* job, I believe." She glared at the bouncer. "If you're slower than a mortal, maybe I hired the wrong man."

"No, no! I'm going to take care of Max. I just thought I'd better warn you about—"

"What are you planning to do?" Vanda felt a sudden twinge of alarm. She didn't want any more deaths on her conscience.

"I was going to teleport him far away and warn him to leave you alone," Hugo grumbled. "And I thought I might punch him in the gut, if you don't mind."

"Oh. I guess I can live with that." She nudged her way back through the crowd. Everyone moved back when Hugo came through.

Phil was still holding down the struggling Vamp

as if he were detaining a small child in time-out. Max didn't seem to be in any pain, since the silver chain was against his clothes. If it had come into contact with his skin, there would have been some nasty, smelly, sizzling flesh.

Phil glanced up at her. "What do you want to do with him?"

"Hugo will take care of him."

On cue, Hugo growled deep in his throat. The crowd jumped back.

Max gasped as Hugo lumbered closer like a huge bear. "No! Let me go. I'll leave Vanda alone, I promise."

"You were told to leave her alone at the coven meeting." Phil glared down at him. "Obviously, you can't be trusted."

"You're in violation of the restraining order." Vanda wrapped her whip around her waist and tied it off. "I believe you owe the court five thousand dollars."

Max spat at her boots. "You bitch! You're the one who owes me money!"

"Enough." Hugo reached down and seized Max around the neck. "I've got him," he told Phil. "You can let go."

As soon as Phil jumped to his feet and lifted the silver chain, Hugo teleported away with Max. Phil stuffed the silver chain into his pants' pocket, and the female Vamps moved in.

"You were amazing." One of the girls pressed close.

"I do declare." Cora Lee wrapped a hand around his arm. "I've never seen such a vigorous, manly display."

"The show is over," Vanda grumbled.

Phil's eyes twinkled with amusement as he leaned over to pick up Max's dagger. "You might want to step back, ladies. This is a dangerous weapon."

With a sigh, the women moved back.

Phil focused on Vanda. "May I talk to you in private?"

"I . . . suppose." She turned stiffly and led the way to her office. Her nerves tensed at the thought of being alone with him again. But she needed to do this. She needed to apologize for causing him so much pain in the past.

She glanced at him briefly as he strode into the office, then shut the door. "Thank you for protecting us."

"You're welcome." He placed the dagger on her desk. "You might need this."

She stifled a shudder. She didn't need a reminder of how bad things could have been. "At least Max didn't bring that damned snake."

Phil turned to face her. "Snake?"

"A fifteen-foot-long python. Max dances with it. Or he tried to. The snake had other plans." She took a deep breath. Thank God Phil wasn't a Vamp and couldn't hear her heart pounding. There was something about him, and apparently she wasn't the only one feeling it. All of the women were reacting to him. And that was making her feel strangely possessive.

He'd affected her from the start. At nineteen he'd

been lean and lanky, but he'd still exuded an earthy sexiness that had appealed to her. Now, at twenty-seven, he'd filled out that lanky form with muscle and an aura of male power. Every nerve ending in her body seemed aware of him, drawn to him, on fire for him.

She had to be out of her mind. Hadn't she endured enough pain in her life? She would apologize and then let him go. She took a deep breath and met his steady gaze.

He stepped toward her. "I need to apologize."

She blinked. He'd stolen the words right out of her mouth. "But——"

He raised a hand to stop her. "I need to say this. I was on the sidewalk, waiting for a cab, when I realized I was a hypocrite. I volunteered to help you handle your anger, but I wasn't handling my own. I was rude—"

"But you had every right to be angry with me. I tormented you. I made you miserable. I shouldn't have treated you like that."

His eyes softened. "I could suffer far worse things than having a beautiful woman come on to me."

The blueness of his eyes made her chest feel tight, like it was hard to breathe. "You're being kind, but I don't deserve it. You were right. I was bored, and you seemed like a safe diversion. I'm really sorry."

"I'm sorry, too. I was coming back inside the club to apologize when Max appeared."

She recalled her bouncer's strange warning. "I heard you reacted very quickly."

"I've been working for MacKay S & I a long time,

so I've learned a few tricks." He touched his pocket. "Like carrying a silver chain with me. It's the only way to keep a vampire from escaping." He tilted his head. "Do you have any kind of security?"

"Of course. I have Hugo."

"I meant away from the club. Who's guarding you while you're in your death-sleep?"

She shrugged. "Pamela, Cora Lee, and I share a condo, and the building has really tight security. They never let anyone near our apartment during the day. We're officially listed as day-sleepers."

He shook his head. "That's not enough. Maybe you should move back to Roman's townhouse for a while—"

"No." Vanda lifted both hands as if to ward off evil. "I'm not giving up my independence. I did that once, and it took over fifty years to get it back."

His eyes narrowed. "Why did you join the harem?"

Damn. Now she'd said too much. "It's ancient history. Forget it."

The look on his face made it clear he was forgetting nothing. "I don't think you've seen the last of Max."

"He can't bother me while I'm sleeping. He's just as dead as I am during the day."

Phil frowned at her. "I don't like the thought of you being alone."

"I'm not alone!" she said, louder than necessary, then winced. "I have friends. And I have this club. My life is one big party."

Phil stepped closer, studying her face. "You've been crying."

"I'm *fine*. Now, if you don't mind—" She flinched when he touched her cheek.

"Vampire tears." His finger traced a line down her cheek. "They leave a faint pink stain."

She moved back. "Good night, Phil. Thank you once again for protecting us."

He stared at her. She looked away, her heart floundering under the searching gaze of those pale blue eyes.

"How about giving me a ride home?"

She swallowed hard. Hadn't she been through enough tonight? But how could she refuse? He'd brought her car back. He'd saved her from Max. But the thought of spending more time alone with him was too disconcerting. Her nerves were completely shot. Her emotions were a tangled mess. She wanted to touch him. She wanted to feel his strong arms around her. And at the same time, she wanted him to go far away and never come back.

She pressed a hand against her brow. "I—I'm very busy."

"It will only take a few seconds for you to teleport me. But then, you would have to let me wrap my arms around you and hold you tight. If that scares you too much—"

"I'm not scared!" She clenched her teeth when he smiled slowly. Damn him. He'd manipulated her into this. "You're still getting even with me, aren't you?"

"Actually, I'm making progress with those negative feelings. I no longer have visions of making you suffer."

"Oh, that's big of you."

His mouth twitched. "How kind of you to notice."

Her gaze flitted south, then quickly away. Good Lord, he *was* big. How could he be so turned on? He'd only touched her cheek. Her skin tingled, and she suddenly wanted him to touch her everywhere.

He took hold of her shoulders. "Instead of making you suffer, I'm thinking about all the ways I could give you pleasure."

Oh God, don't melt on him. She locked her shaky knees and planted her hands against his chest, more to steady herself than shove him away. He wrapped his arms around her and pulled her close.

She gasped when his hard shaft pressed against her belly. "Not so close. I have to concentrate to teleport. You don't want to arrive home minus an appendage, and I don't mean your foot."

With a smirk, he eased back. "It is a foot right now."

She groaned. "Caveman." She closed her eyes to focus on Roman's townhouse. Her body started to waver, but when Phil's body remained intact, she stopped. "There's something wrong. You're not coming with me."

"Not enough foreplay, sweetheart."

She swatted his arm. "I meant your body is refusing to teleport."

"Ah." He released her and dug the silver chain out of his pants' pocket. "This must be the problem." He dropped the chain onto her desk. "Now, where were we?"

Her heart executed a little flip when he dragged her back into his arms. She rested her hands against his chest and felt the powerful thudding of his heart. She squeezed her eyes shut, trying to focus, trying to block out all the tingling sensations that zipped along her body.

His arms were so strong. His breath stirred the hair on top of her head. And his scent—clean but earthy, and redolent with male power—filled her head and made her wish for the impossible.

But it was impossible. No matter how tempting he was, she couldn't let herself have genuine feelings for him. She'd had all the pain a person could bear in a lifetime. She would simply teleport him home, then come right back. Alone.

She felt her consciousness tumble into a black hole. She wavered, taking Phil with her, and everything went black.

Phil had never been fond of hitching a ride from a Vamp. It placed him in an inferior role of accepting help, which grated on his instinctive need to be dominant. He put up with the situation since the war against the Malcontents was more important than anyone's ego. When it came to teleporting with Vanda, however, he'd simply wanted an excuse to hold her tight.

They landed in the foyer of Roman's townhouse, and Vanda immediately broke free of his embrace.

She grimaced, covering her ears. "What's that awful noise?"

"We must have set off the alarm." Phil strode to the control panel by the front door and punched in the code to stop the high-pitched wailing. Only vampires and dogs were supposed to be able to hear it, so apparently he was more like a dog than he cared to admit. "The guys usually teleport to the back porch, so they can turn off the alarm before coming in."

"Oh, I didn't know about that." Vanda glanced around. "Place still looks the same."

"It is, though it's fairly empty." Phil pressed more buttons to reactivate the alarm. "We had to tighten security. Couldn't have Malcontents teleporting in to attack us."

Vanda nodded. "Will it be okay for me to teleport out?"

"Just a sec." He pulled a cell phone from his pocket and called Romatech. They would have received an alert about the alarm going off at the townhouse. "Hey, Connor. False alarm. Everything's fine." He hung up.

Vanda shifted her weight, looking impatient. "Can I go now?"

He dropped his cell phone back into his pocket as he walked toward her. "There's no need to hurry off."

Her eyes narrowed. "Not happening, Phil."

"What's not happening?"

She crossed her arms. "Whatever you have in mind."

He stopped in front of her. "There's a lot on my mind. Could you be more specific?"

She glared at him. "Given your caveman tendencies, I assume all your thoughts lead to the same result."

"Well, let me see. I've been thinking about kissing that luscious mouth of yours. And I've given considerable thought to peeling that catsuit off you. And then, of course, I would have to kiss every inch of your body." He grinned. "I believe you're right, Vanda."

She snorted, but he noted the blush creeping up her neck.

He took her lightly by the shoulders. "Come sit down with me for a while."

She shook her head. "I can't. I—I want you to forget about me."

He released her as if she'd slapped him. "*Forget* you? Vanda, I've wanted you for eight years. I could never forget you. And dammit, I don't want to wait another night!"

Her eyes glimmered with tears. "I'm sorry, Phil. I can't." Her body wavered and disappeared.

"What are you afraid of?" he yelled at her fading body.

Why was she running away?

Because she knew he wanted to have sex with her. He had too much pent-up lust to be satisfied with a few little kisses. And no doubt, Vanda knew that, too.

He felt reasonably sure that she was attracted to him. He'd been the one she'd wanted to flirt with years ago. And if Cora Lee could be believed, Vanda had spent a lot of time talking about him. His sense of hearing wasn't quite as good as a Vamp's, but he could still hear her heart pounding whenever he was near.

So why was she afraid of getting involved with him?

He wandered into the kitchen to have a bedtime snack, then proceeded downstairs to the guardroom in the basement. The dormitory looked strange without any coffins in it. The older Scottish Vamps had preferred to sleep in coffins lined with their clan tartan, but they had all gotten reassigned, or in Ian's case, married.

Phineas McKinney, the young black Vamp from the Bronx, slept in a twin bed with red satin sheets. Photos of his family rested on the bedside table.

A second twin-sized bed had been set up for Phil. He'd left his suitcase beside it earlier. He quickly unpacked, hanging his spare uniforms in the walk-in closet that looked oddly bare without any kilts.

There had been a time when the townhouse was a busy place, occupied by Roman, visiting Vamps, a harem of ten women, and a full contingent of guards, both Vamp and mortal. Now, Roman was married with a family, living in White Plains with Connor and Howard Barr as their bodyguards.

Phil showered and set the alarm beside his bed. He'd have to get up at least thirty minutes before Phineas and Jack fell into their death-sleep. It was his job to guard them during the day and provide any assistance they needed in guarding Romatech.

Like any soldier, Phil had learned to fall asleep quickly. Even so, he tossed and turned. At first he assumed it was a case of too much pent-up lust. As the night wore on, he realized it was more worry than lust. He was worried about Vanda being alone and unprotected.

He punched his pillow and went back to sleep. She wasn't alone. Hugo would protect her.

When the alarm went off, he jerked awake and checked the time. It was still dark outside, but the sun would rise in thirty minutes. Vampires all along the East Coast would be seeking shelter. Phineas and Jack would be arriving soon. Vanda would be going to the apartment she shared with two former members of the harem. Her apartment with inadequate security.

And Max would have a window of opportunity to kill her.

Phil threw on his uniform, then ran into the armory as he dialed Romatech on his cell phone. Jack answered.

He quickly explained the situation while he armed himself with a few knives and an automatic pistol loaded with silver bullets.

"I think you're right to be concerned," Jack said. "Go ahead and check on her. I'll have Lara take your place at the townhouse."

Twenty minutes later Phil pulled into a parking space close to Vanda's apartment. He sprinted toward her building as the sun touched the horizon. *Shit*. He was too late.

He ran into the lobby and stopped at the security desk. The uniformed guard slouched in his chair, his body limp and his eyes closed.

Phil checked the guard's pulse. Still alive. No sign

of injury. He appeared to be in a deep sleep. Could be the result of vampire mind control. Max had beaten him here.

Phil paced in the elevator as it slowly ascended to the tenth floor. How could he have been so careless? He shouldn't have slept at the townhouse. He should have camped out in front of Vanda's door. He should have never left her side.

He'd let his lust scare her away. What a fool he was. If lust was all he felt for her, he wouldn't be so frantic right now. His hands clenched into tight fists. *If Max had hurt her—*

The elevator door opened, and he charged down the hall to Vanda's apartment. The door was locked, but that wouldn't have stopped Max from teleporting in.

Phil kicked the door in. The interior was completely dark, all the windows covered with thick aluminum shutters. He flipped on the lights, half expecting to see bloodstains and piles of dead vampire dust.

The room was spotless. Undisturbed. But it was too soon to feel relieved.

He opened a door and turned on the lights. Cora Lee and Pamela Smythe-Worthing lay on twin beds, motionless in their death-sleep. There was no sign of struggle. The women were neatly tucked in, their hands clasped, their faces peaceful. They must have fallen into their death-sleep without knowing that Max had snuck in.

Phil went back to the living room. There was an odd pattern on the carpet, as if someone had vacuumed in a serpentine fashion. The path led straight to another door, which was slightly ajar.

Max had not come alone.

Phil pulled a knife from the sheath buckled to his calf, then slowly pushed the door open wide. Light from the living room spilled into the bedroom, illuminating Vanda's bed. His skin chilled with a shudder.

Max's fifteen-foot-long python was slowly coiling itself around Vanda's motionless body.

Chapter Five

*T*hat evening after sunset, Vanda's heart jolted in her chest, bringing her back to life. A bright light overhead accosted her eyes, and her heart lurched a second time with alarm. She hadn't left the lights on in her room. And what was this heavy thing across her waist?

She glanced to the side and gasped with a strangled-sounding squeak.

Phil jerked awake. "What is it?" In a second he was kneeling beside her with a knife in his hand.

"Phil!" Vanda scooted to the edge of the bed. "What are you doing here?"

"Sorry. Didn't mean to alarm you." He slid the knife into a sheath under his khaki pants. He was dressed in his usual MacKay uniform, minus his shoes. "I must have dozed off."

"In my bed?" She grabbed the sheet to pull it up to her chin, but dropped it when she noticed the sheets were white. What the hell? Her sheets had been purple when she'd gone to bed. And why did her body feel strangely sore, as if she'd been pummeled with brute force? "What—What's going on? How did you get in here?"

"I . . . broke down the door." He held up his hands when she took a deep breath to yell at him. "It's okay! I had it fixed. Everything's fine."

"The hell it is!" She realized with a shock that she was wearing her green pajama top and shorts instead of the purple ones she'd gone to bed in. Good Lord, how desperate could Phil be? "You broke into my apartment to sleep with me?"

He snorted. "I did a lot more than sleep."

"Oh my God!" She jumped out of bed.

"Oh, come on." He rose to his feet with an indignant look. "You think I would have sex with you while you were sleeping?"

"I was *dead*, Phil. That makes it really creepy."

He gave her an incredulous look. "How can you believe I would do that?"

She plucked at her T-shirt. "You changed my clothes."

"Well, yes. But I tried not to look." His gaze drifted south and his mouth curled up.

His attempt had obviously failed. She waved a hand to snap him out of the dreamy-eyed trance he'd fallen into. "Hey! Pervert!"

That got his attention. He stiffened and his eyes flashed with anger. "I didn't molest you, Vanda."

She pointed at the bed. "You changed my sheets."

"I had to. They were covered with . . . stuff."

She gasped again.

"Not *mine*," he growled. "Now, sit down and listen."

She remained standing so she could glare at him. When she crossed her arms over her chest, the soreness made her wince.

His annoyed expression changed into concern. "Are you all right? I checked for broken bones and you seemed okay, but I was worried you might have some cracked ribs."

Her skin chilled with goose bumps. "What happened—" A hunger pain slammed into her gut, nearly doubling her over. The room swirled around.

"Hold on." Phil scrambled across the bed and caught her by the shoulders.

"No." She pulled away and stumbled, nearly falling down. He smelled too good, with his blood coursing rapidly through his veins. Her gums tingled. "I need to eat."

Her hunger was always strongest when she first awoke. She weaved toward the foot of the bed and recognized the scent of blood. Strange blood, not human.

"Vanda." Phil grabbed her arm. "You're too weak. Lie down, and I'll bring you some breakfast."

Another hunger pain shot through her, and she wrenched herself away. "Dammit, Phil. Get away from me or *you'll* be my breakfast." She lunged around the end of the bed.

"*Aaack!*" She stumbled back.

Phil caught her from behind, clasping her upper arms.

There on the floor were her purple sheets. And in the middle was a pile of bloody cut-up snake. Her purple pajamas lay in the pile, slimy with snake guts and blood.

She struggled to breathe. Her body started to shake.

"Don't worry," Phil said behind her. "It can't hurt you anymore."

The room spun around, a room filled with snake guts and horrific imaginings. Her knees buckled, and Phil swung her up into his arms.

"Vanda?" The bedroom door swung open to reveal Cora Lee in a pale pink nightgown, holding a glass of synthetic blood. "Oh, I didn't you realize you had comp—" Her gaze dropped to the mutilated snake. *"Eek!"* Her glass tumbled to the floor, spilling blood as it went.

"Why on earth is everyone screaming?" Pamela barged inside. *"Aack!"* Her teacup fell to the floor, too.

Vanda covered her mouth as her stomach churned. She'd never experienced such an awful mixture of hunger and nausea at the same time.

"Go back into the living room," Phil ordered her friends as he carried her to the door. "Can you fix Vanda some breakfast? She's very weak."

"Of course." Pamela rushed back to the kitchen, her long blue nightgown rustling around her legs. Cora Lee followed close behind.

While they warmed up more synthetic blood in the microwave, Phil settled Vanda on the leather couch.

He sat beside her. "Are you all right?"

She shook her head. She closed her eyes, but the image of the cut-up snake was still in her head.

"Here, dear." Pamela pressed a warm mug into her trembling hands. "This will soon have you feeling up to snuff."

Vanda took a small sip of bland Type O. When it didn't threaten to come right up, she took another sip.

Cora Lee sat across from them in the blue upholstered chair and drank from her new glass of synthetic blood. "Now what in tarnation is going on?"

Vanda shuddered. She wasn't sure she wanted to know. Phil stretched an arm across the back of the couch and patted her shoulder.

"Indeed. We must be apprised of the situation forthwith." Pamela sank gracefully into the matching blue chair. As a Vamp dating back to Regency England, she preferred her blood in a dainty teacup. She took a sip and returned the cup to the saucer with a little *clink*. "And we must brace ourselves, ladies, for I fear whatever events occurred here were horrid. Simply horrid."

Cora Lee shivered. "That's Max the Mega Member's snake in there, isn't it?"

"Yes," Phil replied quietly.

Vanda shifted on the couch to face him. "Max tried to kill me?" His gaze met hers, and her heart melted at the tender look in his blue eyes. She had no doubt he'd saved her life. Again. He was as brave and noble as any of the fairy-tale heroes she'd read about as a child. The type of hero she'd given up on ever existing in the real world.

With a smile, he tousled her short hair. Then, he shifted his gaze to her friends. "When I woke up this morning, I realized you would be coming here for your death-sleep, and Max would have an opportunity to do Vanda some harm. I arrived just after sunrise, and the guard in the lobby was in a deep sleep, caused by vampire mind control. I knew that Max had been here."

Vanda shuddered, and Phil gave her shoulder a squeeze.

"But we never saw him," Cora Lee protested.

"I believe he was hiding with his snake in the coat closet." Phil motioned to the closet by the front door. "After you came in, and he heard you retire to your rooms, he let the snake out, cracked open Vanda's door, and teleported back to his place."

"Leaving that horrid snake to deliver the deadly vengeance he so craved," Pamela added dramatically. Her hand shook, and the teacup clattered against the saucer.

"Land sakes," Cora Lee whispered.

Phil looked at Vanda and rubbed her shoulder. "I found the snake coiling itself around your body."

"Oh God." She covered her mouth as a wave of nausea swept through her.

"I cut off the head first, but the rest of the snake was continuing to squeeze you, so I hacked it into pieces as fast as I could." He gave her an apologetic look. "I tried not to cut you, but I was . . . in a hurry and the snake was so tight against you that I nicked you a few times. And then there was all the—"

"You don't have to explain." Vanda grimaced. She'd seen the pile of guts and blood. She'd seen how awful her pajamas looked. And she knew her body had been squeezed too tightly. Even with the healing power of death-sleep, she was still sore.

"I didn't want to leave you lying in all that mess," Phil continued, "so I tried to clean you up. And the bed, too."

Vanda nodded. "I understand."

"I took the shower curtain from your bathroom and piled everything nasty on top," he said. "Then I cleaned up the carpet and the walls—"

"*Walls?*" Pamela asked.

Phil winced. "I was throwing the snake parts as fast as I could cut them up."

"Lord have mercy," Cora Lee whispered.

Vanda tried to shut out the terrifying images that flitted through her mind, but she couldn't.

"I was really . . . upset," Phil admitted with a frown, "so I took the snake's head and went in search of Max."

Vanda swallowed hard. "Did you find him?"

"He was in his apartment in his death-sleep." Phil stared into space, scowling.

Cora Lee leaned forward, her eyes wide. "What did you do to him?"

Phil took a deep breath. "I left the snake head on

the pillow next to Max and turned his head so it would be the first thing he would see when he woke up. Then I wrote a note that told him if he ever came near Vanda again, I would kill him."

Cora Lee slumped with a sigh. "That's all?"

"I pinned the note to his thigh . . . with a knife."

Cora Lee brightened up. "Now that's more like it."

"Indeed." Pamela sipped from her teacup. "I say, old boy, good form."

Phil snorted. "I'm so glad you approve. Then I dropped by Roman's townhouse to shower and change clothes, and I made my report. Roman should be hearing about it soon, and he can make a decision on how to handle Max."

"They should lynch him," Cora Lee said, her eyes sparkling with excitement. "We should have a hanging like the good old days."

"Quite." Pamela sipped from her cup. "Now that was entertainment."

Vanda shook her head and finished her mug of blood before it turned cold. Cold-blooded like a snake. She shuddered.

"I had the door fixed, and I left three new keys on the counter." Phil motioned toward the kitchen. "I kept a key for myself so I wouldn't have to bust your door down again."

"Of course." Pamela bowed her head. "We're extremely grateful for your bravery and chivalry."

"That's for sure," Cora Lee added. "Why, if he hadn't come when he did, that snake would have crushed our poor Vanda to smithereens. Imagine waking up to find every bone in your body broken, not to mention all that nasty internal damage. And what if that snake had tried to *eat* her?"

"Enough!" Vanda made a face at her. "I don't want to hear about it."

Cora Lee huffed. "I'm just saying you would probably be dying in agonizing pain right this minute if Phil hadn't come to your rescue."

Vanda gritted her teeth. "I am aware of that. I can't move any part of my body without feeling some soreness."

Pamela tsked. "You poor dear. Hopefully, another round of death-sleep will have you back to feeling tip-top."

Cora Lee nodded. "And you'd better take it easy tonight. Don't worry about the club. Pamela and I can handle it."

"I'm perfectly capable of working," Vanda protested. If she did nothing all night, she'd keep imagining that horrible snake coiling around her while she lay helpless in her death-sleep.

Cora Lee was right. If Phil hadn't saved her, that snake could have remained wrapped around her all night, preventing her body from healing itself. She could have woken to find every bone in her body crushed. Or worse.

Her stomach roiled, and she quickly shoved the grisly images aside. She focused on her hands in her lap and took deep breaths. Father Andrew had taught her this exercise to help calm her anger. Hopefully, it also worked to calm horror.

"What are we going to do with the snake?" Cora Lee asked.

"I'll bag it up in a big garbage sack," Phil replied. "And I'll ask one of the Vamp guys to teleport it out. I would have taken it myself, but I didn't want to look like I was hauling a dead body out of the building. If security asked to see what was inside, it would be hard to explain."

"Yes, much better to simply teleport it away." Pamela returned her empty teacup to the kitchen.

A cell phone rang, jerking Vanda out of her deep breathing exercise.

Phil dug his phone out of his pants' pocket. "Hello . . . Yes, she seems to be all right." He glanced at Vanda and whispered, "It's Connor."

With her superior hearing, Vanda could make out most of what Connor was saying. Jack and Phineas had gone to Max's apartment to arrest him, but the ex-dancer was nowhere to be found. She wasn't surprised. After all, Max had woken with a note stabbed to his thigh with a knife. Even Max, with his minimum brain, could figure out this was a clue that he was in big trouble.

Connor had issued a bulletin to all the minor coven masters under Roman's jurisdiction to be on the lookout for Max. He was now a fugitive from Vamp justice.

"I'll ask her." Phil hung up and turned toward Vanda. "Roman wants to know since you're the victim, what kind of action will satisfy you once Max is captured?"

"Leave him staked outside so he'll fry to a crisp when the sun rises," Cora Lee suggested as she retrieved the dropped glass and teacup from Vanda's bedroom to take them to the kitchen.

"Off with his head," Pamela said as she washed the dishes. "Preferably with a dull axe."

"Banishment will be enough," Vanda said quietly.

"Are you kidding?" Cora Lee advanced toward the couch with an incredulous look. "That bastard tried to kill you. Aren't you angry?"

"Indeed," Pamela called over the sound of running water. "Where is your infamous anger now?"

"Banishment will get rid of him," Vanda mumbled. Max wouldn't be able to show his face or get employment anywhere in the eastern United States that fell under Roman's rule. He would have no choice but to move far away.

Phil watched her curiously. "Are you sure?"

She shook her head. "I don't want any more deaths on my conscience."

His eyes widened. "What deaths?"

She winced inwardly. Now she'd said too much. "I don't want to talk about it." She started to get up to take her empty mug to the kitchen, but a sharp pain creased her ribs. "Ouch."

"Stay put." Phil grabbed the mug from her hand and passed it to Cora Lee.

Vanda pressed a hand against her ribcage. That damned snake had done more damage than her body could heal in one day.

Phil watched her, frowning. "I want the three of you to move back into Roman's townhouse."

She glared at him. "No way."

"It's not safe for you to remain here, not as long as Max is on the loose and blaming you for all his problems," he argued. "I can't watch you here and do my job at the townhouse at the same time."

"He has a point." Pamela dried her hands on her favorite tea towel from London.

"Better safe than sorry," Cora Lee added.

Vanda groaned.

Phil patted her leg. "It's for the best. If you ladies will pack your bags, I'll drive you over to the townhouse."

"Of course." Pamela strode toward her bedroom, followed by her roommate.

"Cora Lee, could you pack a bag for Vanda?" Phil asked as he rested a hand on Vanda's shoulder to prevent her from getting up.

"Sure." Cora Lee slanted a wry smile at Vanda. "Gee, I wonder what I should pack for you? Maybe a black catsuit? And the purple catsuit? And what else?" She tapped her chin, thinking. "Oh, right! The other black catsuit."

"Very funny," Vanda muttered.

"Such a dreadful lack of variety," Pamela said as she marched into her bedroom.

"That's for sure." Cora Lee followed her inside.

The door shut, and Vanda found herself alone with Phil.

"They're just envious," he whispered.

"Of what?"

"That you look so incredibly good in a catsuit. Not many women would."

She felt a blush warming her cheeks.

"That's better." He touched her face. "You were looking so deathly pale before."

For good reason. She'd come too close to dying a horrid death. "I—I want to thank you for saving my life. Again." Her blush deepened, and she clenched her hands in her lap. "It must have been awful for you. I feel so . . . stupid that I was just lying there helpless while you had to do battle with that disgusting—"

"It's all right. I'd fight any sort of creature to protect you." He rested his hand on top of hers. "You're worth it."

Tears sprang to her eyes without warning. She pulled her hands away from his. "Don't say that." She covered her eyes with a trembling hand. *Worth it?* Would he say that if he knew the truth about her?

"Vanda," he whispered, "I'm only telling you how I truly feel. And now that we're alone, I need to tell you something else."

Oh God, no. Her fears were true, and he'd killed Max. That's why no one had found the dancer. Phil could have turned him into a pile of dust and scattered the remains. Was her life always to be tainted with murder? And now she'd dragged Phil into her legacy of death. "There's no need to talk about it. I understand the kind of rage that leads a person to—to take a life."

Phil tilted his head, studying her. "What are you referring to?"

"Max," she whispered. "You . . . " She noted the confused look on Phil's face. The clear blue eyes of an innocent man. "You didn't kill him?"

"No. Believe me, I was sorely tempted, but—"

"Phil." She touched his face. Her heart swelled with relief. "Thank you."

"You're welcome." He took her hand in his. "What I wanted to say was, this morning, for a few minutes, I thought I was too late to save you. I—I was frantic. That's why I busted the door down. I could have picked the lock, but I didn't even think about it. I panicked."

"It's okay. I'll pay for the new lock."

"No, you won't. And I'm trying to make a point here." He squeezed her hand. "I was terrified I was going to lose you. I completely lost it. I was slinging snake parts all over the place."

She grimaced. "Please—"

"And I nicked you a few times because my hands were shaking. It was suddenly clear to me that I feel a lot more for you than mere physical attraction."

Her tears returned, blurring her vision. "Phil, I—" She didn't know what to say. *Forget me? It's hopeless?*

"I want to be here for you. Always."

She shook her head, and a tear escaped. "It wouldn't be always. You're . . . mortal."

"Let me worry about my own mortality." He brushed her tear away. "You're the one I want."

"I'm a vampire."

"I know." He kissed her brow.

"I could lose control and bite you."

"I'm not afraid of your teeth." He kissed the tip of her nose.

"I have a terrible temper."

"You're beautiful." He touched her lips lightly

with his own. Then again. He molded his mouth against hers.

It was such a sweet and gentle kiss that it made her heart ache. If he'd pounced on her with lust and hunger, she could have met him head on and dismissed the whole encounter as a mere physical release from the emotional trauma she'd just endured.

But this was so sweet. She had no defense against this. A tiny fracture cracked in her armor. With a whimper, she wrapped her arms around his neck and threaded her fingers through his soft, thick hair.

Growling, he deepened the kiss. She could no longer think of reasons why she needed to reject him. She couldn't think at all. She could only melt.

Her mouth opened, and he invaded her with his tongue. Phil. Her handsome, strong, brave hero. Not afraid of her fangs. Not repelled by the taste of blood that lingered in her mouth. And boy, could he kiss. Could a man be any more perfect?

"Oops," Cora Lee whispered.

Pamela cleared her throat.

Vanda broke the kiss with a groan. She'd never hear the end of this. Everything was tinted red, which could only mean that her eyes were glowing, a sure sign of desire. She looked away, hoping Phil hadn't noticed. She spotted her friends parking their rolling suitcases by the front door.

"Pardon the intrusion." Cora Lee headed toward Vanda's bedroom. "We'll just pack your bag now."

"Yes, don't mind us. Carry on." Pamela nudged

Cora Lee and muttered, "No need to pack her vibrator."

Cora Lee burst into giggles as they scurried into the bedroom and shut the door.

"I don't have a vibrator!" Vanda yelled after them, then glanced at Phil. "It's a back massager."

He grinned. "You won't need it."

She groaned. What was she getting into? How could she live under the same roof with this man? He was too great a temptation. And this was a no-win situation. If she rejected Phil and never saw him again, it would hurt. Like hell. If she got involved with him and he died, like all mortals do, it would hurt. Like hell.

She sighed. "Phil, it's over."

"Sweetheart, it's been a long time coming."

"I disagree."

"Not a problem." The corner of his mouth curled up. "I enjoy the chase."

Chapter Six

*S*he was avoiding him. Or at least it seemed that way to Phil. By Thursday evening Vanda had hardly spoken more than two words to him. To be fair, he knew she wasn't entirely to blame. She couldn't help being noncommunicative during the day.

When they had first arrived at the townhouse Wednesday night, he'd given the ladies some time to settle into their bedrooms on the second floor. He called Phineas to ask him to teleport the snake out of Vanda's apartment. He also asked him to drop by the nightclub a few times during the night to make sure the ladies were safe. Phineas was happy to volunteer when he heard the Horny Devils was full of hot chicks.

When Phil went back upstairs to check on the ladies, they had already teleported to the club. Pamela had left a note to let him know they would return by five-thirty in the morning. No note from Vanda.

He set his alarm for 5:00 A.M. so he could shower, shave, and dress before she returned. The ladies arrived at the back door just before Phineas and Jack. Then all of them wanted a bedtime snack before retiring to their rooms for their daily death-sleep. He wasn't able to flirt with Vanda in front of the other guys. He was trapped once again in the role as her guard. He was also her anger management sponsor. That made her twice as forbidden.

But he was twice as determined. Thursday evening at sunset he waited in the kitchen for the Vamps to come down for breakfast. Cora Lee and Pamela arrived without Vanda. She'd asked them to bring a bottle to her room. They exchanged amused glances when Phil offered to do it.

He took a warm bottle to her bedroom and knocked on her door. She yelled that she wasn't dressed, to leave the bottle by the door and come back in ten minutes. He came back in five, and she'd already teleported to work.

She was definitely avoiding him. He vented his frustration by taking a long jog through Central Park. Then he picked up a pizza and headed back to the townhouse. He settled in the living room in front of the wide-screen TV to eat. The Digital Vampire Network was on, and *Live with the Undead* was just starting.

Corky Courrant was wearing a tight red sweater to highlight her fake boobs, and it matched perfectly with the red lipstick on her fake smile. She began her celebrity gossip show by attacking one of her favorite targets—the famous fashion model Simone. Apparently, Simone had been dating a rich playboy Vamp from Monaco who had dumped her for another model, Inga. Corky had managed to obtain footage of Simone and Inga having a catfight on the playboy's yacht.

With a sigh, Phil reached for the remote control. His thumb was on the OFF button when he froze. Corky had just flashed up a new picture. It was him, pinning Max to the floor at Vanda's nightclub. An onlooker in the crowd must have taken the picture and forwarded it to Corky.

"Once again, violence erupts at the notorious Horny Devils nightclub in New York City," Corky announced with a malicious smile. "My sources tell me that a former dancer who was sorely mistreated by club owner Vanda Barkowski arrived at the club on Tuesday night, armed with a knife. It's a miracle that no one was killed. Again."

Phil's picture disappeared from the screen, and the camera zoomed in close to Corky's face. She assumed a tragic, pained look. "My dear viewers, this is the same club where I was brutally attacked last December by none other than Vanda Barkowski herself. I still have nightmares about that horrendous attack!"

Phil snorted. Vamps didn't have any dreams at all in their death-sleep. They were dead.

"In case you've forgotten that dreadful event, here it is once again." Corky motioned with her hand and half the screen was taken up with the recording of Vanda screeching and leaping across a table to strangle Corky. While the video played, Corky shuddered dramatically, then slumped on her desk in a swoon.

When the video ended, Corky sat up, perky as ever. "I must urge you, dear friends, to boycott that nefarious nightclub. I repeat, do *not* go to the Horny Devils. It's an evil, violent place, and we can only hope that soon, justice will be served and it will be wiped off the planet. Vanda Barkowski must pay for her crimes!"

"Shit." Phil turned off the television.

He trudged downstairs to the basement to lift some weights. Maybe he should drop by Vanda's club to see if she was all right. She might have heard about Corky's boycott, and as her anger management sponsor, he needed to make sure she didn't do something she would later regret.

With a snort, he began a second set of biceps curls. It was obvious he was desperate for any excuse to see Vanda. And it was just as obvious that she didn't want to see him.

Why was she avoiding him? She'd responded so well to their first kiss. She'd surrendered to her desire, her body trembling and snuggling close to him. She'd kissed him back with a passion that had made his heart soar. And her beautiful gray eyes had turned red. He knew that was a sign of heated desire.

He set down the weights. He'd lost count of how many reps he'd done. It was hard to concentrate with memories of Vanda's naked body flashing through his head. He had tried not to look when he'd changed her clothes and cleaned her up. For about two seconds. Then, he'd seen the bruises caused by that damned snake, and he'd wanted to rip Max apart with his bare hands.

And Vanda had merely wanted to banish him. No more deaths on her conscience, she'd said. And she'd thought he had killed Max. What had been her words?

I understand the kind of rage that leads a person to take a life.

What had happened to her in the past? He knew she was from Poland. Had World War II traumatized her so much that she'd sought the shelter of the harem to recover?

He took a shower while he continued to speculate. According to Connor, Vanda had been angry since he'd first met her, in 1950. She had over fifty years of unresolved, built-up anger, and he felt sure it dated back to some kind of trauma she'd endured in Poland. And chances were good that whatever had caused her anger was also linked to her fear of getting involved with him.

Was it a trust issue? Had someone she loved in the past betrayed her?

He needed answers, and obviously Vanda was not going to supply them. Like any warrior planning to lay siege, he needed to thoroughly study his target and find the weak spots that would crack open her armor. He smiled grimly. Vanda didn't know it yet, but the chase was still on.

When she was in the harem, her best friends had

been Darcy and Maggie. Darcy and her husband were currently serving as day guards for Angus and his team at Apollo's compound. Since they were secretly laying an ambush there, it would not be a good time to call her.

But Maggie would be available. The sun would have set by now in Texas, where she lived with her husband, Pierce O'Callahan, formerly known as DVN soap opera star Don Orlando de Corazon. Phil looked up her contact information on the MacKay database.

Maggie answered the phone. "Phil! How are you? Are you still in Texas?"

"No, I'm back in New York now." Phil explained how Vanda was required by the coven court to undergo anger management. Then he told her about the incident with the snake.

"Sweet Mary and Joseph!" Maggie gasped. "I should be there for her. Do you mind if I teleport over to see you?"

"No, not at all." He strode to the security console by the front door to turn off the alarm.

Meanwhile Maggie informed her family of her emergency trip to New York. A few minutes later she appeared in the foyer.

"Phil!" She grinned at him. "Look at you. I believe you've gotten more handsome than ever."

He smiled as he reactivated the alarm. "And you've gotten more Texan."

Maggie's usual short skirt, clunky goth boots, and tight sweater had been traded in for a pair of jeans, cowboy boots, and an embroidered denim shirt. A fringed leather handbag was looped over her shoulder.

"That's what happens when you lead the glamorous life of a rancher." She hugged him, then stepped back with a gasp. "You're a shifter!"

Phil was so surprised that he could only stare at her for a moment. "You know about shape shifters?"

"Yes. Pierce's uncle is a were-coyote and his sister's a were-jackrabbit." Maggie made a face. "You can imagine how tense it gets around the house when the moon is full. No one wants Uncle Bob to gobble down his niece."

Phil winced. "That is awkward. I guess they were bitten?" Otherwise, members of the same family wouldn't shift into two such different creatures.

"Yes." Maggie gave him a sympathetic look. "Is that what happened to you? Did you get bitten in Texas, too?"

"No, I was born a shifter."

Her eyes widened. "Really?" She ran a hand through her black hair, which was still cut in a short bob. "I guess I never realized it 'cause I didn't know about shifters till I moved to Texas. I recognize the scent now."

"A lot of Vamps don't know. And we'd like to keep it that way, if you don't mind."

"Of course." Maggie pretended to zip her lips. "Now, tell me all the latest gossip about the ex-harem."

Phil ushered her into the kitchen, and she warmed up a bottle of Chocolood in the microwave while he explained his quest for information about Vanda's past. "You see, I believe she has unresolved issues that she's been avoiding for years. If we can force Vanda to confront them, we might be able to cure her anger problem."

"Very interesting," Maggie murmured as she poured hot Chocolood into a teacup.

"Well, I've studied a lot of psychology, so I think my theory is sound."

"I wasn't referring to your theory." Maggie set her cup and saucer on the kitchen table and took a seat. "I find it interesting that I asked for news about all the harem ladies, and you talked only about Vanda."

Phil shrugged. "I'm concerned, naturally, because I agreed to be her sponsor."

Maggie sipped her Chocolood. "And why did you agree?"

"Someone had to do it. No one else volunteered, and I do have some experience in psychology." When Maggie just stared at him with a knowing look, he raised his hands in a surrendering motion. "All right, I admit it. I'm hopelessly attracted to her. Always have been."

Maggie grinned. "I always knew there was something between you two. But why do you say it's hopeless?"

He took a can of beer from the fridge and popped the top. "At first I couldn't get involved with her because I was her guard, and frankly, I just thought she was playing with me because she was bored."

Maggie nodded. "She *was* bored, but I think she was genuinely attracted to you."

"I've just recently become aware of that." He

thought back to their kiss, and the way she'd surrendered in passion. And then he recalled the years he'd wasted when he could have been pursuing her. With an inward groan, he guzzled down some beer.

"It shouldn't be hopeless now," Maggie said.

He sat across from her at the table. "I'm her anger management sponsor, so I'm not supposed to get romantically involved. And I'm her guard again. Technically, she's forbidden."

"Technically?"

He shrugged and drank more beer. "I'm not a very technical person."

Maggie's mouth twitched. "A man of action, eh? That could be exactly what Vanda needs."

He plunked the beer can on the table. "She's avoiding me. I think she's . . . afraid."

"Ah." Maggie traced her finger along the rim of her teacup. "She was always very cautious about forming new relationships. She knew me for over ten years before she would even admit we were friends. But once she calls you friend, she'll fight like a tiger to defend you. Do you know she threatened my husband once if he didn't treat me right?"

Phil smiled. "That sounds like her. She tried to defend Ian, too, last December."

Maggie nodded. "She told me once that Ian looked a lot like her youngest brother. But when I asked about her family, she refused to talk about them."

"Do you know what happened?"

"No, not really. When she first came to the harem, she was like . . . a wounded animal. She wouldn't speak to anyone. Wouldn't look at our faces. It was so sad." Maggie grew silent, frowning as she remembered.

"Tell me more," Phil said softly.

"I was afraid she would starve to death. There were nights when she refused to go out for . . . food." Maggie gave him an apologetic look. "That was before synthetic blood."

"I understand. And Vanda would refuse to hunt? Wasn't that painful for her?"

"Oh yes. Something awful. I would beg her to go hunting with me. Even when she did, she would barely take enough blood to stay alive. I always had this terrible feeling that she was punishing herself."

"Why would she make herself suffer?"

"I asked her, but she would never say." Maggie finished her Chocolood, then took her dishes to the sink to rinse them out. "She reminded me of a sparrow with broken wings. All brown and downtrodden. She wore this old brown dress, and her hair was brown, too. A lovely brown, streaked with dark red highlights, but she pulled it back severely in a bun. It was like she wanted to crawl into a hole and never fly again."

Phil sat in silence. This was not the Vanda he knew. As far as he could tell, she had suffered from a case of post-traumatic stress syndrome and depression. She might still be suffering from the aftereffects. After all, she'd gone from one extreme to the other, from the broken brown sparrow to a purple-haired, whip-toting, wildcat prone to violent outbursts. The real Vanda—the one she was afraid to be, lay somewhere in between.

He finished his beer. "She never confided in anyone?"

"No," Maggie set her cup and saucer in the dishwasher. "Her first year in the harem, she hardly spoke at all. George, the Coven Master back then, gave us a small monthly allowance. Cora Lee, Pamela, and I would go shopping or to the movies. Vanda spent her money on art supplies."

Phil sat back, surprised. "Art?"

"Yes. She painted. Every night. All night." Maggie grimaced. "Ghastly pictures. Red paint everywhere. Blood, dead bodies, swastikas, barbed wire, wolves—"

"*Wolves?*"

"Yes." Maggie shuddered. "She painted them with such huge, vicious teeth."

He swallowed hard. What the hell did wolves have to do with the war? Or with Vanda?

"Then one night she went crazy," Maggie continued in a low voice. "She piled all the paintings in a heap in the backyard and set them on fire. She burned her art supplies, too, and never painted again."

Phil crumpled the empty beer can in his fist. "Did she ever say why she stopped painting?"

"Just that she didn't want to remember anymore." Maggie sighed. "But of course, she still remembers. We all remember the painful memories from our past."

His own painful memories crept out of hiding, brought to mind by Maggie's words. It had been nine years since his father banished him. Nine years since he'd seen his family. During the first few years, he'd received letters from his sister. She didn't know his whereabouts, so she left the notes in his hunting cabin in Wyoming, hoping he would find them.

He hadn't been to the cabin in four years. What was the point? He could never go back to his father's pack. That part of his life was over.

Maggie suddenly brightened. "I know what might help. Darcy interviewed the harem girls for that reality show a few years back. There might be a copy here somewhere."

Maggie dashed from the kitchen to the living room. *"Eew."* She wrinkled her nose at the leftover pizza sitting on the coffee table.

"I'll get it." He closed the box, then hurried back to the kitchen and stuffed it in the fridge. By the time he returned, Maggie was sliding a disk into the DVD player.

"I found it!" She showed him the case titled *The Sexiest Man on Earth.*

"I remember that show." Phil settled on the couch. "That's when the ladies won the money that financed the nightclub."

"And Darcy won the Sexiest Man," Maggie added with a laugh. She located Vanda's interview on the menu, then sat on the couch next to Phil.

Vanda's image came on the TV screen. She was smiling at the camera, her lovely dove gray eyes twinkling, her lips full and sweetly shaped. The zipper on her purple catsuit was pulled down just low enough to show some cleavage. Phil found himself smiling back.

Maggie chuckled. "You're so smitten."

He hushed her when Darcy's voice came on, asking Vanda to tell the audience about herself.

Vanda began, her clear voice showing just a hint of accent. She was born in 1917 in a small village in southern Poland. Her mother died when Vanda was eighteen, and as the oldest daughter, she'd taken over the care of her large family. A father, four brothers, and two sisters.

Her smile started to fade when she talked about her mother's death. She was frowning by the time she told how the Germans and Russians invaded Poland in 1939 and her father and brothers marched off to fight.

Her face grew pale. "My father urged me to escape with my two younger sisters. I packed some food, and we fled south to the Carpathian Mountains. I'd been there before, and I knew there were some caves where we could hide. I . . . never saw my father or brothers again."

"How terrible," Maggie whispered.

Vanda continued, describing their long trek into the mountains. The youngest sister, thirteen-year-old Frieda, took ill, and by the time they found a shallow cave, she could hardly walk. Vanda stayed with her and sent her other sister, Marta, to fill up their water bags.

Marta didn't come back. The next morning, Vanda made her sick sister as comfortable as possible, then went to fetch water. By that evening she was frantic with worry. Marta was gone and Frieda was failing fast.

She went in search of her sister, and squealed with joy when Marta stepped into her path. But Marta attacked her, bit her, and with superhuman strength carried her off to a cave. The vampire who had turned Marta was there, and he changed Vanda, who was too weak from hunger and blood loss to fight off two vampires.

"The next evening," Vanda said, "I was still reeling in shock from what had happened. But I rushed back to my little sister to see how she was. She had died. All alone."

Vanda covered her face, and Phil could tell the film had been edited. The camera rested on Darcy for a moment, and when it returned to Vanda, she was composed once again.

She quickly explained that the war had been so difficult that she'd joined the harem to find a little peace and relaxation. Then she smiled and said she was happy to participate on the show, and the interview ended.

"Poor Vanda." Maggie sniffed. "She lost everyone."

"Not quite." Phil used the remote to turn off the television. "She has one sister who might still be alive."

"Marta?" Maggie made a face. "Marta should have helped her save their sister."

Phil nodded. "Vanda may feel that her only surviving relative betrayed her."

Maggie took a deep breath. "Well, at least you know why she's so angry now."

"There's still a lot she didn't say. She was transformed in 1939."

"Oh, you're right." Maggie sat up. "And she didn't come here till 1948. That's eight years unaccounted for."

"And she merely called it 'difficult' in the interview. I have a feeling she went through hell."

Maggie's eyes filled with tears. "Of course she did. It was in her paintings. Dead bodies, swastikas, barbed wire, blood."

And wolves. Phil swallowed hard. How would he ever gain Vanda's trust if she was terrified of wolves?

Maggie touched his arm. "I want to see her. Even if all I can do is give her a hug."

"Of course. She'll be at the Horny Devils."

"I've teleported there before, so I know the way." Maggie rose to her feet. "Would you like to hitch a ride?"

"Yes." He wrapped an arm around Maggie's shoulders. Vanda wouldn't be able to avoid him now. "I'd appreciate it if you didn't tell her about my being a shifter."

Maggie frowned at him. "You'll have to tell her if you intend to have a future with her."

"I will." But not now. She was already looking for a reason to run away from him.

Phil and Maggie threaded their way through the crowd at the Horny Devils. When Maggie spotted Pamela at the bar, she squealed, and the two women spent five minutes hugging and laughing. Phil could hardly hear them over the noise.

He lifted a hand in greeting. "Big crowd tonight."

Pamela grinned and handed him a beer. "Isn't it marvelous? That awful Corky told everyone not to come because we were so nefarious and evil." She laughed. "And of course, they just had to see for themselves."

"Does Vanda know about the boycott?" he asked.

"No, thank heavens, and we need to keep it that way. She might go ballistic, and we can't afford any more lawsuits." Pamela spotted Cora Lee and waved at her. "Look who's here!"

Cora Lee ran over to Maggie, and the squealing and hugging started all over again. Then Maggie produced a stack of family photos from her handbag, and the ladies gushed over how adorable Maggie's daughter was. Phil wondered how she'd managed to have a child but refrained from asking since the explanation might take a long time, and he wanted to see Vanda as soon as possible.

"Hey, bro!" Phineas walked toward him with two female Vamps hanging on his arms. "I dropped by like you asked. You sure were right about the hot chicks."

"Any sign of Max?" Phil yelled over the noise.

"No." Phineas gave his new friends an apologetic look. "I hate to say this, ladies, but I gotta go back to work."

"Oh no, Dr. Phang." The brunette on his left arm stuck out her bottom lip in a pout. "How can you leave us?"

"Duty calls, sweetness." Phineas patted her hand. "But I'll come back every few hours to make sure you're safe."

"Oh, Dr. Phang, you're so brave." The blonde on his right rubbed against him.

"Where do you work?" the brunette asked, trying to draw his attention away from the blonde.

"I can't say, darlin'," Phineas replied. "Top secret stuff, you know."

"Oooh." The blonde shivered. "Are you a spy?"

"All I can say is when danger lurks in the shadows, they call on Dr. Phang." Phineas stepped back and lowered his voice. "I'll be back."

"I'll be waiting for you," the brunette yelled as Phineas disappeared.

The blonde sidled up close to Phil. "So are you a spy like Dr. Phang?"

"We . . . work together." Phil noticed Maggie was headed with Cora Lee and Pamela to Vanda's office. He started to follow, but the two Vamp women had latched onto his arms.

The brunette caressed his biceps. "You seem incredibly strong for a mortal."

"And handsome in such an earthy way," the blonde added.

"Actually, I'm not in Dr. Phang's league." Phil extricated himself from their grip. "He's much stronger than me. And a little dangerous. You should probably stay away from him if you like to play it safe."

The brunette's eyes lit up. "He sounds so exciting."

"Well, he is called the Love Doctor, you know," Phil admitted.

The blonde stepped back. "No offense, cutie, but I'm going to wait for the Love Doctor."

The brunette turned toward her. "No, you're not. I saw him first."

While the two women argued over Phineas, Phil hurried to Vanda's office.

Maggie spotted him quietly closing the door. "Vanda, I hope you don't mind, but I brought Phil with me."

Vanda stiffened and turned toward the door. The smile on her face vanished, and a blush crept up her neck.

He remained by the door. "Hello, Vanda."

The blush rose to her cheeks. "Hi."

Pamela and Cora Lee greeted him with knowing smiles.

He nodded briefly at them, then returned his gaze to Vanda. "How are you?"

"Yes, dear, how are you?" Maggie asked when Vanda didn't answer. "Phil told me about that horrible snake, and I just had to make sure you were all right."

"I'm . . . fine," Vanda said quietly.

"Well, it was mighty nice of Phil to call you up," Cora Lee said to Maggie.

"And we're delighted to see you again," Pamela added.

"It's lovely to be here," Maggie said, smiling. "The club is a huge success. I've never seen such a big crowd."

"Yeah, that'll show Corky Courrant," Cora Lee muttered.

Pamela winced and shook her head.

Cora Lee gasped and covered her mouth.

Vanda frowned at them. "What's going on?"

"Nothing," Pamela and Cora Lee answered together.

Vanda glared at Cora Lee. "Out with it."

"It's nothing!" Cora Lee insisted, then turned to Pamela for help. "It amounts to nothing, right? We have a huge crowd. They all came to see why Corky said our club was violent and evil."

"What?" Vanda yelled.

Phil walked toward her. "It's all right. Corky used her TV show to announce a boycott of your club, but her plan obviously backfired."

Vanda's eyes flashed with anger. "She's trying to destroy me."

"Your club will be fine," Phil said softly.

"Not as long as that bitch is around," Vanda hissed, and she vanished.

"No!" Phil made a grab for her, but she was already gone.

"Land sakes," Cora Lee whispered. "Where did she go?"

"Where do you think, bigmouth?" Pamela snapped. "She went to DVN to let Corky have it."

"Sweet Mary and Joseph," Maggie breathed. "We need to stop her."

Chapter Seven

 $\mathcal{T}$ hey have lousy security," Phil said as he followed Maggie down a hallway at DVN. No alarm had gone off when they had teleported into a costume room. "You'd think they'd be more careful after that incident last December."

Maggie leaned close and whispered, "These guys aren't exactly grounded in reality."

"I see what you mean," Phil muttered. They passed a group of actors in the hallway, and one of them, dressed as a giant chicken, was practicing his squawk.

"That's it!" one of his companions said. "Now do it again, but with more *passion*."

Another actor, dressed as a pirate, joined in. "Yaar, me hearty. Ye must believe that ye be a chicken."

Phil snorted. A chicken with fangs.

"This is it." Maggie stopped in front of a door decorated with a giant gold star. *Corky Courrant* was painted across the star in bright red cursive script.

Maggie listened. "I don't hear any fighting inside."

"That's a good sign," Phil said.

"Unless Corky's already dead," Maggie whispered.

Phil opened the door and marched inside. Corky was very much alive, seated behind her desk, studying photos. In the corner, a little bald-headed man with a camera gasped, then teleported away. No sign of Vanda.

Corky glanced up. "How dare you barge in like that!" She gathered up the photos and shoved them into a desk drawer. "Who the hell are you?"

"Don't you know?" Phil asked. "You posted my picture on your show tonight."

Corky sniffed, then waved a hand in dismissal. Her large jeweled rings glittered under the fluorescent lights. "I'm not interested in the identity of a mortal. Get out of my office."

"I was the man pinning down the dancer at the Horny Devils nightclub. How did you get that photo?"

"I'm a journalist. I never reveal my sources." She glanced at the corner where the little man had teleported away. Her bosom heaved when she sighed with relief.

"Hello, Corky." Maggie strode inside, her cowboy boots clunking on the linoleum floor.

Corky sat back. "Well, if it isn't little Maggie, known for her short stature and her equally *short* career as a mediocre actress. What brings you to

New York?" She eyed Maggie's clothes with disdain. "A little shopping, I hope?"

Maggie approached the desk. "I just had a lovely time at the Horny Devils. Thanks to you, it's the most popular nightclub in the vampire world."

Corky's eyes narrowed into angry slits. "I remember now. You're one of Vanda Barkowski's friends. You can give that crazy bitch a message from me." Corky rose to her feet. "I'm going to destroy her. And her club."

"Try it," Phil said softly, "and you'll regret it."

Corky scoffed. "Am I supposed to quake in fear from a mere mortal and a . . . miniature cowgirl?" She glowered at Maggie. "Don't think I haven't forgotten how you stole Don Orlando from me."

Maggie glared back. "You had already lost him. You treated him like a slave."

"Ha! I made him a star! I made him famous. What could you ever do for him?"

Maggie smiled. "I make him happy." She turned on her heel and marched out.

Corky sputtered. "I could ruin you. And your ranch. You're just so trivial, I haven't bothered!"

Phil paused by the door on his way out. "Leave Vanda alone."

"What are you," Corky sneered, "her guard dog?"

"Close." He took a deep breath and tapped into his inner Alpha power. He knew it would make his blue eyes glow. His body began to shimmer, his form fuzzy along the edges. He could shift in an instant if he wanted, or remain in human form while retaining all the power of the Alpha wolf.

Corky stumbled back, her eyes wide. "Who—What are you?"

Let her wonder. He shut the door in her face and reined in his power. In an instant he was back to normal. "Okay, where do you think Vanda is?"

Maggie stared at him, her mouth agape. "What was that?"

"The power of my inner . . . animal." He started down the hallway.

Maggie stood in place, her eyes still wide with shock. "But don't you need a full moon?"

"No. So where could Vanda be?"

"I—I don't know." Maggie ran to catch up with him. "I've never heard of a shifter who wasn't dependant upon a full moon."

"I can shift at any time." They reached the end of the hall, where it led into an intersecting hallway.

"That's amazing," Maggie whispered. "What kind of animal are you?"

He ignored the question as he inspected the new hallway. No sign of Vanda. "Let's split up. You go right, I'll go left."

"All right." Maggie headed right, then pulled back around the corner, grimacing.

"What's wrong?" Phil peered down the hall to the right. A blond woman was talking to the pirate actor.

"It's Tiffany." Maggie raised her gaze to the ceiling as if in prayer. "Must I see every woman tonight who's slept with my husband?"

Phil recalled that the actor Don Orlando de Corazon had been touted as the greatest lover in the vampire world. "I'm sure he never looked at another woman once he met you."

Maggie snorted, then smiled. "I believe you're right. Bless you. So you're a powerful shifter who knows exactly what to say to a woman? Vanda doesn't stand a chance."

"I hope you're right. But we still need to find her. How about I go right, and you go left?"

"Okay." Maggie hurried down the new hallway, moving away from Tiffany.

Phil strode toward the blonde and the pirate. He tried the first door. A storeroom.

"Aar, me buxom wench." The pirate adjusted his eye patch. "Ye be a glorious sight for me sore eye. Would ye care to go below deck with me?"

"To the basement?" Tiffany giggled. "Sure. I just love your accent. It's so classy. You sound like a prince." She led him to a door at the end of the hall.

Phil smiled to himself. Tiffany certainly wasn't pining over the loss of Don Orlando. He spotted a door labeled: CORKY'S DRESSING ROOM. This sounded promising. He quietly eased it open.

Vanda was seated at a dressing table. There was no mirror above it, but rather, a monitor connected to a digital camera. As a Vamp, this was the only way Corky could see herself to apply the mounds of makeup she wore. The camera was turned off now, and Vanda was entirely focused on her task, snipping at clothing with a small pair of scissors.

He closed the door with a *click*, and she jumped in her seat.

"Phil! What are you doing here?"

"What are *you* doing, Vanda?"

"I'm busy." She returned her attention to a black brassiere and made a small snip at the shoulder strap.

He stepped toward her. "As your sponsor, I suggest you put the scissors down."

"You are *not* my . . . " She paused with a wry expression. "I'm getting a strange sense of déjà vu."

He chuckled. "What exactly are you doing?"

"Nothing." She made a tiny cut between the two massive cups of Corky's bra.

He eyed the pile of clothing on the dressing table. "You're exacting revenge by destroying Corky's underwear?"

"They're not destroyed." Vanda folded several pairs of lacy underwear and returned them neatly to a drawer. "They're just altered a tiny bit. Corky will never notice." She shut the drawer with a wicked grin. "Until it's too late."

Phil sighed. "Vanda, this is not what they mean by anger management."

She folded up a brassiere and stacked it in another drawer. "I don't need anger management. I was sorely tempted to jump that bitch in her office, but then I thought about all the ripped-out hair and black eyes and lawsuits, and I had to ask myself, 'Is it really worth it?' "

He couldn't help but smile. "You're thinking before you act. That's an improvement."

"Thank you." She picked up the last bra and showed him the humongous cups. "Can you believe this? Fill it with rice and you could feed a starving family of four for a week." She folded it and placed it in a drawer. "Do men really find such huge breasts attractive?"

"Yes. Some men do."

She shot him a dirty look and slammed the drawer shut.

"But I don't." He moved closer to her chair. "I have seen perfection, so I could never want anything less."

She eyed him warily. "Nobody's perfect."

"You are. For me."

She jumped to her feet, positioning the chair between them. "I need to go. Corky could come in any minute."

"You've been avoiding me."

"I've been busy." She tightened the whip around her waist. "And I don't think there's anything to talk about, really."

He eased around the chair. "Have you thought about our kiss?"

"No." She lifted her chin. "I completely forgot about it. I figured it was an accident and we should never let it happen again."

"You reached that decision *after* you forgot about it?"

She scowled at him. "Okay. I remember it quite well. But just because it was hot, that doesn't mean we should do it again."

He smiled slowly. "It was hot, wasn't it?"

Her gaze dropped to his mouth. "I . . . can't remember."

"Strange how your memory comes and goes."

She licked her lips. "Some things are best forgotten."

He slipped an arm around her. "Have you forgotten how I make your heart pound?" He could hear it pounding.

She rested her hands against his chest. "I seem to recall something to that effect . . . "

He nuzzled her neck. "Have you forgotten how you tremble at my touch?"

She trembled. "Phil . . . " Her fingers clutched greedily at his shirt. "I don't want to fall for you."

"But you are." He noted the red glint in her eyes. "I know you want me."

"No." She raked her hands into his hair, closing her fists around the strands as if she never wanted to let him go. "I don't want you at all."

"That's a shame." He kissed her brow. " 'Cause I want you."

"You shouldn't." She tugged his head down so she could kiss his mouth.

"Sweetheart, you're giving out mixed signals."

"I know." She pressed her body against his. "I've got to stop this. But God help me, I can't . . . stop."

He took her mouth, kissing her with all the passion that had simmered for eight long years. Her lips parted with a sweet surrender. But this was no passive surrender, not from his feisty Vanda. She stroked his tongue, then sucked on it with a desperation that made his blood boil. His groin swelled and he pulled her tight against him. With a deep growl he discovered just how well her thin spandex catsuit hugged every curve of her body from the sweet cheeks of her rump to the small of her back.

She rubbed against him, and his erection throbbed.

He unzipped her catsuit far enough to allow him to slip his hand inside and cup her breast. "You're so beautiful, so perfect." He flicked his thumb over her nipple, and the tip hardened.

She gasped. "Phil . . . " Her hands rubbed up and down his back.

"Vanda, I want to make love to you."

Her hands stilled. "No." She moved back, breaking his embrace. "I can't . . . love you."

"I won't hurt you, Vanda. You can trust me."

She shook her head. "I can't . . . " She zipped her catsuit shut. Her red-tinted eyes glimmered with moisture.

"I understand why you're afraid. You lost everyone in your family. Except Marta. And you probably felt betrayed by her."

"What?" Vanda stepped back, her face pale. "How— How did you . . . ?"

"The interview you did a few years ago for the reality show. Maggie found it at the townhouse and we watched it."

Vanda stiffened with an appalled expression. "Maggie helped you *spy* on me?"

"We weren't spying. We're trying to help you. If we can find a way for you to deal with the unresolved issues from your past—"

"My past is none of your business!" she snapped.

"It is. I'm supposed to help you learn how to

manage your anger, and we can do that by confronting whatever trauma you—"

"No! I am *not* a psychological experiment. And I have to question your motives, *Doctor* Phil. Are you trying to help me out of the goodness of your heart, or do you just want to get laid?"

He tamped down on his growing anger. "I want you to have a happy, fulfilled life. It is your fear that is causing you to insult me, and we can get rid of that fear by examining the trauma—"

"You leave my trauma the hell alone!" She adjusted the whip around her waist. "I'm not afraid of anything."

He raised his hands in a supplicating gesture. "It's normal for you to resist reliving those painful memories."

She gritted her teeth. "Don't patronize me. I'm not reliving anything."

"Then you want to stay afraid? Do you want to endure life for centuries afraid to love another person?"

She flinched as if he'd hit her.

"Vanda, I'm sorry." He stepped toward her.

"No." She lifted a hand to stop him. "Do you know how many people I've lost?" A pink tear rolled down her cheek. "My mother and father. My little sister. Every one of my brothers. Karl."

"Who's Karl?" Phil couldn't remember that name from the TV interview.

Vanda's outstretched hand curled into a fist. Her voice shook. "The wolves got him."

Phil froze.

Vanda's arm dropped to her side and her face crumpled. "He was my first love. A mortal. The mortals always die." She wiped her face. "Can't you see? I can't go through this again."

Shit. This would be the perfect time to tell her he was a shape shifter who could easily live another four to five hundred years. But she would want to know what he shifted into. "Vanda, none of us are immortal. You came close to dying the other day. Doesn't that tell you that we should seize the moment and live each night like it was our last?"

"But it won't last. And I can't endure the pain. I'm sorry."

"Vanda, we—"

She disappeared, leaving his hand extended close to where her face had been.

He lowered his arm. Poor Vanda. She was fighting a war between desire and fear. Her desire for him was strong. It had caused her eyes to glow red. It had made her clutch at him with passion. But tonight fear had won the battle.

"I'm not giving up on you," he whispered.

Chapter Eight

$\mathcal{L}$ots of people here tonight," Maggie said as Vanda inched her Corvette closer to the entrance of Romatech.

Vanda checked the rearview mirror. She couldn't see herself, but spotted several cars in line behind them. Two in front. All the local Vamps seemed to be here for Jack's engagement party. "I hate parties."

Maggie scoffed. "It'll be good for you. You've been working too hard."

"Friday nights are always busy at the club. I should be there."

"You'll only be gone a few hours. Cora Lee and Pamela were happy to take care of things," Maggie said. "Besides, you need a break. You've had a rough week."

The guard let another car through the gate, and Vanda moved the Corvette closer.

Maggie smoothed the skirt of her red taffeta cocktail dress. "Isn't it fun to dress up for a change? If I was home tonight, I'd be helping my husband shovel bat guano."

"Sounds better than this," Vanda grumbled.

"Don't be such a party pooper. You look lovely in that dress."

Vanda groaned. She should have never agreed to borrow one of Pamela's dresses. Maggie, Pamela, and Cora Lee had ganged up on her, insisting she wear it. But she was taller than Pamela, so the silver satin dress was too short, hitting her at mid-thigh. The bodice was too low. She tugged at a spaghetti strap. "This dress is too revealing."

Maggie snorted. "And your catsuits aren't?"

"They're comfortable. And I like having my whip handy."

"You don't need a whip at an engagement party." Maggie gave her a sly look. "You're just afraid Phil will see you looking so pretty and girlish."

"I'm not afraid." Last night Phil had said she was afraid, and now Maggie was doing it. "I'll prance around the party butt naked if I want. Nothing scares me."

"Then you'll be courageous enough to tell me what happened last night at DVN."

Vanda gripped the steering wheel. "Nothing happened."

"That's strange. Phil said the same thing."

"Really?" Vanda was relieved he hadn't talked about their encounter. She couldn't believe she'd ended up in his arms again, kissing him as if her life depended on it. And she'd come terribly close to surrendering completely. The man was too tempting. And too damned nosy about her past.

Another car drove through the gate, and Vanda rolled the Corvette up to the guard station. She lowered the window and handed the guard her invitation.

He leaned over to peer into the car. "Your names?"

"I'm Vanda Barkowski and this is my guest, Maggie O'Callahan."

He checked his clipboard, then passed the invitation back. "You can go in."

Vanda raised her window and started down the long driveway to Romatech. "So I guess you teleported Phil back to the townhouse last night?"

"Yes. I offered to take him to the club, but he thought you wouldn't want to see anyone." Maggie gave her a worried look. "He seems to understand you very well."

"I don't want to talk about it." Vanda drove into the parking lot and searched for an empty space. "I can't believe you showed him that interview from the reality show."

"It's public record. Besides, Phil thinks you need to resolve some issues from your past."

"I know about his damned theory. It's bullshit." She spotted an empty space in the next row and stepped on the accelerator to get there before anyone else. "And I don't want him digging around in my past. It's none of his damned business!"

"He just wants to help you with your anger problem."

"*I don't have an anger problem!*" Vanda stomped on the brakes when a couple emerged from between two cars. The woman screamed as the Corvette screeched to a halt a few inches in front of them.

The man thumped the hood of her car. "Stop speeding in the parking lot!"

"Oh, yeah?" Vanda lowered her window. "Watch where you're going, you assholes!" She shot them the finger.

The couple marched off in a huff.

Vanda took a deep breath. That had been close.

"No anger problem?" Maggie muttered.

"They asked for it." Vanda pulled into the empty parking space and stuffed the keys into the silver evening bag Pamela had insisted she use.

She climbed out of the car and checked her dress. The damned bodice was cut low enough that the purple bat tattooed on her right breast was exposed. She sighed. It had seemed like a good idea ten years ago. She'd enjoyed shocking all the stuffy old Vamps at the annual Gala Ball. But after a few years the shock had worn off.

Then she'd cut her hair and dyed it purple. That had worked well. Shocked people tended to keep their distance. Then she'd started wearing a whip around her waist. The implied threat of violence kept most everyone away.

Except Phil. He'd never been afraid of her.

"What do you know about Jack's fiancée?" Maggie asked as they walked toward the entrance of Romatech.

"Her name's Lara." Vanda looped the strap of her evening bag over her shoulder. "I heard she was from Louisiana, and she's a cop."

"Then she's mortal?"

"I guess."

"How interesting." Maggie gave her a pointed look. "Isn't it amazing how so many Vamps are finding true love and happiness with non-Vamps?"

"It's ridiculous."

"I think it's romantic."

Vanda snorted. "You married a Vamp."

"I married for love," Maggie insisted. "If my husband had been mortal, I wouldn't have hesitated one second. There's nothing more beautiful than true love."

"I need a drink."

Maggie scoffed. "Denial will not save you when Cupid's arrow finds its mark."

"If I see Cupid anywhere in the vicinity, I'm ripping his chubby little arms off." Vanda yanked the door open to Romatech.

A few Vamps were mingling in the foyer. Connor was standing behind a table, wearing a black and white plaid kilt and black jacket. He finished checking the contents of a lady's handbag, then passed it back to her.

Maggie rushed toward him, smiling. "Hi, Connor."

"Maggie, my bonny lass." Connor leaned over the table to give her a hug. " 'Tis good to see you again."

Vanda crossed her arms. Connor never called her bonny.

"I'll need to check yer bag, Maggie," Connor said.

"You want to see my pictures?" Maggie opened her bag and removed a small stack of photos.

Connor examined Maggie's bag while she shuffled through the pictures.

"This one is Pierce with our daughter, Lucy." Maggie showed it to Connor. "And this is last Halloween when Lucy was a princess. I made the costume myself."

"She's a bonny wee lass." Connor handed her the evening bag. "Ye adopted her?"

"I did." Maggie rushed to explain. "Her biological mother was a voodoo priestess from New Orleans who slipped Pierce a love potion so she could seduce him. Then, after she got pregnant, she erased his memory and abandoned him. And that's when he got changed into a vampire. But he had amnesia and didn't remember who he was or that he'd fathered a baby. And then Corky Courrant found him and brought him to New York, and he became Don Orlando de Corazon, the famous soap opera star on *As a Vampire Turns.* That's when I met him, and then Ian helped me discover his true identity. It's all very simple, really."

Connor's eyes had glazed over halfway through Maggie's story. "I see."

"The old amnesia/secret baby story," Vanda said wryly. "Happens all the time."

Maggie gave her an annoyed look and stuffed the photos back into her evening bag. "It happened to me, and we couldn't be happier."

"Then I'm verra happy for you." Connor turned to Vanda. "I'll need to check yer bag, too."

"I thought you'd never ask." Vanda tossed her bag onto the table. She was ready for him this time.

He opened her silver evening bag. His eyes widened.

She was quite proud that she'd managed to squeeze a pair of handcuffs, a blindfold, her back massager, and a bottle of Viagra into such a tiny handbag. She smiled sweetly. "Something wrong, Connor?"

"I see ye came prepared." He gave her a wry look as he returned her bag. "Enjoy yer evening."

"I will." Vanda strode toward the banquet hall.

Maggie sidled up to her and whispered, "What's in your bag?"

Vanda handed it to her with a smile.

Maggie opened it and laughed. "Girl, I have missed you." She passed the bag back with a sly look. "You must be planning to have sex with someone. I wonder who that could possibly be?"

"It was a joke, Maggie. Don't read anything more into it." Vanda entered the banquet hall.

The High Voltage Vamps were on the dais, playing "That's Amore." Couples were on the dance floor, happily swaying to the music. Vanda groaned.

A line had formed to congratulate Jack and meet his fiancée Lara.

"Oh, she's pretty," Maggie observed. "And she looks so happy. Come on, let's get in line."

Vanda surveyed the room as they strolled to the end of the queue. No sign of Phil. She grabbed a flute off the tray of a passing waiter. It was filled with Bubbly Blood, a mixture of champagne and synthetic blood. She downed it in three gulps.

Maggie frowned at her. "Are you all right?"

"Sure." She exchanged her empty glass for a full one from another waiter. "I'm just hungry."

"I think you're nervous."

"Why does everyone want to psychoanalyze me?"

"I don't know. Maybe it has something to do with the seven lawsuits filed against you in the last year," Maggie muttered with a sarcastic tone. "That could be a sign that you don't handle relationships well."

"I would be fine if everyone would just leave me the hell alone."

Maggie sighed. "You have friends, Vanda. Whether you like it or not, there are people who care about you."

Vanda's eyes burned as tears threatened. "Don't be nice to me. I can't . . . handle it." She gulped down more Bubbly Blood.

Maggie watched her sadly. "Darlin', you can't suffer like this forever. You need help."

Vanda took a deep breath and blinked her tears away. "I'm fine." She was tough, dammit. She started to tighten the whip around her waist, then realized it wasn't there. "Damn, I feel like I'm wearing a nightgown."

"You look beautiful. That silver satin makes your skin look positively luminous, and your eyes are dazzling. Phil looks completely flummoxed."

"*What?*" Vanda glanced around quickly. "Where is he?"

"He just came in from the patio." Maggie pointed at the glass wall at the back of the banquet hall that overlooked the grounds. "Oh, now he's coming toward us."

Vanda gulped. He looked incredibly handsome in a black tux that hugged his broad shoulders and narrow hips. The blond and red highlights in his hair gleamed, and his beautiful blue eyes were focused on her. "Oh my God."

Maggie smirked. "There goes Cupid's arrow. Bull's-eye."

Vanda grabbed Maggie's arm. "Keep him occupied. I've got to go."

"Chicken," Maggie hissed as Vanda hurried away. She skirted the room, ducking behind groups of Vamps so she couldn't be seen. It wasn't fear. It was *panic*. Her nerves had been frazzled ever since Phil had come back into her life.

In a far, dark corner, she found a row of chairs that were partially hidden by some large potted plants and a giant ice sculpture on a nearby table. She rolled her eyes. It was a giant Cupid, carved out of ice. Then she noticed the table was laden with mortal food. No wonder this corner was deserted. Most of the guests were Vamps, so they had no interest in mortal food, unless it was walking on two legs.

She finished her Bubbly Blood and set the glass next to a tray of boiled shrimp. A bottle of red liquid caught her eye. At first she thought it was one of Roman's Vampire Fusion inventions, since it was red like blood. She read the label: LOUISIANA HOT SAUCE. Maybe it was here for Jack's fiancée.

She wandered toward the row of chairs, looped her bag on the back of one and took a seat. No sign of Phil. No sign of anyone. She inhaled deeply. She would try to remain calm, even though she was a jumbled mess of contradictions. She ached with loneliness, but here she was in the middle of a party, trying to be alone. She longed to feel Phil's arms around her, yet here she was, hiding from him.

He was just too tempting. She loved the way she felt in his arms. She felt beautiful, desired, cherished. It had been so long since she'd felt special to someone.

Trust me, he had said. She wanted to trust him, but how could she trust love? She'd always told others there was nothing more sacred than love. She believed that with all her heart, but she knew deep down that love was for others, not for her. Love had always failed her, always brought pain and suffering. *Do you want to endure life for centuries afraid to love another person?* Phil's words still pricked at her.

"Hey, Vanda. How's it going?"

She jerked out of her morose thoughts to see Shanna approaching. "Hi."

The pretty wife of Roman Draganesti was carrying their new baby wrapped in a pink blanket. She swung a diaper bag off her shoulder, dropped it in a chair, then returned to the refreshment table. With the baby cradled in one arm, Shanna used her free hand to load food onto a plate. "I swear I have to breast-feed every hour. It makes me so hungry."

"Yeah." A pang of regret hit Vanda hard. After her mother's death, she had loved mothering her younger siblings. But she could never have children of her own, since as a Vamp her eggs were dead.

"Are you all right?" Shanna gave her a worried look as she added some grapes to her plate.

Vanda gritted her teeth. "I'm great."

"Good. Then if you don't mind . . . " Shanna hurried over and set the baby in Vanda's arms. "Thank you so much."

Vanda stiffened. "But—"

"It's so hard with two little ones." Shanna rushed back to the table and poured herself some punch. "I gave Radinka the night off 'cause she's so worn-out. And Roman is busy with some official coven stuff." She motioned toward the dance floor. "I left Tino jumping up and down to the music. I hope it wears him out."

She downed the cup of punch, then poured another one. "I need lots of fluids. So, are you enjoying the party?"

"Sure," Vanda mumbled. She lowered her gaze, reluctant to even look at the baby. The infant possessed a surprisingly sturdy little body in a pink dress with pink rosebuds embroidered on the collar. Plump pink cheeks. A pink mouth that opened and shut like a little fish. Big blue eyes.

Vanda swallowed hard. Frieda's eyes had been that same shade of blue. Tinged with a bit of green, so they were almost turquoise. "What—" Her voice croaked, and she cleared her throat. "What's her name?"

"Sofia." Shanna popped a grape in her mouth. "After Roman's mother, who died when he was very young."

Vanda's eyes burned. She'd never be able to honor her mother's memory by naming a child after her. With trembling fingers she brushed the blanket off Sofia's head. Black hair. Just like Jozef. The old wound in her heart cracked further open, and she blinked back tears. She couldn't do this. She had to give the baby back.

She looked at Shanna. "I—"

"She likes you." Shanna smiled. "She usually starts screaming if she doesn't recognize whoever's holding her."

"But . . . " Vanda glanced down at the baby. *How can you like me? I'm dying inside.*

Sofia waved a tiny fist in the air and moved her mouth like she was trying to talk.

"There you are, Vanda." Maggie peered around the giant ice sculpture. "I've been looking everywhere for you."

Vanda's heart leaped, then relaxed when she saw that Maggie was alone. She hadn't brought Phil with her. "Where is he?"

"Gee, I wonder whom you're referring to." Maggie circled the table. "Hi, Shanna."

"Maggie, how are you?" Shanna gave her a hug.

"I'm great. And this must be your new baby." Maggie rushed over to Vanda to look at the infant. "Sweet Mary and Joseph, what a beautiful little girl."

"Thank you." Shanna strolled over with her plate of food.

"Where's Phil?" Vanda whispered to Maggie.

"He's on guard duty right now. He said he'd catch

up with you later." Maggie's mouth twitched. "I didn't know you were so good with babies."

Vanda gritted her teeth. "I'm not."

Shanna munched on a cracker. "Sofia's taken a real liking to Vanda."

"She's too young to know any better," Vanda muttered.

Shanna chuckled. "Actually, she has very good instincts where people are concerned. She always spits up on Gregori, and Radinka claims it's because she knows he's a womanizing cad."

"I'm so glad I ran into you, Shanna." Maggie removed a photo from her evening bag. "I've been meaning to talk to you about my daughter Lucy. She's seven years old now. And she's mortal, since Pierce fathered her before he was turned."

"I see." Shanna studied the photo. "She's adorable."

"The problem is, Lucy's in school now," Maggie continued. "And it's hard to explain how her parents are never available during the day. And we worry that she might slip up and mention that her parents are vampires and her great-uncle and aunt are shape shifters."

Vanda flinched, and the baby whimpered.

Shanna leaned over to whisper comforting words to her daughter.

"Oh, I'm sorry, Vanda," Maggie said. "I probably gave you a shock. A lot of Vamps don't know about shifters."

Vanda shuddered. "I know about them." Her

muscles tensed and a black hole of panic threatened to overwhelm her. She gasped for air.

"Are you all right?" Shanna set her plate on a nearby chair. "Do you need me to take the baby?"

"I—" Vanda's gaze met the baby's blue eyes and she froze. Time slowed down and a soft feeling of peace poured through her, trickling down sweet and golden like honey. The panic attack was gone. "I'm okay."

"Good." With a smile, Shanna handed Lucy's photo back to Maggie. "Your daughter is a perfect candidate for the school we're opening in the fall. We'll have a few mortal children there, children who know too much, like Jean-Luc and Heather's girl Bethany."

"It sounds wonderful." Maggie slipped the photo back into her bag.

"Classes will be in the evening so Vamp parents can teleport their children to school." Shanna retrieved her plate of food, then paused with a piece of cheese halfway to her mouth. "Oh my gosh, I just had a terrific idea. You were an actress on DVN. You could teach a drama class to our older students!"

Maggie's mouth fell open. "Me? Teach?"

"Yes!" Shanna grinned. "You could teleport Lucy to school, then stay to teach a class. What do you think?"

"Well, it sounds more fun than shoveling bat guano every night," Maggie murmured.

"There you go." Shanna gave her an encouraging look. "And your husband would be welcome to teach, too."

Maggie nodded slowly. "We could use the extra money."

"Great! Let's get you a couple of job applications and a registration form for Lucy. I have them in my office." Shanna set her plate of food on the table, then glanced at Vanda. "Can you watch Sofia for a few minutes? Thanks!"

"But—" Vanda watched in dismay as Shanna and Maggie dashed off. "Goddammit." She glanced at the baby. "Pretend you didn't hear that."

The baby gazed up at her, wide-eyed and curious.

Vanda sighed. "I guess you're stuck with me."

Sofia made a slurping noise.

Vanda adjusted her hold and waited. And waited. She touched the baby's cheek. The skin felt so soft and new. The last time she'd held a baby was in 1927, when her brother Jozef was born. She'd always thought of him as her baby. He'd been only twelve when he'd marched off with his father and brothers to fight the Nazi invasion.

Her eyes grew moist. She'd begged him not to go. She'd begged him to flee with her and their sisters. But he'd wanted to prove he wasn't a baby, that he was all grown up.

He was so young to die.

"Hi," a young voice greeted her.

Vanda blinked her eyes dry. A little boy with blond curls and blue eyes stood next to the refreshment table. He was dressed in a little navy blue suit, but his shirttail had fallen out and his tie was askew.

"I'm Tino." He grabbed a cookie off the table and bit into it.

She'd seen Constantine Draganesti before but had never talked to him. "I'm Vanda."

He finished his cookie and grabbed another. "Did you know your hair is purple?"

"Yes." Apparently, small children didn't know they should stay away from people with purple hair.

"Have you seen my mommy?" Tino finished his second cookie. "She told me to come here when I got tired of dancing."

"Shanna had to go to her office for a minute. She'll be right back."

Tino approached Vanda, studying her curiously. "What are you doing with my little sister?"

"I have no idea."

He leaned over to examine Sofia's face. "I think she likes you. When she doesn't like someone, she screams." He puffed out his chest proudly. "No one can scream as loud as my sister."

You haven't heard me, Vanda thought.

"You want to see what I can do?" Tino asked, then vanished. "Ta-da!" He reappeared, standing on the chair next to her.

"Wow." Vanda stared at him. She'd heard rumors that Roman's son was special but she hadn't realized the little boy could actually teleport. "That's amazing."

"I know." He smiled smugly. "My sister can't do it."

"I guess you're all grown up," Vanda said wryly, remembering how fast Jozef had wanted to grow up.

"I am." Tino sat on the chair next to her. "I have more power than Sofia."

"Power?"

He nodded. "She wants to help you, but she's not strong enough. You want me to try?"

Vanda eyed him warily. "Try what?"

Tino rested his little hand on her arm. His nose wrinkled as he made a face. "You're hurting real bad."

"I'm a Vamp. I don't get sick."

"It's . . . an *old* pain," he whispered. "In your heart."

She felt a tingling sensation on her arm where Tino was touching her. "What are you doing?" And how the hell did he know about her pain?

The little boy winced. "I'm trying to heal your pain, but it's so deep inside."

"No!" Vanda scooted down a seat, breaking the boy's hold on her. "I need my pain. It's what I am." Dammit, she'd lived with it for so long, she couldn't imagine being without it. "It—It keeps me safe."

"Safe from what?"

"Safe from . . . more pain."

Tino looked confused. "I don't understand."

"It's like . . . having a broken leg. The pain reminds me to be careful not to break the other leg. If you had a broken leg, you wouldn't want to break the other one, right?"

Tino tugged at his crooked tie. "I don't want any broken legs."

Vanda smiled at him sadly. "You're sweet to want to help, but I . . . broke a long time ago. And I don't know how to get better."

"You have to *want* to get better," a deep voice emanated from behind a potted plant.

Vanda gasped as Phil stepped into view. "You— You shouldn't spy on people." Her heart raced. How much had he heard? Did he really think she didn't *want* to feel better? She wasn't a masochist, dammit. She was only trying to protect herself.

"I was doing a perimeter check." His gaze drifted slowly down her body, then back up her legs, past the baby in her lap, and settled on the bat tattoo on her breast. His mouth curled up.

Vanda ignored the tingles shooting down her arms and gave him a wry look. "And does everything check out?"

"Oh yeah." His eyes gleamed. "It's looking good." He smiled at the boy. "Hi, Tino."

"Hi, Phil." Tino squirmed off his chair. "You want a cookie? They're chocolate chip."

Phil tossed some cheese and crackers on a plate and handed it to the little boy. "Trust me. This is what you want."

Tino accepted the plate, frowning. "But I wanted—"

"Tino!" Shanna called to him as she approached with Maggie. "I hope you're eating more than just cookies."

"I am! See?" Tino showed her his plate and stuffed a cracker in his mouth.

"That's my sweetie." Shanna kissed the top of his head, then walked over to Vanda. "Thank you for watching Sofia." She gathered up the baby, who was now sleeping soundly. "I never realized how good you are with children. You should do like Maggie and adopt one."

Vanda's mouth dropped open.

"What a marvelous idea!" Maggie clasped her hands together, grinning.

"No way," Vanda protested. She winced at the amused look on Phil's face. "I run a strip club, remember?"

"What's that?" Tino asked with his mouth full.

"And I have an anger problem," Vanda continued. "Not to mention the fact that I'm dead half the time." She glanced at the boy. Hopefully, her undead status didn't come as a shock to Tino. He had to know that his father was dead during the day.

She wondered briefly if the little boy ever acted up when he knew his dad wasn't there to stop him. She could just picture Shanna telling him, *Just wait till your father wakes from the dead. You'll be in big trouble then.*

Vanda slowly realized that everyone was quietly staring at her. "What?" She glanced down at her dress to make sure she wasn't covered with baby spittle.

"You just admitted that you have an anger problem," Phil said, his pale blue eyes twinkling. "That's the first step toward improvement."

"Exactly." Shanna nodded. "You can't fix a problem until you admit it exists."

"Well, isn't that special." Vanda stood and slung her evening bag onto her shoulder. "I've had enough fun for one evening. Shall we go, Maggie?"

"We haven't met Lara yet," Maggie reminded her.

"And you haven't talked to me," Phil said.

"I don't—" Vanda started.

"Excellent!" Shanna interrupted. "I'll tell Roman that you're following the court decree and having a meeting with your anger management sponsor. He'll be so impressed."

Damn. Vanda couldn't see a way out of this one. But the last thing she needed was another encounter with Phil. She had no self-control around him.

"Come along, Tino. Let's find your dad." Shanna grabbed the diaper bag, then glanced at Maggie. "I'll call you." She walked away with the baby. Constantine waved good-bye, then ran after his mother.

"I need to finish my rounds," Phil said. "I'll meet you back here in fifteen minutes." He hugged Maggie, smiled at Vanda, and strode away.

Vanda couldn't help but admire his gorgeous backside as he crossed the room. Still, she wondered why he'd hugged Maggie and not her.

Of course! He was guarding her at the townhouse and sponsoring her in anger management. He was forbidden to have a relationship with her, and most of these Vamps in attendance knew it. So, as long as she stayed here in the banquet hall, surrounded by other Vamps, he'd have to keep his hands off her.

She would be safe from his seductive maneuvers. And from her own weakness. Vanda smiled to herself. Suddenly, the party didn't seem so dismal after all.

Chapter Nine

What exactly does a bomb smell like?" Phineas asked.

"Trouble." Phil strode through the parking lot outside Romatech, sniffing each car to make sure the Malcontents hadn't planned a surprise for the Vamps.

"How did you learn how to do it?" Phineas followed him. "Did you train with the canine unit at NYPD?"

"Very funny." Phil gave the young black Vamp a shove. "The lot is clear. Let's go back inside."

They headed for the front door. Because of the party, the door was unlocked and anyone could walk in. The guests had been instructed to drive to Romatech, so they were first vetted by the guard at the entrance station. Then Connor checked everyone in the foyer. Howard Barr was in the security office watching the monitors to make sure no one teleported onto the grounds.

Phil and Phineas had taken turns roaming the grounds and the facility. So far, everything had gone smoothly.

Phil had reserved a conference room close to the banquet hall. He'd called the priest earlier in the day to explain his theory about Vanda's past, and Father Andrew had wanted to see the DVD of Vanda's interview. He was in the conference room now, watching it.

Phil strode into the foyer. "All clear," he reported to Connor.

"Good," the Scotsman replied. "Ye can take a break now." He gave Phineas a stern look. "Doona drink too much, lad."

"Aye aye, Captain Connor." Phineas saluted him, then dashed into the banquet hall.

Phil strolled into the noisy hall and glanced at the far corner where he'd discovered Vanda earlier. He smiled to himself, remembering how beautiful she'd looked in her silver dress, how sweet with a baby cradled in her arms. She had so much love to give, if only she could get over the pain from her past.

"Hi, Phil," a happy voice greeted him.

"Lara." He gave Jack's fiancée a hug. "How are you?"

"Exhausted." She brushed her golden red hair over a shoulder. "It must have taken an hour to meet everyone. My jaw is aching from all the smiling, and now I can't remember half the people's names."

Phil nodded. "You will, in time."

"Jack said there was some real food around here somewhere."

"Over there." Phil pointed to the far corner.

"Good. I'll grab a quick bite while Jack dances with LaToya. Did you meet my roommate?"

"Not yet. I've been on guard duty."

Lara cast a nervous glance toward the dance floor. "LaToya refused to be my maid of honor until we told her the truth about Jack, so we told her last night. Jack wanted to be there in case she went completely berserk and needed her memory erased."

Phil spotted Jack on the dance floor with a young black woman in a red dress. "Is she okay?"

"She's . . . a little freaked out. She always knew there was something different about Jack. But she thought he was a superhero, so now she's disappointed. Of course, I think he *is* a superhero."

"Of course."

Lara leaned close. "I didn't tell her about *your* secret."

"Thank you."

"Well, I'd better get some food." She hurried off and waved at Phineas as he returned with a glass filled to the brim with Blissky.

He took a long drink of the synthetic blood and whiskey mixture and winced. "Damn, that's good."

Phil shook his head, smiling. "Connor will know."

"Not if I have one of these afterward." Phineas showed him a roll of Vampos, then slipped the mints back into the pocket of his black trousers.

Phil knew the vampire after-dinner mint got rid

of blood breath, but he wasn't sure it could erase the smell of whiskey. At any rate, it wasn't his problem. He glanced over at the corner where he was supposed to meet Vanda in five minutes. "Any news on Max the Mini Member?"

Phineas snorted. "You renamed the bastard. I like it. But no one's found him yet." He drank more Blissky. "I'm happy to keep going to the Horny Devils to make sure the ladies are safe."

"Like those two women last night?"

"What can I say? The ladies love to hang with Dr. Phang." Phineas adjusted his bow tie. "I look like James Bond in this tux, don't you think? I'll be looking sharp for my date tonight with Lisa. She thinks I'm a super spy."

"Which one was Lisa? The blonde?"

Phineas frowned, considering. "I think so. Or she could be the brunette." He shrugged. "It doesn't matter. The Love Doctor is an equal opportunity babe magnet, and one hot babe is just as bootie-licious as another."

Phil snorted. "One day you'll eat those words." He pictured Vanda in his mind. "One day you'll meet someone special, someone who can cut you off at the knees with a simple smile. Someone who can capture your very soul with just one glance of her beautiful eyes. And in one fell moment your entire world will tilt on its axis to point only at her. And you'll know you have met your fate."

Crash.

Phil jerked back as Phineas's glass shattered on

the floor, shards glittering in a pool of Blissky. The young Vamp's hand was frozen in the air. He looked stunned.

"Phineas?" Phil touched his shoulder. "Are you all right?"

He remained stiff, his eyes wide-open and un-blinking.

"Phineas." Phil shook him, but it had no effect. The young Vamp seemed completely paralyzed.

Nightshade? For a shocked second Phil wondered if someone had slipped the paralyzing drug into Phineas's drink. Was there a Malcontent lurking in their midst? But no, it couldn't be Nightshade. That would have made Phineas fall on the floor before paralysis set in.

"Who?" Phineas whispered so faintly Phil wasn't sure he'd heard it. This was a good sign, though. If Phineas had been dosed with Nightshade, he wouldn't be able to talk.

"Who . . . who is she?" Phineas whispered.

Phil followed the Vamp's line of vision. The dance floor.

There were several couples on the dance floor. Shanna was dancing with her husband. Jean-Luc was dancing with Heather. Gregori was dancing with the fashion model, Inga. And Jack was dancing with . . . "LaToya? The girl in the red dress?"

"La . . . LaToya?" Phineas stared at her.

"She's Lara's roommate."

"She's a goddess."

"She's the maid of honor."

"She's an angel," Phineas breathed.

"She's a police officer."

Phineas blinked. A shudder visibly shook him, and he turned to Phil with an appalled expression. "I—I don't do well with the po-po. I have an outstanding warrant."

Phil winced. "That could be a problem."

Phineas's gaze drifted back to LaToya, and his brown eyes widened with a look of awe. He squared his shoulders. "Nothing will stop me." He stepped forward.

When his shoe crunched on glass, Phil pulled him back. "Wait a minute." He motioned to a waiter to clean up the mess.

Phineas stiffened suddenly and grasped Phil's arm. "Did you see that? She looked at me!"

Phil glanced at the dance floor, and sure enough, LaToya was checking Phineas out.

"I'm in love," Phineas whispered.

That was fast. Phil suppressed a grin. "What about your date with Lisa?"

"Who?"

"Lisa. The blonde . . . or brunette. They're both Vamps like you. LaToya's mortal." Even though a lot of male Vamps were falling for mortal women, Phil knew the guys deeply regretted the fact that they would have to turn their wives at some point, or lose them to the ravages of time.

Phineas sighed. "LaToya is La-One. La-angel."

"All right, Pepe LePew, but you haven't actually met her yet."

Phineas stepped back as two waiters approached with a dustpan, pail, and mop. "I'll meet her now."

He popped a Vampos into his mouth, then stuffed the roll of mints into his trouser pocket. "I need to act cool, man. Turn up the mojo. Impress her with my savoir faire and debonairness."

He unbuttoned his tuxedo jacket to reveal a bright red cummerbund. "The Love Doctor is in the house. Come on, bro. You can be my assistant. Make me sound good."

"I'll do my best." Phil accompanied the young black Vamp to the dance floor.

Phineas had one hand pressed to his cummerbund and was suddenly walking like John Wayne.

"What are you doing?" Phil whispered.

"This is my pimp walk. The ladies can't resist it."

"Are you sure that's the right approach to take with a police officer?"

"Oh yeah." Phineas smirked. "It's working, bro. She can't take her eyes off me."

"I'm not sure that's a good thing," Phil muttered.

The music stopped, and Jack spotted them. "Phil, Phineas, how are you? Have you met Lara's friend, LaToya?"

Phil shook her hand. "A pleasure to meet you. And may I introduce Phineas McKinney, a valued member of the MacKay Security and Investigation team."

"And head of the special Malcontent Terrorist Task Force, but I can't discuss that." Phineas waved a dismissive hand. "Top secret stuff, you know."

Jack gave him a wry look. "That *is* a well kept secret."

LaToya frowned. "Are you for real?"

"Of course." Phineas took LaToya's hand. "Don't worry, sweetness. I won't frighten you with the gruesome details of my missions as super spy, code name Dr. Phang."

"Fang?" LaToya jerked her hand away and leaned close to Jack. "He's a vampire?"

"He's a good Vamp," Jack whispered. "Like me."

"The jury's still out on that," LaToya muttered.

Jack sighed. "And he has excellent hearing."

LaToya turned back to Phineas and huffed when she caught him ogling her. "Don't go looking at my neck, sucker."

"He drinks synthetic blood like the rest of us," Jack said.

Phineas executed a gallant bow. "I could drink in your majestic beauty for an eternity."

"You're not drinking anything from me," LaToya said, then turned back to Jack. "I saw those holes on Lara's neck when she came back from that under-cover mission. I didn't realize what it meant at the time, but if you ever do that again—"

"It couldn't be helped," Jack interrupted. "I was posing as a Malcontent, so I had to act like one."

"I'm just warning you." LaToya waved a finger at him. "If I see any more bite marks on my friend, I'm coming after you like a gator on a dead chicken. And you—" She turned to Phineas. "Don't think you can pull any of that super mojo on me. As far as I'm concerned, you're just another dead carcass trussed up in a fancy tuxedo."

"I'm the Love Doctor, sweetness. I've got the cure."

"You're a *dead* doctor. I don't care how handsome you are. I'm not interested!" LaToya marched off.

Jack winced. "Sorry, old boy. She's a bit sensitive about vampires at the moment."

Phil patted Phineas on the back. "Maybe she'll come around in time."

Phineas smiled slowly. "She said I was handsome. Did you hear that?" He smoothed back his short hair. "Dr. Phang strikes again. The chase is on."

"You should take it slow," Phil warned him, but the Love Doctor took off, following LaToya.

Phil sighed. He couldn't even take his own advice. Now that he knew Vanda was genuinely attracted to him, he was pursuing her as fast as he could. He congratulated Jack, then hurried off to the conference room to make sure Father Andrew was ready.

And then, somehow, he needed to get Vanda there for the meeting.

As it turned out, Vanda didn't need to get in line to meet Jack's fiancée. After she and Maggie retrieved two more glasses of Bubbly Blood, they returned to the corner behind the mortal refreshment table and found Lara there.

Lara filled them in on the wedding plans, then Maggie shared her family photos and described the ranch in Texas. Vanda sat, sipping her Bubbly Blood, while she waited for Phil to return. Not that she was in any hurry to see him. She was still peeved about his snooping around in her past.

Constantine came back, wanting more cookies, so

Maggie distracted him with photos of her ranch.

"Can I go?" Tino asked. "I want to ride a horse."

"I would love for you to visit." Maggie gave him a hug. "I'll ask your mom about it."

Lara filled a plate with boiled shrimp, then drizzled some hot sauce on top. "So tell me, Vanda, what do you do for a living?"

"I run a—" She glanced at the little boy. "A dance club."

"Can I go?" Tino asked.

"No," Vanda and Maggie both answered quickly.

"But I like to dance." Tino skipped over to the table to snatch a cookie.

"It's just for adults," Maggie explained, then her eyes widened. "Lara, it would be the perfect place for a bachelorette party."

Lara's eyebrows shot up. "It's *that* kind of place?"

"Exactly," Vanda replied. "But with male Vamps doing the . . . dancing."

"I want to dance," Tino said.

Lara sighed. "It sounds interesting, but I don't know if we can get my maid of honor to agree. She's a little—"

"I told you to stay away from me!" A loud voice interrupted Lara. "You come after me again, and I'll sucker punch you into next week. You got that?" A young black woman in a red dress strode into the corner area. "Lara, that Blackula dude is stalking me."

"Who, Phineas?" Lara waved at the young Vamp, motioning for him to stay back. She lowered her voice. "LaToya, he's a nice guy. I think he looks like Denzel."

LaToya crossed her arms with a huff. "A *dead* Denzel."

"He was one of the Vamps who rescued me from Apollo's compound," Lara continued. "He helped rescue all the girls. He's brave and loyal—"

"I don't care," LaToya grumbled. "He's still one of *them*. I don't know how you can stand to be around them."

Lara winced. "LaToya, this is Constantine, Maggie, and Vanda."

LaToya smiled at them. "Hey there." She patted Tino on his head. "Aren't you a cutie? Did you come here with your mommy?" She glanced again at Maggie and Vanda as if she were trying to figure out which one of them was the mom.

"Yes," Tino said. "Do you want a cookie?"

"Don't mind if I do." LaToya grabbed a plate and circled the refreshment table, helping herself. "Thank God I found the place where all the normal people are hanging out."

Vanda set her empty glass on the floor underneath her chair. "So what do you have against Vamps?"

"Oh, the usual." LaToya popped a grape into her mouth. "They're dead and slimy, probably stink during the day—"

"That's not nice." Constantine frowned as he grabbed the last cookie.

"LaToya, cool it," Lara whispered. "I'm in love with a Vamp."

"I know." LaToya grimaced as she tossed shrimp on her plate. "And now you want to quit the police force and work for that stupid vampire company."

"MacKay Security and Investigation," Lara said. "I can work alongside Jack."

"I like Jack." Tino stood close to the table, watching the women argue.

"Whatever." LaToya drizzled hot sauce on her shrimp. "All I know is, I came to New York to be a police officer with you, and now you're quitting. I might as well go home. At least there I wouldn't have to deal with a bunch of creepy vampires."

"Where is your home?" Maggie asked.

"New Orleans." LaToya stuffed a shrimp in her mouth.

Maggie covered her mouth to hide her grin, but Vanda wasn't that polite.

She snickered. "No Vamps in New Orleans?"

"Dammit." LaToya set her plate down. "There's no escaping those monsters."

"They're not monsters," Tino grumbled.

"You're right, sweetie." Lara tousled the little boy's curls. "They're real people. And they have real feelings." She gave LaToya a stern look. "You're hurting Phineas's feelings. He doesn't deserve that."

"All right. I'll let Blackula know just how sorry I am." LaToya walked off.

Lara watched her go, then turned back to Vanda and Maggie with a confused look. "That seemed a little too easy. She's usually more stubborn than that."

"Maybe she's had a change of heart." Maggie stood up to survey the crowd. "Where is she?"

"There." Lara pointed to a bar. "She just picked up a Vamp drink."

"Maybe she's taking it to Phineas," Maggie suggested. "It would be a nice gesture."

Vanda walked over to the refreshment table for a closer look. "I don't think she's giving him a peace offering. The hot sauce is gone."

"The red stuff?" Tino asked. "I saw her take it."

Lara gasped. "I've got to stop her." She ran after her roommate.

"We should warn Phineas." Maggie searched the crowd. "Do you see him?"

Vanda scanned the room, then looked down when something tugged at her skirt.

Constantine clenched her skirt in his fist, his eyes wide with worry. "Is something bad going to happen? Why doesn't that lady like Phineas?"

"She just doesn't know him," Vanda explained. "Once she gets to know him, I'm sure she'll like him."

"I see him." Maggie pointed at the dance floor. "He's over there by the band."

Vanda quickly poured a cup of punch and pressed it into the little boy's hands. "Can you take this to your mom? She gets very thirsty."

"Okay." Tino headed back to the dance floor, carefully holding the cup of punch.

Maggie gave Vanda an appraising look. "You really are good with children."

Vanda shrugged. "Come on, let's get to Phineas before LaToya does."

She and Maggie skirted the table, but came to an abrupt halt when Corky Courrant made a grand entrance into the banquet hall. Her cameraman followed, the camera perched on his shoulder as he recorded the scene.

"Oh great," Vanda muttered. "Who invited her?"

"She reports on all the big parties." Maggie pulled Vanda behind a potted plant. "If she sees you, she'll start screeching at you."

"So? I'm not afraid." Vanda moved back into view.

Maggie pulled her back. "She'll try to provoke you into a fight. She wants everyone to think you're violent."

"I *am* violent." Vanda stepped out.

"You don't want to start a scene." Maggie tugged on her arm. "It would ruin Lara's engagement party."

Vanda spotted LaToya on the dance floor, handing Phineas a drink. "Looks like someone else is going to ruin it first."

Meanwhile, she didn't have to worry about Corky seeing her. A group of well-dressed Vamps had gathered around the reporter, no doubt hoping they would appear on her next show.

"Don't crowd me," Corky hissed at them. She wore a glittery black dress with a low bodice that displayed her augmented bosom. The shimmering black skirt hit just below her knees.

Vanda recalled that one of the brassieres she'd sabotaged was black. And she'd altered some black underwear, too. She gave Maggie a sly grin. "Corky might be giving a bigger exposé than she planned."

Maggie frowned. "What do you mean?"

Corky posed in front of the camera and spoke into a microphone, her voice drowning out the low roar of others. "This is Corky Courrant, reporting for *Live with the Undead*. Tonight, I'm attending the posh engagement party of Giacomo di Venezia, known as Jack to his close friends, like *moi*. Recently, some rumors have surfaced. I know the truth, of course, so I will confirm that Jack is actually the son of that famous libertine, Giacomo Casanova."

Corky assumed a tragic face. "I'm afraid the other rumors are true, as well. It grieves me to tell you this, but Jack is, indeed, illegitimate. And not only is he a bastard, but he's fallen for a common mortal. Once again, a rich and eligible male has brought shame upon Vamp society by marrying far beneath himself."

"That's enough!" Jack pushed through the crowd to confront the newswoman. "I won't have my future wife insulted."

"Jack!" Corky grinned maliciously. "How kind of you to grant me an inter—"

"*Aargh!*" a hoarse voice shouted. Glass shattered on the dance floor.

The crowd turned to see what was happening. Phineas had fallen to the dance floor, his hands grasping his throat as he squirmed in agony. Lara kneeled beside him, while LaToya hurried away, circling the crowd to reach the entrance.

"He's been poisoned!" an onlooker yelled.

Jack pushed through the crowd to reach Phineas. Jean-Luc and Roman met him there. Lara whispered to them while murmurs of poison spread quickly around the room.

"We're under attack!" a male Vamp shouted. "Sound the alarm!"

"It's the Malcontents!" another Vamp yelled. "They'll poison us all!"

Glasses dropped all over the banquet hall, the sound of shattering glass accentuating the squeals of fear. Frantic Vamps stampeded toward the foyer.

Connor blocked the entrance, his broadsword drawn. "No one leaves the premises till we find the person responsible."

Vamps screamed at him, demanding to be allowed to leave. Others huddled in groups, shrieking and glancing wildly about.

Vanda shook her head. What a bunch of cowards. She considered going over to Connor to tell him what had happened, but noticed Jack headed toward him.

Corky positioned herself close to a group of wailing Vamps and smiled gleefully at the camera. "Pandemonium has broken out! I've never seen such a disastrous party in all my life!" She waved her arms at the scene behind her.

"Sweet Mary and Joseph," Maggie whispered. "Corky's going to talk about this for weeks."

The newswoman gestured toward Phineas, who lay writhing in pain on the floor. "Will this poor Vamp die? Stay tuned after these messages from my sponsor, Vampos, to find out!"

"Can I hide here with you?" someone behind Vanda whispered.

She turned to find LaToya crouched behind the potted plant.

"Shame on you," Maggie fussed at her. "Phineas is in pain."

"I didn't know it was going to hurt so much." LaToya set the bottle of hot sauce on a nearby chair. "I just wanted him to leave me alone. And now that Scottish dude has the entrance blocked and I can't get out."

"You should tell Connor what you did," Maggie said. "Everyone thinks we're under attack from the Malcontents."

"I think Connor knows." Vanda motioned to where Jack and Connor were whispering to each other.

"Damn." LaToya frowned at Phineas, who still lay on the floor. "I didn't think it would hurt him so bad. I mean, he's already dead. How could it get any worse?"

"We can be more vulnerable than people think," Maggie said. "Poor Vanda nearly died the other day when a snake attacked her."

LaToya's mouth dropped open. "You mean, you two are . . . ?"

Vanda gave her a big smile that showed her fangs.

"Oh shit." LaToya rubbed her brow. "I've really done it now."

"And we're back!" Corky's voice filled the room as she spoke into her microphone. "As you can see, the poisoned Vamp hasn't died . . . yet. But hope springs eternal."

"Miss Courrant." Jack stepped toward her, and the cameraman swerved to record him. "Let me state for the record that this is not a Malcontent attack. One of our guests has accidentally swallowed a little hot sauce. That's all. We expect a quick and full recovery."

Corky eyed Jack with a dubious look. "And if it was a Malcontent attack, would you admit it? Tell me the truth now. Doesn't your disastrous engagement party predict an equally disastrous marriage?"

Jack stiffened. "Of course not!"

Corky sneered. "The evidence is clear. Your marriage is doomed!"

Snap!

Corky jumped as one of her bra straps popped out from her bodice. She looked down just as the second strap broke loose and slapped her in the face. Her heavy breasts sagged down. "*Ack!*"

The crowd, which had been cowing in fear a moment earlier, now erupted with laughter.

"Stop that! I'll see you all ruined!" Corky attempted to cover her breasts as she glared at the cameraman. "Cut!"

Maggie gasped and turned to Vanda. "What did you do?"

Vanda grinned. "I booby-trapped her." She stepped forward for a better view. "And if we're lucky—"

"*Aagh!*" Corky's black panties fell to her ankles. Her face turned red with rage as she scanned the snickering crowd. "Someone sabotaged me! I'll find out and make you pay!"

A strong arm grabbed Vanda and pulled her back.

She stumbled. "Phil! What are you doing here?"

"What are *you* doing, Vanda?" He glanced at Corky, who was now hurling insults at individuals in the crowd. "Don't let her see you. She'll know it was you." He dragged her back.

"I'm not afraid of her. And where are you taking me?"

"There's an emergency exit behind the stage."

Vanda tried to dig her heels in, but her stilettos merely wobbled. "I'm not going anywhere with you."

He shot her an amused look. "Afraid of me?"

"Hell, no." Hell, yes. Whenever she was alone with him, she lost all self-control and ended up kissing him.

He pulled her through some swinging double doors into a deserted hallway. "This way."

"Don't even try to kiss me again. It's forbidden. I could tattle on you and get you in big trouble."

"Or I could give you such mind-blowing sex, you would beg for more."

"Ha! I never beg for anything."

He stopped abruptly and pulled her into his arms so fast, she slammed into his hard chest. The air was knocked out of her and her heart rate jumped into high gear.

He leaned forward, his breath hot against her brow. "Never say never, sweetheart. You like kissing me."

"Do not." Oh God, he felt so good.

His lips skimmed along her cheekbone. "You were forbidden years ago, and I obeyed the rules. I was young and foolish. Not anymore." He nuzzled her neck.

"Phil," she whispered, and pressed against him. He was so strong and warm.

"We don't need the rules. We're rebels." He suckled her earlobe.

"Yes." She wrapped her arms around his neck. "Kiss me. Now."

He leaned back, his mouth curling. "Are you begging?"

"No." She glared at him. "I'll make you beg."

He chuckled. "I thought I was. But first we have some business to attend to." He led her farther down the hall.

"What business?"

He opened a door and ushered her inside. "Your first anger management class."

"My *what*?" She gasped when she spotted her image frozen on a television screen.

"Good evening, my child." Father Andrew stood next to a conference table.

Phil had shown her interview to the priest? How could he do this to her? Rage shot through her.

She picked up a chair. "You want some anger? I'll give you some anger! Manage this!"

Chapter Ten

*G*et down!" Phil shouted at the priest as Vanda hurled the chair across the conference table.

The chair crashed into the wall, denting the Sheetrock six feet away from Father Andrew, who crouched underneath the table. With vampire speed Vanda grabbed another chair, but Phil wrenched it away and seized her by the wrists.

"Let me go!" She kicked at his shins.

She wasn't as strong as a male Vamp, but with her rage in full bloom, she was damned close. Phil struggled to hold on. He could always unleash his inner wolf and take her down in a second, but he refrained. She was upset enough already.

He pushed her back against a wall, pinning her wrists to each side of her head. "As your anger management sponsor, I have to say—"

"You're not my sponsor." She attempted to knee him.

He twisted and took it in the hip. "I have to say you're not managing your anger in a constructive manner."

"Let me go, you traitor!"

"Calm down and I'll release you."

She met his gaze, her eyes a stormy gray. She lowered her voice to the barest of whispers. "I'll tell him."

So, she was threatening to tell the priest that he'd indulged in forbidden kisses with his charge. Phil leaned forward and whispered in her ear, "Do it. Then he'll fire me, and I'll be free to bed you tonight."

Her breath hissed against his cheek. "Damn you." She raised her voice. "I'm okay now. You can let go."

He leaned back. "No more throwing chairs?"

"Only if you're sitting in one at the time."

He released her. "I know you're upset, but we really just want to help you."

She moved away from him, rubbing her wrists. "You call this help? The two of you ganging up on me? I hate this stupid therapy crap. You want to examine all my old wounds and poke and prod at them till they bleed. What is the point? It doesn't make any of it go away."

"Ignoring it doesn't make it go away, either."

"I told you to leave my past alone." She glowered at him. "I trusted you."

"Betrayal of trust," Father Andrew murmured as he removed some papers from a portfolio and placed them on the conference table. "I think that would be a good place to start." He glanced up at Vanda. "I apologize for the . . . unorthodox scheduling of your first appointment, but we feared you might refuse to attend otherwise."

"You're damned right I would," Vanda grumbled. "I don't need anger management."

The priest looked at the cracked Sheetrock where the chair had crashed into it. "I disagree. Have a seat, please." He sat and put on his reading glasses.

Vanda paced toward the end of the table but didn't sit. Phil could feel the tension radiating from her. She was like a wildcat prowling in a locked cage.

Father Andrew made a note on the top sheet of his stack of papers. "I noticed you called Phil a traitor."

She scowled at Phil. "He is."

"After watching your interview, I can understand why betrayal would be a sensitive subject for you," the priest continued. "Do you believe your sister, Marta, betrayed you?"

"I don't believe anything about her." Vanda strode to the television and turned it off. "She's dead to me, just like the rest of my family."

"She changed you into a Vamp," Phil said.

"No!" Vanda spun to face him. "Sigismund changed me. Marta just bit me and drank from me till I was too weak to fight her off. Then she presented me to her new boyfriend like a dinner entrée."

"You definitely harbor some anger toward her," Father Andrew observed.

"Why should I be angry?" Vanda ejected the DVD

from the player. "Marta didn't do anything. She just stood there and watched while her boyfriend changed me, and our little sister lay dying in a nearby cave. She did *nothing!*"

"Sounds like betrayal to me," Phil said.

"I don't want to talk about it!" Vanda snapped the DVD in two and threw the pieces at Phil. "Leave me alone."

He dodged the flying pieces. "I won't." He strode toward her.

She growled and reached for another chair. He grasped it, holding it down, and while they both leaned forward, he engaged her in a staring contest. She arched a brow and refused to back down.

The priest cleared his throat. "I am truly sorry, my child, for the family members you lost. Do you know if Marta is still alive? Or undead, I should say."

Vanda let go of the chair and turned away from Phil. "I don't know. Who cares?"

"She could be your only surviving family," the priest continued. "I think you should see her."

"No way."

Father Andrew clicked his pen and made a note on one of his papers. "I have a good friend in Poland. A priest who went to seminary with me years ago. I'll ask him to check on the whereabouts of your sister."

"I don't want to see her!"

The priest regarded Vanda sternly over the rim of his reading glasses. "I have an assignment for you. I want you to give serious thought to forgiving your sister."

"What?" Vanda looked at the priest like he'd suddenly grown two heads.

"How old was Marta when you fled to the mountains?" Phil asked.

Vanda gritted her teeth. "Fifteen, but—"

"She was a child," Father Andrew said.

"And Sigismund probably had her mind under his control," Phil added.

"I don't care!" Vanda shouted. "She let Frieda die! I won't forgive her. I can't."

Father Andrew removed his glasses. "Forgiveness doesn't mean that you condone her actions. You don't need to forgive her for her sake. You do it for yourself, so you can put all the pain to rest and start living again."

"Why should I live when they're all dead? Everyone I loved is dead! Next you'll be telling me to forgive the damned Nazis." Vanda ran to the door and wrenched it open. "Leave me the hell alone!" She ran down the hall.

Phil paused at the door, watching her. "I should make sure she's all right."

The priest sighed as he shoved his papers back into his portfolio. "Maybe we're pushing too hard." He stood and pocketed his glasses. "I was a bit worried when she blew up, but you seem quite capable of handling her."

Unfortunately, handling Vanda was about all Phil thought about these days. "You gave her a lot to think about. Let it stew for a while."

Father Andrew nodded and gathered up his things. "I'll be in touch, then. Thank you for your help." He patted Phil on the shoulder, then walked toward the banquet hall.

Phil took off in the opposite direction, hunting for Vanda. With his superior hearing, he caught the faint pattering sound of her high heels on the marble floor.

Then it stopped. She must have left the hallway and entered a carpeted room. But which room? Fortunately, he could also rely on his superior sense of smell. He followed the sweet, jasmine scent of her hair gel and tracked her to the end of the hall where the chapel was situated.

Tomorrow night Father Andrew would perform Mass in the chapel at Romatech. About twenty Vamps usually attended, more if they came for the free synthetic blood offered afterward in the fellowship hall.

Phil paused in front of the double doors leading into the fellowship hall. Vanda's scent lingered there, as if she'd stood there for several minutes, debating what to do. He glanced down at the crack below the double doors. Still dark. With her superior night vision, she hadn't bothered to turn on the lights.

He opened a door quietly and slipped inside. His night vision was excellent, too, and he saw several bare refreshment tables in the middle of the room and numerous empty chairs lining the walls. He scanned along the ceiling. No security cameras. Whatever happened here would remain private.

Across the room, Vanda stood by the window, gazing out at the stars. The door clicked softly when he shut it.

She stiffened but didn't turn around. "Go away."

He winced at the pain in the timbre of her voice. She was either crying or close to it. He moved slowly toward her. "I was worried about you."

"You never follow directions, do you? I said *go away*." She whipped around to glare at him. "I also told you not to snoop around in my past, but you deliberately went against my wishes. You even brought the priest into the act. How could you? You don't think I'm screwed up enough? You have to expose my old wounds for the world to see?"

He stopped by a table. "Your wounds are deep. Even Constantine, a young child, could see it."

Her eyes darkened, a storm brewing in their gray depths. "Oh yes, let's help the poor woman before she goes totally berserk. I don't want your pity, Phil!"

The energy from her strong emotions awakened his inner wolf, inciting a surge of power within him. Good God, he wanted to haul her on top of a table and show her how beautiful she was. He balled his fists to retain control. "I feel a lot for you, but none of it is pity."

Her eyes narrowed. "That's what this is really about, isn't it? Your eight years of unrequited lust. You want me mentally healthy so you can screw me."

He clenched his fists tighter. The animal inside him urged him to jump her, but he was an Alpha and master of the beast. "Don't insult me, Vanda. I want you to be happy. I want you healthy enough that you can forge your own future, instead of wallowing in your painful past."

"Is that all?" she scoffed, then strode toward him. "Here's a news flash for you. I can forge my own future just fine. I have all the confidence and guts I need." She stopped in front of him, her chin lifted in defiance.

"False bravado," he muttered.

She slapped a hand against his groin. "Does that feel false to you?"

He gulped. Her roaming fingers had quickly located his cock. Not hard to do as fast as he was swelling.

"This is what you want, isn't it?" She rubbed the heel of her palm up and down the length. "You've wanted it for years."

He hissed in a breath. "I know what you're doing. You're avoiding the meat of the matter."

"I've got the meat right here." She squeezed.

He groaned. It felt so good. But he knew she was using sex to vent her frustrations and throw him off track. It was wrong. It was glorious. He wanted more.

She unfastened his waistband. "You're getting so big." She unzipped his pants. "What an animal you are."

She had no idea. His inner beast strained to break free from the mental control he'd clamped down on it. How could he take advantage of Vanda when she was clearly desperate? What had happened to her in the past that she would rather throw herself at him than discuss it? "I think you should stop."

"Make me." She curled her fingers around the waistband of his briefs and tugged them down.

His erection sprung free. His inner beast howled. *Take her. Take her now.*

"Oh my." She wrapped her hand around the hard shaft. "You're magnificent."

He groaned when her thumb caressed the smooth tip. Moisture seeped from him, and her fingers glided over him, slick and urgent.

To hell with being honorable. He'd been honorable for eight years, and all it had gotten him was continuous hard-ons and cold showers. So what if she was trying to manipulate him with sex? It would backfire on her when she became emotionally attached to him. He could use sex just as well as she could. He wasn't that gangly young man with a boyish crush anymore. He was an Alpha wolf who had chosen his mate. Nothing could stop him from claiming her.

"Hmm, I bet you're yummy." She leaned over.

"Stop." He pulled her straight and captured her gaze with his own. "You want me to climax, fine. But I'm going to do it deep inside you."

Her eyes widened. Her heart pounded so loud and fast, he knew his suspicions were confirmed. He'd called her bluff and upped the ante. She'd intended to only give him a blowjob, thinking that would be enough to distract him. She'd wanted to perform a service on him, not get involved with him. She hadn't planned on having her own body invaded.

Her false bravado kicked in and she lifted her chin. "Why not? It's just sex."

It was not just sex. It was a wolf claiming his mate. It was dominance and power.

His grip tightened on her shoulders. "Fair warning, Vanda. Once you give me your body, I'm taking your heart."

She scoffed. "Fair warning to you, Phil. My body is all you're getting. Now lie down and take it like a man."

"I don't lie down." He grabbed her around the waist and set her on the table.

He removed her high-heeled sandals and dropped them on the floor, then he grabbed her ankles and lifted her legs so her feet rested on his chest. "Look at me."

Her gaze drifted upward with a wary look.

Still gripping her ankles, he suddenly spread her legs wide. She gasped.

"Relax." He rested her ankles on his shoulders. "Like you said, it's just sex."

Her eyes narrowed. "Exactly."

He skimmed his hands down her shins to her knees. "I want to see your eyes turn red. I want to make them glow." He reached underneath her knees and tickled the delicate skin there.

Her legs trembled and she closed her eyes.

"Lie back." He smoothed his hands down the back of her thighs. "Look at me."

She opened her eyes to glare at him. "Stop giving me orders." Even though she snapped at him, her eyes were tinted red with passion.

He smiled. "Sweetheart, if it's not too much of an imposition, I would be forever beholden to you if you could kindly assume a reclining position so I can screw your brains out."

"That's more like it." Her eyes glittered, bright red and defiant. "Make me."

"Gladly." He scooped his hands under her rump and lifted her hips up so suddenly that she fell back with an *Oof*. With one quick move he jerked her underwear down to her ankles. As he slipped the black lacy panties over her feet, he could feel how damp they were. His nostrils flared with the scent of her arousal. His erection throbbed in response, and he tossed the panties onto the table.

He shoved his pants and underwear down to his knees. "You're ready for me, aren't you? You're slick and hot."

Her feet pressed into his shoulders as she tried to wiggle closer to his erection. "Do it. Now."

There was no way he was going to rush through this. After eight long years, he finally had her at his mercy. He'd make her scream, over and over again.

He slowly pushed her dress past her hips and left it wadded up at her waist. Then he skimmed his fingers across her bare stomach. Her muscles rippled with a tiny spasm.

"Do it." She was starting to pant.

He dragged his fingers into her pubic hair. The brown curls glistened with moisture.

"Get on with it." She squirmed.

"Chill. Like you said, it's just sex."

She gritted her teeth. "Stop reminding— *Aah!*" Her body jolted when his fingers slid between her wet folds.

He explored her, exulting in how slippery she was, how engorged she was, and how she trembled and gasped for air. She was already close to coming. His erection hardened painfully, and it took all his control not to drive himself into her.

Instead, he inserted two fingers and rubbed the inside walls of her canal. She groaned and lifted her hips. Her inner muscles clenched at his fingers. Almost there. He circled her clitoris, then tweaked it.

She cried out. Moisture gushed over his fingers, and her body spasmed. He fondled her clitoris and stroked her inside walls, wringing more cries from her, more spasms.

Finally, she went limp. She lifted a hand to her brow. "Oh God. That was . . . that was . . . "

"Just sex?"

She shot him an annoyed look. "Yes."

"Good. How much recovery time do you need?"

"None. I'm fine."

"Good." He tugged her bodice down to reveal her breasts. "No bra? My lucky day." He noticed the tips of her rosy nipples were hard.

"I didn't have one that worked with this dress," she mumbled.

He outlined her purple tattoo with his finger. "You have this little bat to scare everyone away from your heart. It doesn't scare me." He leaned over and kissed the tattoo. "I've always wanted to do that. And this." He sucked a nipple into his mouth.

She gasped. Her legs clamped around his waist.

He suckled one breast, then the other. "I have to taste you." He lifted her hips and enjoyed one long lick along her folds.

She shuddered. "Phil . . . "

He flicked his tongue over her clitoris. Her womanly scent filled his nostrils. Nothing excited his inner wolf as much as smell. The wolf clawed at his control, threatening to overpower him. He couldn't allow himself to go Alpha right now. He could still retain human form while the power of the wolf was unleashed, but it would scare Vanda too much.

He'd reached the tipping point. With a growl, he thrust himself into her. She instantly climaxed, crying out as her inner muscles squeezed him hard. He gripped her hips and pulled her toward him as he ground into her over and over. Her breasts flushed pink. Her breathing was labored.

Their bodies slapped together. He dropped his head back and relished each thrust. This was his woman. He would never give her up. The wolf howled, and his groin grew tight. With a loud groan, he pumped faster and faster.

She screamed and climaxed once again. Her inner muscles clamped down, and he gushed into her. Again and again. He held her tight against him until the last of his spasms faded away.

The dark room was filled with the sound of breathing. His mind slowly cleared. The wolf inside grinned with victory. He'd claimed his woman. The man on the outside wondered if he'd overdone it. He'd intended to attach her to him. What if he'd given into his lust only to chase his loved one away?

She pressed a hand against her chest and closed her eyes as she inhaled slowly and deeply. She seemed calm, but he could still hear her heart racing.

He moved back and slipped out of her body. "Are you all right?"

She opened her eyes, but looked to the side. "Sure."

He touched her cheek. "I've dreamed of doing that for eight years. It was even better than I'd imagined."

"That's good." She struggled to sit up, but her arms shook.

"Need help?"

"No. I'm fine." She reached for her panties.

So, she was going to act aloof. He could take care of that. He pulled his underwear and pants back up. "Thanks, Vanda. You're a great lay."

Her chin snapped up and her eyes flashed. "Don't you dare talk to me like—" Her eyes narrowed. "You're trying to make me angry, aren't you? What kind of anger management sponsor are you?"

"The same kind who engages in forbidden sex. When can we do it again?"

She scoffed. "There's no need to. You got what you wanted."

"You wanted it, too. You screamed at least three times."

Her fingers trembled as she struggled to put her panties back on. "It was . . . just sex."

"It was a hell of a lot more, and you know it."

She gave him a wary look as she scooted off the table. "I need to get back to the club. It's always busy on Friday night." She adjusted her bodice and smoothed down her skirt.

Dammit, they'd just had mind-blowing sex, and

she was acting like it was no big deal. "Don't you want me to hold you for a while? I thought women liked that."

"No thanks." She picked up her sandals, then sat in a chair to put them on. "Do yourself a favor, and don't get your hopes up. I'm never going to love again."

Too late, he wanted to shout at her. She was already his. She just didn't realize it yet.

She finished putting on her shoes. "Karl was my first love, and my last."

Phil winced inwardly. She certainly knew how to throw a punch. A surge of jealousy swept through him. She'd mentioned this Karl before. Logically, he knew Vanda was close to a hundred years old, so it wasn't surprising that she'd been in another relationship or two. Still, he resented this man who had claimed her heart before him. "What was so special about him?"

She shrugged. "He loved me, even though I was undead and filled with rage."

Phil opened his mouth to tell her that he loved her, too, just the way she was, but he stopped. He didn't want to act like he was competing with a dead man. Or any man, for that matter. "Karl is dead."

She glowered at him. "Thanks for reminding me." She turned her head to look out the window. "The Nazis sent their wolves after me, to track me down and kill me. Karl tried to protect me, but the wolves . . . they . . . " She grimaced, then lowered her head into her hands.

Damn it to hell. Vanda had witnessed her lover getting ripped apart by wolves? Thank God Karl had managed to protect her, but shit—how could he ever tell her he was a shape shifter?

"Vanda, I'm sorry." He sat beside her and wrapped an arm around her shoulders. "Karl sounds like a brave man."

She leaned on him, resting her head on his shoulder. "He was. He was the leader of the underground resistance in southern Poland. After he died, I never wanted to love again. Then I met Ian, and he grew on me. He looked so much like Jozef, and it was like having a little brother again. But he came close to dying last December, and it all came back to me. The fear. The pain. That's why I can't love again. Especially a mortal. Mortals always die around me."

Phil rubbed his chin against her brow. If only he could tell her he was a werewolf, that he could live for centuries.

She stiffened. "There's something vibrating in your pants. Either you've learned a sexy trick or—"

"It's my walkie-talkie." He stood to retrieve the small two-way radio from his pants' pocket. "Phil here."

"Come to the security office." Connor's voice sounded urgent. "We just heard from Angus. Casimir and two of his cohorts came to Apollo's compound. There was a battle, but Casimir escaped. We need to discuss our next move."

"I'll be right there." Phil dropped the walkie-talkie back into his pocket. "I'm sorry, Vanda—"

"I understand. Too bad they didn't kill Casimir."

Phil tucked in his shirt, then refastened the waist-band of his pants. "Do you know him?"

"I never met him, but Sigismund spoke very highly of him. He wanted to be Casimir's best friend, but that honor belonged to Ivan Petrovsky and Jedrek Janow."

Phil recalled that Ivan had been the Russian-American Coven Master until two of his own harem women had murdered him. "Jedrek was the guy who attacked DVN?"

Vanda nodded. "He was a big pal of the Nazis. He hunted me for a year after Karl died. I lived in constant terror, always afraid the wolves would tear me to pieces while I lay helpless in my death-sleep." She shuddered.

"Vanda, sweetheart." Phil caressed her cheek. "You're safe now. Shall I take you back to Maggie?"

She took a deep breath. "I'll be fine. You go on, and I'll follow in about five minutes. We don't want people to see us returning to the party together."

He hesitated, reluctant to leave her. "I hate to see you hurting."

"I'll be all right. I'll take Maggie back to the club. I'm always happy there. I feel in control there."

"Then I'll see you before dawn at the townhouse." He leaned over to kiss her, but she turned her head away.

"Good night, Phil."

Chapter Eleven

It's just sex. Vanda doubled over in her chair, resting her head in her hands. Tears threatened to escape. What a fool she was.

It wasn't just sex. It was glorious sex. The best she'd ever had. Her whole body hummed with residual energy. And she wanted more. You would think experiencing three earth-shaking orgasms in a row would be enough, but no. It was like Phil had awakened a lusty beast inside of her. It had lain dormant for over fifty years, and now it demanded satisfaction. It demanded Phil.

She pressed her thighs together, relishing the pressure on her sensitive, still-aroused sex. Oh God, Phil had been inside her. He'd touched her and tasted her. He'd made her scream.

It should have been just sex. She'd thought the physical act would be a welcome release from all the frustration and anger that had hounded her the past week. It had seemed like a good idea at the time. Distract Phil from his anger management duties and curiosity about her past and have a little fun on the side. After all, it was just sex.

She sat up and looked at the table where she'd squirmed and screamed. It had happened. She couldn't take it back.

Damn him. He'd known exactly what he was doing to her. She'd wanted to keep it purely physical and impersonal, but he had demanded that she look at him. And each time she had, her heart had swelled with so much emotion. She could pretend it was lust, admiration, or fondness, but who was she kidding?

Tears streamed down her cheeks. All her attempts to keep the world at a safe distance had been in vain. Phil had swept back into her life and in just a few days, he'd completely overwhelmed her.

There was something different about him. Sure, he'd filled out his large frame with more muscle, and he was more handsome than ever, but there was something else, something deeper and more subtle. Now, he exuded so much confidence and power. An abundance of raw energy and male sexuality simmered beneath the surface, and it called to her. It drew her in, and she was helpless to resist.

She wiped her face. Okay, so the physical attraction was red hot. And her heart was weakening fast. But she still possessed a stubborn mind and strength of will. The coffin of horrors hidden in the recesses of her mind was still shut. There had been a few leaks the last few days, but she would put an end to that. She'd simply refuse to divulge any more information. Her past would be off limits. Her heart would be off limits. And to play it safe, to keep her heart intact, her body would be off limits.

No man would conquer her. Not even Phil.

He was going to win Vanda's heart, no matter how much she resisted. Phil knew she wanted him. She'd responded to his lovemaking so quickly and sweetly. As annoying as it was for her to act aloof now, it was clear to him that it was an act. She was trying to protect herself. She was afraid to fall in love, afraid of making herself vulnerable to more heartache. But love wasn't something she could turn off like a water faucet. It was happening, whether she cared to admit it or not.

The security office was on the other side of Romatech, so on the way, Phil stopped in a restroom to wash off her scent. Vamps had a superior sense of smell, almost as good as werewolves, and he wanted to keep his affair with Vanda private.

He strode into the banquet hall. The band had left, along with Corky Courrant and most of the guests.

"Phil." Maggie approached him, holding both her and Vanda's evening bags. "Where's Vanda? I thought she was with you."

"She was. I took her to an anger management session with Father Andrew, and then we . . . had a talk. She wanted to be alone for a while to think things over."

"A *talk*?" Maggie gave him a dubious look, then

leaned forward to whisper. "Your pants are un-zipped."

Shit. Phil turned toward a wall and quickly yanked the zipper closed.

Maggie looked away to give him privacy. "Is she all right?"

"Yes."

"I know she acts tough, but she's really very fragile. I'll be royally pissed if you hurt her in any way."

"I won't hurt her. I'm in love with her."

Maggie turned to face him. "Did you tell her that?"

"No. I didn't think she could handle it right now."

Maggie nodded slowly. "You're probably right." She peered around the nearly empty room, then stepped closer to him. "I need to tell you something. Earlier, when I was talking to Shanna, I accidentally let it slip in front of Vanda that some of my in-laws are shape shifters."

He sucked in a quick breath. "How did she take it?"

"She turned ghostly pale, and I thought it was from shock, but then she said she already knew about them. I thought you should know."

His earlier spurt of optimism deflated. It might take longer than he thought to win Vanda's heart.

"Where is she?" Maggie asked.

"The room next to the chapel, at the end of the hall-way." He motioned to the double swinging doors behind the bandstand. "She said she would come here soon, but you might want to check on her."

"I will." Maggie hurried off.

Phil strode into the foyer, wondering how much Vanda knew about shape shifters.

Phineas zoomed in through the front door and joined him. "I was just finishing my rounds when Connor called," he said in a husky voice.

"How are you feeling?" Phil asked.

"Better. Roman gave me some Blissky on ice, and that helped with the throat burn." Phineas placed a hand over his heart. "But the pain of betrayal—how could my sweet angelic LaToya be so cruel?"

"Give her time." Phil headed down the hall with him. "She just needs to get to know you."

Phineas grimaced. "That's what I'm afraid of. What if she finds my rap sheet? I'll be lucky if she doesn't try to arrest me. How can love be so cruel?"

"I know what you mean. The lady I love is scared to death of wolves. How can I tell her what I am?"

Phineas sighed. "Fate can be so cruel." He shot Phil a curious look. "Who are you in love with?"

"It's . . . complicated."

Phineas snickered. "You're in love with an *it*?"

"She's a Vamp. I believe you all claim to be somewhat human."

Phineas scoffed. "Then what's the problem, bro? Don't you big bad wolves live a nice long time?"

"She's . . . forbidden."

"Hot damn, bro, that's the best kind."

Phil smiled. "At least she already knows about shape shifters. It won't come as a total shock when I tell her the news."

"Who are we talking about?" Phineas lowered his voice. "It's not Vanda, is it?"

Phil stopped. "Am I that obvious?"

"Only to the Love Doctor. I'm in tune with sweet

love vibrations." Phineas shook his head, wincing. "But I have to tell you, man. I was at Vanda's club when that Jedrek dude attacked and Carlos shifted into a black panther—I mean a real black panther. She was upset, wanted him out of her club. I don't think she likes shape shifters at all."

Phil swallowed hard. "Thanks for the warning."

"Any time, bro." Phineas sighed. "We're so screwed. Vanda hates shape shifters. LaToya hates vampires. How can life be so—"

"Cruel?" Phil finished the question for him, wishing he knew the answer. Life had certainly dealt Vanda some cruel blows. But she was a survivor, and he wouldn't give up hope. He swiped his ID and activated the hand sensor to open the door to the security office.

Inside, it was standing room only. Phil was surprised by the number of nonsecurity people in attendance, like Roman and Jean-Luc and their wives, but obviously everyone wanted the latest news available.

Connor nodded at Phil and Phineas. "I've been catching everyone up. About thirty minutes ago Casimir and two of his cohorts teleported into the main temple of Apollo's compound in Maine. Angus and his team caught them by surprise, and a battle ensued. Casimir ordered his men to defend him, then teleported away while they were left fighting for their lives."

"Typical of the bastard," Jean-Luc muttered.

"Aye." Connor nodded. "One of the cohorts managed to escape, but the second one was captured.

All we know about him is that he used the name Hermes. He refuses to divulge any more information."

Jack snorted. "I'm sure Angus can change his mind."

Connor smiled grimly. "They have Hermes tied up with silver chains to prevent him from teleporting away. Angus wants to transfer him here to the silver room at Romatech, where we have tighter security, but of course they canna teleport him here with all the silver on him. So they're driving him here."

Phil figured the trip from Maine had to be over five hundred miles. "I don't think they can make it here before sunrise."

"Nay, that's why Austin and Darcy will be driving the van," Connor explained. "They'll have Hermes chained and boxed in the back to keep him from escaping or getting burned by the sun. Meanwhile, Angus and the rest of his team will remain at the compound in case Casimir returns with more men to try to rescue Hermes."

"How many Vamps does Angus have with him?" Jack asked.

"Three," Connor replied. "Emma, Dougal, and Zoltan."

"Does he want more?" Jean-Luc asked. "I can go."

"Me, too," Jack said.

Connor smiled. "If ye want to go, Angus wouldna refuse you. But 'tis probably unnecessary. Casimir has never been known to rescue any of his followers."

"True," Jack agreed. "He considers them expendable. Still, I'd like to go just as a precaution."

Lara leaned close to him, her expression worried. "Shall I come with you?"

"You're tired. Get some rest." Jack kissed her brow. "Wait for me at the townhouse. I'll be back before dawn."

Jean-Luc gave his wife a kiss, then he and Jack went into the armory at the back of the office to collect some weapons.

"Yo." Phineas held up a hand. "I want to go, too."

Connor shifted his gaze to the young black Vamp. "I appreciate that, but we have a special assignment for you."

Phineas grinned. "Cool! Lots of action, huh?"

"I requested your help." Roman stepped toward him. "I believe you once supplied the Malcontents with the ingredients to make Nightshade?"

Phineas's grin faded. "Yeah, that's why they transformed me. They wanted a drug dealer." He crossed his arms, frowning. "I don't do that shit anymore. I'm one of the good guys."

"I know you are," Roman replied. "But if we had some Nightshade, we could teleport prisoners like Hermes. When the Malcontents kidnapped Angus two years ago, they paralyzed him with Nightshade, so there was no need for silver chains. Then they were able to teleport him."

"I know." Phineas shifted his weight. "I feel really bad about helping them, but they said they'd kill my family—"

"We doona blame you, lad," Connor said.

"It would really help us to have some Nightshade," Roman said. "Unfortunately, I don't know how it's made."

"Oh, bummer," Phineas mumbled.

"Exactly," Roman continued. "But I think I could figure out the formula if I had the right ingredients. Do you remember them? Can you procure them for me?"

"Yeah, I remember." Phineas grimaced. "We're talking some bad-ass illegal shit."

Connor gave him a wry look. "We have every confidence in you."

"Yeah. Thanks." Phineas leaned close to Phil and murmured, "If LaToya finds out about this, she'll be really pissed."

"No one needs to know." Connor had overheard him. "Once ye have the drugs in yer possession, ye can erase the mortals' memories."

"Look at it this way," Phil said to Phineas. "You'll be taking dangerous drugs off the street."

The young Vamp's eyes lit up. "You're right. I'll be doing the world a favor."

Roman smiled. "Thank you. This could be a valuable weapon in our war against the Malcontents."

"Dr. Phang at your service," Phineas boasted.

"Then off ye go." Connor gave him a pointed look.

"Right." Phineas nodded. "I'll have to drop by the townhouse first to change clothes. Can't go into the hood looking like this." He teleported away.

Connor waved Phil over. "Can ye take Heather and Lara to the townhouse?"

"Sure." Phil frowned. "But I'd rather go with Jack and be where the action is."

"I doona believe there will be any more action in Maine tonight," Connor whispered. "And once Austin and Darcy get the prisoner here, this is where the action will be. I'm counting on yer help with the prisoner, so get yer rest now while ye can."

It was almost like old times with a full house to guard. Phil drove Lara Boucher, Heather Echarpe, and Heather's daughter Bethany to the townhouse. Then he excused himself to go to the basement to get a few hours sleep. He had to stay alert during the day, when he guarded the Vamps.

He was up again shortly before dawn. Vanda, Cora Lee, and Pamela teleported in from the nightclub. Jack and Jean-Luc returned from Apollo's compound in Maine, reporting that there had been no more activity there. Angus and the rest of his team had decided to stay there. Phineas arrived home with good news. He'd managed to find all the drugs Roman needed to figure out the Nightshade formula.

The house grew quiet as the Vamps went off to their rooms to fall into their death-sleep. Around 11:00 A.M., Austin and Darcy dragged in.

Darcy, a former member of Roman's harem, had met Austin Erickson when he worked for the CIA Stake-Out Team. Now a married couple, they were invaluable mortal employees at MacKay Security & Investigation. They'd delivered the prisoner to the silver room at Romatech before arriving at the townhouse. Exhausted, they headed straight to a bedroom.

Howard Barr called around 6:00 P.M. to ask Phil and Austin to come to Romatech and ready the prisoner for questioning. Since the Vamps were still in their death-sleep, Darcy and Lara took over guard duty. Phil regretted that he would miss seeing Vanda. He hadn't had a chance to talk to her since they'd made love. She could call it "just sex" if she wanted, but to him it was making love.

At Romatech, he and Austin went straight to the safe room in the basement. Angus had designed the room, completely encased in silver, to prevent a vampire from teleporting in or out. A wooden crate rested on the floor with Hermes inside.

Phil noted the lid had been nailed shut. A few air holes dotted the lid. Part of the journey from Maine had been in the dark, and during that time the Malcontent would have been alive and breathing.

Austin had left a crowbar in the room earlier, and now he pried the lid open a few inches. Phil grabbed the top and wrenched it off.

The sleeping vampire lay wrapped in silver chains. He looked about thirty-five years old, with a tall, gaunt body. His pale, pockmarked face was accented by deep-set eyes, sunken cheeks, and thinning brown hair. He couldn't have been a very healthy mortal when he was transformed, and now he was stuck looking ill for centuries. But his pasty skin and frail body was deceiving. As a vampire, he possessed superior strength and speed.

Phil peered around the room. "Where do you want to put him?"

"The bed and easy chairs look too comfortable." Austin grabbed a kitchen chair from the dinette set and set it in the middle of the room. "This will do."

Phil helped Austin lift the vampire out of the crate. "He's gotten a little stiff."

They propped the body against the chair with Hermes's feet on the floor and his shoulders against the back of the chair. The body didn't bend to conform to the chair, but remained stiff as a board.

Austin snorted. "Holy rigor mortis."

Phil chuckled. "Maybe we should lay him on the kitchen table. We could chain him to it."

They soon had Hermes chained to the wooden table and the table standing on its edge.

"We could practice throwing knives," Austin suggested. "Like a circus act."

"Good idea." Phil grinned. "But I think it would be more effective after he wakes up." He checked his watch. "That should be in about ten minutes."

"Let's find something to eat." Austin wandered into the kitchen area and rummaged through the cabinets. He found a loaf of bread and some chips.

Phil checked the refrigerator. It was stocked with synthetic blood but also had bottled water and lunch meat.

They sat in the easy chairs, eating their dinner, while they waited for Hermes to wake up.

Austin told Phil about some of the adventures he'd had as a former member of the CIA Stake-Out Team. "One time, I shot a Malcontent full of silver bullets and he was still able to teleport away."

"Really?" Phil bit into his sandwich. "That's interesting."

Austin swallowed a bite from his sandwich. "I asked Angus about it, and he said silver needed to be external to keep a vampire from teleporting. It acts like a boundary that they can't get through. But silver inside a vampire would hurt like hell and eventually kill him. I guess silver bullets would kill your kind, too?"

"Yeah. Silver inside me is like poison. But externally, it's not a problem. I can touch it without it burning me."

"Roman can touch silver, but he's the only Vamp I've ever known who can." Austin took another bite from his sandwich.

"I've noticed that the older Vamps can do things the younger ones can't," Phil said. "I've seen Angus teleport two mortals at once. And Jack and Ian have both managed to teleport me while I was armed with silver bullets." He recalled how Vanda had been unable to teleport him with the silver chain in his pocket.

"Yeah, the older they get, the more powerful. I wonder how old this one is." Austin motioned to the prisoner. "Oh, look. He's waking up."

The prisoner's body jolted. His chest heaved, straining against the silver chain as he sucked in his first breath. His eyes opened, then narrowed on Phil and Austin. His nostrils flared. He struggled against his chains, shaking the table.

"You know." Austin grabbed a handful of chips out of the bag. "I think he wants to bite us."

Phil drank some water. "I've noticed they're extremely hungry when they first wake up."

"Yeah," Austin agreed. "I heard it can get really painful."

Hermes glared at them. "You are inferior creatures," he grumbled with a thick accent. "You think you can hold me? Where have you taken me?"

Austin gave Phil a confused look. "Is he asking questions?"

"Looks that way." Phil finished his sandwich. "Maybe he hasn't realized yet that he's the prisoner, and we ask the questions."

Austin nodded. "They can be amazingly stupid sometimes. You would think they'd acquire a certain amount of wisdom over the centuries, but no—"

"Silence, mortal!" Hermes growled.

A surge of cold air pressed against Phil's brow. The prisoner was attempting to use vampire mind control on them.

You will release me at once.

Phil quickly tapped into the power of his inner wolf to keep his mind protected. He glanced at Austin to make sure he wasn't affected. He'd heard Austin was psychic but wasn't sure how strong he was. "Are you all right?"

"Oh, yeah." Austin lifted a hand, and a bottle of water flew from the kitchen counter to land in his hand.

Phil drew in a sharp breath. "You're telekinetic?

You must have more psychic power than vampires."

"Yep." Austin unscrewed the top of his water bottle. "It really pisses them off when they realize they can't control me."

"I will not be ignored!" Hermes thundered. "Obey me."

He hissed at them, and his fangs sprang out.

"Now that's just nasty." Austin drank some water.

"Really." Phil helped himself to some chips. "Someone should tell him about whitening strips."

Another wave of cold air circled about the room.

Come to me, mortal. I must feed.

Austin gave Phil a wry look. "Do I look like breakfast to you?"

Phil studied the prisoner. "I think the hunger's getting to him. He's sweating."

"And his legs are quivering," Austin added. "I think he would fall down if we didn't have him chained up."

Hermes hissed at them. His arms strained against the chains, his hands fisted.

"If he wasn't so rude, I might offer him a sip of synthetic blood." Phil passed the chips back to Austin. "We've got plenty in the fridge. But he hasn't even told us his real name."

"You will get no information from me," Hermes snarled. "I'd rather die than drink that synthetic piss."

"I guess he wants to die." Austin took the chips back to the kitchen area.

"Well, technically, he's already died once," Phil said. "He should be pretty good at it by now."

The door to the silver room opened and Phineas sauntered inside. "What's up?"

The prisoner glowered at him. "I know who you are. The traitor. Your time will come."

Phineas studied him with a wry look. "Oh yeah, I'm scared."

"Want some breakfast?" Phil walked toward the refrigerator. "We've got Type O, A, AB, whatever you like."

"I'll take some AB Negative. Thanks." Phineas sat in one of the easy chairs. "Can you warm it up, bro?"

"Sure." Phil popped the bottle in the microwave.

The scent of blood permeated the room. Hermes's body racked with a shudder. His face glistened with sweat.

"Here you go." Phil handed Phineas a glass filled to the brim with warmed-up blood.

Phineas guzzled down half the glass, then licked his lips. "Damn, that's good."

"So where's Connor?" Austin sat next to Phineas in the second easy chair.

"He's in the security office with Jack. They're watching us." Phineas motioned toward the surveillance camera above the bed. "Connor's looking through the Malcontent database to figure out who this Hermes dude is."

"I'm done," Connor announced as he strode into the room. He gave the prisoner a challenging look, then referred to the clipboard in his hand. "Hermes is Polish, about four hundred years old, and he fought on the wrong side of the Great Vampire War of 1710."

"Fuck you," the prisoner growled.

Connor arched a brow. "As you can see, his English is somewhat limited."

"What's his name?" Phil asked.

"Sigismund."

Chapter Twelve

*P*hil growled low in his throat as he unleashed his Alpha power. Because of his blue eyes, everything took on a luminous blue tint. His sight sharpened until he could see each vein in his prey's neck. Smell the fear emanating from him. Hear his heart racing like a scared rabbit.

His form wavered on the brink of an instant shift. He controlled it for now as he stalked toward his prey.

Sigismund pressed back against the table. "What—What kind of shifter are you?"

Phil allowed his face to change. His nose and jaw crackled as they elongated. His canine teeth sprang out. He snarled.

"No!" Sigismund fought frantically against his restraints. He shot Connor a desperate look. "Call off your wolf!"

Connor shrugged. "He's no' *my* wolf."

Phil halted in front of the prisoner. A primeval urge to kill swept through him, more powerful than he'd ever felt before. In the past, he'd killed animals while in wolf form. Werewolves always enjoyed a good hunt when the moon was full. And he'd killed Malcontents while engaged in battle. But never had he been tempted to commit murder—till now.

Sigismund extended his fangs in a futile attempt to defend himself. Phil knew if he drew too close, the vampire would snap at him. But he was seized by a murderous rage that dismissed any threat. His body vibrated with raw power. With lightning speed he latched onto the prisoner's neck with one hand. He clamped down, squeezing with his superior strength.

Sigismund twisted his neck, trying in vain to bite.

Phil sent a flood of Alpha power down his arm, and his hand shifted. Fur sprouted. His nails elongated and curled into sharp claws.

Sigismund's eyes bulged with terror. "Call him off! Call—" He choked as Phil's claws punctured his skin.

Austin moved closer for a better view. "Holy shapeshifting, Phil! Only parts of you have shifted. And the moon isn't even full. How can you do that?"

Phil growled. In his current condition his senses were all heightened, but with his head shifted, he could no longer talk.

"He's an Alpha," Connor replied for him. "He has powers other shifters only dream about."

"Damn," Austin muttered. "I'm glad he's on our side."

"Oh yeah!" Phineas punched the air with a fist. "He's big! He's bad! He'll blow your house *down*, sucker."

Phil snarled as the scent of blood reached his elongated snout. Blood dripped down the prisoner's neck where his claws had penetrated.

Connor stepped closer. "Phil, can ye tone it down a wee bit? The prisoner canna answer our questions if he's unconscious."

Through a blue-tinted haze Phil realized the prisoner's eyes had grown dull. He retracted his claws, reined in his Alpha power, and with one last shimmer his body returned to full human form. He let go of the Malcontent and stepped back.

Sigismund gasped for air as he slumped against the chains. "Don't . . . don't let him hurt me. I . . . I'll tell you everything I know."

"Verra good." Connor nodded at Phil with an appreciative gleam in his eyes. "Well done, lad."

"You da man." Phineas gave him a knuckle pound. "Half man, half wolf, half son of a bitch."

Phil snorted. Technically speaking, all male wolves were sons of bitches. He wandered into the kitchen to retrieve a bottle of water from the fridge. He was painfully aware of the admiring glances that Austin and Phineas kept aiming his way. Personally, he was embarrassed. Ashamed, even.

He'd worked hard at the Navajo reservation in New Mexico to achieve his Alpha status. His old shaman friend and mentor, Joe, had stressed the great responsibility that came with Alpha power.

Phil had sworn to be true to the noble character of the wolf and use his powers to protect those who depended on him. He was to hone his skills so he would always be victorious in battle. In all things, he was to honor the wolf.

Never was he to use his power for personal gain or to exact revenge. He was a chosen one, destined to be a leader among his own kind.

And he'd nearly murdered a man out of rage. He recalled Vanda's words when she'd thought he had killed Max the Mega Member.

I understand the kind of rage that leads a person to take a life.

Was that what she was hiding? Had Vanda been so traumatized by the cruelty of war that she'd stepped over the line? She'd mentioned that Karl was the leader of the underground resistance, so it was logical to assume that Vanda had been involved in dangerous activities. The Nazis had sent wolves to kill her, so she'd clearly pissed them off. More of her words came back to him.

I don't want any more deaths on my conscience.

"Where is Casimir hiding?" Connor asked, bringing Phil's attention back to the present.

"He moves around, a different place every night," Sigismund rasped. "I need to feed."

"And I need real information," Connor replied. "Phineas, is there any Blissky in the kitchen?"

"I'll look." Phineas rummaged through the cabinets.

"I'm not drinking that synthetic piss," Sigismund growled.

"Ye doona have a choice." Connor sat in a kitchen chair close to the prisoner.

"Found one!" Phineas opened a bottle of Blissky and inhaled deeply. "I'd better test it to make sure it's all right." He took a swig. "Oh yeah, baby! Now we're talking." He filled a glass to the brim.

Phil located a straw and plopped it into the amber liquid. The fridge was full of plain synthetic blood, but he figured Connor was hoping the Blissky would loosen Sigismund's tongue. Since it was highly doubtful the prisoner had imbibed any whiskey in the last four hundred years, he would be hammered in no time.

"What does Casimir hope to accomplish here in America?" Connor asked.

Sigismund snorted. "What do you think? He came here to be your friend?"

"World domination," Phineas muttered as he approached the prisoner with the glass of Blissky. "You bad guys are so predictable. Don't you get bored with yourselves?"

Sigismund sneered. "We'll take great pleasure in seeing you all dead." He turned his head away from the glass Phineas offered. "Bring me a mortal."

"You don't know what you're missing, man." Phineas swirled the glass under the prisoner's nose. "Smells really good, doesn't it? Tastes like heaven."

Sigismund's nostrils flared and his fangs shot out.

"Hard to stop those reflexes, huh?" Phineas stuck the straw in Sigismund's mouth.

The prisoner slurped down all the Blissky in just

a few seconds. Then he coughed, his eyes watering. His fangs retracted.

Phineas chuckled. "Good shit, huh?"

"Not as good as a mortal." Sigismund eyed the empty glass. "Bring me more."

Phineas snorted. "You don't want to admit it's good." He returned to the kitchen to pour another glass.

Phil noted there was color back in Sigismund's face. "How big an army does Casimir have?"

"Big enough to destroy you. And about to get even bigger." Sigismund smiled. "Casimir knows how to take advantage of your weakness."

"And what would that be?" Connor asked.

Phineas brought another glass of Blissky, and Sigismund drank it down.

He licked his lips. "You claim to be good because you drink synthetic blood. But if you lost your supply, you'd go right back to biting mortals. Then hundreds of vampires would realize how much they enjoy biting and never want to go back. They'll join us. You'll be so outnumbered, you won't stand a chance."

Connor stood. "You're planning to attack our supply lines?"

Sigismund snorted, then hiccuped. "We'll stop you from even making the crap."

All the Romatech facilities were in danger. Phil knew there were several in the United States. The one in White Plains supplied the East Coast, but there were others in Ohio, Texas, Colorado, and California.

"I need to warn Angus." As Connor strode from the room, he yelled back, "I'll send Jack down. Keep the prisoner talking."

"Will do." Phil approached Sigismund. "Did you go to Apollo's compound often?"

"Sure. It was great. All those stupid girls just begging us to bite and screw them."

Phil squeezed his fists to keep from socking him. "The party's over. We set the girls free. We killed Apollo and Athena."

Sigismund glowered at him. "Their deaths will be avenged."

Phil snorted. "You think Casimir gives a damn about his so-called friends? He knows you were captured last night, but he never went back to rescue you."

"He avenges his friends," Sigismund insisted. "He has a hit list. In a week, everyone on the list will be dead."

"Who's on this hit list?" Austin asked.

"The ones responsible for the massacre at DVN and the murder of Jedrek Janow," Sigismund sneered. "At the top of the list there's Ian MacPhie and his mortal bitch, Toni."

"Wife," Phil corrected him. "They're married." And as long as they remained hidden away on their honeymoon, they should be safe. Still, they needed to be warned.

"Next on the list—those bloody assassins, Giacomo di Venezia and Zoltan Czakvar," Sigismund continued. "Then Dougal Kincaid and the traitor, Phineas McKinney."

"Cool," Phineas said. "I'd feel really left out if you forgot me."

"Anyone else?" Phil asked. He knew Carlos Panterra, Howard Barr, and Gregori had also been at DVN that night, but Casimir might not be aware of their involvement.

"There's one more," Sigismund grumbled. "That crazy bitch from Poland. Vanda Barkowski."

Phil's heart lurched in his chest. "That's not right. She didn't kill anyone."

"She was there, causing trouble like she always does," Sigismund growled. "Don't think she's innocent. Jedrek tried for years to kill her off. Casimir just wants to finish the job once and for all."

Phil swallowed hard. "These hits start in a week?" He had to hide her someplace no one would ever find her.

"They'll be dead in a week." Sigismund chuckled. "The hits start tonight."

Phil grabbed Phineas by the arm. "Teleport me to the club now!" He dragged the young Vamp out into the hallway just as Jack stepped out of the elevator. "We're going to the Horny Devils. Austin can fill you in."

"All right." Jack hurried through the open door into the silver room.

"Let's go!" Phil heard Sigismund's mocking laughter as everything went black.

Vanda eyed Terrance the Turgid's sleek, hairless chest and decided life wasn't at all fair. She'd had sex with Phil and didn't even know what his chest looked like. But the rascal certainly knew what she looked like. All over.

Terrance rotated his hips in time with the bongo drums. "Do you like the music I selected?"

"Jolly good." Pamela tapped her foot on the floor.

Vanda sighed. Every month, her performers gave her a preview of the next month's dances for approval. Cora Lee and Pamela loved this part of the job. Vanda used to love it, too, but now she found herself comparing every man she saw to Phil. And they never matched up.

While Terrance gyrated his hips, he ripped apart the Velcro that fastened the fake leopard cape around his neck. He tossed the cape, and it landed on Cora Lee's head. Giggling, she pulled it down onto her lap.

Vanda could now see Terrance's bare shoulders, but they didn't look as broad and muscular as Phil's. Of course, it was hard to tell 'cause she'd never actually seen Phil's shoulders. Dammit. She should have insisted he take off that tuxedo.

Terrance pranced about the office in his sparkly Tarzan loincloth. "You hear the trumpet sound? When it trills, that's when I'll swing across the stage on a vine."

Pamela clasped her hands together. "Capital idea."

"And then, when the music crescendos, I rip off the loincloth!" Terrance flung the loincloth across the office, revealing his tan-colored thong decorated with ivy leaves.

Pamela clapped. "Outstanding!"

"Yee haw!" Cora Lee shouted.

Vanda eyed Terrance's thong. Definitely not in the same league as Phil, and that she could be sure of. It was the one part of Phil's anatomy that she had seen. And touched. He had truly been magnificent. Long and thick. Incredibly hard, but covered with the softest skin. He'd felt so good inside her. Filling her. Stroking her.

She squeezed her thighs together as a sudden yearning ached deep inside her. Damn. How was she going to resist him? With a sigh, she realized she couldn't. She wanted him. Once had not been enough. A hundred times wouldn't be enough. She was falling in love with him. If she had any will-power at all, she'd never see him again.

The door burst open and Phil marched in.

So much for willpower. With a silent groan she turned off the CD player. The jungle music stopped.

"Phil! How nice of you to drop by." Terrance struck a pose. "How do you like my costume?"

He glanced briefly at the dancer. "Good muscle tone. Guard the door. Don't let anyone in."

"Oh, of course. Anything for you, Phil." Terrance scurried out the door.

"Somebody has a crush," Cora Lee murmured in a singsong voice.

"Enough," Vanda muttered. "What are you doing here, Phil?" And why was he looking around so carefully?

He circled her desk. "Phineas and Hugo are check-ing the main room. Have you seen any suspicious-looking people here tonight?"

Vanda shrugged. "Most of our customers look a little strange. What's going on?"

He moved closer to the credenza where her printer and fax machine rested. "You're in grave danger."

Was he sniffing her office equipment? "In danger from what? Overpriced ink cartridges?"

"It must be Max the Mega Member," Pamela whispered dramatically. "He's come to exact the ultimate revenge."

"Ultimate?" Vanda asked wryly. "He's already tried to kill me. How do you get more ultimate than that?"

"He would kill you in an extremely gruesome manner," Pamela explained. "Mind you, it would be hard to top a python, but I'm sure he could come up with something completely horrid."

"Thanks for the thought." Vanda continued to watch Phil. Now he was sniffing around her file cabinets.

"Maybe it's Corky Courrant," Cora Lee suggested. "She's sworn to see you ruined."

"Thanks for reminding me." Vanda stood and wandered closer to Phil. "Are you going to tell me who—"

He stiffened suddenly. "Cora Lee, Pamela, go tell all the customers to teleport away immediately."

"What?" Vanda set her hands on her hips. "Are you trying to ruin my business?"

"There's a bomb in your file cabinet," Phil said softly.

Cora Lee and Pamela both gasped and jumped to their feet.

Vanda's heart stuttered in her chest. She eyed the cabinet. "Are you sure? You didn't even look inside."

He put up an arm to stop her. "Don't open it. That could be the trigger. We can't be sure, though. It could be on a timer and go off any second. Try to remain calm—"

"*Eek!*" Cora Lee ran from the office screaming. She knocked Terrance aside. "There's a bomb!"

Screams erupted from the main room.

Pamela ran toward the door. "I'll make sure everyone leaves. We'll meet you at the townhouse."

"No!" Phil shouted. "The townhouse may not be safe."

Pamela glanced back with a frantic look. "The apartment, then!"

"But—" Phil started to say that the apartment wasn't safe either, but Pamela had already dashed into the main room.

She yelled at the crowd. "Teleport away! Leave immediately!"

Vanda remained still as a cold fog settled over her. *A bomb.* Her club would be destroyed. She couldn't let that happen.

"Come on." Phil grabbed her arm. "Teleport us out of here now."

She stared at the filing cabinet. "How do you know it's in there?"

"I'm an expert in bomb detection. Come on. Let's go."

"You're an expert? Then turn it off!"

"It's not that simple." He pulled her toward the

door. "Just opening the drawer might set it off. We have to get you someplace safe."

"But—But—" She looked around as they entered the quiet warehouse. Everyone had teleported away. The laser lights flashed, highlighting the empty dance floor, the stage, the bar. How could she leave? She loved this place. It was everything to her.

Phil flung her onto his shoulder and ran for the entrance. His desperation penetrated the cold fog that had marred her thinking. Someone wanted to kill her. Someone wanted to kill her so badly they hadn't given a second thought to killing a hundred or more innocent bystanders.

Once again she was being hunted.

Phil sprinted down the alley, then turned onto the street. She clutched at his shirt. She needed to teleport them farther away.

Boom!

The explosion deafened her ears. She screamed. Bricks flew into the air and flames shot toward her face.

She flinched from the heat, and their bodies were thrown. She held onto Phil as the world went black.

Chapter Thirteen

O of." Vanda landed on the floor of her apartment with Phil sprawled beside her.

He rose to his knees. "Are you all right?"

"Yes." Maybe not. Her face felt terribly hot. But at least they hadn't been burned to a crisp.

"There you are! Thank God!" Pamela rushed toward them and helped Vanda to her feet.

"We were afraid you hadn't made it." Cora Lee's eyes widened. "Land sakes."

Vanda touched a burning hot cheek. "Is it that bad?"

"No, no," Pamela and Cora Lee said quickly, then exchanged looks.

Great. Vanda ran a hand through her hair and felt the singed ends. For once, she was glad she couldn't see herself in a mirror. But it was embarrassing for Phil to see her this way. Luckily, he wasn't looking at her. He'd hurried straight to the big plate-glass window, where he was opening the aluminum shutters.

Vanda joined him there and saw the smoke billowing up from the club two blocks away. Her club. Sirens sounded in the distance. A fire truck raced down the street below them, its lights flashing and horn blaring.

Her club was gone. All her dreams of an independent life gone up in smoke.

"Are you in much pain?" Phil asked softly.

Her throat felt tight, tense. "Yes."

"Your skin will heal during your death-sleep."

Her vision blurred with tears. "But not my heart."

He touched her shoulder. "You shouldn't stand here by the window."

"I have to see." She could at least be close to her club as it burned down to nothing. Along with her dreams.

"Vanda, you can't afford to be seen." He pulled her away from the window. "And we shouldn't stay here long. If they realize you weren't killed in the explosion, they'll come here looking for you. But for now, they probably assume that you're dead."

"Who are they?" She had one last glimpse of the column of smoke before Phil closed the shutters.

"I'm betting on Corky." Cora Lee removed a big bottle of warmed-up Chocolood from the microwave.

"I think it's Max the Mega Member." Pamela set

out three cups and saucers on the kitchen counter. "But it could be any of a hundred people you've managed to piss off over the years."

"I haven't pissed off hundreds." Vanda thought back to make sure that was true.

"I'll explain," Phil began. "We got some information from the prisoner Angus caught last night."

"Oh, right." Cora Lee poured Chocolood into the three cups, then handed one to Vanda. "Darcy told us about that. She and Austin took him to Romatech."

Vanda settled on the couch and took a sip of the hot blood and chocolate mixture. Her friends sat across from her in two easy chairs.

Phil paced about the room. "The prisoner told us that Casimir has a hit list—Vamps who took part in what the Malcontents call the Massacre at DVN. He wants to avenge the death of his friend Jedrek Janow."

Vanda winced. Her friends Ian and Toni had killed Jedrek Janow. She set her cup and saucer down on the coffee table. "Are Ian and Toni on the list?"

"They're at the top," Phil admitted. "But as long as they remain hidden on their honeymoon, they should be safe."

Cora Lee sipped her Chocolood. "Who else is on the hit list?"

"Jack, Zoltan, Dougal, Phineas." Phil looked at Vanda. "You."

She gulped. "Casimir wants me dead? Why? I didn't hurt anyone at DVN. I never even went inside."

"That's true," Pamela insisted. "Vanda was only there for moral support."

"Apparently, Casimir knows about Jedrek's attempts to kill Vanda in the past," Phil said. "He's trying to finish the job, perhaps to honor his friend's memory."

Vanda clenched her hands together. Casimir had thousands of followers. Thousands of vampires who were eager to do his bidding. Panic bubbled inside her, growing and threatening to overwhelm her completely. She'd been hunted before. Jedrek and his wolves had hounded her for over a year. It had been terrifying, but at least there had only been a half dozen of them. Now there could be thousands . . . and no place to run. No place to hide.

Phil touched her shoulder, and she jumped.

"It's okay." He rubbed her shoulder. "They'll think you were killed in the explosion. We'll just keep you hidden—"

"I can't hide for centuries!" Vanda jumped to her feet and paced across the room.

"Oh dear." Pamela stood and dug a cell phone from her pants' pocket. "This is horrid, simply horrid."

"Are you calling for help?" Cora Lee asked.

"I'm seeing if Princess Joanna is still awake in London." Pamela punched in a number. "I'm feeling a little homesick for jolly ol' England."

Vanda strode toward her. "You're running out on me?"

"No offense, dear, but you're not the safest person to hang out with— Oh, Joanna! How are you? Would you mind terribly if I came for a visit?"

"I want to go, too." Cora Lee rose to her feet. "I've always had a hankerin' to see England."

"Did you hear that, Joanna?" Pamela asked. "Yes, there'll be two of us . . . Oh, I quite agree. It'll be a lovely holiday."

"I can't believe you're abandoning me!" Vanda yelled.

"One moment, please." Pamela pressed the cell phone to her chest. "Vanda, you know we love you, but there's simply no point in our staying. We'll just get in the way."

"That's true, actually," Phil said. "It's easier for me to protect one than three. And you wouldn't want your friends to be in danger."

Vanda glared at him. Dammit, he was right. She didn't want Pamela or Cora Lee in danger. But this hurt. She'd expected a little more loyalty from her friends.

"The club is gone, too," Cora Lee added. "You don't need us now."

Vanda's heart squeezed in her chest. Yes, her club was gone, but Cora Lee mentioned it like it was no more important than losing a broken plate. Didn't they realize it was her life? It was her great accomplishment. It was her freedom, her independence, her worth, her security. And she'd lost it. "Go ahead, then, and go! Who needs you?"

Pamela winced. "I'm afraid we're not as brave as you."

Cora Lee's bottom lip quivered. "I always wanted to be brave, but I'm too scared."

Vanda turned away to keep them from seeing the

tears in her eyes. She'd lost the club. She was losing her friends.

"Phil," Pamela whispered. "Promise us you'll take care of her."

"I will. You have my word."

"God be with you, Vanda," Pamela said.

She glanced back just in time to see both Cora Lee and Pamela lean toward the cell phone to concentrate on Joanna's voice. Then they vanished.

She collapsed on the couch. Her club gone. Her friends gone. The nightmare had started again. The nightmare where she lost everyone she loved, and the bad guys hunted her down to kill her.

A clattering noise drew her attention. Phil had taken all the cups and saucers to the kitchen. A sudden realization hit her. She wasn't alone. Phil was with her. He'd sworn to protect her. Her heart expanded with tenderness and warmth.

Then another realization struck her, and her chest clenched tight. Karl had protected her, too, and it had cost him his life.

She couldn't do this to Phil. With a pang that reverberated through her entire body, she knew for certain that she loved him. And she couldn't let anything happen to him.

"You——" She cleared her throat. "You don't have to clean up after us."

"Actually, I do." He loaded the rinsed dishes into the dishwasher. "We can't leave any signs that you were here. And we need to leave soon. If they decide to verify your death, they'll come here first."

She needed a place to hide. But where? She'd spent

most of her time in America safely sequestered in a harem in New York City. She couldn't hide in London with her ex-harem friends without putting them at risk. She couldn't hide in Texas with Maggie without endangering her and her family. "You don't think the townhouse is safe?"

"No." Phil walked toward her. "The Malcontents know about it. It has a good alarm system, but that doesn't stop them from invading."

"Romatech?"

"All the Romatechs are in danger." Phil retrieved a cell phone from his pocket. "Howard has a cabin in the Adirondacks. I've been there a few times for . . . hunting trips. I'll call, and the answering machine will pick up. Then you can focus on Howard's recorded message and teleport us there. Okay?"

"No."

Phil paused in the middle of punching the number. "What?"

Vanda stood. "I'm not going with you."

His eyes narrowed. "I'm not giving you any choice."

She lifted her chin. "I'm the one doing the teleporting. I can go wherever I please. On my own."

He stepped toward her. "Where are you going?"

She shrugged. "I . . . know the Carpathian Mountains really well."

"You plan to hide in caves? Sounds comfy."

"Once I'm in my death-sleep, a dirt floor isn't any different than a soft mattress."

He moved closer. "And who will guard you during the day?"

"No one." She tightened the whip around her waist. "I survived like that before. I can do it again."

His jaw shifted as he ground his teeth. "You were alone before. You are *not* alone now."

"I was alone because Karl died protecting me. I'm not going to let that happen to you."

"It won't happen. I'm a hell of a lot tougher than Karl."

"You never even knew him—"

"I know enough! And I will not allow you to go through this alone."

"You don't have a choice." She searched her psychic memory for a cave in the Carpathians.

He grabbed her by the shoulders. "Don't do it. It could be daylight there."

Damn. He might be right. Teleporting to the east was a very risky business. "It won't be daylight in the cave."

"How long has it been since you were there? Over fifty years? The cave could have changed. You could end up teleporting into solid rock."

She swallowed hard.

"You're teleporting to the cabin and taking me with you." He punched in the number. "End of discussion."

She glared at him. "Are you always so overbearing?"

"When it comes to your safety, yes." He held her tight and lifted the phone to her ear. "Do it."

She concentrated on the recorded message, and in a few seconds they materialized in a dark room. Phil released her then, and pocketed his cell phone. She glimpsed brown log walls and the gray stones of a huge fireplace. Moonlight filtered through windows and glinted off . . . eyeballs.

She gasped, then spun around, looking for Phil. He was moving through the kitchen to the back door. "Phil?"

"Right here." He flipped on the lights.

She turned back to the eyeballs. The head of a deer was mounted on the wall. A giant moose head hung over the fireplace. And some sort of wild pig with tusks hung over the bookcase. "There are dead animals on the walls."

"This is a hunting cabin."

She shuddered. "They're looking at me." *And saying*, you're *next*. "I'm surprised you don't have a bearskin rug on the floor."

He winced. "Howard wouldn't go for that. And they're not looking at you. Those eyeballs are glass." He opened the fridge and peered inside.

"I guess you and Howard killed them?"

"Yeah." He set a bottle of beer on the counter and unscrewed the top. "We're . . . hunters."

She wrapped her arms around herself. She'd been a hunter once, too. She'd started off using her teleportation skills to hunt for her father and brothers in the prison camps. But then she'd seen the hideous cruelty, and something had snapped. Instead of hunting for those she loved, she hunted for those she hated. Prison guards, Nazis. A vampire had to feed every night, so why not do it and rid the world of monsters at the same time?

But Jedrek Janow had discovered her scheme, and she had become the hunted one.

She perched on the arm of a brown leather couch. "I'm a little sensitive about being hunted."

"You're safe here." Phil took a drink. "Only Howard, Connor, and I know about this place."

"That's good." She looked around.

On the back of the couch lay a hand-woven blanket with a Native American design. The couch faced the fireplace, with a coffee table scarred and imprinted with drink rings. An old recliner and floor lamp rested close to the bookcase.

A staircase led up to a loft. She could see several beds up there, all covered with colorful quilts.

Phil was still in the kitchen, sipping his beer. The heat from the explosion must have made him thirsty. Close by, a wooden dinette table and chairs sat on a braided rug.

She took a deep breath and tried to convince herself she was really safe. "Is there any synthetic blood in the fridge?"

"No. Are you hungry?"

"Not now, but I usually have a snack before dawn, and I'll be very hungry when I wake up."

"I'll arrange a delivery when I report in to Connor. I need to make sure Phineas got back to Romatech all right."

She wondered if Phil was going to be in trouble for running off with her instead of staying at Romatech. "Where should I sleep? Is there a basement?"

"There is, but it has windows." He opened a door underneath the staircase. "When Connor comes here, he sleeps in the closet."

"Oh. Okay."

Phil smiled and returned to the kitchen. He took a flashlight from a cabinet. "I'll check the perimeter. Make yourself at home." He went out the back door.

With a groan, she glanced at the dead deer. "Life sucks, huh?"

She checked the bolt on the front door. A Malcontent could just teleport inside to kill her, but at least the bolted door would stop any deer or moose relatives intent on revenge.

The closet under the staircase was surprisingly roomy. It was bare except for a row of shelves at one end. She pulled a blanket and quilt off a shelf and spread them on the wooden floor. Then she wandered through the small kitchen. Some clean clothes were stacked on top of the dryer. Flannel pajama pants, T-shirts, a navy terry-cloth bathrobe.

A nearby door opened onto a small bathroom. She grabbed the bathrobe and locked herself inside. She glanced at the mirror above the vanity. Nothing. The only thing she could see reflected was the claw-footed old bathtub behind her. She kicked her boots off. Good Lord, she hated mirrors. They made her feel like . . . nothing. Small and worthless.

I think, therefore I am, she reminded herself. She had feelings, hopes, and dreams, just like a live person.

But her dreams had just been crushed. Her eyes misted with unshed tears.

She untied her whip and slipped out of her catsuit. While the tub filled with hot water, she rinsed out her underwear and bra in the sink. She hung them to dry on the towel bar.

She settled in the deep tub, letting the hot water seep into her cold bones. She closed her eyes, hoping to relax, but her mind filled with a vision of smoke and fire.

She'd loved that club. She'd designed it, furnished it, decorated it. She'd auditioned the dancers and hired the waiters. It had been her refuge from the cruel world. A place where she controlled everything, and everyone did as she commanded. It was a sanctuary where she never had to feel small and never had to endure the pain from her past again.

Tears rolled down her cheeks. What was she going to do now? Spend the rest of eternity hiding, quaking in fear, with nothing to do but relive the horrors of her past?

She shampooed her singed hair, then ducked under the water to rinse it off. Her face burned. That was her fault. She shouldn't have waited so long to teleport herself and Phil away from danger. But she hadn't quite believed his story about the bomb. How on earth could he have known it was in her file cabinet?

She climbed from the tub, dried off, and put on the terry-cloth robe. It was obviously made for a man. The shoulder seams hung halfway to her elbows, and the sleeves fell past her fingertips. She rolled up the sleeves, belted it tight around her waist. The robe was designed for a man's broad chest, so she flipped the collar inward to help cover her cleavage.

She grabbed her whip and padded into the kitchen. The lights had been turned off, and a big fire blazed in the hearth. She dropped the whip on the coffee table. Was Phil trying to make the place look romantic? Candles flickered on the mantelpiece. And the moose that had been overhead was now gone. She whirled around. The deer and wild pig were gone, too.

A door creaked open, and she spotted Phil at the top landing of stairs that led down into the basement. He switched a light off, then stepped into the main room.

He smiled, his blue eyes gleaming as he looked her over.

Her knees grew weak, but she covered it by sitting suddenly on the couch. She ran a hand through her short, wet hair. "What happened to the animal heads?"

"I moved them to the basement. I figured you wouldn't mind."

"No." She curled her feet underneath her on the couch and adjusted the bathrobe to make sure she was covered.

He moved closer, still looking at her and still smiling. "I checked the perimeter. We're in danger from two vicious-looking raccoons living under a wheelbarrow." His gaze shifted to the coffee table. "Thank God you have your whip."

She knew he was trying to lighten the mood, but the few tears she'd shed in the bathtub had only been the tip of what felt like a giant iceberg in her chest. She turned her head away so he wouldn't see the tears in her eyes.

"I called Connor to let him know we're here. He was relieved to know you're safe."

She started to say a snide remark about Connor, but was too tired to think one up.

"Phineas will come before dawn to bring you a supply of synthetic blood," Phil continued. "So you won't be forced to bite me after all."

She nodded. Relief swept through her, threatening to make her tears overflow. If only Phil would do something awful, then she could scream and throw a fit. She winced inwardly. Was that what she'd been doing all these years? Relying on anger to keep from dealing with her real feelings?

"Vanda." He waited till she cast a furtive glance his way. "Sweetheart, it's going to be all right."

Tears burned her eyes, and she looked quickly away.

"I'm going to wash up."

She heard the bathroom door creak shut. Dammit. She wasn't going to cry. What was the point? She stood and paced to the kitchen table and back. Nothing to keep her mind off her troubles. No television. No computer.

She stopped in front of the bookcase. *How to Gut a Fish in Five Easy Steps. Taxidermy for Dummies.* A romance novel? She pulled out the paperback and studied the half-naked couple embracing on the front cover. She smiled to herself, wondering who had brought this book to the cabin. Howard, Phil, or Connor? Maybe they read the love scenes to pick up a few pointers. Not that Phil needed any help in that department.

He had been incredible. So intense. So sexy. He had made her melt.

"Are you too hot?"

She jumped, and turned toward his voice. He'd just emerged from the bathroom. Bare-chested. The book tumbled from her hands.

He nodded toward the fireplace. "I wanted to make the place more cozy, but the fire might be too hot for July."

"It—It's fine." She grabbed the paperback off the floor and stashed it on a lower shelf, stealing one last glimpse at the hero's chest on the cover. No comparison. The model looked fake. Posed. Waxed.

Her gaze drifted back to Phil. Now that was a chest. Broad across the shoulders. Brown hair, still glistening from his bath and curling as it dried. A thin line of hair dissecting six-pack abs and disappearing under the plaid flannel pajama bottoms he wore low on his hips.

He walked toward her with something clasped in one hand. "I found something in the bathroom that might make you feel better."

Did it require batteries? "What is it?"

He showed her the clear bottle filled with a greenish liquid. "It's aloe vera. Good for burns."

"Oh." She touched her face. "I'll heal during my death-sleep."

"Which is about seven hours from now." He sat on the couch and patted the cushion next to him.

She perched on the edge and lifted a hand to take the bottle. To her surprise, he didn't pass the lotion to her. He squeezed some onto his palm, then set the bottle on the coffee table next to her whip.

"Hold still." He moved closer, then dabbed some lotion on her chin with his finger.

"I can do it myself."

"You can't see where the bad spots are." He smeared some across her forehead.

It did feel wonderfully cool. "I must look awful."

"You're always beautiful to me." He smoothed some lotion over her cheeks. "You've been crying."

Just the mere mention of tears brought the dreaded things back to her eyes. "I lost everything. My club. My friends."

"Your friends still care about you. You haven't lost them." He dabbed some lotion onto her nose.

She sniffed. "I lost the club. It was everything to me."

He rubbed his hands together to coat them with aloe vera, then smoothed his palms down her throat. "It wasn't everything."

"Yes, it was. I designed it myself. I made all the decisions. It was my creation. It was . . . perfect." His hands felt perfect, too.

"It gave you a great sense of accomplishment."

"Yes. Exactly." She was so glad he understood. "I was happy there. I felt . . . safe and secure."

He leaned back against the sofa cushions. "It was brick and mortar. Wood and cement. Nothing more."

She stiffened. He didn't understand at all. "Did you listen to anything I just said?"

"I did. You felt a great sense of accomplishment. You felt happy and secure. And those feelings were all attached to your club."

"Yes." A tear ran down her cheek.

"Vanda, the club didn't hold your feelings. You do that in your heart." He brushed her tear away. "Nothing—not a Malcontent or an explosion or a fire—can take your feelings away from you."

The iceberg lodged in her chest melted away, and more tears streamed down her face.

"Do you know what I see when I look at you?"

"A crazy undead lady with purple hair and a mean disposition?"

He smiled and ran his fingers through her damp hair. "I see a beautiful young woman who is smart and brave and can accomplish anything she sets her mind to."

"You think I can be happy?"

"I know you can."

More tears escaped. "You say lovely things, Phil."

He kissed away the tears. "Actually, I'm more a man of action."

She could imagine what actions he had in mind. "Phil, it will kill me if anything happens to you."

"I'll be fine." He kissed her brow. "Trust me."

"That's why I refused your help, you know. It's not that I'm ungrateful or stubborn. It's that I . . . I . . . "

He kissed the tip of her nose. "You've grown a little fond of me?"

"Yes." Her face felt hot again. "Just a little."

"Good." He grabbed the Indian blanket off the

back of the couch and spread it on the floor in front of the fire. "I'm a little fond of you, too."

Her gaze drifted to the bulge in his flannel pants. "And yet, you show it in such a big way."

He grinned. "Come here. I want to kiss some part of you that doesn't taste like aloe vera." His blue eyes glimmered with heat. "I'm sure I can find just the spot."

She knew he could. She circled the coffee table and stood in front of him.

He touched her cheek. "Vanda, I love you."

Her heart cracked wide open. "Phil." She threw her arms around his neck. "What would I do without you?"

She was falling in love. She hadn't wanted to. But he was proving far too irresistible. And sweet. And sexy. "Will you make love to me? Now?"

"I thought you'd never ask." He bent his head down.

Chapter Fourteen

*V*anda leaned into Phil as he kissed her. It was a languid, leisurely kiss. No doubt he intended to make love to her slowly and thoroughly. But the rhythmic stroking of his tongue against hers, the feel of his soft skin under her roaming hands, and the earthy, manly scent of him filling her senses—it made her bones melt, her heart race, and her desire spiral out of control.

She dug her fingers into his back and arched into him. She pressed her hips against his groin, rubbing his hard length. The aching emptiness between her legs grew hot and demanding.

To hell with leisurely lovemaking. They could do that the second time. Or the third.

She broke the kiss. "Let's get on with it." She fumbled with the knot on her terry-cloth belt. Everything was tinted red, so she knew her eyes were glowing.

"Sweetheart, I love the eagerness, but we need to talk first."

"You've got to be kidding." She yanked her robe off and tossed it on the floor.

He sucked in a breath. "Good God, you're beautiful."

"Thank you." She noticed his groin was even larger. "Enough chitchat." She grabbed hold of the waistband of his flannel pajama bottoms.

He clasped her wrists to stop her. "We really do need to talk."

"Why?" She yanked her hands from his grasp and glared at him. "Are you dumping me?"

"No! I love you. I want to spend my life with you."

Her heart swelled. "Really?"

"Yes, really."

"Then what's the problem? I can't get pregnant. I have no diseases. Your gorgeous body will not be harmed in any way." She grabbed her whip off the coffee table. "Unless, of course, you piss me off."

He laughed.

She huffed. "That was supposed to scare you into submission. The whip or personal love slave—which will it be?"

His blue eyes twinkled. "You don't have to resort to threats. I gladly volunteer."

She tossed the whip onto the table. "Then stop talking and kiss me. Make me scream. That's an order."

He shifted his weight. "I have to say something first."

Vanda groaned with frustration. She should have used the damned whip.

"Remember how you mentioned that the Nazis sent wolves after you?"

She froze. Her skin chilled with goose bumps, in spite of the blazing fire nearby. "I don't want to talk about it." She couldn't let Phil know. He'd never look at her the same way again. "The past is gone. There's no point in talking about it."

"But this—"

"No! You love me, don't you?" Tears sprang to her eyes once again. "Isn't love supposed to be enough?"

He searched her eyes. "I hope it is."

"It is." She wrapped her arms around him. "Please. Just take me as I am. Love me."

"I do love you. More than anything."

"Good." She tugged his pants down. "Then hurry."

"We have all night. Don't rush me."

But he was ready. So ready. "I want you." She reached out to touch him.

"Wait a minute." He lowered her to the floor, and she immediately locked her legs around his waist.

"Love slave." She lifted her hips to rub herself against him. "Take me now."

He pushed her hips down. "Not now."

"Yes, now. What about the term 'love slave' do you not understand?"

He chuckled. "I was the first one to declare my love. So I get the first turn."

"We're taking turns?"

"Yes. Me first."

She suppressed a smile. For a love slave, he was very domineering. But even their little power struggles turned her on. "You think you're in charge here?"

"I know I am." He fished her terry-cloth belt from her robe.

"Maybe I just let you think you're in charge." She frowned as he looped the belt around her wrists. "What are you doing?"

"I intend to explore you thoroughly. I can't do it if you keep rushing me." He pulled her arms above her head and tied the terry-cloth ends around a leg of the coffee table.

She tugged at the belt, then smiled. He'd tied her so loosely, she could free her hands whenever she wanted. "So who made you the boss?"

"I did. Feel free to register your complaints."

"I will. You—You're—" She sucked in a breath when his tongue tickled her neck. "You're overbearing."

"Mmm-hmm." With his tongue, he licked a path down to her breasts.

"You're a caveman." She shivered as his tongue circled her nipple. "Pushy and completely ob-ob—"

He sucked her nipple into his mouth.

"Obnoxious!"

He tugged on the hardened tip, and she moaned.

The ache between her legs grew more desperate. "Phil, please."

"You're not begging, are you?" He nibbled down her belly.

"Never."

"Good, 'cause it won't sway me. This is still my turn, and I'm not done with you." He slipped two fingers inside her.

She jolted.

"You're so wet." He waggled his fingers. "So beautiful."

She panted, gasping for air. Oh God, it felt so good.

Her legs tensed. Her hips lifted.

And his fingers withdrew. The building crescendo keeled over and fell flat.

"Ack!" She'd never felt so desperate. "What was that?"

"Trust me." He dove between her legs.

She squealed at the feel of his tongue. He tickled and teased, suckled and nipped.

The tension slammed back into her full force, stealing her breath away. Oh God, if this was how he took his turn, he could take the whole night. A whole fortnight. Her sight dimmed. Her ears hummed. All feelings, all thoughts, zeroed in on his wicked mouth.

She screamed as a massive convulsion racked her body. She writhed, oblivious to everything but the delicious shudders.

She gasped when he entered her suddenly. "Phil." She freed her hands from the belt. "Are you trying to kill me?"

He smiled and kissed her brow. "Hang in there, sweetheart. It's still my turn."

Several hours later, Phil lay flat on his back in a sated stupor.

"Phil," Vanda whispered in his ear.

He groaned. Was it his turn again? He'd lost count. After his last turn, he'd thought he was completely spent. He'd been half asleep when she'd started massaging him with a warm, wet washcloth. She was so gentle, he'd floated in a drowsy, semiaroused state.

But then she took him into her mouth. In a flash he was fully awake and fully erect. She tortured him till he begged for mercy, and then she straddled him. He didn't know what was more exciting: feeling her hot sheath sliding up and down his penis, or watching her make love to him. He'd adored watching the expressions on her face, the flush on her skin, and the bounce of her breasts. He'd relished hearing the soft moans and hoarse cries. He had never experienced anything so beautifully erotic.

She'd nearly killed him.

"Phil," she whispered again.

He moaned.

"You fell asleep. It's four in the morning."

"That's nice." He pried his eyes open, but they fell shut again. "I sleep at night. Guard during the day."

"I know. But all that exercise left me with an appetite."

"That's nice." He drifted off.

"Phil."

"Mmm."

"I'm *hungry*." She traced his carotid artery with her finger.

His eyes popped open.

She grinned. "I thought that would get your attention. I was going to call Connor, but I thought I should let you know first, in case one of the guys teleports here with synthetic blood and sees you sprawled naked on the floor."

He sat up. "I see what you mean." It would be obvious that he and Vanda were engaging in forbidden activities. He blinked, realizing for the first time that she was wearing flannel pants and a man's T-shirt. "You're dressed."

"Yes. I found these clothes on the dryer. And I took another bath. Vamps have a really strong sense of smell."

Werewolves did, too, and Vanda's scent was all over him. "I'd better wash up." He hurried to the bathroom to scrub himself clean.

When he came out with a towel wrapped around his hips, he discovered she'd loaded the washing machine with the blanket and everything else that smelled of sex.

She paced around the room. "I think I got everything. I don't want to lose you as my guard. If Connor figures out what we're doing, he might reassign you."

"Then I would quit." Phil found one last T-shirt and pair of flannel pants on the dryer. He pulled them on. "I'm not leaving you."

"Phil." She looked at him with so much love in her soft gray eyes. Then her gaze shifted to his neck.

Her eyes gleamed, and she turned away. "Make the call, please."

"Right." He wasn't afraid of Vanda's fangs, but he knew if she bit him, she'd realize he didn't taste like a normal human. That wasn't the way he wanted her to learn the truth. He'd tried to tell her earlier, but she'd refused to listen.

He was halfway to the bathroom to retrieve the cell phone he'd left in his pants when he remembered it never got good reception at this cabin. It would be dangerous to have a Vamp teleport here using an unstable beacon. He went back to the phone on the kitchen counter, then punched in the number for the security office at Romatech.

Connor answered. "How is it there?"

"Quiet. Vanda's hungry, so we could use a delivery."

"I'll send Phineas. Expect his call in a few minutes." Connor hung up.

Phil frowned as he set down the receiver.

"Something wrong?" Vanda asked.

"Connor seemed more . . . curt than usual. There must be something going on. We'll find out when Phineas comes."

Vanda nodded and paced toward the fireplace. The fire had dwindled, leaving a few glowing coals in a heap of ash.

The phone rang, and he grabbed the receiver. "Hey, Phineas. I'm glad you made it out of the nightclub."

By the echoing sound of his voice, he realized he was on speaker phone. He continued to talk so his voice could guide Phineas to the right place. When the young Vamp appeared, his arms filled with a big cardboard box, Phil hung up.

"Hey, bro." Phineas set the box on the kitchen counter and turned to greet Vanda. "Whoa, dudette. Looking a little crispy."

She gave him an annoyed look. "Thanks a lot." Her expression softened as she approached the kitchen. "Actually, I do want to thank you. Not just for bringing the food, but for helping everybody get out of the club."

"No problem," Phineas said. "Sorry about it blowing up. You know, your bouncer was really pissed. Insisted on teleporting back with me to Romatech so he could volunteer to fight the Malcontents. Angus was glad to hire him."

"Angus is at Romatech now?" Phil asked.

"Oh yeah." Phineas removed a plastic case from the box and set it in front of Phil. "These are some weapons Connor wanted you to have."

"Good." Phil opened the case and found two handguns and numerous clips.

"I wish I could have brought you some silver bullets," Phineas said, "but I couldn't teleport with them."

"I understand." Phil loaded a clip into a handgun.

"What about my food?" Vanda peered inside the box.

"Right here, Miss Toasty." Phineas began unloading bottles of synthetic blood and setting them on the counter.

Vanda grabbed one, yanked off the top, and chugged the contents down.

"Whoa, baby." Phineas slanted an amused look at Phil. "I wonder why she's so hungry?"

Phil ignored him and stashed the rest of the bottles into the refrigerator.

Phineas looked back and forth between Phil and Vanda. "Matching lumberjack outfits. How . . . interesting."

Vanda plunked her empty bottle on the counter. "Stow it, Dr. Phang, before I get creative with this bottle."

"Ooh, kinky." Phineas grinned. "I like it."

Phil loaded another handgun, switched on the safety, and offered it to Vanda. "Have you ever used one of these?"

"No." She eyed it warily, then gave Phineas a sardonic look. "But I know where to aim for target practice."

"Ooh, kinky and freaky." Phineas winked.

"Will you get serious?" Phil grumbled. He offered the gun once more to Vanda. "You need this."

She took it reluctantly. "I prefer my whip."

Phineas snorted. "I bet you do."

"Do I need to knock your fangs out?" Phil growled.

"All right, all right." Phineas held up his hands in a surrendering gesture. "The Love Doctor's just having a little fun, that's all. Things are so . . . grim back at Romatech. It's a lot nicer here at your little love nest."

"It's a hunting cabin," Phil corrected him.

"Phil and Howard are hunters." Vanda strode to the coffee table and set her handgun down next to her whip. "Phil moved them all to the basement 'cause I didn't like them, but there used to be animal trophies mounted on the walls."

"Yeah, I know what you've been mounting," Phineas muttered. When Phil elbowed him, he whispered, "Don't worry, bro. I won't tell anyone."

"Now that's weird." Vanda pivoted as she scanned the cabin. "I just noticed there aren't any hunting rifles here. How did you kill those animals?"

Phil winced inwardly. No rifles had been necessary. A fully shifted bear and wolf could kill the old fashioned way.

Phineas let out a slow, whistling breath and gave Phil a knowing look.

Phil cleared his throat. "Howard never keeps rifles here. Someone could break in and steal them."

"Oh. I see." Vanda perched on the arm of the couch, apparently satisfied with his answer.

"So what's happening at Romatech?" Phil changed the subject.

Phineas moved the empty box to the floor. "Angus arrived a few hours ago. He converted the conference room across from the security office into a war room."

"*War* room?" Vanda asked, her eyes wide.

"It's highly probable that things will escalate," Phil explained. "Especially now that Casimir is in America."

She made a face. "Why couldn't he stay in Eastern Europe? That's where all the creepy vampires hang out."

Phil winced. He needed to tell Vanda that the creepy vampire, Sigismund, was here, too. "It makes sense for Casimir to come to America. He wants to destroy all the modern, bottle-drinking Vamps, and this is where the majority of them live. The power base is here."

Phineas nodded. "Angus was saying the same thing."

"Well, the leaders might be here, but the followers . . . " Vanda groaned. "Did you see those guys at the party last night? When they thought Phineas was poisoned by Malcontents, they freaked out and wanted to run away. Our side has a bunch of wimps!"

Phineas stiffened. "I'm not a wimp."

"And neither am I. We have plenty of good fighters," Phil insisted. But he knew Vanda was making a valid point. The Vamps who chose to drink bottled blood did it because they disliked attacking mortals. By their very nature, they were peaceful, law-abiding creatures.

Casimir's followers, on the other hand, were aggressive and violent. They'd been murderers and thugs as mortals, and as vampires, their cruel natures had worsened. Give a criminal super speed, strength, and mind control abilities, and the result was a vicious monster with allusions of grandeur and invincibility. How could the Vamps hope to defeat them? But if they didn't, there would be no one to stop the Malcontents from terrorizing the world. The Vamps had to fight, like it or not, not just for their own survival, but to protect the mortal world.

Phil strode to the back door and slipped on some rubber boots. "I haven't checked the perimeter in a while. You want to come?" He gave Phineas a pointed look.

"Yeah, sure, bro."

Phil smiled at Vanda. "This will take just a few minutes."

She crossed her arms, frowning. "I get it. You want to talk about gory war stuff without scaring the little lady. Well, I've been through war before, you know. I'm tough, dammit."

Not nearly as tough as she pretended. Phil wished he could take her in his arms and kiss away the frown lines from her brow, but he couldn't in front of a witness. "We'll be right back." He slipped outside with Phineas.

He waited on the back porch a few seconds while his eyes adjusted to the darkness. Then he descended the stairs to the gravel walkway. The moon, three-quarters full, hung low over a dark silhouette of evergreens. A breeze rustled the branches, filling the air with the scent of pine.

He strolled down the walkway, the gravel crunching under his rubber boots. Phineas walked beside him, peering into the dark woods.

"This way." Phil turned to make a clockwise circle around the cabin. Their footsteps became soft on the grass. He listened carefully. Birdsong, the scurrying of little paws through the underbrush.

"How bad is it?" he asked.

Phineas kicked a pinecone. "The Russian Malcontents attacked the townhouse. No one was there, but the alarm went off at Romatech, and by the time we got there, they all teleported away."

"Cowards," Phil grumbled.

"We're going to bunk down at Romatech till things settle down." Phineas sighed. "If it ever settles down. That Sigismund dude made it sound like all the Romatechs were in danger. Angus sent Mikhail, Zoltan, Jack, and Dougal to the other facilities to beef up security."

Phil glanced at the cabin's front porch as they passed by. "I'd appreciate it if you didn't mention Sigismund in front of Vanda. I want to break the news to her myself."

"Does she know him?"

"He's the one who changed her and her sister."

Phineas whistled. "Hot damn, bro. No wonder you nearly squeezed his head off. That was really awesome, though, the way your hand turned into a paw."

"I'd appreciate it if you didn't mention that either."

Phineas halted. "You haven't told her yet?"

"No. I tried, but . . . " He groaned inwardly. He should have tried harder. Vanda had been so adamant in her refusal to talk. What was she trying to hide from him?

Phineas resumed their walk around the cabin. "Connor wanted me to pass on a message. Keep your furry paws to yourself while you're guarding Vanda."

Phil gazed into the dark woods, saying nothing.

"Obviously, Connor's warning is too late," Phineas muttered.

"I'm not discussing it." Phil rounded the corner of the house and headed for the back porch.

"You don't have to, bro. The Love Doctor senses these things. Besides, you're an animal. You're going to act like one." Phineas howled like a wolf.

"Enough," Phil growled. "This has nothing to do with my animal nature. I love Vanda. And I think she loves me."

"Dude, she doesn't even know you. Not until you tell her the truth."

Phil winced inwardly. "Okay. You made your point." He could only hope his shape-shifting nature wouldn't make a difference. Vanda claimed his love would be enough. But she hated shape shifters. And she was terrified of wolves.

As they neared the back door, he heard the phone ring inside. "Hurry." He rushed to open the door. "I'd rather Vanda not answer it."

Phineas zoomed inside at vampire speed, beating Vanda to the phone. "Hello?"

As Phil locked the back door, he noted the shocked expression stealing over the black Vamp's face.

"How—How did it happen?" Phineas asked. He grimaced as he listened to the response.

Vanda retreated to the fireplace, a worried look furrowing her brow. She crossed her arms, her shoulders hunched.

"All right," Phineas said quietly. "We'll be right there." He gently replaced the receiver, then turned slowly to face them. He still looked stunned.

"What happened?" Phil asked.

Phineas swallowed audibly. "The Romatechs in Texas and Colorado were bombed. Fourteen Vamps are dead. More were injured."

Vanda sucked in a breath and pressed a hand to her mouth.

Phil felt a tightening in his chest. For the last few years there had been tension between the Malcontents and Vamps. There'd even been a few minor skirmishes. But nothing on this scale.

He looked across the room at Vanda. Somehow, he had to keep her safe. And he also needed to fight. "The war has begun."

Chapter Fifteen

*W*ar.

Vanda shuddered. The nightmare was back in full force. At the age of twenty-two she'd lost her home, her family, and her mortality. War had ripped her life to shreds, and she'd ended up all alone, hunted and hiding in caves.

And now, years later, she'd lost her club and friends. Once again she was in hiding, hunted by the Malcontents. Once again war was destroying her world.

A surge of rage shot through her. How could this happen again? Was she cursed? Her hands curled into fists. She wanted to punch something. Throw something. *Scream*.

She grabbed her whip off the table. Let one of those Malcontents find her. She'd flay his skin right off his face. She'd kill the bloody— The whip tumbled to the floor.

Oh God, she didn't want to kill again. What was she doing? She'd let monsters get to her before. She'd let them turn *her* into a monster. *No.* Tears burned her eyes. Never again.

"Vanda?" Phil approached her with a worried look. "Are you all right?"

What a selfish fool she was. She'd nearly thrown a fit out of self-pity, when there were other Vamps who had lost their lives tonight. Fourteen dead. There were Vamps in mourning. Vamps who were injured. Her anger wasn't helping them or herself.

She took a deep breath. "I'm all right. I—I felt really pissed for a while, but—"

"You took control." Phil's eyes softened, glimmering with love.

Her heart swelled with warmth. This nightmare was different from the last one. This time she had Phil. And she didn't have wolves chasing her.

Phineas cleared his throat. "I hate to break up the tender moment, but Phil and I have been ordered to return for a strategy meeting."

Phil stiffened. "I'm not leaving Vanda alone."

"She could come if she wants." Phineas turned to Vanda. "You know how to get to Romatech, right?"

"No thanks," Vanda said. "You two go on without me."

"Are you sure?" Phil asked.

She scoffed. "Gee, should I teleport to Romatech when the bad guys are bombing Romatechs? That's a tough one. I'll just stay here."

"I'll be back before dawn," Phil assured her.

"Then you'd better hurry up and go." She glanced at the clock over the kitchen sink. "It's already four-thirty."

He nodded. "Just a minute, Phineas. I need to put my uniform back on." He dashed to the bathroom.

Vanda strolled into the kitchen and retrieved two bottles of blood from the fridge. She handed one to Phineas.

"Thanks." He unscrewed the top and drank.

"Thank you for bringing it." She lowered her voice to a soft whisper so Phil wouldn't hear. "I know you suspect Phil and I are . . . involved, but please don't tell anyone."

"Sweetness," Phineas whispered back, "When it comes to you and Phil, I'm up to my eyeballs in secrets. But my lips are sealed."

"Thank you." Vanda clinked her bottle against his. She turned when she heard the bathroom door open.

Phil exited, wearing his MacKay uniform of khaki pants and navy polo shirt. "Okay, Phineas. Let's go."

She gave Phil an encouraging smile as he teleported away with the young black Vamp. And then she immediately felt lonely without him. How quickly and thoroughly he'd invaded her heart and her life.

She sipped from the bottle and wondered what kind of secrets Phineas was keeping. There was no way he could know her darkest secrets. She'd never admitted them to anyone. So he had to be referring to Phil. Was there something about Phil she didn't know?

She thought back to when she'd first met him. He'd been a tall nineteen-year-old college student with beautiful blue eyes, a quick wit, and a charming smile. Even then there'd been an aura of earthy sexiness to him, a strong hint of the man he was to become, and she'd felt attracted to him from the start.

Now, as a twenty-seven-year old man, he'd far surpassed that earlier hint of manliness. He exuded masculine power, strength, and confidence. He drove her wild with desire. He inspired trust and a sense of security. But how well did she really know him?

A few memories flitted through her mind. Phil discovering a bomb in her file cabinet without actually seeing it. Phil capturing Max in her club and having enough strength to pin a vampire to the floor. Her bouncer complaining that he moved too fast.

She shoved those thoughts away. Phil was a sweet and wonderful man. She shouldn't doubt him. She ought to be grateful he was so strong and fast. If he hadn't detected that bomb, she'd be dead. If he hadn't killed that snake, she'd be dead.

His love for her was genuine and beautiful. And she was falling in love with him. That was all that mattered.

The atmosphere in the war room was grim. Phil took a seat at the conference table next to Connor. He nodded at the others sitting around the long table: Jack and Lara, Austin and Darcy, Howard, Phineas, Emma, Laszlo, Gregori, and Carlos, the Brazilian were-panther. Some additional chairs had been brought in to line the walls. Hugo, the ex-bouncer from Vanda's club, was sitting beside Robby and Jean-Luc, who must have teleported in from Texas. Angus paced around the table, deep in thought.

In the corner of the room, Sean Whelan was sitting alone. As head of the CIA Stake-Out Team, Sean's mission was to identify and terminate vampires. That mission had grown a bit complicated when his daughter, Shanna, married Roman Draganesti, and even more complicated when his team members, Austin and Emma, switched sides. Sean's gaze darted nervously about the room.

Phil scanned the room once more and realized Shanna and Roman were absent. He leaned close to Connor and whispered, "Did Angus send the Draganestis into hiding?"

"Nay," Connor replied. "He wanted to, but they insisted on staying here. Dougal and Zoltan are teleporting the injured Vamps here, and Roman and Shanna are in the clinic, patching them up."

"How did the Malcontents manage to infiltrate the Romatechs?" Phil whispered. "I thought Angus tightened security."

"I did," Angus grumbled, overhearing. "We doubled security on the ground, but they attacked from the air. Rockets fired from helicopters."

"Army helicopters?" Phil asked.

"We think so," Angus said as he continued to pace. "They must have used mind control to infiltrate nearby military bases."

"I'll alert the military," Sean Whelan said. When a dozen heads turned to him with alarm, he lifted his hands. "Don't worry. I won't tell them about vampires. I'll just say there's a radical group of psychic terrorists on the loose, using mind control to infiltrate bases. I'll recommend a lockdown, no visitors allowed on base after sundown. Any strangers will be shot on sight. Maybe that will help."

"Thank you, Whelan." Angus paced down the length of the table. "Let's get started, then. As ye all know, two of our Romatechs were destroyed tonight. One of our top priorities is resuming production as soon as possible in Texas and Colorado. Gregori is working on that."

Gregori nodded. "We're already looking at some rental properties. We still have all the daytime mortal employees, so we hope to be producing again in two weeks."

"Good. Another top priority is keeping the remaining three Romatechs safe. To that end, we have enlisted the help of Shanna's father." Angus motioned to Sean Whelan. "Ye have the floor, Sean."

"Thank you." The CIA operative stood and gazed warily about the room. "As much as it grieves me to associate with your kind, I am convinced an alliance with you is in the best interest of *living* Americans."

"Thank you, Sean." Emma smiled at him.

He scowled at his former employee. "I've contacted the army, and they've agreed to provide extra security at your facility here and in Ohio and California. They'll also provide antiaircraft missile launchers, radar equipment, and the necessary personnel to man the equipment. They'll start setting things up tomorrow."

"How did ye explain this to the army?" Connor asked.

"I told them it was a routine exercise to combat domestic terrorism," Sean replied. "Which is true, in my opinion. Those damned vampires are the worst terrorist threat our country has ever faced. If there's anything else I can do to wipe the Undead off the face of the planet, just let me know."

An uneasy silence pervaded the room.

"Well, we're verra grateful for yer help, Sean." Angus shook hands with him. "Now, perhaps ye'd like to visit yer grandchildren? They're across the hall in the nursery with Radinka."

Sean gave him a wry look. "I'd rather stay here and see what your plans are."

A flicker of annoyance shone in Angus's eyes before he motioned to a chair. "Of course. Have a seat."

Angus resumed his pacing. "Roman's busy taking care of the wounded, so he canna report on his most recent project, discovering the formula for Nightshade. Laszlo, do ye know if he's made any progress?"

The small chemist sat up. "Yes, sir. He's completed two test serums. The problem, of course, is finding a test subject. At best, the serum will paralyze a vampire. Worst case scenario . . . " He grabbed a button on his lab coat and twisted it. "It could be fatal."

Connor leaned back in his chair. "Och, luckily, we have a volunteer. He's waiting in the silver room."

"The prisoner?" Laszlo plucked at his button. "That—That doesn't seem very humane."

"He's not human," Sean Whelan hissed. "He's a monster."

Angus sighed. "I'm actually in agreement with you there, Whelan."

"Hell must be freezing over," Connor muttered, then raised his voice. "We might as well put the prisoner to good use. He doesna appear to have any more information for us."

"And I hear ye've been working on something new, Laszlo?" Angus asked.

"Ah, yes." The chemist tugged at his button. "You see, I was talking to Jack last night at the party, and he told me about a device the FBI put into a hair weave for Lara in order to track her. Unfortunately, Jack could hear it, so he had to remove it. But then the Malcontents kidnapped Lara, and he was unable to find her for days."

"Aye, we know," Angus grumbled impatiently. "Get on with it."

The button popped off onto the table. Laszlo grabbed it and stuffed it into a pocket. "I started work tonight on a tracking device that would be completely undetectable to vampires and shape shifters. Then we could all be tagged, and if anyone gets kidnapped, we could rescue them quickly."

"Sounds like a great idea, buddy." Gregori gave the small chemist a thumbs-up.

Laszlo blushed. "Well, I was kidnapped once myself, so I know how frightening it can be."

"How exactly would ye tag us?" Connor asked.

"The device would most likely be inserted beneath the skin." Laszlo started fiddling with a new button. "The incision would heal during our death-sleep, so no trace of the surgical implantation would remain."

"How far along are you?" Angus asked.

"I—I just started tonight. I need a few nights—a week perhaps."

"Right. Good luck to you." Angus motioned to the door.

Laszlo blinked. "Oh. Of course. Thank you." He scurried out the door.

"All right, we need to talk strategy," Angus said.

Phil raised a hand. "Something just occurred to me. We could take Laszlo's tracking device, implant it in Sigismund while he's in his death-sleep so he won't know it's there, then pretend to be moving him and accidentally allow him to escape—"

"The devil take it," Angus exclaimed. "He might lead us straight to Casimir."

Excited murmurs spread about the room.

Sean Whelan jumped to his feet. "If we discover where he's hiding, I could send a special task force to stake Casimir and all his followers in their death-sleep!"

The murmurs stopped. Phil winced at the appalled looks on the Vamps in the room. If Sean felt it was entirely acceptable to stake Malcontents in their death-sleep, what would stop him from doing it someday to the Vamps?

Angus cleared his throat. "We appreciate yer help in matters of security, Whelan. But when it comes to killing Casimir, we'd rather do it with honor. Face-to-face on the field of battle."

Sean snorted. "You think those monsters have any comprehension of honor?"

"Perhaps no', but we do." Angus turned to Phil. "Ye have a great idea there, lad."

"Aye, but 'twill be a week or so before Laszlo has the tracking device ready," Connor said. "We canna wait here, twiddling our thumbs, while Casimir continues his attack."

Angus nodded, and resumed his pacing. "We need to act."

"If we can't find Casimir, we let him find us," Jack said.

"A trap," Angus murmured. "Go on."

"We should set the trap far away from the remaining Romatechs," Emma suggested. "Draw his attention away from them."

Phil nodded. "Then we'll be taking control of the situation."

"Verra good," Angus said. "We just need to bait the trap. Dinna Sigismund give us a list of Vamps that Casimir wants to kill?"

Phil clenched his hands into fists underneath the table. He couldn't let them use Vanda as bait.

"I have the list here." Connor retrieved a sheet of paper from his folder. "Ian and Toni. They would do it."

"But they're still on their honeymoon," Emma protested. "Is there anyone else?"

"Zoltan and Dougal." Connor read from the list. "They were at the Romatechs that were bombed tonight. They have some burns and scrapes, but they'll recover during their death-sleep."

"Good," Angus said. "Then we have two."

"I'm on the list." Jack raised a hand. "I'll do it."

His fiancée, Lara, winced. "Then I'd better go, too. You guys will need a day guard."

"Actually, Jack, we have another assignment for you," Angus said. "I want Roman and his family to go into hiding tomorrow night. Usually Connor and Howard go with them, but I think it makes more sense for you and Lara to go."

Jack stiffened. "But I'll miss all the action. I'm the best swordsman you have. No offense, Jean-Luc."

The French Vamp waved a hand in dismissal.

"The two of you are the perfect choice," Connor explained. "Ye can guard at night, and Lara during the day. And ye'll still be alive for yer wedding."

Lara looked relieved, but Jack was grinding his teeth.

Connor gave him a sympathetic look. "I know how ye feel, lad. I've been there myself. But keeping Roman safe is verra important. If he succeeds in making Nightshade, it could be our greatest weapon in combating the Malcontents."

Jack heaved a resigned sigh. "All right. We'll do it."

Lara took his hand and squeezed it.

"Who else is on the list?" Angus asked.

"I am." Phineas raised a hand proudly. "Dr. Phang at your service."

Angus smiled. "Verra good, lad."

"I'll go, too," Robby announced. "They should have backup, someone Casimir isna expecting."

"Like a secret weapon." Angus nodded. "Good idea."

"Look, guys," Gregori spoke up. "I'm not a warrior, but I know marketing and publicity. You guys from the hit list can sit on a hill for a week, but if Casimir doesn't know about it, he'll never show up. You've got to stage and promote this deal without it looking like it's been staged and promoted."

Angus folded his arms. "What do ye suggest?"

"A believable scenario." Gregori rubbed his chin as he considered. "Zoltan and Dougal just narrowly escaped death tonight, so it would be logical for them to go out and celebrate. They would go to a Vamp club. The most popular one is Vanda's, but it was destroyed tonight. Is she all right?"

"She's fine," Phil replied quietly.

"Good." Gregori flashed him a smile, then grew serious again. "When it comes to Vamp clubs, I've been to most of them. We need a dark, seedy place, perfect for an ambush." He snapped his fingers. "I've got it. Vampire Blues in New Orleans."

"I like it," Angus said. "And the Coven Master there is a good friend. Colbert will help us out."

Gregori tapped his chin, still thinking. "We'll need publicity."

"What about Corky Courrant?" Emma suggested. "She does celebrity gossip on her show."

"Yeah, but let's face it," Gregori said. "Dougal and Phineas aren't celebrities. Corky wouldn't care what they're doing."

Phil felt a heaviness in his chest. There was a sure-fire way to get Corky's unwitting participation. He glanced at Connor, and the Scotsman was giving him an apologetic look.

Connor cleared his throat. "There was one more name on the list. Casimir wants Vanda Barkowski dead. And Corky hates her with a passion."

Phil's heart squeezed in his chest. *Damn*. He didn't see any way out of this.

Gregori winced. "There has to be another way. Vanda lost her club tonight. She's suffered enough."

"But she's a feisty lass, no?" Angus asked. "She might want revenge."

"She does have an anger problem," Gregori admitted. "But we've been trying to help her get over it."

"Her anger might be just what we need," Connor said. "We take her to the club, let it slip to Corky that she'll be there, and let Vanda throw one of her famous fits. Corky shows it on air, and when Casimir realizes Vanda is still alive, he rushes to the club, hoping to kill her. And that's when we kill him."

Gregori nodded. "That would work, but we need to make sure Vanda would be safe."

"I'll go with her," Phil said quietly.

"Can ye convince her to do it?" Connor asked.

Phil sighed. Did he have any choice?

Chapter Sixteen

*I*t was close to dawn by the time Phil returned to the cabin. Phineas teleported back to Romatech, leaving him alone with Vanda. She was folding laundry at the kitchen table. He noted the stack of clean towels and clothes, including her purple catsuit.

As soon as Phineas disappeared, she threw her arms around Phil and hugged him. "I missed you."

He held her close and nuzzled his chin against her hair. Connor had suggested he simply invite her to New Orleans for a holiday. No need to let her know what the real plan was. She might refuse to be their bait, and they were too desperate to take that chance. This was war, and a time for desperate measures.

Phil hadn't argued the point, although he'd doubted he could purposely mislead Vanda. Now that she was in his arms, he knew for certain that he couldn't.

"How bad is it?" Vanda asked.

"Bad enough." He took her hand and led her to the couch. "The Malcontents used mind control to get ahold of some military helicopters. They bombed those two Romatechs from the air."

"Oh no." Vanda sat beside him on the couch. "What's Angus going to do?"

Phil described Sean Whelan's plan to help the Vamps. Then he explained Roman's plan to make Nightshade, and Laszlo's plan to make tracking devices. Vanda nodded, listening carefully in spite of numerous yawns.

She blinked sleepily. "I'm really glad to have a safe place to hide, but I feel a little guilty that I'm not doing anything to help." She sighed. "What am I saying? I worked with the resistance in the last war, and it was scary as hell."

Phil hesitated, not sure how to proceed. "The Coven Master of New Orleans has invited us to stay with them for a few nights."

Vanda yawned. "New Orleans?"

"You're about to conk out. Let's get you to the closet." He pulled her to her feet.

She leaned against him as she walked. "I've always wanted to see New Orleans."

"Gregori told me about this club called Vampire Blues. I think you'd like it."

She gazed up at him with a confused look. "It's a vampire club? I thought I was supposed to be in hiding."

Inside the closet, he sat on the blanket and pulled her down beside him. "Vanda, I have to be honest with you. Angus is desperate to draw Casimir out. If we can kill him now, we might be able to avoid an all-out war. Think of all the lives that could be saved."

Her eyes narrowed. "What's going on?"

"They want you to go to this club so you can be seen. You're on Casimir's hit list, so there's a good chance that as soon as he knows you're there, he'll show up to finish you off. There'll be lots of guys there to protect you. Phineas, Zoltan, Dougal, Robby, and me."

"Oh God." Vanda pressed a hand to her chest. "You're using me as bait."

"We didn't want to. The guys wanted to do this without you. Some of them are on the list, too, but we realized we really need you."

"Why? What can I do?"

"If you're there, we can get Corky to announce it on her show."

"Because she hates me." With a groan, Vanda fell back onto the blanket. "Lucky me."

"I won't blame you for getting angry."

She yawned. "I'm too sleepy to get angry."

He brushed her hair back from her brow. "I'm really sorry. I didn't want you to have to do this. But if it can stop Casimir from killing more Vamps, it would be worth it. I swear I'll protect you. I won't let anyone hurt you."

"Right." Her eyes flickered shut. "First thing to-morrow night I'm kicking your ass."

Phil smiled. "It's a date." His beautiful Vanda, so clever and brave.

She took a long shuddering breath and was gone.

A spurt of panic shot through Phil. He'd just watched Vanda die. If he failed her, she could die . . . permanently.

By noon Phil was pacing the cabin like a caged beast. He went outside, but the woods didn't calm him like they usually did. His inner wolf was howling. He had finally won Vanda's love, but now he could lose her.

Connor had assured him the plan was solid. There would be at least a dozen Vamp men at the club in New Orleans. When Casimir showed up, the Vamps would attack, and Vanda would be safe.

But Phil knew plans didn't always work. He couldn't expose Vanda to this danger without a backup plan. He needed a safe place to take her. They could come back here, but what if it was near dawn in New Orleans? It would already be daylight here. Going west would be safer.

And he had a hunting cabin in Wyoming. Or at least he thought he did. He hadn't been there in over four years. The place could have burned down. There was no phone, so no answering machine would pick up and give Vanda a beacon to guide her to the right place.

It had been a present to him on his eighteenth birthday, a bribe to make him more agreeable to his father's control. That had lasted about three months. Phil had tried to break loose, and his father, in a fit of rage, had banished him for life.

He'd gone to the cabin, but after a few months, he

decided that hiding from life was not a life. He left, seeking an environment that was completely different, and he found it in New York City.

The first few years, he'd gone back to the cabin on vacation. That's when he discovered the letters his sister Brynley had left. At first she had begged him to come home. He'd left a note, telling her no, he could never go back. Then she left letters begging him to at least stay in touch. He entered her phone number on his cell phone but never called. About four years ago he stopped going to the cabin.

He punched in her number. No signal. He switched to the kitchen phone. His heart raced. He hadn't heard Brynley's voice in nine years. Would she be willing to do a favor for him? Would she even want to talk to him?

"Hello?"

His heart stuttered. Brynley's voice had acquired the deep, husky tone of a mature female werewolf. Memories flooded back. Growing up, she'd always been at his side. Werewolf cubs were usually born in pairs, so she was his twin. They'd gone through their first change together, their first hunt together. He'd shared his first kill with her. She'd licked the blood off his muzzle, and they'd howled their joy to the moon.

"Hey, I can hear you breathing, you pervert." She hung up.

He stared at the receiver. Now that went well. He started to dial the number again, then the phone rang. "Hello?"

"I star-fifty-nined you, you pervert. Now I have your number, and I'm turning you—"

"Brynley, it's me . . . Phil."

There was silence. He half expected her to hang up again.

"Philip?"

Now she was testing him. Most people assumed his full name was Philip. "No. Philupus."

She gasped. "Oh my God, it's really you!" She squealed, then burst into laughter. "Phil! Thank God! I've been hoping you would call for ages. How are you?"

"I'm . . . good. How are you?"

"Great! Now that you're back. You are back, aren't you?"

He winced. "No, I'm not."

"Phil, you *have* to come back. It's fate that you called just now. I was about to hire a P.I. to find you."

His skin chilled. "Why? What's wrong?" Surely the old man was all right. A healthy werewolf could live up to five hundred years, and his father wasn't quite two hundred.

"Everything's wrong," Brynley grumbled. "Howell is turning twenty next month. He's pressuring Dad to name him Heir Apparent."

Howell was almost twenty? Phil recalled his last memory of his younger brother and sister. Howell and Glynis had only been eleven years old when he'd left. "I didn't realize Howell had grown."

"Well, duh. We didn't stop living here when you left, you know. Howell has asked the Council for permission to become an Alpha."

"That's awfully young to be an Alpha," Phil murmured.

"Tell me about it. He's extremely ambitious, Phil. And if he manages to pull this off, the pack will be so impressed, they'll favor him over you. So you'd better get your furry ass back here to Montana and get your Alpha status. Prove you're the rightful heir."

He sighed. If the pack knew he'd managed to achieve Alpha status on his own, they'd never leave him alone. "I have a life, Bryn, and I like it."

"Are you crazy? Phil, you're a freaking prince here. You can have anything you want."

Except freedom. Or Vanda. The pack would never accept a Vamp as their queen. "Brynley, is my cabin still there in Wyoming?"

There was a pause. "Yeah."

"I may need to go there in a few days. Would you mind meeting me there?"

"I'd love to see you, Phil. I missed you."

"I missed you, too. Can you get there by tonight and make sure the place is stocked?"

"Okay. Are you on vacation? I don't even know where you work."

"I'll explain everything when I get there." He paused. This was going to sound strange, but there was no help for it. "I'll need some bottled synthetic blood at the cabin."

"You're kidding. Why?"

"I'll have a Vamp with me."

"A *vampire*? Shit, Phil. Dad will have kittens."

"Don't tell him I'll be there." Phil gritted his teeth. "I'm serious, Brynley. Don't tell him."

"I'm serious, too. Dad will want to see you. He's not mad at you anymore."

Phil groaned inwardly. Of course his father would be happy to see him. He'd welcome him back like the prodigal son. He'd dig his claws in and never let Phil go. "Brynley, we can talk about this later. For now, I need you to go to the cabin, take some bottled blood with you, and wait for my call. If I call, it will be at night."

"*If* you call?"

"Yes, and if I call, it'll be because we're in serious danger and need a safe place to hide. The Vamp will use your voice to teleport us there."

"Oh sheesh. We heard a rumor that you were working with vampires. I didn't want to believe it."

"Can you do it, Bryn?"

She sighed. "Sure. But the full moon starts tomorrow night. Dad's going to wonder why I'm missing the Hunt."

Ah yes, the Hunt. The highlight of the wolf pack's existence. Every month, on the first night of a full moon, the pack would gather for a hunt. His father's pack was so huge now, encompassing Montana, Idaho, and Wyoming, that only a handful of wolves were selected each month to hunt with the Supreme Pack Master. Other pack members and lesser pack masters would gather locally for their monthly hunt. Being invited to his father's Hunt was a huge honor, equivalent in the mortal world to being presented to royalty.

Phil had grown up seeing other werewolves bow to his father and call him Supreme Pack Master. His dad was the most powerful Alpha wolf in America. By the age of twelve Phil had realized that his father craved power more than anything. He would always want more power and more control over his subjects, including his own sons. And Phil, cursed with the same genetic makeup as his father, was not the kind of wolf who could accept being controlled.

He took a deep breath. "This is really important."

"Yeah, I figured that. Otherwise, you would have never bothered to call."

He winced at the resentment in her voice. "Thank you for helping. It'll be good to see you."

"Oh Phil." Her voice trembled with emotion. "I'd do anything for you, you know that. I'll be waiting for your call. Be careful."

"Thanks." He hung up.

A sense of foreboding settled in his gut. The cabin in Wyoming was the perfect place to hide Vanda. No one in the Vampire World knew of its existence. But the cost of using it might be way too high.

Vanda wrinkled her nose. "Smells like coffee in here."

"It was a coffee warehouse for a hundred years," Robby explained. "The coven used to live in an old wine cellar, but it was destroyed by Hurricane Katrina."

Vanda surveyed the huge rectangular room. Water stains marked the walls, showing how badly the warehouse had flooded. It was dry now, and empty except for a small sitting area that consisted of a sofa and several armchairs.

Robby, Zoltan, and Dougal had visited the New

Orleans coven before, so the warehouse was embedded in their psychic memory. They'd simply grabbed onto Vanda, Phineas, and Phil and teleported them there.

Vanda tightened the whip around her waist. "Where is everybody? I thought they were expecting us."

Phil pointed at a surveillance camera above the main entrance. "They probably know we're here."

"*Bonsoir, mes amis,*" a deep masculine voice echoed across the warehouse. "Welcome to our home."

Vanda looked around, and then up. A balcony spread across the width of the warehouse. From a door in the center, a couple emerged. The man was handsome, dressed entirely in black, and the woman by his side wore a shimmering golden evening gown the same shade as her hair.

"No stairs or ladders," Phil murmured. "A good way to stay safe."

More Vamps filed from the upstairs room. Elegantly dressed, they posed along the length of the balcony. Vanda realized the coven must actually live in the room on the second floor. With no access other than levitation, it kept them safe from mortal intruders.

The man in black stepped off the balcony and floated down, his black coat fluttering around him till he landed gracefully on the ground floor. He bowed. "I am Colbert GrandPied, at your service."

"Vanda Barkowski." She extended a hand.

He leaned over to kiss it. "*Enchanté.*"

As Colbert greeted the rest of the Vamps and Phil, Vanda watched more well-dressed Vamps float down from the balcony.

"I am Giselle." The blonde, dressed in gold, kissed Vanda's cheeks. "We are honored to have you here."

Honored? Vanda didn't see much honor in being bait. And these elegant Vamps looked dressed for the opera rather than a battle with Casimir. "Ah, you do realize there could be a battle?"

Giselle cocked her head. "It was my understanding that the battle will occur at the Vampire Blues. That is the plan, *non*?"

Vanda sighed. "Yes, but—"

"Do not worry, *chérie*." Giselle patted her on the shoulder. "Our best swordsmen will accompany you to the club. Many of them lost loved ones in the Great Vampire War of 1710. They are eager to have their revenge."

"Great." Vanda smiled wryly. "Then everybody's happy." She glanced at Phil. He'd been frowning all night, his gaze darting everywhere as if he expected danger at every turn.

Colbert slipped an arm around Giselle's slim waist. "And where are Scarlett and Tootsie? I thought they'd be the first ones down."

"They were still fiddling with their makeup in the bathroom, the last I saw them." Giselle smiled at Vanda. "They're your biggest fans."

"Fans?" Vanda blinked when a figure ran from the upstairs room onto the balcony. "Wow." The silver dress was completely covered with sequins and

sparkled like a disco ball. It took her eyes a second to adjust.

"That's Scarlett," Colbert whispered.

Vanda's mouth fell open. Scarlett's figure filled out the dress quite well . . . for a man.

"Hot damn," Phineas muttered.

Scarlett looked down at Vanda and gasped. "Oh my God! She's here! Tootsie, hurry. She's here!" She, or he, flapped a hand in front of his face. "Oh my God, I can't breathe."

"Where is she?" Another figure dashed onto the balcony. Hot pink bell-bottoms and a halter top, completely covered with sequins. He wore a hot pink wig to match, topped with a sparkly pink pillbox hat.

"Et voilà." Colbert gestured to the balcony. "Tootsie."

Tootsie pressed a hand to his chest while he stared at Vanda. "It's really her! Oh my God, she's wearing the purple catsuit. And the purple hair." He reached out to grasp Scarlett's hand. "This is so exciting!"

Together the two men leaped off the balcony and landed on the ground floor.

Scarlett wobbled slightly in his six-inch red stilettos, then scurried toward Vanda. "I'm so glad to meet you. I'm your biggest fan!"

"No, I'm your biggest fan." Tootsie squeezed in front. "I'm a full size bigger than Scarlett." He giggled.

"Well, you wouldn't be if you laid off the Chocolood," Scarlett sneered. "Oh, Vanda—may I call you Vanda, please?"

"I suppose. It is my name."

Scarlett giggled. "You're so clever. And brave! We just loved the way you led that riot outside DVN when Ian was in trouble."

"You saw that?" Vanda recalled the event last December. Gregori had brought a camera out to the parking lot, where she'd gathered a group of women to support Ian. But at the time, she'd been a lot more worried about Ian's safety than the possibility of appearing on television.

"We just adore Ian," Tootsie explained. "Such a sweet boy."

"And such a sweet kilt," Scarlett added, but Tootsie slapped his wrist.

"Behave. And we just love the way you tried to help Ian find his true love." Tootsie pressed a hand to his mouth. "It was so romantic. I think I'm going to cry."

"Don't," Scarlett fussed. "It'll make your mascara run. And Vanda . . . " He grabbed her hand. "We just loved the way you attacked Corky Courrant. Don't we, everyone?"

Murmurs of agreement spread through the crowd.

"We have it all on tape," Tootsie explained. "That hideous part when Corky was insulting Ian, and then that lovely part when you went flying across the table to strangle the bitch."

"We've watched it a hundred times!" Scarlett exclaimed.

"Great," Vanda muttered. "It was one of my finer moments."

"We just adore you," Tootsie insisted. "And we love that terrible temper of yours."

"Oh yes." Scarlett shuddered. "It's so raw and fierce."

"Do you—" Tootsie pressed a hand to his hot pink lips. "Oh, I hate to be an imposition, but do you possibly think you could demonstrate one of those glorious fits of rage for us?"

"Oh yes, please." Scarlett clasped his hands together. "It would be such an honor to see you royally pissed!"

Vanda gritted her teeth. "I'm working on it as we speak."

"All right," Robby interrupted. "Enough gossiping. We need to proceed with the plan."

"Oh my." Tootsie looked Robby over. "Another nice kilt."

Robby arched a brow. "If ye come to the Vampire Blues with us, ye must be prepared to fight for yer lives."

Scarlett and Tootsie both gasped.

"Y'all have a fabulous time." Scarlett stepped back, waving good-bye.

"And don't let anything happen to Vanda," Tootsie added.

"We won't," Phil grumbled.

"This way." Colbert and six of his men strode toward the warehouse entrance.

Outside, they piled into two black limousines. Time to set the trap and see if Casimir would take the bait.

Chapter Seventeen

*P*hil ushered Vanda to a table in the center of the club. Vampire Blues obviously catered to a different sort of clientele than her club had. No bright lights or fast, pounding music. No screaming, bouncing girls demanding the next male dancer.

Vampire Blues was a dark, gloomy place that reeked of spilled Blissky. Vampire waitresses, dressed in black satin shorts and camisole tops, glided around the scarred tables. Above the bar, a television was tuned to the Digital Vampire Network. Stone Cauffyn was delivering *The Nightly News*, but the mute button had been turned on.

In a corner, next to the bar, a small jazz band was playing a slow, sad melody, and a couple on the dance floor swayed to the music.

Vanda sat with a huff. "This place is depressing."

"You're supposed to be depressed." Phil sat next to her. "You just lost your club."

"Don't remind me." She looked over her shoulder. "Where did the guys go? They're supposed to protect me."

"They will." Phil noticed how well Colbert and his friends blended into the dark booths at the back of the club. Robby MacKay, with his bright blue and green kilt, was more noticeable. He was sitting at a table, facing them, to keep the broadsword on his back from being seen.

"The first part of the plan is for you to get on Corky's show," Phil explained. "But we don't want your little army to appear on the show."

"Right," Vanda muttered. "Not only am I bait, but I have to look like totally helpless, vulnerable bait."

"Exactly." Phil motioned to a waitress. "If Casimir sees how well-protected you are, he'll know it's a trap. But if he thinks you're unprotected, he's more likely to attack with just a few men."

Vanda sighed. "Okay. Let's get on with this."

The waitress stopped by their table and looked Phil over. With a smile, she leaned over to show off her cleavage. "How can I serve you?"

"You can put on some clothes," Vanda grumbled.

The waitress straightened and shot her an annoyed look.

"I'll have a beer," Phil said. "And my fiancée will have a Blissky."

The waitress turned with a huff and stalked away.

Vanda stared at Phil. "What was that?"

"I know you don't drink liquor much, but you need to appear drunk," he explained.

"I meant the *fiancée* part. Did I miss a conversation somewhere?"

He smiled. "I thought it might keep the waitress from coming on to me. My apologies for using you in such a manner."

Her mouth twitched. "Honey, you can use me in any manner you like." She rubbed a booted foot along his leg.

He motioned with his head toward the other Vamps.

She rolled her eyes. "This forbidden crap is for the birds. I should be able to jump my guard if I want to." She smiled. "And I do want to."

He smiled back. "I want to, too. But we can't allow ourselves to get distracted right now."

A flash of light drew Phil's attention. More flashes. Three Japanese vampires were taking photos of the waitress. She posed for them, smiling.

Tourists, he figured. They each had a digital camera hanging around their necks. They sat at a table close by.

The waitress brought Phil and Vanda their drinks, then turned to the Japanese. "What would you like?"

"We want Brissky! I am Kyo, and I pay."

The waitress nodded. "Three Blisskys, coming up." As she walked toward the bar, Kyo took a picture of her backside.

"Kyo!" One of his friends laughed. "You are too bad."

Vanda sipped her Blissky and grimaced. "*Ugh.*"

"Sorry," Phil murmured. "You're supposed to look like you're drowning your sorrows."

Phineas approached them, talking on his cell phone. "Yeah. Okay, bro. Way to go." He snapped his phone shut and sat at the table with them. "That was Gregori. He's at DVN, pretending to be arranging a new commercial for Vampire Fusion Cuisine, and he let it drop a few times that Vanda was here wallowing in self-pity."

Vanda scoffed. "I don't wallow."

"It's all part of the act, sweetness," Phineas whispered. "Any second now the news will reach Corky."

"And she'll want to show me wallowing on her show," Vanda grumbled. She took another sip of Blissky and made a face.

Phineas frowned. "Sweetness, you don't look very drunk."

"I'm not. And if you call me 'sweetness' one more time, I'll cram my whip down your throat."

Phineas raised his hands in surrender. "Dudette, I'm just saying that I have some experience in matters of extreme intoxication. First of all, you need to look like you're enjoying that Blissky. Let me show you." He grabbed her glass and guzzled down half the contents.

He slammed the glass down and thumped the table. "Damn, that's good. Now, secondly, you need to look intoxicated. Slouch over in your chair and leave your mouth hanging open."

Vanda arched a brow at him.

Phil noticed the bartender answering the phone. A short bald man appeared, teleporting in with a small camera. Corky's spy, the same guy Phil had spotted in her office a few nights ago. The man scurried off to a nearby booth.

"Showtime," Phil whispered. "Corky's spy is here."

"Where?" Vanda turned her head.

"Don't look," Phil growled.

She gazed at him, her eyes wide with worry. "What now?"

"You do your anger thing," Phineas said. When Vanda did nothing, he added, *"Sweetness."*

She frowned at him.

"I bet you just hated watching your club burn to the ground," Phineas continued. "I bet it made you really mad."

She took a sip of Blissky.

Phineas leaned closer. "I bet it filled you with uncontrollable rage."

She gave him a bland look. "I know what you're doing."

Phineas huffed. "Do something, Phil. Insult her. Make her mad."

Phil shrugged. "Nothing comes to mind. I think she's . . . perfect."

She gave Phil an angelic smile. "Thank you."

"Oh come on." Phineas glared at them. "Can't you two have a lovers' quarrel? Is the camera on us?"

Phil glanced at the booth where the short bald man was sitting. His camera was aimed right at them. "Yes, it is."

Phineas smirked at Vanda. "You know, you really

shouldn't wear those catsuits. The camera adds ten pounds."

She gave him an annoyed look. "You guys talked me into being a sitting duck, but I didn't agree to be a trained monkey."

"Dammit, woman," Phineas snarled. "Everyone knows you're crazy. Start acting like it!"

Vanda shrugged. "Sticks and stones."

Phineas glowered at Phil. "What kind of anger management sponsor are you?"

"A successful one, apparently."

"Shit," Phineas muttered. He glanced at the Japanese vampire tourists and his eyes lit up. He reached under the table, then heaved it at the Japanese Vamps.

The table crashed on top of the tourists, sloshing them with spilled Blissky and beer. They jumped up, hollering in shock and outrage.

Phineas leaped to his feet, giving Vanda an appalled look. "Vanda! Why'd you do it?"

"What?" She stood.

Phineas slapped a hand against his brow. "You can't attack these people just because you hate Naruto!"

"Who?" Vanda asked.

"She hate Naruto?" The tourist named Kyo glared at Vanda, his face turning red.

"You ruined my shirt!" A second tourist wiped at the Blissky stains on his red silk shirt. He glowered at Vanda. "You evil woman."

"Hey, she did you a favor," Phineas yelled. "That shirt belongs on a woman."

The tourist gasped.

"She has insulted your honor, Yoshi," Kyo declared. "And she insults Naruto's honor."

"Hai!" All three Japanese vampires assumed attack poses.

"What the hell?" Vanda jumped back and quickly untied the whip from around her waist.

Phil glanced at Corky's cameraman. He was still recording. They would have to fight.

The Japanese charged with an impressive series of kicks and spins. Yoshi kicked at Vanda, but she managed to dodge it. She snapped her whip at him, and he backed up.

Kyo came after Phil, but he'd had enough martial arts training to block all the kicks and punches. He quickly discovered that a kick aimed at Kyo's expensive digital camera would always make the tourist jump back.

Still, he knew they needed to put on a show for Corky. Phil slung a chair at Kyo, purposely missing him and shattering the chair on top of a table. Customers screamed and ran from the building. Others stayed and laid bets.

Finally, the cameraman vanished. Phil assumed he had a deadline to keep in order to get the video on Corky's show. *Live with the Undead* was due to start in fifteen minutes.

"All right!" Phil shouted. "The show's over."

Phineas and Vanda stopped fighting. The Japanese Vamps stood there, panting, with confused looks on their faces.

"Congratulations!" Phineas grinned at them. "You guys just got punked. You'll be on a TV show."

"What?" Kyo glanced at the television. *The Nightly News* was still on. "We American movie stars now?"

"Television stars," Phineas corrected him. "You're going to be famous. And dudes, we love Naruto."

"Who's Naruto?" Vanda whispered.

"Let me buy you some drinks," Phil offered.

Ten minutes later Phil, Vanda, and Phineas were sharing a table with their new friends: Kyo, Yoshi, and Yuki. Robby, Zoltan, and Dougal came over to introduce themselves and congratulate them on their fine martial arts skills. Colbert and his men introduced themselves and gave the tourists more compliments on their fighting. Colbert paid the club manager for the damages, then bought everyone a round of Blisskys.

When Corky Courrant's show came on, the bartender turned up the volume. The jazz band and all the customers settled down to watch the show, *Live with the Undead*.

"Greeting, dear viewers." Corky smiled grimly at the camera. "Tonight we have shocking news. As you know, last night we showed you the utter destruction of Vanda Barkowski's notorious nightclub here in New York City."

Half the screen displayed the burned and charred remains of Vanda's club.

Phil patted her leg in sympathy underneath the table.

"It's no secret that I was celebrating last night while Vanda's club was burning," Corky continued. "But I must confess that I had nothing to do with it. It was simply a matter of divine justice. Now, we had thought Vanda had died a horrible death in the explosion. Indeed, everyone hoped and prayed that she was dead, but tonight, in late-breaking news, we can confirm that Vanda Barkowski is still alive!"

A picture of Vanda flashed on the screen.

"Ah, Vanda." The Japanese bowed to her. "You are famous celebrity."

She groaned and shook her head.

"You see, dear friends," Corky continued, "I have exclusive footage that proves Vanda is still alive. And not only is she still breathing, but she's engaging once again in disgusting and violent behavior! Just moments ago my operative filmed this scene at the Vampire Blues club in New Orleans. Vanda was there, so drunk and disorderly that she attacked three unsuspecting tourists from Japan!"

The video played. The Japanese cheered.

"We're famous!" Yuki shouted.

"Brisskys for everyone!" Kyo yelled.

Phil stood. "Guys, I hate to break up the party, but we need you to leave. We're expecting trouble any minute now."

"Trouble?" Kyo asked. "What kind of trouble?"

Yuki lifted his chin. "We do not run from trouble."

"Dudes, the Malcontents are coming," Phineas explained. "They want to kill Vanda."

Kyo jumped to his feet. "No one kills Vanda."

"We will fight!" Yoshi punched the air with his fist.

"They'll have swords," Phil warned their new friends.

"We not afraid," Yuki declared. "We fight."

Colbert and the other Vamps gathered around the

table, their swords drawn and ready. The remaining customers ran from the building.

Two hours later they were still waiting.

Vanda sighed. "I was scared to death a few hours ago, and now I just want to get it over with."

"What's taking them so long?" Phineas asked.

Phil shook his head. "I don't know. Maybe they smelled a trap."

"Or they were busy doing something else." Robby called Angus, then reported that no bombings had occurred. The Malcontents appeared to be taking the night off.

"They're up to something," Zoltan muttered.

But three hours later it looked like they weren't.

Phil had started drinking coffee to try to stay alert.

"Maybe they missed Corky's show," Phineas suggested.

"Some Malcontent somewhere must have seen it," Robby said. "Perhaps it's a problem of getting the news to Casimir. He may be hiding so well, some of his own people doona know where he is."

"That could be it," Colbert agreed. "I say we come back here tomorrow night. Casimir could still come, looking for Vanda."

The Japanese stood and bowed. "Then we will come back tomorrow to fight."

They headed for the door, but Phil stopped them on the way. "Are you serious about helping Vanda?"

"Of course," Kyo said. "She famous American celebrity."

Phil whipped out his cell phone and added Kyo's

cell phone number to his directory. "Thank you. If I ever need your help, I'll call."

"It would be an honor." Kyo bowed and left with his friends.

Vanda sat on her assigned cot in the upstairs section of the coffee warehouse where the New Orleans coven lived. She unwound her whip and set it on the cot while Scarlett and Tootsie perched on a neighboring cot, entertaining her with stories of their crazy antics.

She glanced across the dormitory at Phil, who lay sleeping on his cot. The poor guy was so exhausted, he was sleeping with all the noisy Vamps chattering around him.

But not all the Vamps were talking. Vanda had spotted a few private rooms behind the kitchen. Colbert and Giselle had retired to their own room. Vanda had been tempted to ask for a private room for her and Phil, but there were too many MacKay S & I employees here. She couldn't let them know she was indulging in a forbidden affair with her assigned guard.

Scarlett stood. "I'm going to have a warm cup of Chocolood before bed. Would you like some, Vanda?"

"Yes, thank you." Vanda leaned over to unzip her boots.

"*Intruder!*" a man by the surveillance monitors shouted. "Intruder alert!"

In seconds the Vamp men had grabbed their swords and were dashing out the door. Vanda hurried to the monitors to see what was happening. A dozen men, armed with swords, had arrived in the huge room on the ground floor.

Colbert ran into the dormitory, barefoot, his shirt unbuttoned, but with a sword in one hand. Giselle followed him, wrapped in a bathrobe. The coven women gathered around her.

"Oh my God!" Scarlett grabbed Tootsie. "What do we do?"

Colbert glanced at the two men as he hurried out the door. "Guard the women!"

Tootsie gasped. "I thought we *were* the women."

Phil sat up and rubbed the sleep from his eyes. "What's going on?" He grabbed his shoes and quickly put them on.

Vanda ran to him. "The Malcontents are here."

"Shit." He strapped on a shoulder holster and inserted his handgun. "Stay here." He grabbed a sword from the stash by the surveillance monitors, then he sprinted for the door.

"Phil!" Vanda ran after him. The damn balcony was about three stories up. She'd had to levitate him up earlier. "Wait." She reached the balcony just in time to see him leap. She squealed. Good God, he'd kill himself.

She peered over the edge and gasped. He'd landed nimbly and was already challenging a Malcontent with his sword. How on earth had he managed that jump?

She flinched when a sword thrust narrowly missed him. Her heart lurched up her throat. How on earth could he possibly survive in a battle against a vampire? Good God, Hugo was right. Phil moved incredibly fast.

Her blood chilled as she surveyed the scene. Vamp fighting vampire. Swords clashing. Shouts of victory and screams of defeat. Men howling in agony before crumbling into piles of dust.

"Revenge!" someone yelled over the clash of swords.

She spotted the shouting man. He was completely surrounded by armed Malcontents. They fought furiously around him while he remained safely co-cooned. He held a sword in one hand, his other arm cradled against his chest at a strange angle.

"Casimir," she whispered.

A scream jolted her. One of Colbert's men had been skewered. He turned to dust.

Hands grabbed Vanda's shoulders and she jumped.

"Come inside." Giselle pulled her back from the edge of the balcony. "Don't let them see you."

"But I have to know . . . " Vanda searched the flail-ing arms and swinging swords, looking for Phil. He was still all right. He had a different opponent now. He must have killed the first one.

She spotted a Malcontent lurking in a dark corner with a cell phone to his ear. A dozen more Malcon-tents appeared around him. "Look at that!"

Giselle gasped. "We'll be outnumbered!"

"We need to call for backup." Vanda grabbed Gi-selle's arm. "Get me a phone. We'll call Angus."

"It's already daylight on the East Coast." Giselle's eyes filled with tears. "They can't come."

Damn. That was probably why the Malcontents

had waited so long before attacking. Vanda grimaced when another group of Malcontents teleported in. Good God, there had to be twenty of them.

Casimir barked with laughter. "Revenge for the Massacre at DVN!"

Giselle burst into tears. "God help us. This *is* a massacre."

Vanda stood frozen on the balcony, afraid to watch, afraid not to watch. Her heart raced, pounding in her ears. If only there was something she could do. But she'd never trained with a sword. It would be suicidal to jump down into the melee.

She spotted Robby and Phil fighting their way through the newly arrived batch of Malcontents. Robby skewered the guy with the cell phone. The Malcontent turned to dust, his phone falling to the floor. Phil stomped on it.

A flash of brown hair caught Vanda's attention. One of the newly arrived Malcontents spun about to ward off an attack. A long brown ponytail whipped through the air. A woman.

Vanda stepped closer to the edge of the balcony. There was something about the way the woman moved. She turned again, and Vanda's heart lurched.

Marta.

As if Vanda's thoughts could be heard, Marta glanced up at the balcony. Her eyes narrowed.

Vanda stumbled back. "No, no."

"Are you all right?" Giselle dragged her into the dormitory.

Scarlett hovered just inside the door. "You look like you've seen a ghost."

"I have." Vanda stumbled to her cot. Her heart ached in her chest. Marta. Fighting for the Malcontents.

Tootsie screamed.

Vanda spun around. A Malcontent had entered the room.

Giselle ran to the huddle of whimpering women at the back of the room.

The Malcontent spotted Vanda and raised his sword. She grabbed her whip off the cot.

With a shout, he charged. She leaped over a cot and snapped her whip at him.

Scarlett threw a pillow at him, then squealed when the Malcontent turned and stalked toward him. Scarlett pressed against the wall, trembling.

Tootsie teleported, landed right behind the Malcontent, and clonked him on the head with a Blissky bottle. The Malcontent tumbled onto the floor.

Scarlett leaped into Tootsie's arms. "You saved me!"

Giselle and the women screamed. Two more Malcontents had entered the room.

Colbert charged after them, killed one and engaged the other in battle. "We called a retreat!" he shouted. "Teleport to our country place now!"

The women began teleporting away.

"God be with you." Tootsie hugged Vanda, then he and Scarlett teleported away.

With a quick thrust through the heart, Colbert turned the second Malcontent to dust. He spotted the unconscious Malcontent on the floor and finished him off, too.

"Colbert!" Giselle ran into his arms.

He hugged her, then extended a hand to Vanda. "You should come with us."

"No!" Phil sprinted into the room.

Vanda grimaced at the bloodstains on his shirt. But thank God he was alive. But how he'd managed to get to the second floor on his own, she couldn't imagine.

He grabbed his cell phone he'd left on his cot. "Go ahead, Colbert. Leave while you can. We're leaving, too."

"God be with you." Colbert teleported away, taking Giselle with him.

Phil opened his phone and punched a number. "We've got to go, Vanda."

"But where?" she cried. "We can't go east."

He put the phone to his ear. "Brynley? Keep talking. We'll be right there." He wrapped an arm around Vanda and pressed the phone to her ear. "Trust me."

Vanda heard a strange woman's voice on the phone. Three Malcontents charged into the room. She gasped, and everything went black.

Chapter Eighteen

*V*anda stumbled. Her concentration was off, making for a messy landing.

Phil quickly regained his balance and steadied her. "Are you all right?" He snapped his phone shut and pocketed it.

"I—" She blinked. For a second she thought they were back in Howard's hunting cabin in the Adirondacks. But that couldn't be right. It was daylight in New York.

"Phil!" A young woman ran toward him, smiling.

He turned and grinned. "Brynley!"

She halted with a gasp. "You're bleeding. You've been injured."

He glanced down at his ripped and bloody polo shirt. "Just a few cuts. No big deal."

"It *is* a big deal." The woman cast a suspicious glance at Vanda, then grabbed Phil's arm and dragged him away. "Let me patch you up. Dear Lord, look at you." She touched his cheek. "You've gotten so handsome."

Vanda's hand curled tighter around the handle of her whip. Who the hell was this woman? With her long, gleaming hair and skintight jeans and tank top, she was bound to be a bitch. How come Phil let her touch him like that?

Phil took her hand and squeezed it. "I missed you."

Vanda cleared her throat.

He glanced at her. "Brynley, this is Vanda."

She noticed this time he didn't call her his fiancée. "How do you do?" *Bitch.* She glared at the beautiful *Brynley.* What kind of stupid-ass name was that anyway?

Brynley glowered back. "So this is the vampire you mentioned? Somehow, I thought it would be male."

Vanda's temper flared. "Who are you calling an 'it'?"

"Brynley," Phil said quietly, "Vanda and her friends are very good friends of mine."

"Friends?" She motioned at his bloody shirt. "What kind of terrible mess have these 'friends' dragged you into?"

"Phil's more than a friend." Vanda stepped toward the bitch. "He's my anger management sponsor. He can tell you how dangerous I get when I'm royally pissed!"

"Oh yeah?" Brynley stepped forward.

"Enough." Phil put out a hand to stop her. "Vanda, this is my sister. So cut the crap."

Vanda's mouth fell open. His sister? She looked

past the gorgeous hair and perfect skin and noticed the pale blue eyes, just like Phil's. "I didn't know you have a sister."

"*What?*" Brynley stared at Phil. "You never told your friends about me? I'm your twin, dammit!"

"*Twin?*" Vanda gazed at her, then at Phil. "You hypocrite! Always hounding me to tell you about my past, and you don't even tell me you have a twin?"

Phil shifted his weight and glanced back and forth between the two women. "I—I'm bleeding, you know. I thought you might want to patch me up?"

Brynley crossed her arms. "Patch yourself up."

"Fine." Phil stalked into the kitchen area.

Vanda suppressed a laugh. "Good for you."

Brynley's mouth twitched. "Thanks."

Vanda's smile quickly faded when Phil removed his shirt. Cuts and slashes marked his chest and torso. "Oh no." She ran toward him.

"Damn, Phil." Brynley rushed to the kitchen sink and worked the old-fashioned pump. "Clean towels in the drawer there." She motioned with her head.

Vanda set her whip on the counter, then took a towel from a drawer and handed another one to Brynley. Water spewed from the pump, and she dampened her towel.

Phil winced as she cleaned the blood off his chest.

"How did this happen?" Brynley dabbed at a bad slice on the side of his torso.

He lifted his arm to look at the wound. "A war has started between the Vamps and the Malcontents, or you could say the good vampires and the bad ones."

Brynley snorted. "Since when are there *good* vampires?" She glanced at Vanda. "No offense."

Vanda ignored her. She was too upset at seeing Phil's beautiful skin all cut up. Too upset that her own sister could have caused one of the wounds. "Phil, you can't do this again. Vampires are too fast and strong for mortals like you. It's a wonder they didn't kill you."

"Mortals?" Brynley narrowed her eyes.

"Are there any bandages here?" Phil asked. "I need to get back to business."

"What business?" Brynley opened a cabinet and pulled out a box of Band-Aids in assorted sizes. She handed a few to Vanda.

"Urgent business." Phil pulled the cell phone from his pocket. "Like I said, we're at war."

"The vampires are at war," Brynley corrected him. "It has nothing to do with you."

Vanda stiffened. "Phil is a very important member of our society. We couldn't manage without him." She stuck a Band-Aid over one of his cuts.

"Enough." He stepped back and punched a number on his phone.

"But you still have cuts," Vanda protested. "And that long one on your side might need stitches."

"It's nothing." His eyes glistened with moisture. "This is nothing. I saw a lot worse."

Vanda's skin chilled. Had one of their friends died? "What? Who?"

"Dougal." Phil grimaced. "His hand was cut off."

Vanda gasped. "But—But they can sew it back on, right? It'll heal during his death-sleep."

Phil shook his head. "It was completely sliced off. It turned to dust."

Vanda doubled over as nausea slammed into her stomach.

Brynley touched her shoulder. "I'm sorry. He's a good friend?"

Vanda took deep breaths. "I've known him a long time." He'd been a guard at Roman's townhouse for over thirty years, always shy and quiet, except when he was playing the bagpipes. Now, he'd never be able to play again.

"Howard?" Phil spoke into his phone. "Have you heard what happened?"

Phil launched into a description of the events in New Orleans. Vanda could tell his sister was listening carefully, for she gasped at all the appropriate moments.

For the first time, Vanda had a chance to check out the cabin. It consisted of log walls and a stone fireplace like Howard's cabin, but it was smaller and more primitive.

The water over the kitchen sink had to be pumped. There was no refrigerator, just a big ice chest. As far as she could tell, there was no electricity at all. A fire and a few oil lamps illuminated the room. A tank of propane gas was hooked up to a stovetop. No curtains at the windows. No rugs on the wide-planked wooden floor. No staircase. A wooden ladder led to the loft.

"Where are we?" she asked quietly.

"Wyoming," Brynley answered. "This is Phil's cabin."

"I didn't know he had a cabin."

"Yeah. Well, there's a lot you don't know about him." She frowned at Phil. "But I guess the same goes for me. I had no idea he was involved with vampires."

"He's a day guard," Vanda explained. "We're vulnerable during the day when we're in our death-sleep."

Brynley regarded her curiously. "And who are you, exactly?"

Vanda shrugged. "No one special."

"And yet Phil seems to be risking his life to keep you safe. Are you some kind of vampire . . . princess?"

Vanda scoffed. "Far from it."

Brynley picked up the whip Vanda had set on the counter. "You're fighting in the war."

"Only because I have to. The Malcontents want to wipe us off the planet."

Brynley handed her the whip. "Why? What did you do?"

"We invented synthetic blood so we wouldn't have to bite mortals. We took jobs so we wouldn't have to steal money from mortals." Vanda wrapped the whip around her waist and tied it off. "We just want to blend in and pretend we're normal. I guess that sounds strange."

Brynley frowned. "No, not really." She wandered toward the ice chest. "I brought some bottled blood. Would you like one?"

"Yes." Vanda heaved a sigh of relief. "Thank you." She accepted a bottle and unscrewed the top.

It would be cold, but a whole lot better than biting her hosts.

"All right, Howard." Phil finished relating the news. "Call me if you hear anything." He closed his phone and glanced around the cabin. "The place looks good. Have you been keeping it up, Bryn?"

"Yeah." His sister settled in an old worn armchair and propped her cowboy boots on the coffee table. "I've been coming here every now and then."

"Thanks. I owe you." He began to pace up and down the room.

Vanda sat on the old couch and sipped from her bottle. Phil's sister wasn't so bad after all. She obviously didn't like vampires, but she was loyal to her brother. Vanda couldn't claim any loyalty from her sister Marta.

Damn. She rubbed her brow. How could her sister do this?

"I wonder where they went," Phil muttered. "I wonder how Dougal is doing."

Vanda shuddered. "He must be in shock. And a lot of pain. You don't know where they teleported to?"

Phil shook his head. "It's not like they could tell me when the enemy was all around us."

"Oh, right." Vanda sipped more blood from her bottle. It had been close to dawn in New Orleans, but here in Wyoming she'd acquired more time of darkness. "I heard Colbert tell his coven members to go to their country place."

"He's the guy in New Orleans?" Brynley asked.

She'd obviously learned quite a bit from listening to Phil's conversation with Howard.

"He's the Coven Master of New Orleans," Vanda explained.

"And who's your Coven Master?" Brynley asked.

"Roman Draganesti. He's head of the entire East Coast region. And he's the brilliant scientist who invented synthetic blood." Vanda lifted her bottle.

Brynley looked impressed. "That synthetic stuff saves thousands of lives every year."

"They must have gone to Jean-Luc's." Phil pressed a button on his cell phone.

"Who's Jean-Luc?" Brynley asked Vanda.

"Jean-Luc Echarpe. Famous fashion designer."

"Oh, I've seen his stuff." Brynley nodded. "Really nice, but really pricey. Isn't he in Paris?"

"Texas." Vanda sipped more blood. "He's hiding out so the media doesn't figure out he's a Vamp."

Brynley's eyes widened. "Sheesh."

"Billy?" Phil spoke on the phone. "Did the guys come there?" He listened as he paced. "Great. And Dougal, is he going to be all right?" He glanced at Vanda. "They're okay. The sun just rose there."

Vanda nodded. If Dougal was in his death-sleep, he would no longer be in pain. And the wound would heal.

Phil stopped in his tracks. His face paled.

Vanda sat up. She'd never seen him look so stunned. A frisson of fear prickled her skin with goose bumps.

"Are you sure?" Phil whispered.

Vanda's hand trembled as she set the bottle on the coffee table. Brynley set her boots on the floor and sat up.

"Maybe he went somewhere else," Phil said. "Did you check?"

Vanda stood. "What is it?"

Phil swallowed audibly. "I understand. I—I'll get back to you." He closed his phone slowly. He looked at Vanda, his eyes glimmering with pain.

"What is it?" She rushed toward him.

"Robby . . . he's missing."

Vanda halted as if she'd been knocked in the chest. "He—He teleported somewhere else."

"No, they checked. Zoltan and Phineas called all the major covens in the West. No one's seen him. And besides, he's Jean-Luc's personal guard. He lives there in Texas. He would have gone there."

Bile rose in Vanda's throat. "You think he's dead?"

Phil shook his head. "Everyone remembers seeing him alive. We . . . we think he was captured."

Vanda pressed a hand to her mouth. The cold blood she'd just imbibed churned in her stomach. Oh God, no. The Malcontents would torture him.

"I'm sure Casimir considers him a great catch," Phil continued. "He's the only living relative of Angus MacKay, the general of the Vamp army."

Vanda's eyes filled with tears. She wanted to hit something. "I hate war! I hate this! I never wanted to go through this again."

Phil pulled her into his arms and held her tight. "It'll be all right."

"No, it won't." She wrapped her arms around his neck.

"It was almost daylight there. They can't . . . hurt Robby if they're in their death-sleep." He kissed Vanda's brow. "We have to keep faith."

She nodded. "What can we do?"

Phil stepped back to call another number on his phone. "We'll think of something."

He paced away, talking into the phone. "Howard, it looks like Robby MacKay has been taken prisoner."

Vanda winced. She could hear Howard's booming voice raised in anger.

"Howard, listen up," Phil demanded. "How far along is Laszlo on that tracking device? . . . That's not good enough. Call Sean Whelan. Get some military experts over there and make them finish it. Then get it inserted in the prisoner while he's in his death-sleep."

There was a pause while Phil listened. "Okay, I realize the army can't tell if the device can be heard by vampires. Listen to it yourself. If you're not sure, use the damned Stay-Awake drug on a Vamp and test it on him. We have got to get it ready today. Then, as soon as the sun sets, you let the prisoner escape. Hopefully, he'll teleport straight to Casimir and that will lead us to Robby. Keep me apprised."

He snapped his phone shut and looked at Vanda. "It's a long shot, but I think it's our best chance at finding him."

She nodded. She'd never realized till now what a born leader Phil was. He was incredible. Strong and decisive, loyal and brave. And so beautiful, even with his torso covered with cuts. "I love you so much."

His blue eyes softened. "I love you, too."

"Oh my God," Brynley whispered.

An hour later Vanda scowled at the old horsehair blanket on the cellar floor. Things were already bad enough with Robby captured, Dougal wounded, and her sister Marta fighting with the enemy. But now Phil's sister was treating her like she'd suddenly grown two heads.

Brynley had lashed out at Phil, but he'd simply told her to hush. He would discuss it with her later.

Brynley had ignored that and blurted, "How can you possibly love her?"

"I do," Phil had replied with a stern look. "And we will not discuss it now."

Brynley had sat in her armchair, pouting, while Phil took Vanda down to the cellar to make sure it was safe for her death-sleep. He boarded up the one small window. Then he'd found the horsehair blanket and spread it on the floor.

"She doesn't like me," Vanda whispered.

"She's not marrying you. I am."

Vanda stared at him, agape.

"Oh, sorry." His mouth twitched. "Guess I forgot to ask. Will this be okay?" He motioned to the blanket.

She nodded. Phil seriously wanted to marry her? Why would a mortal want to marry a vampire? Sure, some of the Vamp guys were marrying mortal women, but the women would probably change over eventually, and for now they could give the guys children. She couldn't give Phil anything. She wasn't rich and charming like the Vamp guys. She was a neurotic, barren Vamp with purple hair and a nasty temper.

She felt the first tug of sleepiness as the sun neared the horizon. "I'm tired."

"Good night, then." He kissed her cheek. "I'll check on you every now and then."

She hugged him tight. "I'm not going anywhere."

"I love you, Vanda."

How can you possibly love her? His sister's words echoed in Vanda's mind. "Good night."

She watched him climb the ladder and step through the trapdoor onto the cabin's ground floor. He hauled the ladder up, then lowered the trapdoor shut. The cellar turned pitch-black.

In a moment Vanda's eyes adjusted and she scowled at the scratchy blanket. If Phil married her, they could never share a bed like a real couple. Unless he didn't mind sleeping next to a corpse.

How can you possibly love her?

Vanda paced across the small cellar. She had no doubt that Phil loved her. For now. But what if he discovered her darkest secrets? What if he learned about her terrible sins? He hated the Malcontents who fed from mortals, killing them in the process. He hated the Malcontents enough to risk his life fighting them.

But she'd done the same things a Malcontent did. Good Lord, he would hate her, too.

Another pull of sleepiness swept through her. She trudged toward the blanket.

Then she heard Brynley's voice overhead, loud with anger. Phil responded, much more quietly. It was a private conversation, none of her business.

But they were talking about her. *Damn.* She moved underneath the trapdoor, then levitated close to the ground floor.

"You can't marry her," Brynley said with an urgent tone. "Dad will never accept her."

"I don't give a damn what he thinks," Phil replied. "He has a narrow mind, and a narrow vision of the world."

"He's got a lot of power."

"And what does he use it for?" Phil demanded. "Raising cattle and sheep. Buying more land. Raising more cattle. More sheep. And the highlight of his existence is going out once a month to kill a defenseless animal."

"It's what we do. You enjoy hunting, too."

"It's not enough!" Phil shouted. "There's a whole world out there."

"A world of vampires?" Brynley sneered. "No thanks."

A wave of sleepiness hit Vanda, and she dropped a few feet. She shook it off and levitated once more to the trapdoor.

Phil was explaining how important it was for the Vamps to defeat the Malcontents. "This is huge, Bryn. If the Malcontents win, they could take over the entire world."

"Fine," Brynley snapped. "Help your good Vamps win. But don't *marry* one of them! This is crazy, Phil. You're a freaking prince, for God's sake."

Prince? Vanda shook her head. She couldn't have heard that right.

"And what about Diana?" Brynley continued. "You were betrothed to her years ago."

Vanda gasped. Her concentration broke and she tumbled to the floor. "Ouch." She winced as she stood up. Her ankle had twisted.

She limped to the blanket. At least the stupid ankle would heal during her death-sleep. She stretched out on the blanket. Prince? Prince Philip? Engaged to Diana? This was Wyoming, not bloody Britain. This couldn't be right.

Death-sleep tugged at her again, stronger and more pervasive. She yawned and closed her eyes. Images flitted through her mind. Phil pinning down Max the Mega Member. Phil leaping off the balcony and landing neatly. Phil fighting the Malcontents and surviving. Moving so fast.

Too fast. She gave up the struggle and succumbed to death-sleep.

Vanda awoke with a jolt. She stared into the darkness, unsure for a few seconds where she was. Oh, right. Phil's cabin in Wyoming. She fumbled beside her and found her whip.

A heavy feeling of dread swept over her, so heavy it took some effort to sit up. The war had started. Robby was captured. Marta had betrayed her once again. Dougal was handicapped for life. And Phil's sister hated her.

She rose to her feet. The ankle had healed. She tied the whip around her waist. It was quiet upstairs.

Quiet outside. She levitated to the trapdoor and pushed. It creaked open a few inches.

"Oh, you're up." Phil pulled the door open the rest of the way and smiled at her. "I don't suppose you need the ladder?"

"No." She levitated through the opening in the floor.

He took her hand and pulled her toward him. Her feet landed on the floor, and her arms wrapped around his chest.

"You look like a cowboy." She smoothed a hand over his plaid western shirt.

"Brynley went into town today and bought us some clothes." He kissed her. "Do you want to look like a cowgirl?"

She snorted. "How are you? Are the cuts still hurting you?"

"I'm fine. I got some sleep during the day, while Brynley was here."

Vanda looked around, but the cabin was empty. "Where is she now?"

"She's . . . taking a hike outside."

"In the dark?"

"It's a full moon. Do you need some breakfast?" He led her toward the ice chest. "Brynley brought us some more ice."

"That's good." Vanda grabbed a bottle of blood from the ice chest. She thought about asking Phil if he was really engaged to some lady named Diana, but she didn't want to admit that she'd been eavesdropping.

She took a long drink. "So what's the latest news?"

He leaned against the kitchen counter, frowning. "They weren't able to finish the tracking device before sunset. So we have no idea where Robby's being held prisoner."

"Oh, God. Poor Robby." She set the bottle down on the counter. She didn't feel like drinking when Robby was probably being tortured. "What will they do to him?"

"Make him go hungry, for starters. I've heard it's very painful."

"It is."

Phil tilted his head, studying her. "Maggie told me you used to go without. You made yourself suffer. Why?"

"I—I don't want to talk about it." Vanda walked across the room. "Is there a bathroom around here?"

"There's an outhouse behind the stable."

She scoffed. "You have a stable but not a bathroom?"

He shrugged. "The stable is empty. And I haven't needed a bathroom. I haven't been here in over four years."

"Why not?"

He gave her a wry look. "I don't want to talk about it."

"Well, aren't we a secretive pair?"

"Yeah, we are. I think it's time we had a long talk." He motioned to the couch just as his cell phone rang. "Hello? . . . Yeah, Howard. I'm sure Angus is beside himself. Any progress with the tracking device?"

While Phil talked, Vanda paced about. She really needed to go. Mortals didn't usually understand that, but a vampire only needed the red blood cells to survive. The plasma part of blood became waste, along with any added ingredients like the whiskey in Blissky.

She could find the outhouse on her own. She stepped outside onto a wide front porch. A cool breeze swept past her, making an old wooden rocker sway with a creak.

A small pasture spread out in front of the cabin. The full moon shone down, gilding the grass with a touch of silver. In the distance, a forest of tall trees reached to the clear, starry sky. The air was crisp and cool.

She rounded the cabin and saw the stable. It was almost as big as the cabin. She strode past it and found the outhouse. Just like the old days in Poland. She took a deep breath and did her business as quickly as possible. A roll of toilet paper sat on what looked like the end of an old broom handle.

She left the outhouse and strode past the stable, adjusting the whip around her waist. An eerie howl echoed around her. She gulped. Okay. So there might be a wolf or coyote in the woods. That was normal for Wyoming, right? She hurried around to the front of the cabin.

Was that something moving out of the woods? She inched toward the front porch steps.

Another movement captured her attention. And another. Animals. Perhaps a dozen. They moved from the dark shade of the trees and into the moon-lit pasture. She stiffened.

Wolves.

The moonlight gleamed off their silver gray coats. They slowly stalked toward her. Their eyes glinted. Their teeth were bared. A low growl rumbled across the pasture, freezing her with fear.

Light spilled suddenly onto the porch. Phil had opened the door.

"Vanda, come inside," he said quietly.

She willed her feet to move but they remained frozen to the ground. The nightmare was back. She was hunted once more. And the wolves had been sent to kill her.

They inched closer. Her heart stilled. This was it. They would kill her.

"Shit." Phil strode down the porch steps and into the pasture. "Go inside, Vanda."

She jolted out of the fear that had paralyzed her. Oh God, no! Phil would try to protect her just like Karl had. The wolves would kill him.

She ran to him and grasped his arm. "Come with me. Hurry."

He peeled her hand off. "I'll handle this. Trust me. Now go inside." He pushed her gently toward the stairs.

She hurried up the steps. The wolves howled. With a shudder, she turned to watch.

Phil had pulled off his shirt. All the cuts on his torso had healed. How had he managed that? His body began to shimmer.

She gasped. What was he doing?

The wolves charged.

Phil spread his arms wide, threw his head back, and howled.

Vanda stumbled back, knocking against the cabin wall. Light from the open door illuminated Phil. Fur sprouted across his back and shoulders, then spread down his arms. His hands turned into paws with long sharp claws. His head crackled, the jaw elongating into a long snout.

The wolves stopped in their tracks and hunched down to the ground. They were afraid, Vanda realized. But not as terrified as she was.

Phil was a werewolf.

Chapter Nineteen

$\mathcal{T}$ ime came to a screeching halt. Vanda couldn't breathe. Couldn't think. She was plastered against the cabin wall, unable to move.

A werewolf. Her beautiful Phil was a werewolf.

She began to shake. Panic swirled in her gut, then shot through her chest and erupted from her mouth with a strangled cry.

The werewolf turned to her. How many times had she seen those vicious jaws and snapping teeth? Always coming after her. Hunting her relentlessly.

She dashed into the cabin and slammed the door shut. With trembling hands she slid the bolt across the door. She stepped back, her knees shaking. Her gaze darted to the windows. He could crash right through the glass. That's how the wolves had invaded the safe house where she and Karl had taken shelter. The wolves had ripped him apart.

Footsteps pounded up the porch steps. Vanda stepped back. Her heart raced, thundering in her ears.

The doorknob turned. The door shook. She pressed a hand to her mouth as a terrified sob escaped.

"Vanda." His voice was soft. "Let me in."

She moved back. Thoughts jumbled in her head. She'd never heard of a werewolf who could talk. Or turn a doorknob. He had to be human.

But she'd seen him change. Or rather, she'd seen half of him change. He'd definitely had the head of a wolf. And the teeth.

Dammit, how could he do this to her? Rage flooded through her, a welcome relief from the terror that had made her weak.

"Go away!" she screamed.

The door shook again. "We need to talk."

"Go to hell!" _Dammit_. She'd made love to him. She'd let him inside her body. Inside her heart. A sense of betrayal twisted in her gut. First her sister, and now Phil.

She wanted to throw something. Rip something apart. She spotted the wooden ladder propped against the loft, the same ladder Phil had inserted through the trapdoor to descend into the cellar. She kicked a boot through some wooden rungs, then grasped the ladder in her hands and snapped it in two.

"Vanda."

She spun toward his voice. He'd raised a window and was peering in at her. How dare he look so normal? He'd completely fooled her.

"As your anger management sponsor, I have to say—"

"Leave me alone!" She hurled a splintered piece of wood at him.

He dodged the missile and it flew through the window. He peered inside again. "We're going to talk. There's no escaping it."

No escape? She opened the trapdoor and floated down into the cellar. She paced back and forth. She could teleport away, but where? Her apartment wasn't safe. The Carpathian Mountains were probably in daylight. London might be, too, so that left out Pamela and Cora Lee. She had no idea where Ian and Toni were. Maggie?

Vanda winced. She was still on that hit list. She couldn't put Maggie and her family in danger. But wasn't there a cave on their property? She could hide there. Unfortunately, she'd never been to Maggie's ranch, so she didn't know the way. She needed to call. She needed Phil's cell phone.

"Vanda, come back."

She glanced at the trapdoor. Phil was there.

She scanned the cellar and spotted a shovel. That would keep him away. Keep his *paws* off her. She grasped the handle.

He jumped. Her heart clenched as she watched. He landed, his cowboy boots hitting the wooden floor with a thud, his knees bending to absorb the shock.

He straightened slowly. The jeans hung low on his hips. His bare torso and chest rippled with muscles. Oh God, how she had loved his hard chest and broad shoulders. There was no trace of the injuries he'd suffered the night before.

His thick brown hair gleamed in the light that filtered down from the open trapdoor. Highlights of gold and auburn glinted. His pale blue eyes watched her, glimmering with strong emotion.

He was so gorgeous. How could he be a werewolf? And how could he be human now? The only time she had seen a wolf change back to human form was when Karl had killed one. As far as she knew, once a werewolf became a wolf, it stayed that way for the entire night. She'd certainly never seen one that could change only half of its body.

She pointed the shovel at him. "What are you?"

His gaze flitted to the shovel, and his mouth thinned. "I'm Phil Jones, the same man I was yesterday." He stepped toward her.

"Stay back!" She raised the shovel. *"What are you?"*

His chin lifted. "I'm an Alpha werewolf. I can change completely or partially whenever I wish, day or night. I have super strength and speed and heightened sensibilities. If I'm cut, I can change and instantly be healed. I can call on the power of my inner wolf without changing physical form. And one more thing . . . "

He leaped toward her so quickly, she barely had time to jab the shovel at him. He grasped the handle and yanked, pulling her toward him. In a tug of war, she dug in her heels and pulled the handle back. He yanked even harder, throwing her off balance. When she stumbled forward, he tossed the shovel aside, swung an arm around her and slammed her hard against his chest.

"One more thing," he growled. "I love you."

She shoved at his chest. "Let go of me. You—You lied to me."

"I was going to tell you tonight. Hell, I tried to tell you the other night at Howard's cabin, but when I mentioned wolves, you refused to talk."

She winced. She'd been so intent on keeping her own secrets, she hadn't let Phil tell his. "But you should have told me." She pounded at his chest.

"Why? So you'd have an excuse not to fall in love with me?" He grabbed her hands and pinned them behind her back. "Whatever happened to my love being enough?"

Her eyes burned with tears. "But I hate wolves. I hate shape shifters."

"You love this one."

She shook her head. "I—I can't. You scare me."

His mouth ticked. "Haven't I saved your life enough times for you to trust me? I love you, Vanda. I will always be there for you."

A tear escaped, rolling down her cheek. It was true. He had saved her. Several times. He'd stopped Max the Mega Member at the club. He'd killed the snake. He'd detected the bomb. He must have been able to smell it with his heightened werewolf sensibilities. But how could she get past him being a werewolf?

She shook her head. "I've been afraid of your kind for too long."

His grip tightened on her hands. "What exactly

scares you? Is it my teeth? I've nibbled on you before without hurting you."

She shuddered.

"Is it the claws?" He released her hands. With one arm wrapped around her shoulders, he showed her his other arm. It shimmered with a bluish light. Fur sprouted on his hand, and it changed into a paw. Claws extended, sharp and deadly.

Vanda flinched. She turned her head away and squeezed her eyes shut. "Don't."

"Don't what? Do you really think I would hurt you?"

She jumped when she felt something touch her cheek. *Fur*. Soft and warm. He stroked her cheek, then skimmed down her neck. She sneaked a peek and saw him caressing her with the back of his paw.

"I'm in complete control," he said softly. "Trust me."

He turned his paw and slipped a claw beneath the zipper of her catsuit. He pulled it down and sliced right through her bra.

She gasped.

The paw shimmered and turned back into a hand. He peeled back the catsuit and bra to reveal her breasts. Her nipples tightened. Her breasts heaved as she struggled to catch her breath. Her skin tingled, aching for him to touch her.

She shook her head. How could she want him now? But there was something about him. An animal magnetism that overwhelmed her senses. He was raw and powerful, and it made her ache for him. Even her fear made it seem more exciting.

He cupped her breast and squeezed gently. She moaned.

He rubbed a thumb over the hardened tip. "I think, in time, you'll come to appreciate my dual nature. I can make love like a gentleman. Or I can rut like a beast." He tweaked her nipple.

She jolted. Moisture pooled between her legs. God help her, she wanted him.

"Which would you prefer tonight? The gentleman or the beast?" His mouth twitched. "In human form, of course."

She smoothed her hands over his broad shoulders. "I'd like one of each."

He smiled slowly. "That can be done." He leaned closer and whispered in her ear, "But the beast wants to go first."

Before she could even react, he had unwrapped her whip, dropped it on the floor, and tugged her catsuit and underwear down to her ankles. "You do have super speed."

"And strength." He picked her up and lay her on the blanket. In another second he had her boots off, as well as his own cowboy boots.

She eyed the bulge in his jeans. "You appear to be super-sized, too."

He smiled as his jeans and underwear hit the floor. "It's the animal in me." He crouched at her feet. His nostrils flared. "I can smell your heat."

Her thighs squeezed together as more moisture seeped from her.

He lifted a foot and nuzzled the arch. Then

he licked her toes and nipped at them. Her leg twitched.

"Are—Are you sure you should bite?" She thought that was how a werewolf was made.

He nipped at her ankle. "Are you afraid of turning furry, sweetheart?"

"Well, I think I have enough problems already, just being me."

He chuckled. "I love you just the way you are." He licked a path up her calf. "I would have to bite hard, break the skin, and get my saliva into your bloodstream."

He tickled the back of her knee with his tongue. "And I'd have to be in wolf form at the time. So, you're reasonably safe."

"Reasonably?"

"You can't reason with a beast."

Her heart stuttered when he growled low in his throat. He moved around her body on his hands and knees, nuzzling her naked body, rubbing his nose across her tingling skin, licking her, tasting her. No part was off limits. Her ears, her neck, her armpits.

With another growl, he pounced on her breasts. He licked them, squeezed them, suckled the nipples hard. They turned red, the tips distended and tender. She groaned, arching up into his mouth.

And then, with a push of his hands and his nose, he flipped her over. Her breasts, overly sensitized, scraped against the horsehair blanket. She pressed her legs together, close to climaxing.

He nuzzled the back of her neck, tickling the tiny hairs and making her shiver. Then he licked a path down her spine. He kneaded her rump, licked and nipped till she was squirming.

She gasped when he pulled her onto her side and nudged his head between her legs. With his head pillowed on her thigh, he lapped at her.

She squealed and pressed her thighs against his head. With a growl, he nuzzled his face deeper into her. His tongue seemed to also have super speed. She screamed, her body shattering with a massive convulsion.

"You're mine." He nipped at her bottom, then pulled her onto her knees.

"Wait." Her knees were rubbery. Her body was still throbbing with aftershocks. She rested her forehead against the blanket, struggling to catch her breath.

"I've got you." He grabbed her hips, supporting her with his hands as he plunged into her from behind.

She cried out. He was incredible. He filled her completely. He pulled out slowly, dragging the sensation, setting her on fire. "Phil!"

He plunged back into her. He supported her with one arm, then leaned forward to nuzzle her neck and hold her hand. He pumped faster. The tension started to build once more. He growled in her ear, then reared up onto his knees, taking her with him.

She leaned back against his chest. His hands slid up her body and squeezed her breasts.

"You're mine," he whispered in her ear.

"Yes."

He reached between her legs and tweaked her clitoris as he ground into her vagina from the back. She screamed when the orgasm slammed into her. He let out a hoarse cry, eerily similar to the howl of a wolf. As he tumbled onto the blanket with her, she knew her future had been decided. The beast had claimed his mate.

"Are you all right?" Phil asked when her breathing finally slowed.

"Yes." She cuddled against his body.

He was flat on his back, still in the cellar. He wrapped his arms around Vanda and rubbed her back. He was relieved she knew his secret, but now he had another problem.

Brynley had seen his display of Alpha power. She'd been the leader of that damned group that had scared Vanda so badly. No doubt that had been Bryn's intention—to scare Vanda out of his life. Where his sister had managed to find the rest of those young cubs, he had no idea.

They were probably in the woods now, hunting fox or rabbit. As normal werewolves, they would be in wolf form all night, changing back to their human bodies shortly before sunrise.

The last thing he'd wanted was to let Brynley in on his secret. Achieving Alpha status was a major event in the Lycan World. She'd let Dad know about it as soon as possible.

The firstborn son was Alpha. Phil had proven his worthiness to be Heir Apparent.

"How did you become a werewolf?" Vanda whispered.

"I was born this way."

"So you were a beastly child?"

He snorted. "Lycan children don't usually have their first change until puberty. I was thirteen."

"It must have been scary. And painful."

"Yeah, a little. But we were prepared for it. When you've heard the stories all your life, about the rush of freedom you'll feel when running through the woods, the thrill of the hunt, and the victory of the first kill, then you're really happy when it finally happens."

She stroked her fingers through his chest hair. "How did werewolves get started? Was there some kind of strange, rabid wolf that bit a human?"

"It's a very old story. I remember sitting in front of the fire, listening to my parents tell it." He rubbed her back. "Would you like to hear it?"

"Yes." She rested her head on his chest. "Tell me."

"My family are the descendants of an ancient line of Welsh royalty."

She raised her head. "So you're a prince?"

"I wouldn't go that far. These ancestors were more like wizards than kings. They possessed many strange powers, and one of them was the ability to transform into any sort of animal. Over time they developed personal tastes for what sort of animal they liked to change into. The favorites were wolf, bear, wildcat, and hawk."

"The hunting animals," Vanda murmured.

"Exactly. Why change into a mouse when you can be a lion? My direct ancestors preferred the wolf. Everything was fine until the Romans invaded. The Celtic tribes were falling in defeat. My ancestors realized they could escape Roman rule by living as wolves."

"Did others live as bears, wildcats, and hawks?" she asked.

"Yes." Phil assumed that was the beginning of Howard's family of were-bears. "While my ancestors were in wolf form, they mated. They discovered those children were bound permanently to the wolf. They could no longer choose which animal they wanted to turn into."

"And werewolves were born," Vanda whispered.

"Yes. Every now and then the Romans would kill a werewolf, and it turned back into human form. They were superstitious and fearful of some sort of supernatural retaliation if they didn't keep our secret. They called our tribe the Philupus for those who loved wolves. The name has been passed down in my family for centuries. It's *my* name, actually."

She gave him an incredulous look. "Philupus?"

"Now you know why I prefer Phil. After the Romans left, my ancestors thought it would be safe to go back to living in human form. But a few generations had passed and they found they couldn't stay human all the time. They changed on the first night of a full moon."

"So they were doomed to turn into wolves every month for eternity," she whispered.

He smiled. "I wouldn't call it 'doomed.' I've never met a werewolf who didn't love that burst of freedom we get every month when we can toss all human rules and conventions out the window and act like . . . animals."

"You find it liberating."

"Yes." Phil sighed. "Or it should be. There are some among the Lycan World who think we should adhere to our own traditions. Supreme Pack Masters can be very powerful, and they try to force everyone to do as they say."

Vanda sat up. "You had trouble with someone like that?"

He nodded. "My father."

She winced. "I'm sorry."

"It's all right." He caressed her arm.

"He wouldn't approve of me. Your sister doesn't either." Vanda glanced at the trapdoor. "When is she getting back? That's an awfully long hike—Oh." She slapped her forehead. "Your sister's a werewolf."

"She was one of those wolves who scared you."

Vanda made a face. "She really doesn't like me."

"She doesn't know you yet. And don't worry about her. I'll have a good talk with her."

"Were all of those wolves werewolves?"

"Yes, but they won't bother you again. They know you're under my protection." Phil sat up. "So how come you're so afraid of werewolves?"

She flinched. "I—I told you. They were hunting me."

"You never said why."

She slipped her underwear on. "You know, you ruined my bra. I hope your sister has one I can borrow."

"She bought some clothes for us. Come on, Vanda. I told you my secrets. It's time you told yours."

"You'll hate me." She stood and walked away.

Chapter Twenty

*V*anda levitated through the trapdoor, landing on the ground floor of the cabin. A cool breeze prickled her skin, and she rushed to close the window Phil had left open.

She heard a sound behind her and turned. Phil was standing by the trapdoor. "You can jump that high?"

He nodded.

So that was how he had managed to get upstairs at the warehouse in New Orleans. She glanced warily at the windows flanking the cabin's front door. No blinds. No curtains. Welcome to the Wyoming Peep Show. She crossed an arm over her breasts. "Someone could see us in here."

"A lucky squirrel maybe." Phil smiled. "The nearest neighbor is miles away."

"The werewolves are out there." She moved

quickly to the kitchen area, which had no windows.

Phil followed her. "Lycans always strip before changing. Nudity is not a big deal for us."

Her gaze flitted down his naked body. "Easy for you to say when you look like that. But I would imagine some of the guys would be a little uneasy about displaying their . . . shortcomings."

He snorted. "Lycan men don't have shortcomings."

"Right. You're as big as your egos, which is fairly huge." She removed a kitchen towel from a drawer and grasped the pump handle.

"Here, allow me." He worked the pump, and water spewed from the spout onto her towel.

She scrubbed her face and neck, wincing at how cold the water was.

"What happened to you in Poland after you became a vampire?"

She swallowed hard. The coffin of horrors took shape in her mind. "I—I need more water." She held the towel under the spout.

He pumped more water for her. "What happened?"

She washed her chest and torso. "I buried my little sister." The coffin rattled, trying to break open. "More water."

He gave her some more. "And then what?"

She wiped her arms. "I had borrowed a shovel from a nearby farm. I was returning it to the toolshed when the farmer found me. I was instantly overwhelmed with hunger."

"You bit him?"

She leaned over to wash her legs. "I ran outside

and bit his cow. For the first few weeks I was so confused. So hungry, and so terrified that I might kill someone. I didn't know what to do. I hid in caves and fed off animals. I felt like I'd become an animal, too."

"Your . . . sire didn't help you to adjust?"

"Sigismund?" She snorted with disgust. "I wanted nothing to do with him or Marta. I left them the night I awoke."

"There's something I need to tell you." Phil frowned. "The prisoner at Romatech, the one they captured at Apollo's compound—it was Sigismund."

Vanda's breath caught. Her skin chilled. "Are— Are you sure?"

"Yes. He was one of the Malcontents masquerading as a god in order to feed off the girls and . . . rape them."

She sighed. That had been one more reason she'd fled from Sigismund. She had known he would abuse her. She could tell he had abused Marta, although her sister had seemed to want it. "I ran into him a few times when I was hiding in the caves. He would always laugh at me and say I was doomed. There was no way I could escape the almighty Casimir. Then I would teleport away before he alerted Jedrek Janow." She shuddered. "Sigismund is an abusive pig. I hope you guys made him suffer."

"We did," Phil said. "When I found out who he was, I nearly killed him."

But he didn't, she thought. Phil only killed in self-defense. He was an honorable person, unlike her.

Vanda rinsed the towel. "Marta's in America. I

saw her at the warehouse in New Orleans, fighting with the Malcontents."

Phil winced. "That must have been a shock for you." He took the towel from her and rubbed her back.

She closed her eyes, enjoying the feel of his hands.

"How did you get involved with the underground resistance?" he asked.

Her eyes flew open. Good Lord, the man never gave up. "Do you know where your sister put those clothes she bought?"

"The bag's on the kitchen table." He set the towel on the counter. "You're avoiding the subject."

"You bet I am." She strode to the table and removed the items from the plastic bag. Underwear and bra, close to the right size, jeans and a western-style shirt.

"I realize it must be painful."

"Dressing like a cowgirl?" she asked wryly.

"No, talking about your past."

"Oh, do you think so? Can you imagine losing your father, your sister, and four brothers to war? Jozef was only twelve! I couldn't find out if they'd died in battle or were taken prisoner. I hoped they were prisoners, that they were still alive, but when I saw the concentration camps, I almost wished they were dead."

She strode back to the kitchen sink. "I learned how to teleport by accident. I was standing outside a camp one night, staring through the barbed wire and wishing there was a way I could get inside to see if my father or brothers were there. And the next thing I knew, everything went black and there I was, inside the camp."

She pulled off her underwear and rinsed it out in the sink. "I rushed through the bunkhouses, searching for my family, but they weren't there. I couldn't believe what I was seeing. So many prisoners, crammed in so tight."

The coffin cracked open. God, no, she didn't want to remember. All those prisoners, those gaunt, emaciated bodies, those haunted eyes filled with pain and despair.

"What happened then?" Phil whispered.

"A guard caught me." Her eyes blurred with tears. "I was so upset from seeing all the prisoners, and so hungry. I bit him." Tears streamed down her cheeks. "I lost control and killed him."

She glanced at Phil through her tears, expecting to see disgust in his eyes. It wasn't there. This had to be a mistake. He didn't understand the magnitude of her sins. "I had to feed every night. Why torment some poor unsuspecting cow when I could kill a Nazi? And I did. Every night. I joined the underground. I would teleport into a camp, free some prisoners, and kill a Nazi all in a night's work."

Phil said nothing, just watched her intently.

She paced away. *Dammit.* The coffin was fully open now, and all her terrible sins had crept out. "One night, after I'd killed a guard, a vampire appeared before me. He said he'd been watching me for several weeks. He congratulated me for being a natural born killer. He gave me an ultimatum—join the True Ones or they would kill the leader of the resistance."

"Karl," Phil said softly.

She nodded. "The vampire was Jedrek Janow. He told me about the True Ones, the ones we now call Malcontents. He said they were in league with the Nazis. Once the Germans controlled the world, the True Ones would control the Nazis. I could be a part of it all. I could rule the world."

She rubbed her brow. "All I could think about was my father and brothers who were probably dead from fighting the Nazis. I told Jedrek to go to hell. And that's when he said he would send his personal pets to destroy me." She shuddered. "His wolves."

She paced back to the kitchen. "I ran to Karl to tell him what had happened. Three wolves came that night, and I managed to teleport Karl away. But every month when the moon was full, they would come after us. And there would be more and more of them. Then one night Karl killed one, and it changed into a human."

"And that's when you realized they were werewolves?" Phil asked.

"Yes. Karl bought us some silver bullets."

"Did you ever see the werewolves in human form?" Phil asked. "Other than the one you killed."

"No."

He nodded. "That explains it, then."

"Explains what?"

"Why you never recognized my scent. Shape shifters don't smell like normal humans. But we only have that unique scent when we're in human form. When we're wolves, we smell like wolves."

She sighed. "You talk about it so matter-of-factly, but you're not getting it. I was *terrified*. Every month we would find a new place to hide, and the wolves would track us down. They were relentless."

"I saw how frightened you were outside."

"I saw them rip Karl apart! They would have gotten me, too, but I managed to teleport away. And then I was all alone, hiding like a rat in the caves, searching for my father and brothers and never finding them, feeding off Nazis every night. I—I killed so many." She slumped in a kitchen chair and covered her face as tears ran down her cheeks. "I'm a monster."

The room was quiet except for her sniffles. She'd done it. She'd let him see inside her coffin of horrors. Let him see her for what she really was. And now he would look at her differently. Instead of seeing love in his beautiful blue eyes, she would see utter disgust.

"Vanda." He crouched beside her.

She covered her eyes so she couldn't see.

"Vanda, you lived through a hell no person should ever have to endure. You lost your family, your lover, your mortality. In those camps, you witnessed the worst kind of cruelty a human can inflict on another. You lived in constant fear and despair."

She lowered her hands. "I killed them. I didn't have to. I acted just like a Malcontent. I'm no better than they are. I know you hate them. So, I know you'll hate me."

"Come." He took her hand, pulled her to her feet, and led her to the sink. He pumped water onto the kitchen towel. "You were at war, Vanda. War is an ugly monster that forces people to do terrible things they would normally never do."

"It's no excuse."

"Yes, it is." He wrung out the towel. "When you came across those guards in the camps, you were an intruder. They would have killed you if you hadn't killed them first. It was self-defense." With the towel, he wiped the tears from her face.

More tears seeped from her eyes. "You—You can forgive me?"

"Of course. I—" He tilted his head. "Oh, I see."

"See what?" That she didn't deserve to be loved?

He dampened the towel once more. "I see why you have so much anger and frustration. It's not because you need my forgiveness. I have nothing to forgive." He wiped her face again. "Vanda, the problem is within you. You're not able to forgive yourself."

She blinked. "I did terrible things."

"It was war. And you did what you had to do to survive."

"You don't think I'm a monster?"

"No. I think you're an incredibly brave and beautiful woman."

A surge of relief swept through her. It flooded through her, washing away a heavy load of guilt and remorse. "I was so afraid you would hate me."

He smiled. "I love you. And I'll keep saying it till you believe me."

For the first time she actually did believe it deep inside. For the first time in many years she felt worthy of love. She smiled back. "I do believe you. And I love you, too."

Still smiling, he dampened the towel with water. "I'm glad you finally told me everything."

Vanda nodded. The coffin in her mind was wide-open. It was still there, and it always would be, but it didn't look scary anymore.

She gasped when the wet towel was suddenly pressed between her legs. "What are you doing?"

He rubbed the towel against her. "I believe you requested two rounds of lovemaking: one with the beast and one with the gentleman." He rinsed the towel off, then began washing himself. "The gentleman is at your service."

"Phil, wake up." She nudged him. "The phone's for you."

He jerked awake and sat up.

"It's Connor." She offered him the cell phone. When it had started ringing, she'd moved with vampire speed to find it. It had been in his jeans in the cellar.

She'd answered it while levitating back to the ground floor. Then she'd levitated again, to the loft where she and Phil had made love a few hours earlier.

"Hey, Connor." Phil listened on the phone. He sat up straighter. "That's great!"

Vanda perched on the edge of the bed, listening. From what she could overhear, it sounded like Laszlo had completed the tracking device. It would be daylight on the East Coast in about five minutes. As soon as Sigismund was in his death-sleep, the device would be implanted in him. Then they would accidentally let him escape right after sunset. They hoped he would lead them straight to Robby.

"Yeah, I'll fight," Phil said. "Just send someone to get me."

Vanda swallowed hard. Of course, Phil would want to fight. He was probably good friends with Robby. They'd both been stationed at Jean-Luc's place in Texas.

If something happened to Phil, how could she bear it? She'd lost so many loved ones to war.

"I'll need a sword," Phil continued. "I only have a handgun here."

He wouldn't die like Karl had, Vanda told herself. He had super strength and speed. For the first time, she realized how grateful she should be that he was a werewolf. A normal mortal wouldn't stand a chance.

"Right. I'll be ready." Phil hung up.

"So the battle will be tonight?" Vanda asked.

"We hope so." He looked her over. "Your hair's wet."

"I got bored. There's nothing to do here. At least, not when you're asleep." She poked his foot. "I found some shampoo and washed my hair in the kitchen sink." She'd also put on the western clothes Brynley had bought.

She stood. "How do I look?"

He smiled. "You're the best-looking purple-haired cowgirl I've ever seen."

She huffed. "I should take my whip to you."

"I should peel those jeans off you."

Her mouth twitched. "You have a one-track mind."

"I can't help it. I'm an animal." He pulled her onto the bed, and she giggled.

He tugged at her shirt, popping the snaps open.

"Wait." She rested a hand on top of his. "Do we have time? I'd hate for your sister to walk in."

"Let me check." He climbed out of bed and peered out the little window in the loft. He might be looking at the full moon, but Vanda was scoping out the heavenly body. Strong back, gorgeous rump. Her skin began to tingle. Good God, she could get excited just looking at him.

"We have almost an hour." He turned to face her.

She sucked in a breath. He was already thick with arousal. "You started without me."

His gaze drifted to her jeans and his nostrils flared. "No, I haven't."

She struggled to unsnap and unzip her jeans. Meanwhile he strode to the foot of the bed and removed her boots. His bare skin took on a red tint from the glow of her eyes.

He seized the hem of her jeans and yanked them

off. "You have five seconds to remove your underwear or I'll shred them."

She wiggled out of her panties and feigned a shudder. "Oooh, I'm scared. The big bad wolf's in town."

With a grin, he stalked toward her on his hands and knees. "My, what sweet legs you have." He nipped at her thigh.

"The better to squeeze you with, my dear." She sat up to remove her bra.

His eyes gleamed blue. "What sweet breasts you have."

"The better to entice you with, my dear."

With a growl, he shoved her back on the bed. He drew a nipple into his mouth and suckled.

She moaned. "What a great tongue you have."

He looked at her with twinkling eyes. "The better to eat you with." He nibbled down her belly.

Moisture rushed to the apex of her thighs just in time to meet his inquisitive, insistent tongue. Within seconds she was squirming and panting. He teased her clitoris with the ruthlessness of an animal.

She squealed as a climax jolted through her. He watched her, a wolfish grin on his handsome face.

"Ready?" He moved between her legs.

"Wait." She rested her hands on his shoulders. "After dressing like a cowgirl, I have a strange desire to ride."

He chuckled and fell onto his back. "Saddle up, sweetheart."

* * *

An hour later Vanda sat in bed relaxing and drinking from a bottle of cold synthetic blood. She stretched her legs, feeling the pull of sore muscles. She couldn't even recall how many orgasms she'd had over the course of the night. It had been one long delicious, forbidden night of sex, mixed with heart-wrenching confessions that made the love-making even sweeter.

She felt the tug of sleepiness. The sun must be nearing the horizon. She sipped more blood. Phil had brought it up to her in the loft. He'd washed up at the sink and gone to the cellar to put his clothes back on.

From the clunk of cowboy boots and clanking of pans, she could tell he was in the kitchen now. Her nose twitched, catching the smell of coffee.

She hoped morning had already come to Robby, wherever he was. Death-sleep would not only put him asleep, but also his torturers. His body would heal while he slept. She hoped his mind would, too.

With a sigh, she sat up and began to dress. She had just finished zipping up her jeans when she heard booted feet at the cabin's front door.

"Phil!" Brynley shouted. The door shook. The bolt was still in place.

Vanda heard Phil's footsteps approach the door. She slipped on the western shirt and fastened the snaps.

The door creaked open.

"Phil!" Brynley's voice was full of excitement. "You're an Alpha! It's so amazing! How on earth did you do it?"

"Bryn, we need to talk."

"We are talking. You wouldn't believe how excited the guys are. We were talking about it all the way back to the cabin, and the only thing we can figure is that somehow you managed to go Alpha on your own. Is that true?"

"I wasn't alone, but I wasn't with a pack either."

Brynley squealed. "This is so freaking fantastic! No one's ever done that before. Dad is going to be so—"

"Don't tell him."

"What?"

"I mean it, Bryn. Don't tell him. It's none of his business."

"Of course it is! Phil, every Lycan in the territory is going to want you for the next Supreme Pack Master. I can see it now. Dad will throw you a giant party to welcome back the long lost prince."

Prince? There it was again. Vanda padded to the edge of the loft. Brynley was back in her jeans, tank top, and open plaid shirt, but Vanda noticed a few leaves in her hair and a bloodstain on the shirtsleeve, as if she'd wiped her mouth on it.

Brynley's gaze shifted to the loft and her eyes narrowed. "She's still here."

"Yes." Phil crossed his arms. "And you owe her an apology."

Brynley snorted. "For what? Being myself?"

"For purposely trying to scare her away," he replied.

Brynley scowled at him. "I was doing her a favor. She needed to know the truth about you."

"Yes, I did." Vanda was tired of being talked about like she wasn't in the room. She grabbed her bottle of blood and floated down to the ground floor. "Thank you for scaring the crap out of me."

"Any time." Brynley smiled grimly. "So why are you still here? Can't you get a job in Hollywood? I hear vampires are all the rage right now."

"She's under my protection," Phil said. "This is my house, and it will be a sanctuary to Vanda whenever she needs it."

With a huff, Brynley stomped to the kitchen. She grabbed a cup from a cabinet and poured a cup of coffee.

Vanda sat at the kitchen table and sipped from her bottle. Another wave of sleepiness swept through her.

Phil strode to the kitchen. "Who were those puppies with you last night?"

Puppies? They'd seemed plenty big to Vanda.

Brynley sipped her coffee. "They're friends."

"They're underage." Phil sat at the table next to Vanda. "They're supposed to be with their pack when they shift."

Brynley snorted. "Since when do you follow pack rules? The boys can't shift with their pack. They can't even live with their families. Or go to school. They've been banished. I'm sure you understand how that happens."

Vanda gave Phil a questioning look.

He shrugged. "I was banished at eighteen. After a year of near starvation, I found Connor, and he gave me a job and a place to live."

Vanda winced. That was when he'd worked at the townhouse and she'd tormented him. "How could you be banished? I mean, if you're really a *prince*, who would have the power to do that to you?"

His mouth thinned. "My father."

Brynley waved a dismissive hand. "He just wanted you to learn a lesson. He expected you to come back in a month or so."

"With my tail between my legs," Phil muttered. "What kind of Supreme Pack Master would I make if I was that big of a wimp?"

Brynley sighed. "I know it's hard to submit to Dad's every wish and command. That's the sort of thing that got these boys in trouble. They challenged their pack masters' authority. Then their masters appealed to Dad, the Supreme Master, and he kicked them out."

"Sounds like dear old Dad hasn't changed," Phil murmured.

"They're just teenagers," Brynley continued. "They had nowhere to go. I knew your cabin was empty, so I let them stay here."

Phil snorted. "They're your Lost Boys? Are you sure your name isn't Wendy?"

She made a face at him. "They're more a pain in the butt, actually. It takes half my monthly allowance to feed them. They're bottomless pits. And rowdy as hell."

"Wouldn't you be in big trouble with your father if he knew what you're doing?" Vanda asked.

Brynley's eyes narrowed. "Are you threatening to tell on me?"

"No. I just find it interesting," Vanda said. "It

sounds to me like you're rebelling against your father just like Phil did."

Brynley scoffed. "Believe me, if Dad says jump, I ask how high. I . . . I just felt sorry for these boys. They have nowhere to go." Her eyes lit up. "But that's all changed now that Phil's back. Phil, they want you to be their pack master!"

He looked stunned. "I . . . can't do that."

"Of course you can," Brynley insisted. "You can't be an Alpha without a pack."

"I have other things to do. Important things. There could be a battle after sunset tonight."

"A *vampire* battle?" Brynley's eyes flashed with anger. "You're going to help them and ignore your own kind?"

"I'll do what I can to help the boys, but I can't be their master."

Brynley made a noise of frustration. "You haven't even bothered to meet them. They're so excited about you, Phil. You're the first sign of hope they've had in months."

He stood. "Where are they?"

"In the stable. Don't be surprised if they cheer for you when you walk in. You're their hero."

"Great." He gave Vanda a wry smile. "Just what I needed."

She smiled back. "You're my hero, too."

He leaned over and kissed her brow. "I'll be back soon." He strode out the front door.

Brynley refilled her coffee cup, then moved to the kitchen table and sat across from Vanda. "Alone at last. We need to talk."

Chapter Twenty-one

*W*ell, you'll have to make it quick," Vanda said. "In about five minutes I'll be falling into my death-sleep."

Brynley nodded. "This battle Phil talked about, how bad will it be?"

Vanda was surprised. She'd expected Phil's sister to tell her to get lost. "We're at war. The Malcontents want to kill us."

"I've heard that vampires have the power of mind control. Is Phil under their influence, or does he really want to do this?"

Vanda tamped down her growing irritation. "Everyone I know in the Vampire World has the utmost respect and fondness for Phil. They would never control him. They consider him family."

"He has family here."

"His family here banished him."

Brynley took a sip of coffee. "Did he tell you about himself?"

"He told me how your ancestors became were-wolves."

"Ancient history." Brynley waved a dismissive hand. "Did he tell you about his life here?"

Vanda was tempted to ask, *What life?* but she was too curious to brush Brynley off. "Is he really a prince?"

Brynley nodded. "A direct line from the old Welsh princes. Dad came from Wales about a hundred and eighty years ago and started his first ranch in Montana. Some of the clansmen followed him here. Over time the clan grew, and Dad became more and more powerful. He owns over fifty ranches now, spread over Montana, Idaho, and Wyoming. The entire western territory—that's over sixty packs—swears allegiance to him as Supreme Pack Master. No one dares disobey him."

"Except Phil."

Brynley shrugged. "It's hard for someone like Phil to submit. Dad understands that. Believe me, he'll be so proud when he finds out that Phil acquired Alpha status without the aid of a pack. It's never been done before. Phil is truly amazing."

"I have to agree with that." Vanda yawned as sleepiness tugged at her.

"And since Phil's one of the most powerful were-wolves in the country, it's obvious that he has an important future with us."

Vanda rubbed her brow. "You want him to come home."

"Yes." Brynley leaned forward. "He belongs with us. Did you know he was betrothed to a werewolf princess?"

So, Princess Diana was a werewolf? An image flitted through Vanda's mind of a mangy wolf wearing a diamond tiara. "He never mentioned it."

"He was ten years old when Dad arranged his betrothal to Diana. She was two."

"How romantic."

Brynley snorted. "Diana's father is the pack master for Utah. And he owns several ranches. She's an only child, so that makes her a very powerful and wealthy heiress."

"Good for her."

Brynley's eyes narrowed. "She can give him children. The royal line would continue."

Damn. Vanda closed her eyes.

"I'm sure you're a nice person, Vanda. My brother wouldn't care for you so much if you weren't. But try to look at this with an open mind. If Phil comes back, he can be a powerful leader. If he stays with you and your kind—what sort of life would he have? He would always be an employee, at the beck and call of a vampire. What would you wish for Phil: a life as a leader where he has wealth, power, and children? Or a life of servitude where he can't have children at all and his life is in constant danger?"

Vanda swallowed hard. The sun drew close to the horizon, dragging her into death-sleep. But she knew the heaviness in her heart wasn't caused by drowsiness.

"I've heard enough." She stood and trudged toward the trapdoor.

"Think about it, please," Brynley said. "If you love him, you should let him go."

As Phil walked back to the cabin, he noted the pink and gold streaks brightening the sky. The sun was breaking over the horizon, so Vanda would already be asleep. Dammit. He trudged up the porch steps. He would have liked to discuss this new problem with her.

He opened the door, and Brynley greeted him with a big smile.

"Well, did they cheer for you?"

"Yes." He glanced at the trapdoor. "Did Vanda make it into the cellar all right?"

"Yeah, she's fine. We had a nice talk."

He arched an eyebrow at his sister. "You didn't try to scare her away?"

Brynley snorted and strode to the ice chest. "Would you like some breakfast? I could scramble up a few dozen eggs."

"A few dozen?"

She removed two cartons from the ice chest. "I told you the boys are bottomless pits. They took down an elk last night, but I bet you they're already hungry again."

He filled up his coffee cup. "What do they do when you're not here?"

"I leave as much nonperishable food as possible. And they have hunting rifles. They manage."

Phil sipped some coffee. He'd had a good talk with the boys. There were ten of them. The youngest was thirteen. The oldest, seventeen. They'd all regarded him with a look of wonder, as if he were the answer to all their problems.

A surge of anger shot through him that his father would banish children and let them fend for themselves. "How long have they been here?"

Brynley cracked eggs into a mixing bowl. "The youngest, Gavin, came about a month ago. The oldest, Davy, came two years ago."

"He's been here for *two years*?"

She turned on the gas and lit a burner on the stove. "Davy was fifteen when he came here. What else could he do?"

"He could finish school, for starters. None of those boys have a high school diploma."

She banged a frying pan down onto the burner. "I can't enroll them in school. I'm not their legal guardian. I'd teach them myself, but I'm only qualified to teach elementary."

"You got your teacher certificate? I didn't think Dad was going to allow you to go to college."

She sighed. "He was worried I might get involved with a non-Lycan. But I was able to go to the local community college."

Where Dad was on the board. "Aren't you sick of him controlling every aspect of your life?"

"I'm happy with my life. And in case you didn't

notice, Dad doesn't control everything I do. He has no idea I'm helping these boys."

"You're not helping them. You're enabling them."

"What?" She poured the eggs into the frying pan. "I gave them a home."

"They're doing nothing, Bryn. They should be finishing school, getting jobs."

"The only jobs around here are on ranches that are either owned by Dad or someone he controls. The boys are stuck."

"As long as they're here, yes. They need to leave."

Bryn gasped. "You would kick them out?"

"No." He drank some coffee. "I'll think of something."

"Like being their pack master?" She gave him a hopeful look. "They need a father figure. They need you."

He began to pace. The last thing he wanted was to act like a father.

He had wanted to go away to college, but his father hadn't seen any point in a higher education. Dad had every detail of his life already mapped out—the ranches he would run, the female werewolf he would marry, and his eventual ascension to the role of Supreme Pack Master in about three hundred years. All the wealth and power would be his, if he could just behave himself and do as his father said for a few centuries.

Maybe it was time for a change. Roman Draganesti had revolutionized the Vampire World when he'd invented synthetic blood. Modern Vamps, no longer shackled with the need to feed every night, were now engaging in careers in science, business, entertainment, whatever they wanted.

Maybe it was time for a similar revolution in the Lycan World. He'd broken free from the pack and all the old traditions and restraints. Maybe these boys could do it, too.

Phil spent the day preparing for the battle that night. He borrowed Brynley's car and drove to the nearest town, where he purchased more clothes and bottled blood for Vanda and more ammo for himself. It occurred to him that she might need more than a whip for protection, so he bought her a handgun plus a hunting knife with a sheath she could strap to her calf. And if anything happened to him, and she ended up on her own, she would need a cell phone to help her teleport.

On the drive back to the cabin, he charged his cell phone and Vanda's new one. Then, at the cabin, he downloaded all the contact numbers from his phone onto hers.

He heard the boys outside and peered out the window. They'd divided into two teams and were playing touch football in the meadow.

He stepped onto the porch.

Brynley was sitting in the rocking chair, creaking it slowly back and forth. "So are you really going to fight in that battle tonight?"

"Yes. I'm leaving Vanda here. I'd appreciate your help in keeping her safe."

Bryn nodded. "I can do that."

Phil leaned against a post. "How long can you

stay? Don't you have a teaching job you need to get back to?"

She frowned. "Dad didn't want me to work. He thought it was beneath me."

Phil shook his head. "I know a school that would love to hire you. The boys could go there, too, and live on campus."

Her eyes widened. "Where?"

"The location is kept a secret 'cause the students are . . . different. Some are mortal children who know too much, some are half-vampire children with special powers, and others are were-panthers. I think these boys would fit right in."

She frowned. "I don't know. It sounds so far removed from the Lycan World."

"They can't have a life in the Lycan World, Bryn. They were banished. There's no going back."

"Hey, Mr. Jones." The youngest boy jogged up to the porch. "You want to play?"

"Sorry, Gavin. I need to conserve my energy."

"I told you he wouldn't," Davy grumbled. "He doesn't want anything to do with us."

Phil frowned. "That's not true."

"You refused to be our master!" Davy shouted.

Phil shot his sister an annoyed look.

She shrugged. "They wanted to know. What else could I tell them?"

"I said I would help them." Phil turned to the boys, who were clumped together in the pasture, watching him with injured expressions. "Okay, listen up. You were all banished because you challenged the authority of your masters, right?"

Davy lifted his chin. "So? You got a problem with that?"

"We wouldn't challenge *you*," Gavin insisted, his eyes pleading. "We think you're totally awesome."

The boys all murmured in agreement.

"Is it true you went Alpha without a pack?" a red-headed boy named Griffin asked.

"Yes." Phil held up his hands to quiet the boys, who were growing too excited. "Look. There's a good reason why you challenged your masters. It's because you all have natural leadership abilities. Each one of you has the strength, courage, and intelligence it takes to be a pack master, and your masters knew it. You're their worst nightmare—young Alphas in the making. The only way they could keep control was to get rid of you."

"Yeah, so we're tough," Davy growled. "We already knew that."

Phil smiled. "I'm sure you do. You also have the confidence it takes to be a leader. But consider how the Lycan World is set up now. With Alphas in charge who can live to be five hundred years old, how can someone like you become the leaders you were born to be? You're a threat to the leaders in power now, so they kicked you out. And all that's left in the Lycan World are the wimps and weaklings who are happy to submit. Over time the Lycan World will become weak and ineffectual because they rejected the strongest and fiercest of their youth."

"That sucks," Griffin mumbled.

"Do you know why I don't want to be your master? Because you would accept me, and it would hold you back. Each one of you has the potential of becoming Alpha, and I intend to help you achieve it."

The boys gasped.

"We could be like you?" Gavin asked.

"But there can only be one Alpha in a pack," Davy protested.

"According to the old rules, yes," Phil said. "But the old ways rejected you. Why should you follow them? Why should you accept being less than you can be?"

Gavin stepped forward. "I want to be an Alpha."

"You can do it." Phil looked each boy in the face. "You can all do it. I know a school where you can go."

"School?" Davy wrinkled his nose. "Who needs school?"

"You do. You need a high school diploma at the very least," Phil explained. "And then you'll be free to follow whatever aspirations you might have."

Davy snorted. "I want to kick ass."

Phil smiled. "I know the perfect place for you. It's a security and investigation company that would hire you in a second. But you'll have to learn how to fight."

"We know how to fight." Griffin elbowed the boy beside him, who pushed him back.

"You'll have to become experts in firearms, martial arts, and fencing. There's an enemy out there that wants to take over the world, and they tend to fight with swords."

"Cool," Davy said.

Phil snorted. "This is not like a hunt. You'll be up against a foe that actually fights back."

"Awesome," Griffin whispered.

Phil gave him a stern look. "They fight to the death. They're an evil group of vampires we call the Malcontents. They have super speed and strength."

"So do we," Davy insisted. "We can take them on."

Phil smiled. "I'm sure you can. But first you have to be trained. Each one of you can achieve Alpha. Take that power. Seize it and make it your own. Together, we can change the outcome of this war. We can save the mortal world. We can defeat evil. What do you say?"

The boys cheered.

Brynley leaned close to him and whispered, "If you get one of them killed, I'm going to be royally pissed."

He gave her a wry look. "Why don't you come work at the school, then you can watch over them?"

"Dad would never allow it."

"You're twenty-seven, Bryn. Time to break free."

She sighed. "I'll think about it."

"I'll leave you the number for Shanna Draganesti," Phil said. "She's in charge of the school. If anything happens to me, call her and get the boys enrolled."

Brynley scowled. "Don't you dare get yourself killed."

"I don't intend to."

Chapter Twenty-two

*E*arly that evening, Phil had just finished eating one of the two dozen hamburgers Brynley had cooked for supper when his phone rang.

"Are ye feeling up to a fight, lad?" Connor asked.

"I'm ready." Phil glanced out the window. It felt strange to hear Connor's voice while the sun was still shining.

"Good. We need every available man. We doona want to be outnumbered like that fiasco in New Orleans."

"Did you get the tracking device implanted in Sigismund?"

"Aye. And we let the bastard escape. So far, he's gone to the Russian coven in Brooklyn."

"Do you think Robby could be there?" Phil asked.

"Nay. Sean Whelan has the place bugged and his

team watching it. There's been no mention of Robby's whereabouts. Or Casimir's either. We think Sigismund is biding his time, waiting for nightfall in the West before he moves. Och, wait a minute . . . "

Phil could hear Connor discussing something with Howard.

"He just made a big jump on the radar. He must have teleported. Do ye have a fix on him, Howard?"

"Chicago," Howard answered with his booming voice.

"Good," Connor said. "Phil, as soon as the sun sets in yer location, I want ye to call Phineas. He'll pick you up. By then we should know where Sigismund has stopped, and we'll be gathering there to attack."

"Will do." Phil hung up. He drummed his fingers on the table. It would be another hour or two before the sun set in western Wyoming.

As soon as night fell, Phil jumped into the cellar to see Vanda. He heard her first gasping breath as she came back to life. "Hey, sweetheart."

She sat up. "What's going on?"

"I have to leave soon. Phineas will come to get me."

She rose to her feet. "Then the battle is tonight?"

"Yes. I bought you some weapons today, just in case, and a cell phone so you can teleport. I want you to know you can stay here as long as you like. If anything happens to me—"

"No!" She dashed toward him at vampire speed

and threw her arms around his neck. "Nothing's going to happen to you."

He held her tight. "I love you, Vanda."

"I feel the same way about you," she whispered. "I know you have a great future ahead of you."

He started to kiss her, but she jumped back.

"I need to eat." She levitated up to the ground floor.

He jumped through the opening and shut the trap door. Vanda was already pulling a bottle of synthetic blood from the ice chest. Brynley was standing by the kitchen table, where he'd left his weapons. He embraced her, then strapped on a shoulder holster and inserted his handgun.

He picked up his cell phone and called Phineas.

Within seconds the young Vamp was there. "Yo, wolf-bro." He shared a knuckle pound with Phil. Then he noticed Vanda and winced. "Oops, hope I didn't blow the big secret."

"She knows." Phil looked at Vanda and smiled. "She loves me the way I am."

Vanda smiled back. "Yes, I do."

"This is my sister, Brynley." Phil motioned to her.

"Whoa, a lady wolf. Dr. Phang at your service." Phineas shook her hand.

Phil noticed the boys on the front porch, peering through the windows. "And this is the young wolf pack. Future employees of MacKay S & I."

"Excellent." Phineas waved at the boys. "Looking good, dudes."

Vanda approached the kitchen table, sipping from her bottle of blood. "Phineas, how is Dougal?"

"He's okay. He's learning how to fence with his left hand." Phineas frowned. "He insisted on coming to the battle tonight, and Angus let him. Angus is worried about us being outnumbered, but we have more than seventy Vamps there now."

"Where?" Phil asked.

"A campground just south of Mount Rushmore," Phineas said. "Are you ready?"

"Yes." Phil gave his sister a quick hug and Vanda a quick kiss. "Remember, I love you."

She nodded, her eyes glimmering with unshed tears.

"Let's go." Phil grabbed onto Phineas, and everything went black.

They landed in a small clearing next to a stream. The moon shone overhead, still full. It glittered on the gurgling water and reflected off large gray boulders. The air was fresh with the scent of pine.

"The campground is farther down this stream," Phineas whispered. "Come on, let's get you a sword." He led Phil upstream to a pile of boulders. Dougal was standing guard by a stash of weapons.

Phil greeted him quietly and clapped him on the back.

Dougal gave him a wry smile. "They doona trust me to fight yet, so this is my job."

"It's a damned important job," Phineas muttered. He selected a sword.

Phil picked one that felt good in his hand.

"Angus sent Ian to scout the campground," Dougal whispered.

"Ian's back from his honeymoon?" Phil asked.

346   *Kerrelyn Sparks*

Dougal nodded. "He and Toni came back when they heard about Robby. In fact, about every MacKay employee I've ever met is here."

"Come on." Phineas led Phil to a nearby clearing where the Vamps had gathered.

It was true. Every male Vamp Phil had ever met was here, plus others whom he'd never met. Even Laszlo was here, nervously fidgeting with a sword. Emma was sticking close to him like a protective mother hen. Colbert GrandPied had come with four men. Phil recalled he'd had six men in New Orleans. Two must have died in the battle there.

Phil stopped next to the other shifters.

"If things get bad, I'm going to shift," Carlos said. "I'll be a lot more effective as a panther."

Phil nodded. He would stay in human form as long as possible, but draw on the power of the wolf for super strength and speed.

"Ian's back," Howard whispered.

Ian, dressed entirely in black, slipped noiselessly into the clearing. With his sword, he drew in the dirt. "The campground has a central open area with a fire that's been lit in the middle. The buildings surround the area like a square. The main lodge is on one side, and there are nine cabins on the other three sides."

"How many Malcontents did ye see?" Angus asked.

"I spotted fifteen Malcontents in the lodge," Ian continued. "They're holding a group of mortals prisoner—the original campers, I assume. Each cabin was occupied with another three or four Malcontents."

"So there are about fifty of them," Jean-Luc concluded.

"And we have seventy-four," Angus said. "Any sign of Robby?"

"Nay, but I did see three Malcontents leaving the campground, going east, so I followed them." Ian drew a line in the dirt. "They went into a cave. I think Robby could be in there."

"They probably use the cave for their death-sleep," Jean-Luc said.

Angus frowned. "There could be more Malcontents in there. We could still be outnumbered." He looked at everyone in the clearing. "I canna guarantee how safe this will be."

Jack waved a hand in dismissal. "Battles are never safe. I came here to rescue Robby. I'm not leaving without him."

The others nodded in agreement.

"Verra well, then," Angus said. "We'll divide into five groups, captained by Jean-Luc, Connor, Jack, Colbert, and myself. My group will attack the lodge. Jean-Luc, Connor, and Jack—your groups will take the other three sides of the square. Colbert, you'll take the fifth group and station yourself here." Angus marked an X in the dirt. "Halfway between the camp and the cave, so you can kill anyone coming or going. Let's go."

There was some quick shuffling while the five captains selected their groups. Jean-Luc asked Roman, Phil, Ian, and two other Vamps from Texas to join him.

All five groups moved stealthily through the

woods and into position. Phil crouched behind some bushes between Roman and Ian. He heard Roman murmur a prayer, and he added a silent amen.

When Angus bellowed a war cry, they charged.

Phil rushed through the back door of a cabin. Four Malcontents jumped up from a card table. He skewered one. The other three were quick to grab their swords. Phil and Roman each engaged a Malcontent in battle. The other one ran out the front door, into the central open area.

Phil killed his second opponent. Roman's opponent, realizing he was alone with two swordsmen, teleported away.

"God's blood," Roman muttered.

Phil ran out the front door. Several Malcontents from each of the nine cabins had escaped out the front door when the Vamps had invaded through the back. The Malcontents formed a huddle close to the bonfire. More Malcontents dashed from the lodge, narrowly missing execution by Angus and his group.

Phil estimated about twenty-five Malcontents were left in the open area. They'd lost perhaps half their original number. As far as he could tell, all of the Vamps had survived the initial assault. Seventy-four to twenty-five. Victory was within their grasp.

The Vamps surrounded the Malcontents and closed in.

"*En garde!*" Colbert ran toward the open area with his three men. He was bleeding from a chest wound. "They're coming from the cave. There must be a hundred of them!"

Phil swallowed hard. He and his friends were in deep shit.

Vanda paced about the cabin. She had a bad feeling about this battle. If the Vamps fell, the war would be over. The Malcontents would win.

And how could she do nothing while Phil fought for his life? How could she live with herself if he died?

She stopped at the table and looked through the weapons he'd bought for her. In an instant she knew what she had to do. She rolled up a leg of her jeans, strapped on the sheath, and inserted the knife.

"Are you going?" Brynley asked.

Vanda nodded. "I have a bad feeling about it."

"Then I'm going, too. You can teleport me, right?"

The door swung open and all the boys barged in.

"We want to fight," Davy announced.

"No," Brynley said. "You're too young."

"But we can shift," Griffin insisted. "We can really tear into them as wolves."

"You can shift?" Vanda asked. "I thought that was last night."

"The full moon cycle affects us for three nights," Brynley explained. "On the first night we shift involuntarily for the whole night. On the next two nights we can choose whether or not to shift."

"And we want to shift!" Davy looked at Vanda. "If you can get us there, we'll fight."

"Please," Gavin pleaded. "Mr. Jones believes in us. We want to show him we're worthy."

Brynley sighed. "Okay. But if any of you gets

wounded, you pull out. You stay safe." She turned to Vanda. "How many can you teleport at once?"

Vanda winced. "Just one."

The boys groaned.

"Wait a minute." Vanda grabbed her new cell phone. Relief swept through her when she saw a long list of contacts. Thank God Phil had planned ahead. She called Maggie. "Maggie, this is Vanda. I need you and Pierce to come here right away. Bring some weapons."

"Are you in danger?" Maggie asked. "We'll be right there."

Within seconds Maggie and her husband appeared in the cabin. Maggie was holding a cell phone and a revolver, while Pierce was toting a shotgun. They both had knives stuffed in their belts.

Vanda quickly explained the situation. "You don't have to fight if you don't want to, but we need you to help transport."

"Not a problem." Pierce looked at the group of boys. "You're sure you want to do this?"

"Yeah, let's go," Davy insisted.

"Where exactly are we going?" Maggie asked.

"Phineas said it was a campground south of Mount Rushmore. I thought we'd call some of them and teleport straight there."

Pierce frowned. "If they're fighting, they're not going to answer their phones."

"We've got to try." Vanda studied the list of contacts on her cell.

Brynley whipped out her own cell. "There's got

to be a wolf pack living around there. I'll try to find them."

Vanda's eye caught on the name Kyo. The Japanese tourist and his friends had offered to fight before. She punched in his number.

"Kyo, this is Vanda. I don't know if you remember—"

"Ah, Vanda, the famous celebrity. I am honored."

"Kyo, could you and your friends teleport to me? And if you have any weapons, could you bring them?"

"You in trouble? We be right there." Kyo, Yuki, and Yoshi appeared, all with samurai swords.

Vanda explained the situation once again and introduced everyone.

The Japanese gaped at Pierce.

"You Don Orlando de Corazon!" Yuki shouted. "You very famous."

"We are honored to fight with you." Kyo bowed.

Brynley covered her phone with one hand. "I called my sister, Glynis. She's looking up the phone number for the nearest wolf pack to Mount Rushmore."

"Mount Rushmore?" Yoshi asked. "Big mountain, big heads?"

"We were there," Kyo said. "We have very nice photos. You want to see?"

"We want to go there." Vanda wrapped her whip around her waist and shoved the handgun under the waistband of her jeans. "Do you know the way?"

"*Hai.*" Kyo nodded. "We take you."

"Never mind." Brynley told her sister, and hung up. "Let's go."

For the first trip, the three Japanese teleported Vanda, Maggie, and Pierce. Then they all teleported back. It took them two more trips to transport Brynley and all the boys.

They heard the clashing of swords to the south and ran toward the sound, weaving through trees. The clashing sounds grew louder, punctuated every now and then with a shout of victory or a cry of pain.

Vanda saw the light of a bonfire ahead. She stopped behind a cabin and peered around the corner. Brynley looked over her shoulder.

Phil and the Vamps were completely surrounded and fighting for their lives. A panther was dashing around the perimeter, taking down Malcontents and dragging them away to maul them to death.

"The panther's on our side?" Brynley asked.

"Yes." Vanda narrowed her eyes. "Where did the bear come from?"

"That's Howard," Maggie whispered.

"Sweet Howard is a *bear*?" Vanda winced when the huge bear took a swipe at a Malcontent with his mighty paw and ripped the vampire's head off.

"Cool," Davy whispered. "Come on, guys, let's shift."

"Make sure you attack the bad guys," Vanda warned them. "Our guys are in the middle."

"Yeah, they're surrounded." Davy pulled his shirt off. "But not for long."

Brynley and the boys stripped and started shifting.

Vanda grabbed Maggie and ran to hide behind another cabin. "Maybe we can find Robby."

Pierce followed them, carrying his shotgun. "I'm not letting Maggie out of my sight."

A series of howls and war cries echoed through the camp. Vanda peered around the cabin. The werewolves and Japanese had attacked.

The Malcontents, taken by surprise, suddenly found themselves fighting on two fronts. Their line thinned and faltered. Screams of pains filled the air. The grass was littered with piles of dust that were quickly scattered as the warriors trampled over them.

Vanda saw a group of four Malcontents break away and run down a path. She narrowed her eyes. She'd recognized Casimir and Sigismund. They might be escaping, fearing that the battle had turned against them, or they could be going to Robby.

"Let's follow them," she whispered to Maggie and Pierce.

They stayed in the shelter of the trees and followed the path Casimir had taken. It led to a cave where two Malcontents were standing guard at the entrance. Sigismund and Casimir must have gone inside.

"How good are you two with knives?" Vanda asked.

"Very good." Maggie took the knife from her belt. "I've got the one on the left."

Her husband held a hunting knife. "On the count

of three." He counted softly, then the knives spun into the air. They landed with a thud in the chests of the two Malcontents.

Pierce's was a direct hit to the heart, and the Malcontent turned to dust. Maggie's victim fell to the ground. Pierce rushed forward at vampire speed, yanked the knife out, and plunged it into the surviving Malcontent's heart. He turned to dust as well.

He handed the knife back to Maggie before they entered the cave. A lit torch was attached to the cave wall every ten feet. They progressed quietly, then halted when the main tunnel divided in two.

"You guys take the right," Vanda whispered. "I'll go left."

"Are you sure?" Pierce asked.

"Yes." Vanda removed the knife from the sheath on her calf and hurried down the narrow tunnel. It grew darker, so she removed a torch from the wall to light her way. The tunnel opened into a room with stalactites dripping from the ceiling. She weaved through the stalagmites. No Malcontents. No Robby.

She heard a moan and whirled around.

"Robby?" She barely breathed the name, hoping the sound wouldn't carry too far.

She heard the moan again. She held up the torch and peered around slowly. There, a narrow crack in the wall. She turned sideways and squeezed through.

It was another room. And there, in the middle, was Robby tied to chair.

"Robby," she whispered, rushing to him.

He lifted his head, and she halted with a jolt. Good Lord, they'd beaten his face black and blue. One eye was swollen, the other one cut above the brow. Blood trickled down.

"Oh Robby." She wedged the torch between two rocks. Bile rose in her throat as she saw the slashes across his chest.

"Hungry," he whispered.

Oh no, she should have thought to bring some bottled blood. "Don't worry. I'll teleport you out of here straight to a supply of blood." There was plenty at the cabin. She could take him there.

She set down her knife, then grabbed at the chain across his chest. She cried out when it burned her fingers. Of course, silver, so he couldn't teleport away. She winced at the burn marks on Robby's chest.

She looked around for something to insulate her hands. Socks? She glanced down at Robby's feet. They were barefoot and bloody. Dammit. Was there no part of this man that they hadn't tortured?

"Hungry," Robby whispered.

"I'll get you out of here." She pulled off her shirt and wrapped it around her hands. Then she unfastened the chain around his chest and neck. She saw his hands, tied with silver behind the chair. They were burned and dripping blood.

He started to shake, and she realized he was fighting a compulsion to bite her.

"Just a little longer, hang in there." She unhooked the chain that strapped his thighs to the chair.

"*No!*" Robby cried.

"It'll be all right," she assured him.

Something sharp poked her in the back, and she straightened with a jerk, glancing over her shoulder.

Sigismund stood behind her, his sword pressed into her back. "We meet again, Vanda. For the final time."

Chapter Twenty-three

Vanda glanced at her knife on the ground. She'd never get to it in time. And she couldn't unwind her whip in time either. She let her shirt drop to the ground, then she curled her hand around the pistol she'd wedged under the waistband of her jeans.

Sigismund grabbed her suddenly, pulling her back against his chest. He swung the sword around and pressed it to her neck. "I should have killed you years ago. Jedrek insisted on doing it himself, but he's gone now. You and your nasty friends will pay for his murder."

Vanda held her breath, afraid the sword would cut her throat if she so much as inhaled.

He pinched the sword tighter against her neck.

"Maybe I'll have some fun with you first. I always did want to fuck you, you know."

He grunted in her ear. His sword clattered to the floor. Vanda spun around.

Sigismund was a pile of dust. Her sister stood there, staring at his remains, a sword trembling in her hand.

"Marta?" Vanda whispered.

"I—I'm finally free," Marta whispered in Polish. Her gaze lifted to Vanda. She dropped her sword with a clatter.

Vanda took a deep breath. "You saved my life."

Marta's eyes filled with tears. "I killed our little sister. I didn't mean to. I didn't want to." She looked at the pile of dust. "He controlled me for so long." With a sudden cry, she stomped on his dust. She stomped and stomped, crying, "I hate him! I hate him!"

"Marta." Vanda grabbed her by the shoulders. "It's okay. We're together now."

She blinked through her tears. "Can you forgive me?"

"Yes." Vanda pulled her tight and hugged her. Marta was trembling in her arms. "Can you help me get Robby out of here?" She released her sister and moved behind Robby to unfasten the chains around his wrists.

Marta stood still, staring at Robby with tears running down her face.

"Robby!"

Vanda heard Angus shouting in the cavern room. "We're in here!"

The Scotsman squeezed through the narrow

opening. He halted when he saw Marta and lifted his sword.

"It's okay, Angus. She's with me." Vanda released the chain binding Robby's wrists, and he slumped forward.

Angus rushed forward to grab him. "Och, Robby, my lad."

"Hungry," Robby whispered.

"Of course." Angus fumbled in his sporran and pulled out a bottle of blood. He ripped off the top and put it up to Robby's mouth.

Robby guzzled it down.

"How is the battle going?" Vanda asked.

"'Tis over," Angus replied. "The Malcontents dinna like being skewered by us and mauled by wild animals. They teleported away. Where did those wolves come from?"

"I brought them," Vanda said. "They wanted to prove themselves to Phil."

"Och, they certainly proved their worth to me." Angus realized the bottle was empty. He pulled a flask from his sporran. "Here, lad. A little Blissky will help with the pain."

"I got it." Robby took the flask in a shaking, bloody hand. His grip faltered.

Angus grabbed the flask and held it to Robby's mouth. "We were so verra worried. I'll kill the bastards that did this to you."

"Robby!" More shouts came from the cavern next door.

"In here!" Angus yelled.

Jean-Luc, Connor, and Phil slipped inside. Vanda's

heart leaped at the sight of Phil. He had a few cuts and scrapes, but otherwise, he looked absolutely wonderful.

He didn't seem surprised to see her. He must have realized she was here when the wolves had joined the battle. He grinned at her, then looked at Robby and his smile faded.

"Och, lad." Connor kneeled in front of Robby. "Let's get you back to Romatech and clean you up."

"Did ye find Casimir?" Angus asked.

"Nay," Connor said. "It looks like the bastard teleported away."

"I'll tell everyone we found Robby." Jean-Luc patted Robby on the shoulder, then left the small room.

"Hey, Robby." Phil touched his knee, then looked at Vanda. "Are you all right?"

She nodded and pointed at the dust scattered about the room. "Sigismund tried to kill me, but my sister saved me." She pulled Marta forward. "She's on our side now."

"Welcome." Phil shook Marta's hand. "Thank you for saving Vanda."

Marta nodded with tears still streaming down her face.

Vanda felt tears in her eyes, too. She had her sister back. And Phil had survived the battle. "I'm glad you're all right."

He nodded. "I'm glad you're all right, too." His eyes glimmered with love and longing.

"Och, go ahead and hug her, lad," Connor growled. "Ye're no' fooling us."

Phil grabbed Vanda and held her tight. "I was so

scared when I realized you were here." He kissed her brow. "But thank you for coming. The boys and the Japanese were a great help."

"I'd like to talk to the Japanese," Angus said. "Phil, can ye ask them to come to Romatech with us?"

"Sure." Phil released Vanda. "I'd like to bring the boys there, too. They need a home and a school."

"Are they orphans?" Angus asked.

"Banished like I was," Phil replied. "They have no home."

"They do now." Angus helped Robby to his feet. "I'm taking him to Romatech. Bring the others." Angus wrapped an arm around Robby's shoulders, and they vanished.

"Let's go." Phil took Vanda's hand.

She pulled back. "I—I'm going to take Marta to Howard's cabin. We have some catching up to do. I'll see you later."

Phil tilted his head, looking a little worried. "Are you sure?"

"Of course. We'll be fine," Vanda insisted. She blinked back the tears in her eyes. "I'll always love you, Phil. I know you have a great future ahead of you."

His eyes narrowed.

She grabbed her sister and teleported away.

Two hours later Phil left the boys in a conference room at Romatech, filling out registration forms for Shanna's school. He headed down the hall to the clinic to see how Robby was doing. The room was full of people waiting for some news.

He sat next to Brynley. "What are you doing here?"

She shrugged. "Waiting for one of these Vamp friends of yours to give me a ride home. How are the boys?"

"They're getting registered for school. You sure you don't want to apply for a teaching job?"

She frowned. "I don't know. I have a good life back in Montana."

"You could live on campus, see the boys every day."

"And never see my parents again? Or Howell and Glynis?" She gave him an annoyed look. "You don't even want to see your younger brother and sister?"

Phil sighed. "This is my home now."

Brynley looked about the room. "Where's Vanda? I thought you two were inseparable."

"She wanted to be alone for a while with her sister. I tried calling her, but she didn't answer."

"Great. She finally saw the light."

Phil cocked his head. "What did you say to her?"

"I explained who you are. I told her you have a great future ahead of you."

"She said that to me twice."

Brynley shrugged. "I guess she understands where you belong now. You'll be an important leader someday."

"Maybe. In about three hundred years," Phil growled. "Did you tell her that?"

"You're better off without her. She can't even give you children."

"You think I care?" Phil shouted, then realized everyone in the waiting room was looking at him.

He lowered his voice. "I love her, Bryn. I'm going to marry her. And there's not a damned thing you can do about it."

Brynley glowered at him. "You could have everything. Wealth, power, and prestige. You would give it up for a vampire woman—"

"With purple hair," Phil finished her sentence. "Yes, you bet I would."

He left the waiting room and paced around the hall. He could have Phineas teleport him to Howard's cabin. And then what would he do? How could he convince Vanda that she was the perfect woman for him?

She'd always been the one for him. Years ago, when he'd rebelled against his father and ended up at the townhouse, he'd met Vanda for the first time. With her purple hair and bat tattoo, he'd known right away that he'd met another rebel. Another outcast. They were two of a kind, both hiding a passionate, angry beast deep within.

"Phil, how are you?"

He turned to see Father Andrew coming down the hall. "I'm fine, Father. How are you?"

"Good. I've been meaning to talk to you." The priest pulled out his day-timer and thumbed through the pages. "I was researching Vanda's family to see if I could locate her sister."

"We found her. Vanda's with her now. They're working things out."

Father Andrew glanced up, smiling. "Excellent." He tore a page from his day-timer and handed it to Phil. "I thought you might find this interesting."

Phil read it, and his heart expanded in his chest. This was the perfect way to win Vanda back. "Thank you, Father."

"You're welcome, my son." He patted Phil on the back. "So will I be officiating another wedding soon?"

Phil gulped. "You knew?"

The priest's eyes twinkled. "That you were engaging in forbidden acts? Don't worry. I believe in forgiveness."

Forgiveness. If Vanda could forgive her sister, maybe it was time he forgave his father. After all, if his dad hadn't banished him, he wouldn't have ended up in the Vampire World. He wouldn't have found Vanda. "I believe in forgiveness, too. And love."

Father Andrew smiled. "Then you are truly blessed."

Epilogue

Three nights later . . .

*V*anda looked up when Phineas teleported into the cabin with a box. "Oh, you brought us some food. Thank you." She'd called Connor a few hours before, asking him to please send some bottled blood.

She wasn't ready to return to the city yet. She and Marta had more than fifty years of memories to catch up on. And according to Connor, Casimir was still somewhere in America, and she was still on his hit list.

He would want Marta dead, too, so it was better for them to stay hidden at Howard's cabin. Besides, Vanda knew she wasn't ready to be seen in public.

She still broke into tears at unexpected times. She still ached with loneliness for Phil.

He'd stopped calling after that first night. She could only think that he had realized he was better off without her.

"Hey, sweetness." Phineas grinned at her as he set the box down on the kitchen counter. "Hey, dudette." He nodded at Marta.

"Hi, Dr. Phang." Marta ran to look in the box. "Did you bring any Chocolood? I love that stuff."

Vanda smiled. Her sister seemed to be adapting well to synthetic blood and Vampire Fusion Cuisine.

"Here you go." Phineas handed a bottle of Chocolood to Marta. "Can you get the rest of this stuff put away? I have a top secret mission to go on."

"Really?" Marta unloaded bottles from the box. "What kind of mission?"

"The sort of mission that requires the expertise of the Love Doctor." Phineas sauntered over to Vanda. "Don't worry, dudette. I'll be right back."

"What?" Vanda started when Phineas grabbed her. "What are you doing?"

Everything went black.

Vanda stumbled, and Phineas steadied her.

"Okay, wolf-bro. Mission accomplished." Phineas gave Phil a knuckle pound, then teleported away.

"What is going on?" Vanda looked at Phil, then around them. "Where are we? In a closet?" She frowned at the shelves filled with antiseptic cleansers and dust cloths.

Phil touched her shoulder. "I had to see you, Vanda."

"In a closet?"

He grinned. "I had to tell you how much I adore you. I love you. I refuse to live one more night without you."

Her heart squeezed in her chest. "But you have a great future—"

"Yes, with you."

Vanda pressed a hand to her chest. "You're destined to be a great leader of your people."

"Maybe, in about three hundred years. My sister wasn't entirely up front about the timeline."

"Oh." Vanda's heart raced. He still loved her. He still wanted her. And he could live for hundreds of years.

He smiled. "I want to show you something."

"In a closet?"

With a chuckle, he opened the door. "I asked Phineas to teleport you to the closet so your arrival wouldn't look suspicious."

He led her down a plain white hall. Their footsteps echoed on the gleaming linoleum floor. The smell of cleansers was heavy in the air.

"Where are we?" she asked.

"Cleveland." He led her toward some double swinging doors. "This is a retirement home."

"Sheesh, Phil, I'm not that old."

He chuckled and squeezed her hand. "I missed you."

She frowned at him. "You didn't call me."

"I was waiting for the perfect day. Today, they're having a party, and I wanted you to see it." He opened the double doors. "This is the recreation room."

She noted the table with a big birthday cake and a bowl of punch. Mortals milled about, chatting and laughing. Some children pranced around the table, admiring the cake and trying to sneak tastes of the icing. An elderly woman with a cap of gray curls shooed them away, laughing.

Vanda frowned. "I don't know any of these people."

Phil dragged her forward. "I want you to meet the birthday boy. He's eighty-one years old."

Vanda spotted an old man sitting in an armchair. He was looking down at the little girl in his lap. His face was lined, his head bald on top. He held the little girl with wrinkled, age-spotted hands.

"You want a piece of cake, Pawpaw?"

"Yes, Emily, that would be lovely."

The little girl squirmed off his lap and ran to the table. The old man lifted his face to watch her, and he smiled.

Vanda gasped. Those blue eyes. Her gaze flitted over him quickly and spotted the numbers tattooed on his forearm.

Jozef.

She stumbled back. Her heart lurched. She covered her mouth with a shaky hand.

Phil held her shoulders, steadying her.

"Jozef," she whispered. A flood of tears came to her eyes.

"He survived the war," Phil whispered. "He immigrated here in 1949 and married a few years later. He has four children, ten grandchildren, and three great-grandchildren."

Vanda turned away and furiously wiped at the tears streaming down her face. "I can't let them see me cry. Not with my pink tears." Oh God, she was actually related to all these people.

"Do you want to meet him?" Phil asked.

Vanda pressed a hand to her racing heart. "What will I say?"

"You'll think of something." Phil escorted her to her brother.

His mouth twitched when he noticed her hair, then he looked at her face and frowned. "Do I know you? You look so familiar."

She blinked back her tears. "I—I— My name is Vanda."

His blue eyes widened. "I had a sister named Vanda. You look so much like her."

"She was . . . my grandmother."

Jozef stiffened suddenly and grabbed at his chest. Vanda gasped. Good Lord, she was going to kill him.

The elderly lady rushed over. "What's going on here?" She glared at Vanda. "Who are you?"

"I'm all right," Jozef insisted. "Gertie, you remember how I used to talk about my sister Vanda?"

"Yes, she was the one who raised you after your mom died. You said she died in the war."

Jozef looked at Vanda with tears in his eyes. "She lived! This is her granddaughter."

"Oh my!" Gertie grabbed Vanda's hand. "Bless you."

Jozef took Vanda's other hand. "How is she? Is she still with us?"

"She passed away," Vanda said quietly. "But she always talked about you. She loved you very much."

"I loved her, too." Jozef shook her hand. "This is the best present ever."

"Yes, it is." Vanda glanced at Phil and smiled. "Thank you."

Jozef laughed. "I like your purple hair. That's something my sister would have done."

Phil stepped forward. "Sir, my name is Phil Jones. It's an honor to meet you."

Jozef released Vanda's hand and shook hands with Phil. "Are you here with Vanda?"

"Yes, and since you're Vanda's oldest living male relative, I thought I would ask you for her hand in marriage."

Jozef blinked. "An old-fashioned sort, are you? I like that." He looked at Vanda and his blue eyes twinkled. "Do you love this man, Vanda?"

"Oh, yes." She stepped close to Phil and put her arms around him. "I love him very much."

Gertie clasped her hands together. "This is so sweet."

Jozef cleared his throat and gave Phil a stern look. "Do you have a job, young man?"

"Yes, sir. I'll take good care of her. I love her with all my heart."

Jozef chuckled. "Don't know what you need me for. You two go on and get hitched."

Vanda laughed. "We will. I promise."

Phil pulled a diamond ring from his pocket and slid it onto Vanda's finger. "To our great future together."

She slipped her arms around his neck as his mouth met hers in a long, lingering kiss.

"Oooh, Pawpaw," Emily whispered. "They're kissing."

Vanda heard her brother laugh, and her heart soared.

"How can I ever thank you for this, Phil?"

He gave her his wolfish grin. "We'll think of something."

STEAMY, SENSATIONAL VAMPIRE LOVE FROM
NEW YORK TIMES BESTSELLING AUTHOR

KERRELYN SPARKS

ALL I WANT FOR CHRISTMAS IS A VAMPIRE
978-0-06-111846-3

Toni's best friend has been locked up in a mental hospital
because she said she was attacked by vampires. The only
way to get her out is to prove that bloodsuckers really do
exist, so Toni takes a job for the undead, but damn sexy,
Ian McPhie.

FORBIDDEN NIGHTS WITH A VAMPIRE
978-0-06-166784-8

Vanda Barkowski is a vampire with a hot temper, and
now her employees at the nightclub she owns have filed
complaints, sentencing her to anger management class.
Worse, Phil Jones has agreed to be her sponsor, but can
she resist her attraction to this forbidden mortal?

THE VAMPIRE AND THE VIRGIN
978-0-06-166786-2

FBI psychologist Olivia Sotiris is in dire need of a
vacation, and cool ocean breezes on a Greek island are
exactly what she needs. But when a deadly criminal from
a case back home tracks her down, it's up to sexy
bloodsucker Robby MacKay to save her life.

KSP1 0310

MORE DELECTABLE VAMPIRE ROMANCE FROM
NEW YORK TIMES BESTSELLING AUTHOR

LYNSAY SANDS

THE ROGUE HUNTER
978-0-06-147429-3

Samantha Willan is a workaholic lawyer. After a recent
breakup she wants to stay as far away from romance as
possible. Then she meets her irresistible new neighbor,
Garrett Mortimer. Is it her imagination, or are his mysterious
eyes locked on her neck?

THE IMMORTAL HUNTER
978-0-06-147430-9

Dr. Danielle McGill doesn't know if she can trust the man who
just saved her life. There are too many questions, such as what
is the secret organization he says he's part of, and why do his
wounds hardly bleed? But with her sister in the hands of some
dangerous men, she doesn't have much choice but
to trust him.

THE RENEGADE HUNTER
978-0-06-147431-6

When Nicholas Argeneau, former rogue vampire hunter, sees
a bloodthirsty sucker terrifying a woman, it's second nature
for him to come to her rescue. But he doesn't count on getting
locked up for his troubles.

LYS2 1009

At Avon Books, we know your passion for romance—once you finish one of our novels, you find yourself wanting more.

May we tempt you with . . .

- **Excerpts** from our upcoming releases.
- Entertaining **extras**, including authors' personal photo albums and book lists.
- Behind-the-scenes **scoop** on your favorite characters and series.
- **Sweepstakes** for the chance to win free books, romantic getaways, and other fun prizes.
- Writing **tips** from our authors and editors.
- **Blog** with our authors and find out why they love to write romance.
- **Exclusive content** that's not contained within the pages of our novels.

Join us at
www.avonbooks.com

AVON

An Imprint of HarperCollins*Publishers*
www.avonromance.com

Available wherever books are sold or please call 1-800-331-3761 to order.

FTH 0708